Against the Grain

Against the Grain: a novel by Suwarsih Djojopuspito

The Lontar Foundation
Jl. Danau Laut Tawar, Blok A/53
Bendungan Hilir, Tanah Abang
Jakarta 10210, Indonesia
www.lontar.org

Design and layout by Cyprianus Jaya Napiun
Cover illustration by Sudjana Kerton

ISBN 978-623-7150-24-4

MODERN LIBRARY OF INDONESIA

SUWARSIH DJOJOPUSPITO

Against the Grain

a novel

translated by
George A Fowler

with an afterword by
Gerard Termorshuizen

LONTAR
Jakarta, Indonesia

Contents

1

Her manuscript had been rejected. Its return made that clear. For two years now, Sulastri had been preoccupied to utter distraction with her hope for its publication, and now, all for nothing. She reread her manuscript page by page, recognizing in it so many memories woven into this work from the very beginning, even the ink and paper purchased with her last money. She thought of the nights she and her husband took turns reworking and refining it; then finally submitting it. The cost of its delivery was barely squeezed from their tight shopping budget. They were so very poor at the time.... Oh, what was the use of all those memories? They're all too painful and humiliating.

She rubbed her forehead as if to erase all those recollections from her mind.

"I need a good cry now. I feel like I've been beaten up. Oh, there I go drifting between Sundanese and Dutch. It's obvious that they, the ones I loved, have kicked me out. They've made me feel hopeless and think that I worked all for nothing. Still, my work wasn't all that bad. I wasn't just teaching then; I had given voice to my heart and feelings. Was that wrong?"

Sulastri frowned and held back her tears.

"It's so strange to see myself clearly. Lastri, you are so stupid. Don't be conceited. You aren't the least bit smart. All you've done is make a big mess."

"But I'm going to try all over again!" And she kept on like this in her head. "How ironic: I've been writing, not for other people's pleasure, but for my own."

She gave a sour smile and shivered for a moment, as though wanting to toss these awful feelings far away. She forced back a feeling of nausea, but it kept returning. Then she made herself stand in the back doorway. The stars were out in the blue sky and she thought, "How clearly they sparkle and glitter. It all looks so calm and awesome."

She could almost hear the stars breathing. Their lights looked so clean and seemed to speak to her. "We know what you're feeling," they said inaudibly. "You feel beaten, though you always wanted to be praised. From these vast blue skies, we pity you. But we have to laugh at you sad, petty, inferior things. You're all so niggling, shut up in your own melancholy. You don't know why we display ourselves to you in our millions on nights like this; why we light up the heavens above you and lavish our brilliance to brighten the darkness of nights like this. It's all wasted on you, because you're such stupid creatures."

It seemed the stars were amused and softened their dazzling light a little. Did Sulastri really feel ashamed because the manuscript had been rejected? Was it really a humiliation? No, she was extremely angry. And devastated. A voice inside her said, "Stars, return to me all those memories that you've kept for so long. My manuscript's been returned. They think it's bad. It seems they think the writing is stupid."

The stars were still out there, clear and glittering with clean faces. Memories came with jokes and bantering or with sweet smiles. Or they took Sulastri's breath away, to her utter fascination.

"Do you remember?" they whispered. "Do you recall when..."

Sulastri grew uneasy, stood up and paced back and forth along the veranda, hands behind her back. She turned her gaze toward her husband who was near the fence, lackadaisically puffing smoke up into the air. Abruptly, he felt his wife watching him, and he turned toward her.

"Out of hope now?"

He said this indifferently and Sulastri, glaring, was surprised at herself and lowered her head.

"He doesn't know," hissed a whisper in her ear. "He doesn't know how shattered I am."

"Lastri," Sudarmo's voice sounded like it came from far away. "Are you so sad that your manuscript's been returned to you? Isn't that just normal? The only thing Balai Pustaka is interested in publishing is things for the general public. What would that be like? It should be useful, meaning instructive, educational, with well-shaped sentences, and... charming, in a word. Your story is useless. It doesn't have a traditional form, so isn't charming, and it doesn't provide answers to the childish dreams of a village schoolteacher. The way I see it, write in any language at all. Sundanese at the most will always be just a regional language. Anyway, the important thing isn't the language, but what you want to say. Write, if you want to write an article. It doesn't matter how you write."

Sulastri answered, resentfully, "I can't accept their decision. I know how hard I worked on it. I feel... I'm sure."

She emphasized her words, and without finishing her sentence, pressed her fingernails into the palm of her hand and bit her lip.

"What are you saying?" Sudarmo nonchalantly put his left hand into his trousers pocket and, looking quizzically at his wife, nodded several times. He couldn't really understand her disappointment. For him there was no doubt that their assessment of the manuscript needn't be taken seriously and might even be worthless. There was no reason to call his wife's work bad just because of them, even though he himself wasn't competent to evaluate it. He was very sure of her ingenuity as a writer. He had an unlimited—and unconscious—faith in his wife's ability, even if in other things he had to admit that she was sometimes annoying and the way her mind worked was a bit silly. Like that display of feelings now. Why did she have to feel so stricken, when it was clear that a general evaluation didn't bear the slightest significance. It might be significant a hundred years after the writer's demise—and if it wasn't, so what? Previously, they had discussed whether it wouldn't be better to return to Sundanese, their own language. In the end, Dutch was nothing more and nothing less than a foreign language, and what's more, he felt, all Indonesian thoughts written in Dutch would only have meaning for the short term, while if written in *our own language*, such a work could live longer. We could enrich our own language and in doing so contribute to our own literature. This was terrific in theory, but in reality...

"Dar, this is a turning point in my life. I am separating myself from the Sundanese language."

"Do as your heart tells you. Sometimes one's intuition is more correct than the sharpest mind."

They sat there silently on the bench. The little tree in the corner of their garden cast a faint shadow on the short grass. When the first rains fell, this grass would grow quickly and luxuriantly and become the haunt of snakes and lizards. The banana palms with their fat trunks raised their fronds to the light of the stars and swayed, ever so slowly and serenely. The skies looked even more deeply blue and the stars were like a sweet cape of flowers, fresh and dew-drenched. From next door came a shrill, nerve-rattling song that disturbed the quiet ambience.

Popsicles, just young coconut ones
Push your cart here, boss, and give us some!

"Just listen to that!" said Sudarmo. "It sets every bit of our nerves on edge. People nowadays get on like the voice of that singer. Chaotic, hysterical. Parliamentary promotions! Raise funds as fast as you can! Oh, back in the time of Sukarno, people who now say bad things about us were delighted to call us their friends. Now they're happy that Wicked Karno is unable to sweet-talk them into abandoning their jobs, and so now they mock us, knowing they can say anything at all. We're above them intellectually, but financially, our social circumstances are about the same as the other people in our alley. Every day I hate this situation. And what's more, we know that we're almost drowning. We're weak and broken down. And the time might even come when they beat us to death. These days, it's what's useful that's valuable. The rest is worthless, maybe useful just as tools."

Sudarmo stopped speaking. Sulastri answered slowly, "That's true. Only money has value. The rich and powerful are good people and are above criticism. The old people say that you get rewarded according to your services. So be it then, the rich and powerful can only be good people, and the down-and-outers like us are bad."

Sulastri stroked her husband's shoulders. She very rarely displayed such affection.

"Do you remember Marti's letter? I could never bear having to live like that. Eating, sleeping, having children. If that's what you call life, ah, there's no meaning in going on living. It'd be better to just be savages."

Sudarmo scoffed and laughed. Then he went on, "Even a mother's love is now measured by how much money you send to your family. And because we are in this thing.... Do you remember when you were sick?"

"Shush!" Sulastri cut him off. Unspeakable pain tore at her heart. "Don't talk about that, Dar. Shush!"

Once again Sulastri hugged her husband and gazed at him with a look that was so sharp that he made a face.

"All that's long gone," she said, "We have to be able to bear this life. And perhaps our souls will grow because of it. Everyone's life has its own meaning. Nothing happens for no reason. Our luck will improve, Dar. Do you remember what your uncle said? He could tell fortunes and he told us ours. Strangely, I believed him.

I felt at ease. But sometimes I feel a loneliness that just gets worse and worse. If there were no children. But everyone gets lonely. I just feel it more than you. And in fact, everyone wants to free themselves from that feeling."

"It depends on the kind of person you are, Lastri. The more mature one's soul, the more deeply one will feel that loneliness. We can't dissolve into others."

"Deep inside, we're also shrouded in that loneliness. I love you, Dar. But sometimes you're a stranger to me. It's as if you and I can't punch through the wall of isolation between us. Love and affection aren't enough to make us united in spirit and body. We only think of ourselves as individuals. Whatever the suffering, it can be defeated, if there is a pleasant breeze around us. Fresh air."

Sulastri took a breath, feeling the coolness of the night breeze. The scent of yellow jasmine wafted by them. She loved that fragrance. She saw the old tree, its branches sticking out everywhere. It was in last flower, white as snow, its fragrance pervasive. The radio had gone off air for the night and the streets were quieting down. Occasional bicycle lights shone in the darkness and then were gone. The dark houses with faded colors had an appealing charm, as if veiled in dark shadows and dim light. The lights looked hazy and secretive, not unlike overhearing someone breathing in their sleep.

She stood up, stretched, and then leaned against the wooden wall of the house. Sudarmo's cigarette was finished and he lit up another. The light of the match illuminated his face for just an instant. His face was boney and lined, revealing a stubborn quality in the firmness of his jaw against his cheek, though his lips were soft and eyebrows almost invisible.

"He's suddenly looking like an old man, this husband of mine," thought Sulastri. She heard him going on, a certain anger in his voice. "Who has time to think? No one. People line up in their uniforms. And then they plunge forward as if into some kind of painful walking race. Everybody wants to think the same and move the same. The masses, just a herd of sheep. Not allowed to have their own opinions or points of view. And so, we're farther than ever from our independence."

"Oh, independence. Who is truly independent…? But, not like that," Sulastri corrected him. "That's how people become Buddhist, and we haven't achieved the luxury to meditate in spiritual peace. I take back what I said just now. Let's not cleanse ourselves by becoming just spectators. That's right, spectators, what's called bookworms. Practical people, people who are capable of action, think our clever brains should be just kept in a museum. The way they see it, we're useless. On the other hand, the young spend their time just partying, playing sports, and fooling around. Is this generation cursed to live like flirty butterflies? I don't know. But there is something that strikes me as a warning: that we are flying in the clouds. Relations with the common people? No. Respected by the officials who lead peaceful lives? No. Oh, I don't know what tomorrow holds for us."

"We feel smashed to bits, Las. That's the problem. Everyone suspects everyone else. There's no courage among us. If there were just one person who dared to... but leaders aren't born every day. Or if they were, they might disavow the obligation. Strange to say, Marti wants to swim against the tide of the times and take her boat upriver, but in fact she's being carried by a swift current. She's become bourgeois. Head to toe bourgeois. She greedily devours the old, superannuated honors, like a prima donna examining the pictures of her youth, and revels in outdated praise. And she regales her guests with those same stale victories. What a shame. She can't free herself from her environment. Too bad, when we look back on how she could attract people with her deep conviction. Now she's just down-to-earth. I hate that term. Working for something good and wanting to make a little sacrifice, that's not down-to-earth. Criticizing someone as being stupid for not having money anymore or for getting married for love and affection, that's not down-to-earth, or..."

Sulastri gave a little pout and laughed. "Everyone nowadays only chases after pleasure and therefore supposes they can buy brilliance."

She laughed again because she remembered a colleague at work who felt proud to mix Sundanese with Dutch words; but she spoke Dutch in such a way that her students secretly laughed at her. She also spoke grandly of how her husband had cheated on her. Seated casually on a chair, she giggled as she spoke of scary things and, covering her mouth with a plump hand, announced that she hated her husband. But she kept directing her speech to the naughty husband and it was like she was living again in her memories, which seemed very saddening and gloomy, as she related them. But why did she always titter and act so coyly? That was such nonsense to Sulastri, because she herself wouldn't talk about all the ins and outs of a divorce and a husband's treachery. Sulastri thought she'd be better off keeping quiet if she were ever in that situation. Her colleague delighted in talking about how "he" was not being looked after properly by his young mistress and even had to do all the housework.

"This is *her* time," thought Sulastri, "people only think about saving money so they can get rich fast. They scrimp and save so they can have fun in life. I'm not the way I used to be. Can one hold back the course of time?"

She continued along this line of thought and didn't realize the breeze was getting cooler. Sudarmo stood up and touched his wife's shoulder.

"Let's go inside. It's gotten late," he said. The clock struck eleven o'clock. They went into the house and locked the front door.

Their bedroom was dim and dusky, even in the daytime, for it had no windows. It received light from the children's room, because the wall between the two rooms did not reach the top of the low ceiling. In bed now, Sulastri covered herself with the blanket and drew close to her husband. He was smoking a cigarette again and sending up puffs of smoke to the top their mosquito net. From the beginning of their marriage, Sulastri couldn't get used to his habit of smoking in bed. Early in the morning, when he had gotten up, she felt nauseated at the sight of cigarette butts by the bed and all the ashes mottling the floor.

But now in the present environment, the clouds of smoke actually drew them close and made her feel their fates were shared. Sudarmo didn't notice his wife watching him from the side. He gave a start when she gently covered his eyes. He moved her hands away and said more sourly than he intended, "Act your age."

"What are you thinking about?" she asked.

"Oh, your manuscript. Last night, when you came in with the mail, I had hoped its contents would be different. I worried this would happen, but I tried to suppress it. That's just the way people are, hopeful about something while actually feeling the opposite will happen. Have you ever felt that way?"

Sulastri frowned and probed her feelings the previous day as deeply as she could. "No," she said definitively, "Something did tell me that this was going to happen. I couldn't sleep. I felt hot and restless."

"That's not the reason. You're fibbing, Las."

Sudarmo looked at her face and winked playfully. Sulastri blushed and hid her head under the pillow. She turned away from him, angry at him for spoiling the tender atmosphere.

"I'm just teasing you." Sudarmo pulled at his wife's hair and whispered something in her ear. Sulastri relented and went on speaking rather moodily.

"Don't joke like that. Of course that's the reason. I tried to think of other things by reading a book. But the words just flashed through my mind. And the book was so good! Early this morning, I sensed a kind of emptiness in my chest and I felt nauseated. I saw everyone dimly as if they were enveloped in thin clouds and I could barely make out their faces. I had to smile at the ignorance of the children. And normally I'm not like that. And a hidden voice kept echoing in my mind: your manuscript has been returned. When I held that mail at nine o'clock, I looked at it with an unnatural calmness and a bitter taste on my tongue. Then I became very painfully aware: *you've worked all for nothing.* And after that, I thought of just giving up and felt an amazing lethargy come over me." Sulastri stopped, fascinated by her own words. Sudarmo could still hear the trembling voice of his wife.

"Las, my dear," he thought with fondness. "You're on the threshold of your life, so it's hard for you to bear this disappointment. Even so, you've got your sadness under control. And that's good. Your time will come. But for me, everything's too late. Too late."

A feeling of his own desolation made him embrace his wife affectionately. He rested his head on her shoulder and, feeling her warmth, his gloominess went away.

"If one could always take shelter in his belief," thought Sudarmo. There were times when people acted like children and had to cry and dispel their sadness with a flood of tears. And that weakness would freshen the heart, be cooling and disperse anxiety.

Sulastri didn't move. She just whispered in a voice that was soft, as if far away.

"Dar, do you remember how we took turns rewriting that draft? Sometimes you didn't understand what was written there. You made fun of the words, and over and over asked me what they meant, so I got mad and left you to work by yourself. When you got tired, you laid down on the sofa. And then it was my turn.

You wrapped yourself tightly in the blanket because of the way the cold wind blew in through the cracks in the wall. When I wrote I never paid attention to the letters themselves, I was so keen on finishing the manuscript. Some sentences I just wrote off the top of my head. I kept feeling the wind on my frozen legs. I didn't know what to do so I folded them under me. Sometimes I turned my eyes to the lamp so I wouldn't fall asleep.

"I wrote and wrote. That's what hurts, that the work was all for nothing. And to keep from falling asleep, I kept going over to sit next to you. You slept so soundly. I would calm down hearing another person's breathing in the quietness. I was also quite scared, even though, with my rational mind, I don't believe in ghosts. But in the deep of the night, my sense of fear was awful. I'd sneak in under your blanket, shut my eyes tight and try to calm my heart, it was beating so hard. There were so many of those sorts of things we experienced together. Could you ever divorce me?"

Sudarmo hugged his wife ever more tightly and felt her heart beating, softly conscious of her breath on him. Then all of a sudden he realized how he'd feel if he ever lost her.

"I remember it all, Tri. Don't even think I could forget it. I barely realized what love was, though, then."

Sulastri answered almost inaudibly, "Because of our life together, we can appreciate all this. Friendship, love. Maybe it's better like this. We can't deny the hidden meaning behind everything that happens."

They still felt those memories anchored in the past. Now came the recollections that mocked all that, sometimes with looks of confusion. Sudarmo and Sulastri lay side by side, silently lost in their own thoughts of the past. Outside, the night watch patrol struck their bamboo clackers. Guavas fell on zinc roofs. A cuckoo cried out plaintively, a hair-raising sound in all that solitude. Now the stars glittered majestically until the dawn light would make them pale and look ashamed. Tick, tick, tick, the silver wall clock sounded, indifferent to everything.

Sudarmo slept next to her, his arm covering his head. He had to be asleep now. Softly Sulastri pulled the blanket down and carefully she crossed over her husband's outstretched legs and left the bed. She closed the mosquito net again as if she were a mother standing over the bed of her child. She closely monitored the outside sounds as she stood in the doorway. Then she stepped lightly into the inner room. She had to bind those memories together, right now, because if not, they would vanish again.

"Come to me, memories," she whispered above the blank piece of paper. She pressed her hands against her chest and then bowed her head.

"Inspiration, come to me. Oh no, no. My own life must be my inspiration. I only reminisce. I've got to recall it."

Dim forms seemed to become clear, like memories standing there, with bright, enthralling faces.

"I'll write about you," she whispered. "Forgive me if I want you to be prettier... or funnier. Forgive me if I beg you to stay with me forever."

The paper accepted the images moving from Sulastri's hand as she quickly wrote. The letters merged into words, into sentences that sought to sequester her memories in their innumerable ranks. She didn't feel time marching on, didn't feel her body's exhaustion. That night, she began new pages—this writing must replace the rejected manuscript, must be made into the instrument to avenge her defeat.

2

In 1933, Sulastri walked into her new home. Various pieces of furniture, such as a table, chairs, wardrobes and dressers, had earlier been delivered here to Bandung from Purwakarta. These had been the household furnishings of her girlhood home and, for the time being, the possibility of buying new things would be unthinkable for her. Where her life was going now, she didn't know. There was a vague reminder of the misery and lack of money that warned her to get used to her new life as quickly as possible. She was proud of having to follow her husband into a life of impoverishment. And it was out of pride that she felt far apart from other people. Higher than them, people whose marriages were based on calculations of mere profit and loss. This made her happy and she saw everything else as shallow. She'd laugh derisively if someone told her that in real life she would be weighted down with other problems. And that people couldn't just ignore the values and habits of living according to custom. She'd disagree, saying, "Doesn't Sudarmo work in the interest of the nation? I would be ashamed if I weren't by his side in his work."

That's how she'd defend herself. And she'd ignore how her father, uncle, and sisters would frown to think of what would happen to her in the future.

"Let Sudarmo arrange your home however it appeals to him, just so long as you don't let your job go because of him. In a year or two, you both will lose your home and jobs if you get involved with working in the nationalist education schools. You know yourself that Sudarmo is no leader, no matter how he sees himself. Everyone is allowed his or her ideals. But by themselves, everything has to accord with reality. And if you two lose everything, we're going to have to feed you."

Her brother-in-law, an intelligent and quick-witted man, had said all that with total certainty and, in the end, Sulastri naturally did just the opposite.

She loved her husband, didn't she? Everything was crystal clear. Besides, there was another consideration at that time. People who quit their jobs and thereby sacrificed their salaries so they could throw themselves into the service of nationalist education or the hustle and bustle of political activism, all which demanded their sweat and energy, were called fighters, warriors. The spirit of Sukarno ignited flames in the consciences of the youth. Many of them resigned from their jobs. And those who still worked as civil servants gave clichéd reasons for their attitudes.

"Yes, we're forced to stay at work as government workers, but when conditions permit, we'll act differently...." History bore witness that such words later became "Lucky we're still government workers."

A thousand excuses pressured Sulastri's brother-in-law into staying with his job. She and Sudarmo's friends just gave a little smile. Martilah, Sulastri's older sister, felt disrespected and she gave an even more passionate speech before the members of her women's association. Of course, the times were strange. Marriages were contracted according to political convictions between men and women who previously would never have met. Youngsters married without asking about lineages and titles. There were no masters and servants. Everyone was a friend and comrade. No one would dispute it, because Sukarno, Bung Karno himself, treated his servants as members of his own family. As far as valuing someone... whoever orates loudly in a general meeting, that is a fighter, man or woman. A man chooses as his partner for life a woman fighter, a Srikandi, and not a Sumbadra. And obviously, Sumbadra was the aristocratic married woman in spirit.

It wasn't in the least surprising when Sulastri chose Sudarmo without first finding out about his position and salary, while Marti had entered a very different family setting. There were certain advantages, while the disadvantages didn't matter at all, they were so insignificant. They both were still young and didn't need anyone else in their lives except each other.

Sudarmo was a director of the nationalist education school in Bandung. This consisted of a primary school and a MULO, which were located in two school buildings and provided food to fifteen teachers. They often went for months short of money even to buy food. But there were times when they received sufficient support. The question of holidays and vacations was most important. Sudarmo arranged it in such a way that the days of time off would fall at the end of the month. There was another difficulty, an invoice of *f*200 for the purchase of books.

Sudarmo didn't know about that debt when he accepted the position of director. He was shocked and forced to adopt a new strategy. For a while there was a risk of all the school assets being seized, but after a long conversation between the school head and the bookstore owner, the outstanding amount could now be paid in reasonable installments, so it wouldn't be too long before books could again be bought on credit. The textbooks that he had bought previously couldn't be used, and, even worse, had gone missing in all directions.

Sudarmo didn't underestimate his responsibilities and obligations. And he pressured Sulastri into lightening his job by helping to teach. She quit her own job and gave lessons in Sudarmo's school. Sulastri had a lot of faith that they would succeed. And so she came to Bandung, full of hope. Before leaving, she wrote this letter to her sister.

Marti,
Pray that I can work full of ideals. You recall that our bond as sisters must perpetuate our loyalty to our oath: work for those who are oppressed and for Indonesia, the motherland of both you and me.

Lastri

The reply came with a piece of advice. Her brother-in-law penciled in additional admonitions as well.

But Sulastri crumpled up their letter. And on one brilliant morning, after rather energetically closing the door of the taxicab that brought her there, she stood in front of a lodging house in Bandung. At first, she was surprised at how unkempt the garden and everything around it was. It was like getting a slap across the face, and she was shocked and hurt. The *cemara* tree at the edge of the yard looked like it was there just for the birds' nests. Dry leaves piled up under the trees. Purple bougainvillea spread out everywhere. The grass was excessively high, nor was it regular in its growth and there were patches of red earth. The windows and door of the main house had been painted any which way and clashed with the tin-bordered windowpanes on the front. An areca palm tree with its red petals stood taller than the tiled roof and its fronds swayed with great passion, the petals a glowing red. The climbing jasmine ornamented the rooftiles with ranks of beautiful deep yellow blossoms. But such adornment of the rather old building was in vain.

Sulastri walked as quickly as she could along the gravel path to a pavilion far to the rear of the first building. She felt a tightness in her chest and her breathing was difficult, only partly because of the heat of the sun. She turned around and signaled to Sudarmo to hurry along. She felt alien here and gazed doubtfully at the solid-looking front door. It had been painted a yellowish color and because dust had gathered in the cracks of the door panels, the yellow looked darker. The key was rusted, so Sudarmo had some trouble opening the door.

"Huh," grumbled Sulastri. "The trip was tiring and my head is spinning. But what's that?" She took up a pestle from the table and, peering at it closely, decided that it was used to make *rujak*.

"Why is this thing here? *Aduh*, on the front veranda table! Aren't you ashamed, Dar?"

Sudarmo shrugged and replied indifferently, "That's none of my business. Jamil's made rujak. Nothing unusual. Our laurel tree produces lots of fruit. And, oh, so what? It's all the same if you make rujak in the kitchen or here. The results are the same."

Sulastri just stayed silent. She knew that tidiness in a home was said to be bourgeois. And could you go against public opinion? The door was open. Sudarmo entered the house and opened the side windows. Sunlight came into the room. What in dimness didn't look so bad, in sunlight appeared very unsightly and depressing. Sulastri was surprised at the sight of such a messy room, because, apart from its slovenliness, the person who lived there was an intellectual. She saw books scattered all over the place and a big bookshelf leaning against the wall full of books with colorful covers. Socks, shoes, and clothing were strewn everywhere. Spider webs accumulated around the light bulbs like spools of thread. There were two chairs, one of which had a broken seat, that were being used as a rack and a place to hang clothes. And, from the piles of cigarette ash and butts in front of it dirtying up the fine floor tiles, a sofa covered by a piece of batiked cloth appeared to have been used more as a place to sit than to lie down on. A high window let in sunlight. The ceiling, painted an off-yellow color, stood rather high; the floor felt cool and refreshing. Sulastri went straight over to the window. She wanted both to cry and laugh. Oppressive feelings suddenly hit her, and her eyes glistened.

"I'm crazy," she thought, holding back her tears. Then she smiled at her husband and turned around.

"It's very nice here."

"You're not fibbing, are you?" With a disbelieving expression, Sudarmo looked carefully at his wife. But Sulastri paid no attention to his look and replied lightly:

"What more is there to say? The air's cool and you're near me. What more would I want? Even if...." She fell silent in hesitation and Sudarmo understood. Then they both suddenly burst out laughing.

"Oh, it will all get fixed up. Only, one thing, Tri. The people here are real hairsplitters. I mean, we will quickly be branded bourgeois."

"Oh, who cares! Don't talk nonsense."

Sulastri put her finger on Sudarmo's shoulder and said, "Okay, I want to see everything." They went to look at the back room and then the kitchen, which was quite big and whose walls had been painted blue. It felt fresh and pleasant.

"This'll be our dining room." Sudarmo had immediately decided on how the rooms in their new residence would be used.

"The rooms in back belong to three teachers. You know Jamil, right? Well, that's where he sleeps. Oh, here he is now. Speak of the devil—"

"—and for sure you'll tread on its tail," chuckled Jamil. With his big head, he looked like a wild bear, and when he spoke, his head would tilt somewhat. He fortified his words with a clenched fist or by nodding his head.

"Our agriculture expert, Tri. For days now, he's been constantly thinking of making a school garden."

"I can help with it, Mas. I enjoy making little gardens."

Jamil nodded and, putting his forefinger on his forehead, said thoughtfully, "The problem is, I can't work with that lazy school servant. He's fat and lazy and spends the whole day singing... and just slacking off. What should I do? And now that he's member of the Marhaen Party, he calls me 'Bung'. For every order I give him, he asks for an official statement for it from the faculty meeting."

"Oh, don't make a big thing out of this. I am very satisfied with him," said Sudarmo. He had to laugh at Jamil's sourpuss look; he was such a pessimist. His friends teased him because he talked like a fortune teller or an agricultural expert who sometimes got off track when he spoke.

Jamil himself defended his expertise in botany and animal husbandry. He had attended class three of animal husbandry school. Sulastri felt friendly toward him, even though she always disliked his know-it-all attitude. While they were discussing all this, a young man passed by with head bowed.

"It's Harjono. Mas Harjono, come on over!" He joined them, a youth with a shy and daydreamy look. His shoulders were hunched, and his mouth showed signs of his basic gloominess. His eyebrows were always furrowed.

"Um, I'm glad to meet you," he said. "I still have work to do."

And he went off, rather touched by this, with his head bowed and the same dull steps, as if carrying a heavy weight on his shoulders.

"He never smiles," said Jamil.

"We've betted on making him smile. He never does. And he's shy in front of women."

"He takes everything so seriously. If he jokes, he never laughs. But... he's good enough at teaching his students. He teaches Dutch, German, English and French. He went to AMS, and majored in Western Literature and he was in the highest class there."

With all the zest of revealing some secret, Jamil took up the lead.

"Dar, one time in MULO he was reading a French poem. It was

clear no one understood it. He was a bit nutty—if he gave a lesson, he never moved his gaze from the book and stuck to his high chair like a rusty nail."

Jamil laughed happily at his own story.

"Don't talk about Harjono," said Sudarmo. "And when it comes to you, Mas Jamil, everyone complains that you're always grumbling like an old bear." Sudarmo winked at Sulastri and then looked over at Jamil in pretended earnestness.

"Oh." Jamil's face darkened red in embarrassment. "To hell with those kids. They're all dumb. They can't tell the difference between a root and a tuber." He stroked his chin, where a few beard hairs gave him a manly look, or so he thought. Then he continued with hurt feelings.

"And not just kids. Mas Dar, for example..."

"Oh, oh, that business of the beans. Pooh!" Sudarmo burst out laughing and shook his head like a water-sprayed cat. Then he turned around. Sulastri was delighted. And Jamil, seeing the amusement in Sulastri's eyes, went on. "He, I mean Mas Dar, he said those beans were tiny tubers, and I said to him that no, they were tiny fruits. He wouldn't believe it. What would you say, Zus Tri?" He paused for a bit, waiting for Sulastri's answer.

"Tiny tubers," Sulastri blurted out, not quite sure.

Jamil laughed uproariously and then explained. "Beans are fruit. When pollen lands on the pistil, the flower droops and the farmer's got to cover it over with soil. And that's when its fruits grow."

Sulastri didn't want to believe it. Then Jamil said, "Lodgers, we're going to plant beans."

"Hmm," intoned Sudarmo. "Jamil thinks he knows about everything about everything. Isn't that so?"

"If you want, I'll swear to it. It wasn't for nothing that I studied to be—"

"A vet," Sudarmo broke in.

Sulastri and Sudarmo laughed at Jamil. Then another person joined in their laughter, a young man, wide-shouldered and tall, with very large hands and feet.

"And there's Waluyo," said Sulastri to Sudarmo.

"Yes, I know him. We've gone on excursions together with other people to this place and that. And he often visits Marti. How are you, Bung?" she greeted Waluyo. A broad grin showed on his thick, slightly protruding lips. He presented an air of nonchalance with his head rather tilted back.

"I'm fine. And how are you, Zus? You're a *nyonya* now." Waluyo gave a little laugh. Sulastri wasn't pleased. There was something untrustworthy about him. He had sat in second year at the Technical School. He had had a messy life and in the company of his fellow party members, he was labeled as a flip-flopper. Nonetheless, he was an excellent propagandist, while his courage at rallies gave him slight victories in front of the masses whenever the police moved to keep the peace. In that way, people at rallies awarded him a high degree of respect. Even though they were fellow party members, Sudarmo didn't particularly like him because Waluyo wouldn't go along with him; and he was very lazy. In this school of theirs, he worked in administration because he had been banned from teaching by the government. Waluyo should have been grateful to Sudarmo for allowing him to keep working at their school, but instead he stirred up friends and enemies to oust Sudarmo from his job. The reason for this was because Sudarmo had once criticized his laziness. Sudarmo had required Waluyo to be at the school from 8:00 am to 12:30 pm, but Waluyo still just came and went as he pleased. You had to go find him or wait for him to arrive to pay the school's fees. This contributed to a shortfall in school fee payments.

That's why the atmosphere grew tense when Waluyo came over to them. He and Sudarmo exchanged stinging and unpleasant words.

With a mocking smile, Waluyo said, "Dar got married the same way he'd go to the washroom. He said tomorrow he was getting married and then nothing more after that. Kind of funny, right?"

"What's even more funny was when you telegrammed me from Batavia on the day of my wedding. And just because of that—because one of the teachers had to appear before the PID, my wedding had to be postponed one day. You could have fixed it yourself. And as a result, I inconvenienced everyone."

"Oh, isn't Mas Dar the school principal?"

"Yes, but that didn't mean that I had to be called back on that day." Sudarmo shrugged his shoulders, then laughed and said, "Let's wait for the truck outside on the bench. It's sure to be coming."

The four of them sat on the bench. Waluyo kicked at small stones, then stood up, straightened himself and began to talk, oblivious to all.

"There's a teachers' meeting tomorrow. I think all the teachers will be complaining about the low pay. I usually pay them right on the 15th. After that I divide the remainder among us all, according to the regulations set by the teachers' meeting. But they complain it's not enough for them, let alone for Harjono and Mas Prawira."

"Yes, those two." Sudarmo was chatting again with Waluyo, while Sulastri and Jamil stood under the *buni* tree. "Harjono's deep in debt and a lot of people are coming after him. Why did he ever have the idea of buying a gramophone?"

"He's interested in the arts, according to what he told me," explained Waluyo.

"He enjoys classical music. Listen, he's playing another record now."

They heard Beethoven's minuet in G major. Over the window curtain they saw Harjono's head with its wavy hair.

"An odd fellow. He's really fallen for Kurani, a girl in the second year at MULO."

Sudarmo frowned. "In love with a student? I don't believe it. But it could be...," he said slowly.

Jamil heard their conversation. He left Sulastri and joined in with gusto. "Yes, I knew that too. The children bother Kurani about it. Embarrassing! Naturally he thinks it would be easy to get her. Well, now I've got *you*!"

"That's Mas Jamil for you!" Sudarmo said. "A guy who collects slanderous stories. Oh, here we are talking gibberish. A bunch of bourgeois, that's what we are." Sudarmo drew near to Sulastri and picked a berry from its twig.

"Delicious!" He put the fruit into his mouth and chewed it for a while, then spat out the seeds, one by one.

"Look at your tongue. Black. How's mine?"

Sulastri stuck out her tongue. Jamil and Waluyo snickered in disgust and joked, "Don't imitate him. Ignore him, he's become a dictator."

Sulastri couldn't fathom the logic behind this string of sentences, but she did see a dark shadow flit over Sudarmo's face. Then his face regained its light, the visage of a young man.

A truck came bringing the furniture, and Jamil and Waluyo helped them unload. The workers who accompanied the vehicle labored hard. Sulastri frequently had to press herself against the walls to avoid blocking their way. She followed her husband everywhere, even though she couldn't work. The messy pavilion now gradually took on a different look. The atmosphere was as if a young person had returned. Potted plants covered the dirtiest places. The inner rooms with their soft chairs, red satin lampshades and the gold-striped, brown door curtains displayed an ambience that was tolerable, while all the books behind the curtains appeared inviting. The veranda took on a fashionable look because of the pots of plants set on the low wall. The floor tiles began to shine, thanks to the mop of Sulastri's servant, who had joined in, a local Batavian who usually broke out in a broad smile in response to any request by Sulastri.

Waluyo and Jamil sat in the living room with outstretched legs and didn't give any impression of leaving. When the school servant Urip came with a tiffin carrier of food, Waluyo stood up, stretched, and went home. Jamil heartily joined in the meal, while Sulastri ate without much appetite.

Afterward, Sudarmo chatted with Sulastri. He was lying down as he talked. Sulastri sat on the sofa before him as she carefully folded her sarongs.

"This is a new life for you," he said. "I ask you to help me in everything, and you can help me if you stay cheerful. Because hard days are definitely ahead. They didn't want you to work here, actually. They think I ordered the transfer of a female teacher to be replaced by you. But that's not true. It smears the good name of our school. And now you're here, Tri." And Sulastri listened to him as if she were a small child.

"Sometimes I want to leave all this," her husband went on. "I've got lots of enemies. You know, I, a member of the Marhaen Party and nationalist education movement, would like someone else to become the school principal. They think I have too many people influencing me: Jamil, Waluyo, and Kardi are members of the Marhaen Party leadership and are very active outside the school. My own responsibilities are heavy and grueling. The teachers complain about their salaries. And I myself can't be said to be living in luxury on 40 guilders. The school's heavy in debt and I've felt obligated to fulfill all our promises, Tri, even if we have to pay monthly instalments of 150 guilders, or even more. Dearest, you won't be adding to my burden, right? More than anything else, Tri, I have got to have your understanding and help."

Sulastri looked straight ahead without blinking. Unexpectedly, a single teardrop fell on her hand. "Dar, I promise to help in everything. But forgive me if my mental condition doesn't meet with your wishes."

"We can bear the lack of funds, Tri. But this atmosphere of everyone suspecting each other sucks the blood out of my chest. I feel like I'm not living. I lash out right and left and I'm only hitting the air. You can bet, if the enemy is right there in front, but can't be seen, it can't be grasped. I feel like I am losing ground, step by step. You'll see that yourself. Even so, I work hard and give all I've got. My fellow-workers can only gripe and moan. They call me a dictator. That makes me sad because they misunderstand my determination. I mean well. Now you're here, Tri. You are my comrade. It's my hope never to lose a single member of my party as a comrade."

Sulastri felt as though suddenly the sunlight had been covered by dark clouds.

"I'll help you," she replied, almost in a whisper. "May Allah grant me the strength and fortitude." They fell silent. Then Sulastri said, "Dar, I'm happy you need me. Rest assured, I'll always be by your side, even when enemies attack, as long as you tell me everything plainly and openly, everything. Are you willing to do that? We have no need to lie to each other. Because if that's not the case, we cannot love each other."

They discussed many things: love, the future, and after that, everyday matters. Then, feeling greatly reassured, Sudarmo closed the window, so that the sunlight wouldn't come in during their afternoon nap. All the sounds outside slowed down. Sulastri heard her husband's pocket watch in his jacket.

"Roses in the sunshine," she thought, "I picked them one by one when I was a little girl. Those were lovely times." She saw in her mind the sunlight passing through the clove tree and making splotches of brightness under the *kedongdong* tree. She imagined clearly hearing the hissing of the train whistle. She saw her mother. Then all these images and people's faces faded. Sulastri fell asleep and breathed easily as if she had no fear of tomorrow.

The next day they got ready to visit Mas Prawira at his home.

"Finished, Tri? Let's go."

She fixed something on her chignon, smoothed some powder over her cheeks and then put a caramel-colored shawl over her shoulders. Sudarmo looked at her uneasily.

"Way too much," he said disapprovingly. "You've got to learn to dress simply. This is an ordinary visit."

"Never mind," Sulastri said, offended by the harshness in his voice. "I like dressing nicely. And I'm not bothering anyone."

"No," he replied, "but it disturbs people's sensibilities if you arrive in some impoverished milieu wearing clothes that fine. Don't wear that dress anymore. It's too good for here."

Sulastri looked at him coolly. She was angry to be the target of griping when in fact they had only just gotten married. And what was she going to do with those clothes? She hadn't bought them; they were gifts from other people. As they wrangled thus, they walked across the grass to the house next door.

That was where Prawira, an older colleague of Sudarmo's had been given a place to stay. They passed under a low doorway and were in the back of the school building, where Prawira's family were living in several rooms. The front of the building was for the classrooms, where at that moment there was no one. The veranda alongside those back rooms was used as a guest room as well as a dining room. The bedroom was dark, and crammed with beds, cabinets and all sorts of things, to the point where it was nearly impossible to move around in there. Prawira had seven children, three nephews and nieces, and an old uncle who had to look after the children who were still little. At night the boys slept on a mat on the floor. It was always in turmoil there, with the young ones shouting and yelling, the old man grumbling, while the older boys roughhoused. In the morning they fooled around in the washroom, spraying water everywhere and paying no attention to their father's angry threats. Their father would wait patiently at the doorway and then patiently return to his cup of coffee.

That is why Prawira usually arrived late at the school. Every day had to apologize, saying his watch was slow. All the pupils would grin, and once they composed a song to annoy him: "*Pak Prawira comes late... late.*" At the words "late... late," the kid up front would be poked in the back and the song would be performed in rhythm, which gave the opportunity to sway most pleasantly and clomp their right foot on the floor.

His colleagues at school secretly laughed, but none of them forbade the children to do that. Wasn't it a very amusing prank?

Prawira's wife smiled awkwardly at Sulastri. "Oh, I can't tell you how happy I am that you're here. Sudarmo's really happy, for sure. We're lucky to have you so close by." And she went on with many more pleasantries. That was the way Indonesians were toward guests and it shouldn't be taken seriously. Prawira's wife looked a lot older than she should have. But despite the creases and crevices of her wrinkled face, one could see the loveliness of her youth. Her hair was still wavy and neatly covered her ears. Her face spoke of her hardships. In the expression of her child-like eyes flitted dark images of daily suffering. Sudarmo remained silent, rather bored and mentally drifting, as he listened to the beautifully rhythmic Sundanese language of the woman. Then Prawira himself arrived, stooping and bowing, and apologized for having neglected his guests so long. He stood in the doorway, which was low and narrow and provided a dim view.

Sulastri wound up the dirty yellow mosquito nets that enveloped the beds. In front of her was a table with little boxes, a string, and a broken doll. Then she saw in another glance a display cabinet, the prettiest piece of furniture in the house. The floor tiles looked in bad shape because of the dust and the tracks of the children's dirty feet.

There was a well near this veranda, where could be heard both rowdy voices and covered whisperings. For an instant, Sulastri saw the face of someone peering at her, which quickly disappeared. In the back next to the kitchen were tomato and red pepper plants. Two of the boys were kicking at each other; their mother abruptly stood up and ordered them to be quiet. Then she took over the baby from her uncle's shoulder sling and breastfed it in front of her guests. Prawira turned to Sulastri, rather embarrassed but with a calmness, and said, "So this is our situation on the occasion of your first visit. I feel ashamed."

He cringed once more, and, stroking his face with his hand, he began again, "Uh, hmm, Pak Sudarmo, I've read the all the rules, eh, your recommendations and suggestions. Really wonderful, and so right. Oh, you are extremely skilled in expressing them."

Prawira continued in the same tone of voice, scraping the floor as he moved his chair to sit together. And he didn't forget to cringe when answering Sulastri in a way that she felt derisive and unnerving. Prawira's mottled face was the earthy brown of the *sawo* fruit. His smile seemed to be camouflage. Sulastri suspected Prawira would go on cringing and smiling like that, even upon hearing his own death sentence pronounced. But she knew that Prawira also worked hard and went into debt to feed his family. Nor would he ever leave the nationalist education school.

"That's the way our people are," said Sudarmo later. "They want to make sacrifices. They're filled with dedication. But because of the hardship of daily life, it's like they're dead, like they've surrendered themselves to fate. They can't tell the difference between the causes and results of things. They work without reflecting, like automata. There's love in their dedication at first. Then their courage in living crumbles bit by bit and they complain, they sabotage, and then they just keep quiet and conspire with one another."

Sulastri saw the heartrending poverty and she understood their cringing walk, their smiles and tone of voice. When she and her husband took their leave that afternoon and passed through that low door, she sensed sharp relief in a certain person's smile and all the suffering hidden behind it. They returned home in silence. Sulastri wrapped her shawl around her. She was filled with vague thoughts and, as she leaned back in the reclining chair, she still heard the rhythms of Ibu Prawira's voice.

"That's the way I'll be," she thought, "if I'm not careful. She used to be young. And now?"

"Tri, are you daydreaming again?"

"No," she answered harshly. "It's just that I've seen my future face."

3

"Comrades, on the blackboard you can see my proposals for managing the sources of our livelihood. Starting now, we can hope to receive 850 guilders. We need to make monthly outlays of 370 guilders to pay for rental, loans, lighting, water, school staff and much else besides. That leaves us about 500. These are the arrangements I will make: everyone will get at least 25 and if there still remains any distributable surplus, that will be divided among us as shown on the blackboard."

Sudarmo pointed to the board and continued. "I will act democratically in as perfect a manner as possible. You won't be able to say this distribution is unfair. Do you agree with it? You certainly will if you examine coolly and objectively what I'm proposing here."

He leaned back in his high chair, crossed his legs, knitted his fingers together and ran his eyes over all the teachers. For the moment they were tensely silent. Then Jamil raised his hand hesitantly. "I say it's not fair if someone has to sacrifice because of what others have done, their irresponsibility. I mean... uh... what I think is...." He stumbled on. Then noticing Sudarmo's questioning look, he went straight to the point. "You all know I don't have any children. Mas Prawira has seven. Why should I, though I work as hard as Mas Prawira, get less than he does, because he has seven children? Do you understand, comrades?" Jamil directed his look toward all the silent attendees. He felt the clumsiness of his speech and his ears had reddened, for he saw their censorious looks.

Sudarmo stood up. "Mas Jamil is against. I can see what he is getting at. And I can guess the reasons why. I understand. I ignored his diploma and the years spent in study, that is to say, giving him a recognition that was lower than it should have been. As to the standard we take: every person gets 25 guilders. One year's study after MULO will earn 5 plus guilders. For one child, 2.5, and for a wife 7.50. So Mas Prawira would get 25 guilders + (7 x 2.5) + 7.50 = 50. The highest salary is 50 guilders. Is this not fair, when a person who has the biggest family gets more than a single unmarried person?"

Jamil: "Do we get a subsidy for a second wife?"

Waluyo interrupted here: "It just looks like a wedding present."

Sudarmo was stung, because he could see that Waluyo was indirectly making fun of him, and so answered sharply, "I've just gotten married and can't make a regulation advocating polygamy. Comrades, let's be serious."

Then Jamil, pretending not to understand, said, "Wouldn't you see preventing childbirth as being more sensible?"

Sudarmo flushed a deep red and lashed out, "Do you want to reduce my livelihood and my wife's, too, because we've just been married?"

Jamil laughed in a whinnying sound and they all broke out laughing.

Sudarmo paused a moment and then continued, "So you all have decided that these proposals of mine are appropriately fair, is that it? Certainly as Indonesians?"

They all nodded in agreement, but the tension in the air could not be dispelled. They felt it wasn't fair that Mas Prawira, who had never attended a MULO school and whose diploma was no higher than that of a village school and assistant teacher training school, would now receive what they got, even more than Jamil and Harjono.

Sudarmo went on, "Under these circumstances, we need not think only of our own needs. We're still young. Whatever the case, we can shoulder the weight of this life. But we will feel wrong if we underestimate the obligations of managing a family. We must try to lighten other people's hardships. You lighten my burdens, and I will do the same for you. And doing it this way will be more advantageous for the school rather than complaining about higher levels or demanding rights according to whatever people want."

Waluyo whispered something to Jamil and they both laughed. Then Jamil raised his hand and said with a well-intended smile, "Right, all of that is right. We accept that, it's true. But what if another baby is born, then another? Should I, or better, we, pay for those children? In this way...," he stopped. Everyone was laughing. Normally Jamil spoke straightforwardly. He spoke just as he thought.

"No. Let's be serious here," Sudarmo said. "Let's take the questions calmly. I know there are some of you whose feelings are hurt. But you couldn't say that I show excessive recognition to my wife. She receives *f*25, even though actually, if you consider her diploma and because she's married, she has the right to demand much more."

They deliberated over those proposals. As usual, Prawira looked as if he were indifferent to it all. He felt that the young teachers were dissatisfied and didn't dare say anything, because Sudarmo himself had set a good example.

"So... does anyone else wish to speak? If not, I'll consider my proposals approved."

One teacher raised his hand. "May I suggest something? I ask that the administration office be opened at 7:30 am and closed at 1:00 pm."

This proposal was approved unanimously. Jamil glanced at Waluyo full of amusement. The latter stuck up his hand and asked, "May I be permitted to make an amendment? The teachers also have to be in the schoolyard at 7:30 am sharp." He glanced sideways at Prawira, who was fidgeting anxiously on his bench and scratching his ear. "Yes, every day I get up at 6:00 am," Prawira said a little self-consciously, "but my children make me to wait so long in front of the washroom that I can't get to the school on time. You all understand how much trouble I get from those naughty kids. They fool around in the washroom and even get into fights there!"

His cheeks had reddened. Waluyo took the opportunity to absolve himself. "I also arrive late, because in the afternoon I have to bike to Cimahi to give courses."

People laughed.

"Does anyone else want to speak?" Everyone was silent.

Sudarmo ended the meeting by rapping the bench with a blackboard eraser and everyone went outside. Most of them went home while others stayed to converse on the back veranda. Discussing financial matters was difficult and had to be done cautiously, but every month they felt the shortfall. They weren't satisfied with the results of the meeting, but who would have dared to say they were nonetheless still proud of their diplomas, even if they now lived with the slogan, "Equal rights means equal burdens"?

"Let me tell you," said Waluyo, "don't debate with Mas Darmo. He went to sea-lawyer school and could prove that a black wall was a white one, and the other way around. Don't argue with him. At the end of the day, isn't the solution of the problem in our hands?"

This was the beginning of the sabotage that was so nerve-wracking! It wasn't easy for Sudarmo. He meant well, no matter what; his luck was bad and that stamped everything he did. He wanted to help and was scorned for it. He wanted to bring progress to the school and people condemned him for being a dictator, for urging that four incompetent teachers be transferred to a branch of the nationalist education system in the interior. With that they had to leave. The problem was that Sudarmo had shaken the teachers with all manner of changes, improvements, and rules, while the teachers weren't used to changes and reforms and they worked because they had to. They were confused and didn't know whether to be suspicious of him or to agree with him. In the end, no one is always right. And so, they began to oppose everything, considered all the rules and regulations crazy and stupid, and commenced sabotaging. They all had the same view: "Of course, Sudarmo has always got new ideas and they change from one day to the next. But he throws them in our face just like that and we're forced to accept them. Okay, he's acting for our good, but why doesn't he do it gradually? We're exhausted from all those changes. We can't work in peace and can hardly breathe."

Such was the atmosphere at the school. One day, a "wall newspaper" came out. It was published by the pupils, with its articles written by hand and submitted to the editors before 9:00 am. At that time, the articles were attached with thumbtacks to a board and hung on the outer wall of the school building. There were all sorts of things to read: advertisements for swapping pictures; news of someone losing his wallet; or articles about different things. It was funny and childlike, in three languages: Dutch, Indonesian and Sundanese.

And there was censorship too. You couldn't criticize a teacher. If that happened, it was an offense and a PID committee was formed of several students, ready to punish the offender. These wall newspapers could be very upsetting. It was too bad the other teachers simply shrugged and smiled, even though they paid close attention and were curious about the hustle and bustle of the pupils going back and forth. The children themselves were delighted. "One of Sudarmo's experiments," said someone and laughed mockingly.

"What will we have to face next month?"

The wall newspapers were a great success. But gradually the activity dragged on too long. After two months, there were only a few pieces of paper, written very badly. By the third month, every few days only the paper was visible, and because of the rain it got torn and sodden and finally fell to the ground to be trod on. Sudarmo began a new experiment. Marching. He intended to get rid of the effect of the age-old etiquette of bowing and scraping like slaves. The children lined up and Sudarmo gave the command, "One, two! Left, right!" And he joined the march behind the children, lifting his red sarong high enough for his skinny legs to be showing below it. Then with flushed cheeks and ears, he drew near to Sulastri. His wife laughed patiently; she thought of him as a young boy.

One day, the nationalist red and white flag was raised on its bamboo pole in front of Sulastri's class. She gave the command herself—and she held a bamboo staff to keep rhythm.

"One, two, three! Salute our motherland!"

The children raised their right hands and sang with resounding voices:

See our flag,
Red, white, waving,
Sent waving on this day
With joyful hearts

On a tremulous note, the song ended. The children were rather winded because the note had been too high. There was a moment of silence, then, one, two! one, two! the students marched into the classroom with erect bodies and doughty steps. Sulastri walked behind them, the little staff resting against her shoulder. The lessons commenced and the students bowed their heads and began to write diligently.

Not long afterwards, there was another teachers' meeting during which Sudarmo presented his thoughts. "Are we seeing our income shrinking? Several students have left us and are attending government or other schools. We have to hold onto the ones we have here. Comrades, I have a proposal. We will strengthen the relations between home and school. First, we will hold meetings with the parents. Two or three of us must give presentations on education. Second, we will organize language courses in the evening from 7:00 pm to 9:00 pm for which the parents will pay 0.25 guilders. They can choose English or Dutch, and we will take turns teaching these. Third, all of us will take turns visiting the parents of the students whose classes we teach. We can gain quite a reasonable benefit with just one visit. Remember, you don't love those whom you don't know. This is how we can get to know them. Draw up lists and make your visits precisely according to them. Fourth, we must have a news report. And now I come to the main point. That report will not be profitable for us, and in fact we will have to spend money, the opposite of our language courses. I know that it's hard to take 10 guilders from our meager cash holdings, but I guarantee that those who make their voices heard will be listened to. What this means is that they will get to know us, and this will benefit us. Let me deal with the organization of the news report. I ask your approval for the initial capital of *f*10. You are surely aware that all this depends on us. If the school flourishes, we will pick its fruits. If not everything will go downhill, of course.... And so, with strong inner energy we must try to raise ourselves up. Believe in victory, for there's nothing that can drag us into the mud! Comrades, I hope for absolute approval from all of you."

Sudarmo lit a cigarette and looked questioningly at his colleagues. Not a single one replied. They were perfectly silent, until Prawira raised his hand in opposition. "Isn't that too heavy for us? Demands too much work? Bear in mind the Dutch proverb: *te veel hooi op zijn vork nemen*—Taking too much hay on your fork."

A few of them nodded in agreement. Jamil was drowsing off. Waluyo was drawing little stick figures. The women teachers shifted their stiff feet. One teacher cleared his throat.

"Well, will anyone else express an opinion?"

Sudarmo ran his look questioningly all around. He flicked away the ash from his cigarette and inhaled again as he waited.

Jamil coughed and said, "I have another question. Who has to teach those parents? Not me, I've got too much to do. Mas Harjono, maybe?"

Waluyo nudged Harjono with his elbow and whispered, "Don't say yes. Let him and his wife do it. You're not crazy, are you?"

Sudarmo observed them. He smiled cannily and spoke again, "Mas Jamil is a realist. I have overlooked him. But surely teachers with high-level diplomas must give the lessons. We have to make a good showing of ourselves, right? For example, Mas Harjono, a language expert, has taught in a MULO school. Well then, who better suited for giving English lessons than him? For Dutch, we have many people. Comrades, Mas Jamil teaches with me this month, because we certainly have more than one class. Then in the following month, two other teachers. That'd be exactly right. Then we'll take another look and rearrange it. Do you all agree with my proposals, comrades? Yes. So, everything's settled."

There was no opposition at the meeting. The word "yes" sounded simultaneously and unanimously. Sudarmo had gained another victory.

The next day, he took three thick books on education from his cabinet and placed them on the table in front of Sulastri. Then he said briefly, "In the coming month, you'll give the first lecture with me. This is your reading material. As a topic you will take 'Judgment.' You'll begin now. I will be proud if you, my wife, sets a good example."

Sulastri looked at the books.

"Those look like a lot of work. I don't feel I am up to them. Couldn't you pick someone else?" Doubtfully, she opened one of the books and went through it page by page. Sudarmo got angry, revealing his low spirits. So, Sulastri gave in and said, "All right, I'll do it. I'll take a look at the notebook I made some time ago."

"Forget about that passé material. Study these books."

"I don't know if I can do it. I know a few things, but a lecture? I've never done that before. But if you require it... what's there to say?"

Sulastri at least gathered the books and stacked them on the table for reading in the evenings. She had the feeling that it would be very difficult to sit outside under the trees in the daytime and study those tomes. It would be so much nicer to gaze at the blue sky, enjoying the sight of the sunlight passing through the tree branches and the cool air quenching the heat of her body. In the evenings Sulastri would apply herself to them with perseverance. She was quite afraid of Sudarmo, of the way he would wrap himself in silence, something that had its own meaning. Besides, she wanted the nod of approval from him.

Sulastri pored over the books, making notes, and gradually she made a bit of progress. She felt obliged to fulfill her responsibility. Therefore, she drank coffee if she started to drift off to sleep. Sudarmo felt satisfied and throughout these days he could be heard singing most merrily in the washroom.

4

The pupils had now gotten to know Sulastri. When they arrived at school early in the morning, they greeted her cheerily. "Good morning, Ibu Guru." And they would laugh happily. The mornings seemed full of brilliant hopes. Then, after the bell sounded, they lined up neatly with earnest expressions, ready to study. In two columns and marching firmly in order, they headed into their classrooms. Sulastri was pleased to see their studiousness in drawing and listening to their teachers. She felt something warm inside her, something so subtle and fine which showed only in her eyes and movements. This was because the small children of first grade considered themselves her friends. Maybe also because of the term of address, "Ibu Guru," that was so endearing, a simple salutation that strengthened the bond between child and teacher. They came to Sulastri with their tiny worries and sadnesses, and she gave them advice and encouragement not to give up, while listening to them with complete attention.

During the rest period, Sulastri encouraged them to play by running and fooling around. Children who hadn't had a playful spirit because they felt too grown up for such things, now ran around gleefully on the patch of grass. Sulastri watched the quick movements of their feet and waving hands. Occasionally a boy would climb a tree, actually more than one of them would, if no one was watching. Then naturally Sulastri shouted loudly, ordering them to come down. The other teachers, though, stood talking under the trees and letting the kids play however they liked;

weren't they supposed to teach the children "freedom"? They didn't understand *ngemong*, the word used by Javanese educator Ki Hajar Dewantoro, which they followed scrupulously but unreflectingly. They thought "freedom" meant acting any way you want without considering anything else, whereas the meaning of freedom in education was to teach children in such a way that their own characters and personalities would not be repressed. And so the teachers allowed the children their tree-climbing. "They can't be prohibited, right? Then let them have their freedom in the trees, just so long as they behave in accordance with the traditions and etiquette of the Sundanese people and don't fight with each other. Wouldn't that be the peace and good order we all mean?"

Sulastri felt there was no need to take a stance "à la Rousseau." She usually strolled about the yard to watch whether the children were engaged in mischief, because no matter how happy they were with Sulastri, they were also afraid of her stern voice, which was usually loud and echoed energetically throughout the schoolyard. Then they would stop playing those dangerous games and calmly look for other ways to play until the bell rang and they returned to their classrooms, faces flushed from the heat.

On the other hand, her relations with the school employee Urip didn't go as smoothly as it did with the schoolchildren. Urip, a member of the Marhaen Party, felt he was part of Sulastri's family. And his behavior was unacceptable to her, because it deviated too much from traditional Sundanese ways First of all, he addressed her as "Zus". When she complained about this to Sudarmo, Urip then called her "Ibu" and was unwilling to address her as "Nyonya", because he felt it too demeaning to himself.

He would often look for this or that in the pantry, use butter for his fried rice, milk for his coffee, and eat at the dining table. He egged on Achmad, Sulastri's servant, to take a taste of Sulastri's chocolate liquor which she got from a friend upon her departure.

This Urip fellow was even so bold as to use Sulastri's comb when she was at school teaching and he would comb his hair neatly in front of the mirror and laugh at his own reflection.

This annoyed Sulastri but she didn't dare say anything outright. Why veer away from the ideals of independence and community? And this difficult situation made her feel dizzy—a situation that shook her and got her head spinning. The only thing she could do was just to ignore it as something insignificant. Then she didn't want to speak any more with Urip and in this way irritated Sudarmo. This was because her husband thought there was nothing odd about taking a fraternal attitude with Urip. But that was merely on the surface. Deep inside he felt just as uncomfortable as Sulastri did, because he complained that he couldn't sit anymore on the terrace now that Urip had taken it upon himself to receive his visitors there and felt free to offer them Sudarmo's cigarettes. Achmad, the Batavian, felt put in a strange situation. Urip gave him orders and considered Achmad's own boss to be his friend. So, because he was of sane mind and, being still bound up in the old politesse, Achmad could no longer bear to watch Urip's boorishness and asked to quit his job. He bid farewell, with smiles and faithfulness showing on his face. Sulastri felt she had lost something after Achmad left, the final memories of a past life.

Now came the days where she always had to closely watch Sudarmo, other people, their views, their desires, to think of school, so that she felt her small soul had been imprisoned in an ever-shrinking ring that would never give her the chance to breathe. Still, she felt glad for this sacrifice and pressing financial desolation as a gift from God, as an honor. Happiness filled her when she recalled that she was doing all of this for the motherland, which was symbolized at that time in the images of Sudarmo and the school. There were no other meanings for her, because it was too vast and cloud enshrouded. She was happy because she could work wholeheartedly and because she loved Sudarmo.

But, oddly, Sudarmo was disappointed with Sulastri. Previously he spoke in a patient and sweet tone of voice, but now he'd frequently snap at his wife. Sudarmo conceived of Sulastri's soul as different from what she really was. In your aspirations you usually chase after something perfect. And if its reality diverges from that perfection, you're naturally going to feel disappointed. Sudarmo saw that Sulastri, just like other women, paid attention to clothes and "trivial things." Sudarmo felt he had the right to speak to his wife in a sullen and reproachful way because he was disappointed. In this way, their relationship gradually frosted over. Angry words, spoken with some uneasiness, succeeded in hitting their target, straining the relationship between husband and wife, and making them suspicious of each other. Often they would face each other in silence, or one of them would be engrossed in reading a book while the other would be pacing up and down under the *cempaka* tree, filled with anxiety and mounting anger.

Then, as usual, Sulastri would be the one to begin speaking words of peace, because she felt wrong in causing anyone anxiety. And, by declaring her love and speaking sweet words, she was able to lighten her husband's moodiness. So, after speaking to her sharply, Sudarmo finally felt the tension in his heart dissipate and for an instant became quite happy, until a new quarrel broke out and the lines around his lips that showed his hardness looked even more severe. A very difficult marriage! They both realized they needed love imbued with patience, with mutual forgiveness for wrongs done. But they both were hardheaded people who by a caprice of fate were brought together as a married couple. Sulastri sometimes wondered, "Will our lives together go on like this? I'm devastated by this fighting, but I'm too advanced to lower myself by apologizing to him for the millionth time."

And Sudarmo couldn't restrain himself if Sulastri just followed her own wishes. He felt pierced to the heart and humiliated, because, according to tradition, a woman was lower in status than a man, even though in theory he held modern views on the equality and liberation of women. This was something else. Something we received along with our mother's milk and grew from babyhood to maturity and which was hard to demolish, even after a lot of thought.

What rather lightened this period of discord and quarrels was Jamil's pleasing laughter, his chit-chat about this and that silliness. They drank coffee and laughed uproariously until the tears rolled down their cheeks. Waluyo occasionally came by and joined in. They often made fried rice on the gas stove. Jamil ground the onions. Sudarmo lit the stove according to the manufacturer's instructions, explaining that the vents of this appliance must never get plugged up. And Sulastri would have to hear, "This stove is so dirty. Why don't you order it cleaned, Tri, you lazy child." Sulastri laughed because she felt guilty and then put a lot of butter in the pan. And after the red onions were hissing and fragrant, it was Sudarmo who put his nose near the pan and watched it to see if the spices were cooked.

Looking serious as he stirred the pan and checked if the ingredients were now cooked, he said, "Fried rice tastes best if the rice is put into the pan at just the right time, just when the fragrance of the red onions tells you they're cooked. After that, scatter the rice around nicely and its steam will rise. And keep stirring, then put in the spices."

His mouth watered, so he handed over the work to Sulastri when the rice was ready to be served. Jamil kept breaking out in laughter as he fixed the tablecloth and warned the cooks when the rice almost spilled out of the pan. They ate lustily. And if Waluyo was present as well, the four of them laughed gaily at their own jokes. It was abundantly clear that there just enough of the rice for the four of them and no more, so that Jamil had to eat even more bananas. Sudarmo's face shone with happiness, and he was proud of himself at having taught Sulastri cooking skills. Then, grandly stretching out his hands, he said, "I taught her to make noodles, beefsteak and fried rice. Our fried rice, when I was still a university student, was really renowned, and I used corned beef, crab, prawn, and—"

Sulastri interrupted him quickly. "Right, right. That's what makes the fried rice delicious. With so much butter and all the other things. The skilled cook is the one who cooks delicious things with just a few ingredients, cheaply and tastily."

And Jamil said, "A stone is delicious cooked in butter."

Immediately Waluyo burst out laughing and didn't stop until Jamil patted him on the back nicely and, with a smile, began to talk about Waluyo's appetite for gobbling up good food. Waluyo raised both hands to keep Jamil from talking and then quickly said goodbye. Sudarmo and Sulastri couldn't make out quite what Jamil was talking about. They figured it was something funny, but Jamil, who usually couldn't keep from talking, shut up and kept this as a threat, if Waluyo ever again made fun of him.

For Sulastri, this was the life of a respected artist and educator. She was captivated by it, felt able to accept their circumstances and was happy in this environment.

Once when they were looking for a way out of their arguments, the couple visited Sukarno. He lived on Jalan Astana Anyar in a *rumah panggung*, a house built on stilts. Before they set out, they had another squabble. Sulastri wanted to go another time, but Sudarmo held fast to going on that very day. So that's how they walked there, rather distant from each other and in silence. Sulastri with her short steps tried to walk beside Sudarmo, who made no concessions in his own pace. With anger in his eyes and around his mouth, he didn't turn to look at his wife. He walked erectly, his right hand in his pocket, and stepped very quickly, as if the roadway was burning the soles of his feet.

Sulastri glanced at him sidelong, at his forehead and nose, rather broad jawbone, lips that indicated moderation, and scruffy hair which enlarged his stubborn face. Then she looked ahead and before she knew it, they were at Sukarno's house. She saw Sudarmo stop abruptly in front of her and look at her with a cold dislike. Then her husband walked slowly up the gravel path, gazing upward.

The front veranda was closed. There were doors on its right and left and similarly behind it were two doors. In the middle of the veranda were a set of chairs, pale brown in color. Against the wall there were dining chairs with worn-out seats in unsightly colors. Next to the front door, a potted palm looked untended and dry. A hat rack in the corner was weighted down with various sorts and qualities of hats. An assortment of handles was visible in the umbrella box. The sound of several typewriters could be heard from the study to the left, and from time to time they heard the sweet laughter of a youngster or a husky voice over the sound of the typing. Sulastri hesitated on the steps, between removing her shoes or just going in like that. Then she boldly entered barefooted, putting her shoes in a corner next to the door.

"Hello, Mas." Bung Karno came out of his study with outstretched hand and warmly greeted Sudarmo. Then he turned to Sulastri who felt herself blush. He looked at her for a moment and gently asked, "Do you feel at home here in Bandung, Zus? Are you happy?"

Sulastri nodded quickly. And, again feeling bashful, she felt inside her purse for a handkerchief. Sukarno affably patted Sudarmo's back and invited him into the study, leaving Sulastri standing beside his wife. This woman was seated on a low, broad divan and holding a cigarette that she lifted flirtatiously to her lips. A young boy was sleeping on the divan. A blanket covered him up to his chin, and around his head was wrapped a piece of white cloth. His hands on his stomach looked thin and his bones showed. His cheeks were blackish and quite dirty.

Sulastri was embarrassed and looked around, not daring to lay eyes on the young child. She turned away from the child and, waiting to hear what Zus Karno would have to say, studied the gestures of the other woman's hands. Zus Karno stroked Sulastri's shoulders as a mother would to her child. She smiled and in a rhythmic voice in which every word possessed an enchanting tone and form, said, "So then, dear, are you happy here? And how does life feel as a new bride?"

She pronounced the word "dear" in a soothing voice and looked at Sulastri from the side. Coquettish as she was, on the refined features of her face there was the impression of a mother filled with love. Her face was still pretty, even though Zus Karno was no longer young. Her face was tapering and the delicacy of her features from her nose to her chin, and the full chignon on her still firm and slender neck, gave the impression of a young woman, although rather at odds with the lines and wrinkles here and there, and the expression in her eyes was a bit sepulchral. From a distance, the slenderness of her body and its lively movements would have given the impression of a mere girl. She was stimulating as a conversationalist and in how she engaged with people—a woman who looked for happiness in pleasing others, to say nothing of pleasing her husband. Further, she spoke with a gentle and notably rhythmic voice with its attention to the emphasis of words, and hand gestures as she spoke her flowing Sundanese. This language reminded one of a dancer, refined of gesture, flitting across one's line of vision. Sulastri listened to her with admiration. How smooth and subtle was this pretty woman.

Had Sulastri received word from her sister, was she content with her job, was she able to get along well with her colleagues, and so on and so forth. Questions voiced only for the sake of speaking, and Sulastri sensed that her replies were not all that important. The older woman's hand movements erased any memory of what she said. She moved from one thing to another, from housework to the women's movement to her husband's party work, from rallies to the difficulties of politics—all of these with an agility that made them seem equally important—and all the time exhaling smoke through her nose with a languid, daydreaming look. She paused, not asking a response, because Sulastri only listened with rapt attention when Juhariah entered the room.

Juhariah held a tray in both hands and walked carefully for fear of spilling the drinks. Greeting Sulastri with a smile and the look in her eyes, she placed two cups in front of them on a little table and offered cakes from a jar. Then she amiably told Sulastri to take another cake. She took Sulastri's hand and said quietly, "You've married, right? Lastri, we're fast getting old," displaying her clean white teeth. Zus Karno stood up and fixed the child's blanket. He had now awoken and she asked, "You'd like an orange, of course?"

The child answered by nodding his head then closed his eyes again and crossed his right hand over them, as if ashamed to be in the presence of a guest. Sulastri glanced behind her then turned back to Juhariah, who laughed for no reason at all and Sulastri joined in.

"Shh, be quiet! We've become old housewives. And how about your anti-polygamy movement, Ju?"

Juhariah laughed but restrained herself when Zus Karno looked at her rather menacingly. Juhariah began earnestly, "We've got many members now. Actually, you ought to be the chairman. We really need you."

"Ah, Ju," Sulastri protested, "I cannot. I don't feel I could do it. And... I would only go along if I were one hundred percent sure of myself. I couldn't just sit with the leadership like a doll, right?"

As she looked at Juhariah in her resistance, Juhariah spoke scoldingly, her hand pushing Sulastri's shoulder. "Oh, you! You've always got some objection."

Juhariah was small and the lines from her nose to her lips gave her the face of someone old. Her hair was gathered up in a small chignon close to her ears. There was something simple and childlike about her that people found moving. Anyone who saw her would immediately be drawn to her. This eighteen-year-old girl with the simple, plain face would never be considered noteworthy if she didn't work so hard for the women's movement, travelling everywhere, never paying any attention to the winds and rain, and loyal with all her heart to Bung Karno and his wife.

She and her husband Supardi were greatly loved by Sukarno and lived together with him. Juhariah managed the household and everything else, since Zus Karno, a woman used to being spoiled, was incapable of managing a place so big. Juhariah had been raised there since she was little because her father had been exiled to Digul. When Sukarno and Supardi were imprisoned, Juhariah lightened the suffering of the then-solitary Zus Karno by her extraordinary industriousness. Zus Karno also frequently ran out of money, though luckily there were people who helped relieve her penury. However, more oppressive by far was her solitude, for she had been left all by herself. Where she had usually heard the tender laughter of her husband, now it was Juhariah who dispelled her loneliness. Juhariah counseled her to be patient and gave her new hope. Within only a few months this lovely woman looked old, and Juhariah, who kept a close eye on her, saw how Zus Karno's shoulder blades had become visible under her yellowish-brown skin. Also, it was Juhariah who visited Sukarno and became the lifeline between him and the world across the prison wall.

Juhariah's husband Supardi was dear to Sukarno. This young man had a fresh intelligence and a healthy perspective. He attracted listeners because of his excellence in speaking and the gestures of his hands revealed the ardor flaring in his breast. In addition, he used his pen smoothly with a brilliant and appealing writing style because it was simple and honest. He was loyal, straightforward, and brave. He was also unassuming and ready to forgive the wrongs of others. In him, Sukarno had gained a believer, a friend, and one whom he could trust.

When Supardi was released from jail, he married Juhariah, long his sweetheart. But when Sukarno chose the Nationalist Party after his earlier party had split into two—that is, the Nationalist Party and the Marhaen Party—there was a slight rift between him and Supardi, since Supardi had become a well-known figure in the Marhaen Party. Supardi had written for the party newspaper, spoke at rallies, and gave educational courses. He was tireless in contrast to Jamil and Waluyo, who weren't very serious in their work. Because of that, these two respected Supardi. It was the same with Sulastri's husband, Sudarmo, Mister Clever Guy. Quite unintentionally, he sensed that he was better at getting close to the common people. Supardi didn't debate much, but he performed his work with energy and spirit. He had chosen these obligations as his life. And Supardi sensed no wall separating him from the people to whom he gave courses. Even in his joking he felt himself one of them, so it wasn't strange when they opened their hearts to him.

In Sudarmo, however, they saw a wall, and that was the reason that, in spite of his high ideals and good initiatives, he never won the love of those attending his classes. They withheld their hearts from him. Waluyo knew this and enraged Sudarmo by frequently calling him "bourgeois". This was a word that carried many nuances, such as arrogance, indifference to the feelings of others, egoism, self-exultation, and the like.

The split between Supardi and Sukarno was felt even more deeply by themselves. Therefore, the two young couples intended to move elsewhere. Then they would see how they had to live alone. Sukarno was sad, realizing the situation couldn't be maintained any longer, even more so when tensions sharpened between the youth members of the Nationalist Party and those in the Marhaen Party. Juhariah spoke of it in a near-whisper to Sulastri. "I actually am sorry for Zus Karno, for she's usually incapable of managing a household. But we can't do anything else. We have to go. And besides..."

She smiled and Sulastri took note of her expression. Then she understood and replied, "I understand your difficulty. And when your baby arrives, will you be getting a midwife or going to the hospital?"

Juhariah shrugged. "Oh, it's all taken care of. A shaman-birth attendant will do. My mother wasn't helped by a community midwife, either."

"Goodness, Ju, why are you doing it that way? Aren't we modern women? Do you have the courage to entrust yourself to a shaman?"

"Why not? She has experience. And also, the important thing is she believes in herself."

"But wouldn't she be dirty, disheveled and messy in every way? I'd never be so brave, that's for sure. But... you're not afraid, Ju?"

Juhariah laughed and patted Sulastri on the shoulder.

Amusement was written all over her face and she said, just to annoy her friend, "We're not as spoiled as you, Sulastri. Really, we're not. But, um, you'll be going through it yourself soon. It's the normal condition and in accord with the laws of nature. All women must experience it. I'm so very glad, and I hope he'll look just like Supardi. It's got to be a boy, Tri."

"Yes, I see you with a boy with lots of wavy hair, just like Mas Pardi's." Juhariah laughed again, then jumped up.

"Oh gosh, here I am, talking away. I've got to cook," she whispered, because Zus Karno just then came in. Sulastri also stood up. And then she saw Sudarmo coming too. Her husband smiled at her and signaled to her to bid good-bye. Because of that, Sulastri spoke rather hesitantly to her hostess. "Zus, I have to go. It's already midday or more and no one's at home."

Zus Karno, taking hold of Sulastri's hand, held her back. "Don't go yet. Stay and eat with us. This is the first time you've visited us, dear, and Mas Karno is chatting with your husband. Mas Karno's pleased to have guests. Do stay."

Sulastri couldn't be detained and said good-bye. She went to the kitchen for a moment to say good-bye to Juhariah. Then she went to the study. Sukarno was standing in the doorway.

"Come again, Zus. Zus Inggit is happy to see you. Isn't that right, Git?" he said to his wife. Then to Sudarmo, "Mas, I wish you success in your work. Oh, isn't that school fairly close by? Anyway, go safely, you two."

Sulastri made a shy *salam*, because the personality of Sukarno had the power bind your eyes and that made her feel very small. Sudarmo and his anger disappeared. She only saw two blazing eyes, black and studying, a capable mouth, everything that made that handsome face even more striking.

"Sukarno," she thought and she saw an envelope in which she kept a picture of Sukarno and Hatta. Had she willy-nilly become smitten with him? She viewed it as glorifying someone, something a young girl did in hero-worshipping some romantic figure. She remembered seeing Sukarno before the judge, and beside him, his lawyers in their black robes. Sukarno's eyes were blazing. He was like a lion, in her memory, with a broad chest and a head raised disdainfully. Sulastri and Marti had obtained seats along the back and they listened with rapt attention. But they soon left, unable to stand the body odors of the people there. And it was too sad for them to see Bung Karno brought in a prison van. So Sulastri's cheeks reddened when she had to speak with Bung Karno and could barely find a single word to say, though all the nice words for him had piled up in her heart.

As they walked home, Sudarmo spoke non-stop with her. "So that's the way it is, Tri. He is friendly and affable with people. Everybody recognizes him at the podium. How he orates, with fire in his eyes, and captivates his listeners. I have heard his speeches and I can't forget them. I saw him, as he stood at the podium before thousands of people. When he stepped forward, everyone applauded. He took off his *peci* fez and threw it on the table. Then he would commence, his left hand on his hip, and with his right hand giving emphasis, explaining, strengthening the extraordinary meaning and brightness of his words, because it was *he* who spoke to them. And all those attending listened silently, wide-eyed and breathless, where you only heard the urgency of his thundering voice, the raging of that full baritone sound, that brought you to another world. And you saw how his eyes flashed in the dimness like two luminous spheres, then flaring up again out of anger and hatred of the injustices you suffered. You felt his honesty in the movement of his hand, his voice, his eyes, Tri, the simplicity of his gestures. When he reached the climax of his speech, it was as if everyone breathed from one chest. And you could hear people heaving a deep sigh because their hearts had been greatly shaken. Then came the uproar of applause that made the old walls of the room tremble. Even the policemen were awestruck. Occasionally a government official who had to attend these meetings as a representative of the PID joined in with the applause in spirited pleasure. The wretched fellow would be reprimanded for sure, maybe even fired, I wouldn't know. People knew Sukarno as an extraordinary orator, a really tremendous one, who could speak heart-to-heart and bind the souls of his listeners. But I know him differently. As a friend and brother."

Sudarmo stopped and heaved a great sigh in his enchantment. And Sulastri, in her mind's eye, saw Sukarno return, but it was a different Sukarno, thin and pale. He had at that time stepped out of the prison van and was climbing the stairs of the courthouse. She and Marti greeted him and were shocked at his pallor and very different expression. And, at that time, too, Sulastri saw him before the judges, standing tall and smiling, because he knew that he was not the criminal the court held him to be. Sulastri burned with rage and hatred toward the coiffed judges in their black robes, the cloak of law enforcement, which had to see virtue as evil in the name of justice. Now she knew why she hated the hypocritical and self-serving "Western culture" that invoked God and justice.

Sulastri began to speak, "Dar, you know Mas Karno well, right? Is he really that friendly in his own surroundings?"

"Yes, it's true and I'll tell you about it. I knew Karno up close for a month. Strange to say, the person who can enchant a meeting is rather shy when surrounded by his guests. You saw him yourself, right? He didn't sit down with you, even though he had known you from before. And what was funny about him was that a lock of hair, which somewhat covered his forehead and moved when he shook and nodded his head..."

Sudarmo paused for a moment to laugh, as if he was seeing the face of Sukarno clearly and Sulastri found herself laughing too. She saw that lock of Sukarno's hair and said, "I worship him. Is there anyone like him in this world?"

"It's the easiest thing to imagine a warrior. But you've got to be careful that he doesn't become a statue. In the end, there are little things, realities that you can't avoid. And Karno is just a human being, with an amusing character and faults, so that he can't float about in dream world. Karno also pays attention to pretty faces. Would you disapprove of him if I were like that too?"

Suddenly a dark shadow passed over Sulastri's face. She turned away from Sudarmo and gazed for a while into the distance. The road lit by the sun seemed all at once empty, and the shadows above it were dark and frightening, as if her heart couldn't break out of that grim mood. She felt how everything would end and was sad for the sunshine and other things that had meaning for her. She replied in a quavering voice, "Don't spoil this atmosphere. I don't wish to speak of that. You all usually talk for your own benefit. You can find reasons to forgive your own behavior. I hate you."

"I'm only kidding. That couldn't happen. I love you and we've only just gotten married. Now, more about Karno. Don't you want to hear more about him?"

Sudarmo looked at her tenderly, intimately, so that Sulastri blushed and listened again.

"When I stayed in his house, we'd always sing *Indonesia Raya*. You know that song, don't you?"

And Sudarmo sang a few lines.

"Well," he went on, "we usually sang at the top of our lungs. Karno has a great voice. When he starts to sing, he begins by finding the note first. And it's so funny listening to him doing that. My own voice sometimes goes off-key and he would yell, "Mas, you're flat. Start over." And we would begin again. But what I most admire him for is his desire to please. He can get to the bottom of people's problems. And he's so friendly and nice when he socializes with people. His home is open to everyone. You come and go and return home bringing with you a bit of his huge spirit."

Sudarmo said this in a failing voice. Sulastri nodded and said, also faintly, "Yes, and he prays and takes pleasure in reading religious books."

"Yes," her husband continued, "he frequently burns incense on Thursday evening. Sometimes he fasts on Mondays and Tuesdays."

"What? Really, he does that?"

"Yes, somedays he doesn't join in eating and apologizes, saying he's not hungry. But then, his wife whispers, pointing to his room where he's sitting, 'He's fasting.' Oddly enough, he's got a superstitious nature. But he often says at rallies, 'Even if you burn a ton of incense, that won't bring Indonesia independence.' But maybe none of us is free from superstition, much as we are against it."

"I can understand why he says that to the masses. Those customs and attitudes in the hearts of people kill the desire and energy to rebel. Incense makes you dizzy and enervates you. But for a leader who possesses knowledge and self-awareness, for him it's a different matter."

"Even so, I don't approve of it," Sudarmo began again stubbornly. "I hate all that fooling around with incense. And even though I realize what's good for me and what other people think is good, there's still danger and I couldn't be held accountable for myself. Whatever frightens and shackles us in cowardice must be thrown away. Just imagine if an old master of the occult with his attendant spirits can control us and intimidates us by forecasts and threats of curses. No, I want to stand on my own strong feet and have no wish to try immersing myself in the world of the unseen."

Sulastri laughed at his anger. "Yes," she thought, "we're modern. But deep in our hearts we still keep a little place for burning incense in our moments of despair."

5

The clamor of voices talking gradually receded. Sudarmo stood up and gazed dramatically over those present, sitting on benches in both classrooms. In the classroom on the right side, the lamplight was dim, because the light in the middle of the room fell at a slant. Thus, only shoulders and torsos were visible. Above that, nothing. On the left was a dark passageway leading to the other rooms and the outside. Here, too, people were sitting, their cigarettes flaring like embers of coal, and all seemed enveloped in a cloak of secrecy.

"Comrades!" Sudarmo began. He saw the hope in all the faces there. "First of all, I have to express my thanks for your attention and for your desire to accept our invitation this Saturday night. We, the teachers, welcome you with happy hearts."

He stopped for a moment and, carefully choosing his words, he calmly and lucidly explained the purpose of the meeting. "There must be relations between home and school. Given the circumstances, we can only attend to the children's education from seven-thirty in the morning to one o'clock in the afternoon. The responsibility then passes on to the home environment. Therefore, there is the utmost need for a concordance in education between school and home. But this can only be if between school and home there is a desire to cooperate and a shared recognition that we must teach our children to be good people in general and good Indonesians in particular.

"Now you will ask: Who is a good person? The answer to this is quite difficult, because the word 'good' has many angles to it. For an employee, he is good when he obeys exactly and is loyal to his employer. A religious person is one who prays five time a day and each year pays his or her *zakat fitrah*. A *warung* operator carefully calculates its profit and loss, lives frugally, and has savings. And so, you all see, that what is seen as good by one is not necessarily good for others, good for me is different from good for you. But we cannot deny that that there is one great theme in our problems here. Do we not, in a moment of solitude, give the responsibility to ourselves, to an 'I' which cannot be seen? This invisible 'I' tells us the true situation, even if we often don't want to hear it. The existence of this 'I' cannot be denied and it makes us cover our face because of our sense of shame.

"We Indonesians call this 'I' by the name of *kakak tua*, 'older sibling', who watches over us. Religious people call it an 'angel,' the conscience that can tell good from evil. There's no need to go into this in great depth here because this problem is not for people with stomachs growling from hunger like us. It would be more useful to answer the question, how do we as good Indonesians follow our hopes and dreams? We will say as with one voice, a good Indonesian is someone who develops his or her talents and devotes them to the nationalist movement."

Sudarmo paused and observed the heads nodding in agreement and the attention growing in their faces. Then he continued more confidently and in his eyes was a humorous glint. "Who among us would be interested in being a peasant, let's say working hard growing potatoes to sell to the Dutch at the highest price possible, and rice to sell to the teachers in the national schools at the lowest price possible?"

They burst out laughing and Sudarmo's face lit up while his amused eyes narrowed to a squint. People whispered for a moment, then *shh! shh!* was heard ordering silence and Sudarmo began again.

"Whoever has the talent to be a carpenter, make sturdy furniture for sale as expensively as possible to the Dutch, and strong benches for sale as cheaply as possible to our national schools." There was hearty laughter, while a number of people noted the rather rickety benches on which they were seated. Sudarmo himself laughed at his own joke. He straightened his black *peci* cap and struck the table with his fist.

Their faces grew serious again, notwithstanding that some of them still had smiles on their faces. Sudarmo now explained the goals of nationalist education and finally expressed his thanks to all those present. At that point, he handed his place over to Sulastri. She came forward toward the audience holding her folio of paper. She appeared calm, but inside she was nervous and doubtful about the results her talk would produce. She slowly laid the paper on the table, looked around to gain some composure, and passed her gaze over the heads of the attendees and through the open windows to the garden. Outside, the lamps shone in great circles on the grass. Then she looked at her text and began to speak, the paper gripped in her cold hands. She spoke calmly, as if there was nothing else, only her hope of success.

"Comrades, I hesitate to try to give this lecture, because this is the first time that I have spoken before an audience as attentive as this."

She saw their faces filled with friendly brightness and curiosity. She continued, rather bolder now, her lecture on judgment. She saw the genuinely friendly look on their faces and she let go of her voice, spoke freely, more precisely and concluded in a strikingly downbeat note. "It is easy for us to forgive something, if our spirit is higher than those who are at fault. Who considers themselves to be like God and thinks themselves free from fault? We are all human beings who have feelings of love and also tendencies to do wrong. So that's what we must be able to forgive, and when giving that forgiveness, let's not force the ones who're wrong to state their faults in words. It is enough if awareness of fault is there. There's no need to dwell on the tightness of their lips, for the expression in their eyes will be even clearer in their admission of guilt. And we can fully forgive, with a firm belief that even the most wicked person has feelings of forgiveness and love."

Sulastri's lips were quivering when she finished speaking, for she had been entranced by her own words. She, too, had made a lot of mistakes as a child and then made more, new mistakes. Their applause was pleasing and the looks and gestures were friendly as Sulastri made her way back to her place among them, looking pleased and with her hands crossed.

Sudarmo stood up again and smoothly ran through his plans—plans for the language courses and the school magazine that were to strengthen relations between school and home. Then he related in a comical fashion the strange characteristics of several of the children. They listened with rapt attention, charmed by his amusing manner. Then suddenly there was a voice from the darkness of the alleyway, "You don't think my kid is the naughtiest one in his class?"

Questioning looks appeared on the faces of all present. Then the bass voice continued louder, steadily, "We've got to give another name to our kid, because he's unmanageable at home. Maybe he's like me, because I used to be obstinate like that. I'd like to ask something to Ibu Sudarmo. Can he be admonished with words? At home we usually beat him."

In a loud voice that cut through the riotous laughter, Sudarmo addressed the fellow, "Brother, come forward, so I'll know who your child is."

"No," said the voice firmly, "I don't want to. I'm a bit shy, because he looks exactly like me, like two sides of a split pinang nut. And also..."

The rest of what he said was drowned out in the growing uproar. Sudarmo shaded his eyes and peered into the darkness of the alleyway.

"Oh, I know you. Just get out." He motioned with his hand and smiled amusedly. There was the sound of someone standing up and everyone looked toward the alley. Under the lamp with the dark shadows behind it, with the blinking of eyes set at a slant on his face, a man stood up. He was stocky and sturdily built, and on his forehead was a broad scar, some old wound. When he spoke, his mouth looked askew and his head leaned to one side. People laughed at his ears, which were large below his messily wrapped head scarf. People at the meeting knew him as a fighter who was interested only in brawling and women.

"After you all take a good look at me," the fellow began, "I won't feel comfortable, if I hear 'like papa, like son'. Because I realize that I'm this way because of how my father taught me by beating me all the time. So let me ask, how should I teach my son? If he has to study, he's in the stall with my horses. If I scold him, he throws stones. In short, we've given up on educating him. And he's hard to get up in the morning, until he pisses in his bed."

There was even more riotous laughter when he apologized by saying, "I'm not speaking to be funny. I'm serious. I'm asking you, what should I do? I've lost all hope."

He sighed and it seemed comical to look at such a big fellow in despair over his son, so that people laughed all the more.

Sudarmo raised his hand to ask everyone to stop laughing and then said, "I can't write you out a prescription. I can only say that beating a child as big as yours has to be softened to stern looks only. Even if I can't give you a prescription, you've got to look at all the aspects of a given situation and according to certain rules."

Someone cut in. "So... if you think that you can teach your child to be good by beating him, then you're choosing beatings to educate him. I have another way." People laughed again. The first speaker had gone back into the shadows. There arose the sound of people speaking with each other, friendly conversations about troubles at home with their children.

"Comrades, let's get back to the subject at hand. Who else has questions?" Sudarmo saw several hands raised and gave one of them a turn.

"Two days ago, my child was told to go home because his shirt was messy."

The squeakiness of the voice didn't match the size of the body that emitted it. It should have been a baritone. People laughed rather tentatively, afraid of hurting the speaker's feelings. He passed his small, shrewd-looking eyes over the attendees and turned his mousedeer-like face to Sudarmo. Then he squeaked again, "And I'd like to know, how must he be dressed?" Sudarmo paid no attention to the other's combative look and calmly said, "In my view, blue trousers and white shirt would be the most appropriate. Very practical, and blue twill doesn't tear easily."

"You understand we're just poor people." It seemed the speaker was asking for pity and his face became more tapering with a sly look. "So, we never throw away pieces of cloth, for they have many uses. How about if my wife patches those rents and rips with what's left of those pieces of cloth, surely there'll be no more holes. Why can't we do that? Would you forbid children from wearing clothes like that? We really are poor people."

The tense attention was tangible, and visible from the tension of their backs. Sudarmo answered again, "We have to forbid that sort of clothing. A pair of trousers and a shirt looking like the American flag will disturb the calm of the lessons and..."

Roars of laughter. Several listeners leaned against the wall, wiping their eyes. The speaker sat back down, his shoulders heaving from laughter. Then an elderly man stood up. He was dressed quite fashionably in the Yogya style of sarong and jacket, black with brown stripes and closed up to his neck. In this way he displayed his slender frame to advantage. His jaw was rather tilted forward and his friendly smile made him look younger and rather feminine. Now he had no smile, though, but looking to the right and to the left around him, and his left hand cupped to his cheek to soften his voice, he whispered, "I would like to make a statement."

"Louder, we can't hear you."

"Shh, I am speaking quietly because... because the *danyang* will hear this." His voice faded away and was nearly inaudible. He went on and everyone held their breath. "The danyang of this building will keep on demanding victims if no *tumbal* is provided. Plant two coconut trees in the front of the yard, one on the right and one on the left, and bad luck will be gone. The school will not get ahead if you don't plant those trees. Do you still remember, when one teacher after another was forbidden by the government to teach? And the theft of *f*400, how long ago was that? Isn't that a fact? For as long as the school is located here, some bad thing or another will be sure to happen. You must plant those coconut trees as soon as you can. In the back, in the garden" —he looked around and whispered—"there are two kemiri trees, and demons like to dwell at their tops. I'm have experience with these things. And that's why I'm giving you advice. Drive off those evil spirits as soon as possible."

He stopped. In the silent darkness, the lamp seemed to be shrouded by something. You now could hear the wind noisily blowing through the leaves. No one moved, dominated by something alien and unknowable. Someone put his hand in his pocket and nudged the bench he was sitting on. That sound released them from their tension. Sudarmo said, "I believe those two trees will have to be planted. We'll look into that. But, what connection does that have to... ah, we're living in the modern age and are not going to be scared by demons."

The old man began to hold fast to what he said, but now the atmosphere had been lost. They all even joked, although there were those who spoke in whispers about several proofs of the existence of spirits. One man, wearing glasses and a *peci* and closed jacket, stood up and said, "Wouldn't it be better if this school had its own building? I'd contribute some wood. Maybe other people have other things to give. The rent for this sort of building could be put to use for other needs, and we needn't be linked to the bad things attached to this place."

"That's really a very good idea," replied Sudarmo. "Let's establish a committee for constructing such a building. Everyone's thoughts on this?"

Everyone was for it and discussed the possibility of a committee. By the time people finished talking, the night was well-advanced. Sudarmo expressed his thanks for everyone's attendance and, as well, his hope to meet again on another occasion. Everyone bid each other goodnight, and laughter and uproarious joking were heard again and again. Several people still stayed and praised Sulastri. The swashbuckling man said, "I'm amazed, why does my kid now comb her hair neatly? Is that the influence of her lady teacher?"

Sulastri smiled lightly and answered modestly, "Everyone likes to be appreciated. She is my assistant and so now she's very earnest and diligent."

Sudarmo chatted about ghosts with the old man, who began anew, filled with conviction. In the quiet of the schoolhouse there were only still Sulastri, Sudarmo, Jamil and Harjono. The school employee quickly shut the door. The lights were turned off and they all went outside, feeling their way slowly in the darkness. Eventually, they reached their own rooms in the darkened pavilion, which seemed to be awaiting its residents. The lights were turned on and Sulastri sprawled in a chair.

"Dar, about those ghosts, you don't believe that, do you?"

Sudarmo slowly took off his shoes. He shook his head but then immediately said, "Whether they exist, I don't know. But whether I absolutely don't feel their presence, ah, I do get scared walking through the graveyard at night."

"I believe they exist. I'll say frankly that I feel there's something in this house. I sometimes shiver when I look at the henna tree there. My bapak said there's a spirit there and he ordered it cut down, because bad luck would strike if we let it be."

Sudarmo smiled at his wife's fears and joked, "There you go again with the ghost stories. Don't let yourself be scared, Tri." She didn't reply, just looked straight ahead and thought, "There will come a time when Sudarmo will believe my dad and ask for protection against those ghosts and spirits. Proof will come with time." Convinced of that, she sat silently until she saw that her husband had long gone to sleep.

6

Sulastri was barely aware of the passage of time. She only sensed that household difficulties were growing heavier. And also that Sudarmo seemed in a daze and often didn't hear her speaking to him because his thoughts were elsewhere. It even happened that for a few days he was frequently angry with his wife over little things. Later, he apologized anxiously for his rudeness: "Oh, you don't know what's going on." Nonetheless, Sulastri felt something exhilarating in her heart. And she hummed while she worked in her garden or she let loose with her happiness in a highly musical voice. She saw the leafy plum tree and the flowers hanging on the laurel tree. Then there was a subtle feeling within her body that something was beginning to grow, and told her of happiness to come so that she held her breath and her eyes glistened with restrained tears. And during those joyful days when she felt total happiness, the difficulties of the household seemed insignificant. Sudarmo was interested by Sulastri's joyous moods and watched her more closely, even if other feelings arose, for Sudarmo had his own troubles. The atmosphere of discontent and grumbling among his colleagues at work had spread to the older students. Sudarmo sensed that something invisible and intangible was going to collapse if for some reason it got too heavy to be held up. Now there was a quiet lull, as if before the approach of a great typhoon. Conversations suddenly stopped. Eyes secretly met. Meaningless words were heard but seemed to have hidden clues and purposes. Sudarmo felt oppressed. He concluded that they didn't like him and wanted him to go. But to give up just like that and to lose courage? *No, endure this and strengthen my resolve.*

The way one's body moves, even how we walk has its own meaning. Waluyo, for example, was always slacking off, arriving late and chatting on and on with his colleagues at the school. Usually, people heard his hoarse laughter and footsteps on the side veranda, and the children would get scared and look out the windows, because they wanted to be sure. Now he worked hard, gloom written on his face, and almost wouldn't answer if Sudarmo asked him something; to Sulastri, he said nothing more than a curt "good morning." And Prawira, now more bent over than ever, kept a cold look on his face, even if he always smiled back. He kept away from Sudarmo, and lately if Sudarmo stood at the fence in front, Prawira would greet him respectfully and ask with complete attention, "How are you? I haven't seen you for so long."

It was even worse with Jamil. Good-natured Jamil now wore a sour expression. And when he was given a task to perform, he'd say, "Yes, that's right, of course, ahem, it's only natural," and so forth. In that way he implied that he wanted to do it, but couldn't, because of party work or some other problem. Sulastri felt sad. She had an intuition about such things. And it was she who spoke to Sudarmo about this. She often observed her husband, his eyes always questioning, which revealed his unhappiness, to the point where Sudarmo had to pace back and forth in front of her to get rid of his uneasiness.

Once when they were seated in the darkness of the terrace, Sulastri asked, a bit hesitantly, "Dar, what's happening? Do they hate me? I think I've never taught as well as I do now. You know that the children can now write compositions, good ones. What's wrong?"

Sudarmo just kept silent and smoked his cigarette, tapping the ashes into the ashtray, inhaling again and puffing out the smoke, without saying a thing. Sulastri watched him as he leaned back in his chair. There were dark shadows on his thin cheeks. In the dim light, his forehead showed his stubbornness, an attitude that nothing mattered to him. She sensed he wanted to say, "Stay out of my affairs." Lacing her fingers, Sulastri rested her chin on her hands and thought, as she observed her husband, "If only he'd speak. Why do we have to make such trouble for ourselves?"

Sudarmo got up and sat on the low wall of the terrace. He swung his feet rhythmically—and annoyingly—so that Sulastri couldn't think any more and kicked his foot.

"Stop that. You've really got to be happy. I'm concerned. I swear now, I won't ask you any more questions." Her face was creased with anger. Her gestures, like the movements of a cat, made him stand up and apologetically take her shoulders.

"I didn't mean to make you angry. You don't understand me. I'm so frustrated, I'm exhausted. Oh, Tri, you don't know what I'm thinking."

"Yes, a lot to be thinking about, right? But that's no reason for you to see me as just not there. Like something that means nothing. All right, then, I'm going. I'll leave you by yourself."

Sudarmo had a mean look on his face, now pointy and sharp.

"Go then," he said nastily. "I can't stand you living here."

"All right, I'm going." Sulastri stood up, walked a few steps, then stopped in doubt, sat down again and waited. But she said nothing and assumed a pose of indifference. Crossing her legs and caressing the leaves of their arum plant that was sagging next to the chair, she looked away from her husband and waited for the desolate atmosphere to become too much for them. But it seemed that wasn't going to happen, because Sudarmo kept on smoking and keeping to himself. At times like that, Sulastri would usually begin to slowly move toward peace, but on this night, her lips were locked shut. She said to herself, it's no use acting this way with him. But—and this was the nub of the tension—couldn't she fully understand him? And it was the same with Sudarmo. He regretted the loss of that charming atmosphere... simply sitting on the terrace in the dusky light as they had been when they first sat there. This night was so quiet and peaceful, they could immerse themselves in memories and tell each other about their earlier lives. Why couldn't people behave as they wished?

"Tri," Sudarmo suddenly had taken her hand, "Why are we always quarreling? Let's go sit next to the bougainvillea. The moon will be coming up soon."

"I don't want to," she refused. "I hate it."

"Hate it? Lastri, I am very sorry. Come..."

He drew her by the hand. and she, who at first wanted to refuse him, was afraid to lose good moments like this. So she quickly followed him in her sandals on the sharp gravel and the wet grass. There was a bench near the bougainvillea, where they sat side by side. And when the ambience returned and the warmth entwined them, Sudarmo began.

"I will tell you about this from the start. Don't interrupt me. Just listen. This is the problem. When I came here, I came at the invitation of Bung Karno. Last year, he stayed at our house and he asked me to come to Bandung, because, one by one, a number of teachers had been forbidden to teach. You will surely understand that schools in those days smelled too much of incense and various old-fashioned practices and attitudes. And Bung Karno needed me to create a balance. At the time, he hadn't chosen a party, so there was nothing wrong with him choosing me. I asked him to let me think about it, and I also said that I wouldn't be so happy in a nationalist education school environment. He wrote back saying, 'Nationalist education in Bandung is me.' That meant I just had to come, that I could come without feeling I had betrayed my convictions."

Sudarmo paused and began again in a soft voice.

"I came and stayed at Bung Karno's home. Because the board of directors issued a directive for all the new teachers to be apprentices first to avoid the Education Ban policy, I had to pretend to be an apprentice. After two weeks I returned to Batavia because I wasn't happy with all this apprentice pretense. In October, when the school representative was called to Yogya, I got a promotion letter from Bung Karno, who at the time was the head of the board of the school branch. That's how he had the authority to sign that decision. I became the school principal for three months and I cleaned the place up. Incompetent teachers voluntarily requested transfers. And I must admit, I was the one who persuaded them to do so. But I did not betray them, because I took the opportunity of those conditions that coincidentally arose from the need for teachers from small places, and the ones who requested transfers were better than the ones already in those places. There was so much slander about those transfers. People thought I was Bung Karno's tool. But it wasn't at all like that, because in reality, I was squeezed between several factions. Bung Karno and others of the Nationalist Party wanted a 'frontline guard post' at this school.

"My Marhaen Party friends wanted me to favor them and not to say anything if they arrived late due to party work or even if they didn't show up at all. And Ki Hadjar's people saw me as a Westernized intellectual who had no interest in the culture of the motherland itself and who tried to imitate the West. Strange, right? Did you know that some people even say I have become a religious teacher or a mystical guru? My friends want me to cut my ties with groups that value culture, because in the end, people with rumbling stomachs can't think of culture, let alone appreciate gamelan music and classical dances. Now do you know why I'm in such difficulty? And here you come with all your grumblings. You complain about this and that, instead of standing here bravely beside me." His voice had grown hoarse. Sulastri felt guilty for inflicting this depression upon him.

The areca palm fronds quietly stirred. The *cempaka* tree's dark peak swayed. Flowers fell to the ground like fragrant rain.

"Dar," her voice had a conciliatory tone to it. She leaned on her husband's shoulder and felt his warmth pervade her own body. She was disappointed in herself, at her weak character and felt afraid of herself for frequently upsetting other people's composure.

"Dar, sometimes I get a feeling that your colleagues would like me to leave. So recommend me at another school. Oh, I can't tell you how heavily all of this weighs on me.... Dar, we're not going live as poor as this with our child forever, are we?"

She fell silent and suddenly her eyes were wet.

"Look outside for work? I won't permit it. I'd be too ashamed to do that. What would everyone say about our willingness to sacrifice here? And, about our child, oh, everything will be fine. Don't be like those market peddlers who only think of profit and loss."

"But, Dar, if we're forced to leave here, how would we live?" she sighed.

"It's not a big thing to live in a hut. You're a materialist and it's disgusting how you're always looking into the future. If you loved me, you'd be loyal to me. If you can't stand it anymore, you can leave."

Sulastri didn't argue back. But she was sad and felt alone.

"Sulastri, darling, you look at the present. You're bourgeois. You're unable to adjust to a life filled with household difficulties. I'm ashamed of your pettiness. Why are you still so stuck on your dreams of an easy life? Everyone works and almost no one goes about with a smile. And you only long for happiness and ease?" His inner, real voice seemed to be reproaching and mocking her.

"Dar," she said gently, "I will follow wherever you go. I am so exhausted but even so, I am happy and lighthearted. I don't know why I'm like that. You are no longer the person I married. You're different from what I thought: you're sharp, arrogant, tense. But I will try to be brave and not burst into tears anymore."

She stood up but felt so heavy inside that she stumbled and almost fell. She slowly made her way into the house and was surprised to see the lamps still brightly shining and the flames undisturbed.

That is how it was that night. Not long after this, the tension suddenly broke. One morning, when Sudarmo was teaching at the MULO school, the incident occurred. The MULO school had been moved to another building at the corner of the street. The large rooms in the back were where Prawira, Harjono, and Jamil lived. The result of this was that Sulastri and her husband now occupied four rooms in the pavilion. They could organize their residence better and there was even a guest bedroom. It was exceedingly quiet at night, but they didn't want the din of people around. There was a large garden, and in the solitude of the night with silence and darkness all around them, they could talk about things more freely.

One morning, Sudarmo had noticed something odd in the schoolyard. Ordinarily, the students would have been memorizing their lessons or sitting and talking on the steps, but now it was totally quiet; and when it was time to go into the classrooms, he spotted only one child. When the bell rang, several students did go into the classrooms, giving Sudarmo puzzled looks. He didn't pay any attention to this and he went straight into teaching as usual. But when he went into the classroom next door, he noticed that many of students weren't there. He asked about this, but no one admitted to knowing anything. So he went looking for Prawira, whom he found sitting on the side veranda, drinking coffee. Prawira didn't answer his questions right away, but he was rather dumbstruck and said slowly, his body hunched over, "The boys?

Ah, maybe... oh, wait, there's Atikah. Atikah, do you know where the boys are?"

Atikah stood before them silently pinching her shiny braids. Then she said, "I really may not talk about it."

"Why not? What do you know?"

Sudarmo began to suspect something and looked closely at her.

She hemmed and hawed and finally said, "They... they threatened me, if I went to school now. They're on strike, sir"

"On strike? Ah." Sudarmo shook his head several times. Then he spoke harshly as he looked at Prawira, who wanted to quickly get away from there, with a bag squeezed under his arm.

"Tell me everything, Atikah. Let's go, follow me."

The girl followed into the classroom and told him about the "joke" of the strike. At one point, she let the cat out of the bag. "They wrote a letter. They meant to—" then she stopped in shock and clamped her hand over her mouth.

"What? Go on." But Atikah went stubbornly silent. She kept pinching her braids and didn't dare look up. She flushed red to her ears, and Sudarmo, now annoyed, grabbed her roughly around the shoulders. But the result was that she burst into tears, which further aggravated Sudarmo. He left quickly, threw his books on the table and then went to the pavilion. There he threw himself down on the easy chair and tapped its armrests with his fingers.

When Sulastri asked what was wrong, he snapped at her, "Go away, I'm tired."

Sulastri left him by himself and went to find her colleagues who were talking among themselves. She overheard this: "I actually heard it from a boy in the first year of MULO. He said he actually knew it. They had send out letters."

"What letters?" asked Sulastri.

One of the women teachers replied, "You don't know about this, ma'am? They've sent an anonymous letter to the Board of Directors of Nationalist Education to transfer the boss."

"What? I didn't know. Go on, tell me the rest of it."

And this teacher related what she knew of the matter, which wasn't much, but enough to make Sulastri run to Sudarmo and ask him to explain this. He pretended not to hear her and looked blankly at the pages of a book he had just opened. Sulastri kept insisting.

"What's going on, Dar? Come on, say it!"

"Here," he said, "read this." He angrily thrust a card at Sulastri and she read that the Board of Directors had received an anonymous letter. In it, Sudarmo was slandered. The Board wrote about that letter to Sudarmo and told him it was up to him how he would respond. In addition, the Board had received a telegram from some MULO students. They strongly urged that Sudarmo be transferred immediately.

Sulastri placed the card gently on the table, as if afraid of causing distress to her husband. Then she said, "Who would be so brazen as to slander you. My guess is—"

Sudarmo interrupted her. "It's that traitor, Sanip, the one with all the blotches on his face. I've read his article in one of the lousy newspapers. There he pronounced on the difficulties of this school since I was appointed. I know why they hate me. But I don't care. It's better to be hated because of virtue than to be praised because of vileness."

He lit another cigarette and Sulastri felt relieved. She watched Sudarmo's lips and waited for what he would say next.

"This is a scheme by people in the Nationalist Party. They're taking advantage of this situation. A few days ago, I forbade a student from taking the Sundanese language course for teachers. Also, before you came here, I dismissed one understudy, because he got one of the MULO girls to have improper relations with him. The girl got pregnant, and all that led to this strike. But, Tri, do you suspect Bung Karno is involved in this?"

"You had the right to dismiss the understudy. As to Bung Karno... did he become a party member only to defend his own camp? Do you also think that?"

Sudarmo just stayed quiet, his chin in his hand. Then he got up, patted his wife's shoulder, and left. Sulastri heard his loud steps going toward the study, then crossing the road to the other building.

After eleven o'clock there was a teachers' meeting. Five teachers attended to discuss and set Sudarmo's policy toward the striking students. They agreed that the strike leadership would no longer be accepted as students, while those who just followed along would be given amnesty if they promised not to do such a thing again.

Two days later, the striking students came back, ashamed and unsure. But, because no one paid any attention to them, lessons went on calmly as always. However, the strike leaders did not return and later became extremely energetic propagandists for the Nationalist Party.

7

The school newspaper came out and night classes began. These victories made put Sudarmo in a good mood, and he forgave Sulastri's petty faults. His relationship with his colleagues was freer and more cordial, so that Harjono was pleased to greet Sulastri and smile at her. The attitude of colleagues toward Sulastri was a barometer of their feelings toward Sudarmo. Only Waluyo maintained his gloominess. The student strike made the teachers, who had split into two factions of their party, now come back together again—one united fortress, which would defend the school organization against outside challenges, notwithstanding its uneasiness within. Work at the school proceeded smoothly. Sulastri, who loved the school children as her own, experienced something that was new to her.

First, there was a small girl who sat hunched over near the rain gutter. She held her head in both hands and her yellowish-brown, dust-covered feet close together. Her hair was curly and shoulder-length, and she looked like a skinny little cat, happy to be basking in the warm sunlight. Her friends would shriek and shout and laugh in the schoolyard, but she kept to herself and never moved her head or shoulders.

"What is it, dear?" Sulastri gave a playful tug of the child's curls. The child didn't answer, but when Sulastri lifted the little one's chin and looked at her face beneath the curly hair, she saw two fearful brown eyes. Sulastri exhorted her with sweet smiles to open her heart, and, sobbing, the little one began to tell of her misery. It was the story of a woman suffering in her marriage. Her mother had been abandoned by her husband and this little girl had been the victim. The father had gone, there was no money, and so she had to leave the school. Who could stay calm at the tears of that child?

"I don't want to leave school, to leave you and the other children," she said, her shoulders heaving.

"Must you go, dear?"

"Yes, we're all going to Grandma's. My mother can't stop crying. She's always thinking about Bapak. Our neighbor says he's got someone else. A second wife." This information passed her lips so smoothly.

"A second wife." Polygamy was so normal that a little child thought so too. She only felt sad because her mother was always crying. And so, the girl parted from her teacher and friends and left through the iron gate in front of the schoolyard. She looked very small in the sunlight. She glanced back with a tear-filled smile. Sulastri had a sense of experiencing something new. She could only wave her hand and sadly watch that curly-headed little child leave.

While her pupils were studying, Sulastri noticed one with a very listless expression. His shirt was open and its cuffs were dirty. One day, when the children were monotonously reading boring sentences for the third time, that particular child was dozing off and awoke with a start when Sulastri called his name. His eyes were red, and he gaped as he looked around, his hair all disheveled at being startled, and he was squeezing his cuffs. His classmates laughed at him mockingly. When he himself joined in the laughter, Sulastri got angry. Nonetheless, because she was unaware of the child's situation, she scolded him and didn't understand the fear that showed on his face. But she spoke with him during the rest period and his story came out. It wasn't a happy one. He told it with a bowed head. "I have to take care of my little brothers and sisters up to nine o'clock. After that I can study. My ibu is always busy selling fried bananas and my bapak has to go to the market. So I have to manage my brothers and sisters. I've got to put the kettle on very early and I can go to school only then, Ibu Guru."

"Well, I now understand why you're falling asleep. But can't there be different arrangements at your home? There's no one to help you?"

He shook his head, sad and ashamed, and he tugged his cuffs down to cover up his thin wrists. Because of the unease of the silent boy and Sulastri's anxiety about her excessive clumsiness in approaching him, she signaled the child to go outside. She followed him and placed her hands on his shoulders, lightly and amicably. The boy regarded her with a look of gratitude, and then ran out to the garden in the heat of the sunlight. There he began leap about and frolic with his friends. They didn't know why, but they chased each other around yelling and screaming. And Sulastri smiled at the dust that floated up and dirtied the decorative plants in their pots.

The girls gathered in a group. They chit-chatted about clothes, hair ribbons, and about those who were sweet on boys. They giggled as they twirled on their toes. Those who wore kebaya-style blouses frequently straightened their chignons: they were flirtatious girls who carried on like older women and had a grown-up style. Sulastri found it more pleasant being with the little children. They invited her to the front garden and drew her there by the hand.

The little garden was well-ordered and filled with all sorts of plants. There was bitter gourd, pumpkins, beans, and even a small banana tree. The young children tended their garden well and their voices rang out there each morning, sweet little bird-chirpings. Jamil grumbled about the way they planted things without knowing the proper way. Sulastri just laughed and challenged him to get the same results with the big boys. Jamil accepted the challenge. He gathered the boys to work the soil on the left side of the pavilion.

But they let Jamil sweat it out in the practice lesson while they climbed the citrus tree and shouted peans of praise at their own teacher.

Only now did Jamil get really incensed. He clenched his fists and pulled the boys down by their feet and, one by one, smacked them about their ears. The naughty boys held their hoes full of respect, for they saw the frightening look on Jamil's face. Gradually the garden came into being. Now they discussed what they would plant. Their boisterousness made Sudarmo get involved and he decided they'd plant corn, because corn didn't need tending. Jamil shrewdly explained that corn was the food of the people, so the children should plant it.

While they were busily planting corn, Sulastri candidly said to Jamil that his notion about beans was true. Beans really were a fruit. This made Jamil happy and he promised her a *pikul* of the corn harvest. The plants sprouted and gave forth their first leaves, then flowers, and then their ears, so small and rather round that Sulastri observed this with wonder. The tall stalks were slender and pointed at the tips. "That's because of the soil," Jamil said, "This type takes a while. Don't be surprised, it's a special corn. But I'm amazed, it's very odd."

He shook his head as he looked at the ear of corn and said, "I followed the instructions in the book. The gaps between the holes were measured and everything was counted precisely. Very strange!"

Then he burst out laughing. "It's because of the corn seeds, you know. The harvest is going to be good."

Sulastri's eye's shone with tears of amusement, but she said nothing. She just held one of the ears of corn. Jamil's corn was a laughing-stock. They all made jokes. Jamil joined in the laughter and scratched his head. The harvest was approaching, and one day Sulastri carefully picked a few ears of corn from their stalk and was filled with a sense of reverence. She placed these in an unusually large basket as all the kids gathered around shouting and yelling because of how funny the big basket looked. Her corn practically disappeared inside it.

Jamil was nowhere to be seen. In the evenings, Sulastri peeled the leaves from the ears of corn and Sudarmo roasted the corn over a charcoal fire. There were only a few kernels on each cob and these were quite widely spaced. Jamil sat with them and Sulastri teased him. "These ears are so plain, they've almost got no kernels at all. This is what happens when Bung Jamil plants corn."

Jamil looked at her wonderingly, so Sudarmo explained. "There's a superstition about it that goes like this. Whoever has bad teeth may not plant corn. That's because the ears will be exactly like the jaws of the planter. There'll be almost no kernels."

The three of them guffawed uproariously. Jamil's experience with this corn gave him a cause for complaint. He himself guffawed the loudest and grumbled about the lazy school employees and the boys who couldn't hoe.

"What kind of boys are they? Their hands get blistered after holding the hoe a few times. They don't follow the traditional ways. I recommend teaching them to hoe twice a week. We aren't women. How can we build a strong people like this?" Jamil groused in this manner to everyone.

The practical lessons were continued and were in line with Sudarmo's enthusiasm for the currents in modern education. But, as always, Jamil had a reason for staying quiet in the classroom. The work spirit rapidly diminished. In their botanical studies, the children diligently made notes and the garden fell into disorder. In the interstices of the lawn there were dried up ears of corn. They went there only to pick sour citrus.

Around the time of Jamil's setback, Sudarmo and Sulastri had visitors. One Sunday morning, when they were sitting on a mat beneath the cempaka tree enjoying their coffee, Juhariah and Supardi came for a visit. Juhariah was big around the waist. Her movements were heavy and labored and her face was mottled. The lines of apathy there had grown worse. "A woman in this condition is really ugly," thought Sulastri. "I'll get this way too. Will Dar still love me?"

She felt something sharply stab her in her breast, a sense of desolation all about her. Juhariah noticed Sulastri lapsing into silence and she asked, "What is it, Tri?"

Sulastri laughed. She jokingly took Juhariah by the hand and invited her to the plum tree, so rich in fruit. There they plucked the black fruit off their stems. Juhariah stretched to reach a cluster of big fruit. Supardi laughed happily, just like a youngster. He and Sudarmo came up to their wives, and the two men went on talking.

Supardi said, "Even so, I know that my life will end in some desolate place out there on the edge of the Maluku Sea. But all the wealth in the world isn't going to make me betray the position I have chosen. What's more, in that place of exile, we'll be surrounded by our own people."

He laughed softly and made the others laugh too. His eyes sparkled and he watched his wife with a subtle and strange look in his eyes.

Juhariah protested. "And I have to go with you. And what about our child? Would he have to go to school there?"

Sudarmo, as if he had just awoke, joked, "They can take my wife as the teacher. Most agreeable. The pay there's better than here, right?"

He nodded his head in the direction of Sulastri, who said with bravado, "Yes, let's all of us move there."

Everyone laughed. And they kept talking with even greater amusement. The morning was bright and cloudless. They drank coffee together under the tree, served by a girl who looked to be in her late teens.

"Oh never mind," said Juhariah. "Why do we have to be unhappy? Human happiness and sorrow depend one's attitude toward it."

"I'd certainly follow Mas Dar. What would I do in a land as packed with people as this one if I were all by myself? But, Dar, wouldn't it be foolish to go to that point? And also, don't we have to think of our children?"

Sudarmo said, "We don't need to trouble ourselves with that right now. What do we know about tomorrow? What's clear is that our teachers are being paid on the Gandhi scale."

"What?" Supardi was surprised.

"Yes," Sudarmo explained. "We only get a little bit, so we can't refer to it with the prevailing BBL scale. So, just the Gandhi scale." They again laughed. There was a lot of humor in pitiful things. Stroking his unruly hair, Supardi said, "In three more months, my wife is going to give birth. We're just calling in a *dukun*. Why would we get a midwife, when our common folk have to use a dukun?"

Sulastri and Sudarmo glanced at each other meaningfully. Then Sudarmo, looking at his fingernails, said carefully, "If you don't mind, we'll provide a midwife."

The other two were silent. Then Supardi said in a normal tone of voice, "That's not the problem. No. Mas Karno has also offered us a midwife and we declined. Ah, so why not? Juhariah was also not brought to birth by a midwife."

"Mas Karno has sent me various kinds of medicines," Juhariah said smiling.

"He's always thinking of the hardship of others," said Supardi. "It's just too bad—" Supardi was silent for a moment and he looked straight ahead with some regret. Then he continued listlessly, "We can't go on. It's like we've become different people and he is a stranger to us. In fact, we and he have gone through so much together. There's nothing that he doesn't know about me, and I about him. Like a stranger..."

And speaking very softly, he said, "Even in one's greatness, there's still some pettiness. Maybe I'm the one at fault. It's so strange, why am I seeing him now with different eyes? But, no, he's not like that. It's because of the people around him. People wearing traditional clothes, who make him so petty. He's still great and pure. It'd be too disturbing for us if he weren't."

He stopped, his voice trembling. Now he plucked a blade of grass and gently chewed on it. The three of them were silent. Twisting and turning in its descent, a yellow leaf landed on Juhariah's shoulder and rested there. The garden, which until now had been filled with bright sunlight, now seemed empty and desolate. An eagle's shadow crossed the hot grass. The breeze gently shook the clumps of Japanese red elder flowers, seemingly enchanted and sunk in memories.

"A comrade has left us. A comrade once has now become an enemy," whispered the agitated leaves of the shade tree. And the thought of this enveloped everything with melancholy, as if the sun had lost its light. Such were the feelings of the four of them, sitting in silence on the mat under the tree. And perhaps at that time there were more people who felt the effect of that sadness.

Sudarmo's voice broke the silence. "All right, let's talk about something else. Our newspaper's finished and will be delivered by the children on Monday. I'll give each of them five newspapers and for each one they have to ask for at least one cent; if they can get more, so much the better. I just hope there's nothing in these papers that sets off the police. You know that they check everything, like looking for husks in the rice. They take ordinary words and give them revolutionary meanings."

"Be careful, Mas Dar. It won't be long till they come after you. They're very quick and active imps!" Supardi smiled sardonically and quickly added, "They keep a very sharp watch on things. Two or three of them silently wait in front of my home smoking cigarettes and then walk behind me like they're my bodyguards. You actually have to be pleased, Ju, that there's someone watching my every step. If not..."

Juhariah raised her finger menacingly. "Keep quiet, you, and don't talk nonsense. Men, really, Tri! I've had a lot of trouble with our anti-polygamy movement."

"Not for us, is it, Tri," said Sudarmo. "Actually, polygamy is very practical, if one has three wives who all work. Or if Lastri lets me marry a rich woman...." Sudarmo glanced at his wife with an amused look.

Sulastri made a sour face. She didn't appreciate jokes like that. Especially if they involved Sudarmo. So, she didn't answer him but turned to Juhariah. "In love, I want all of it or none of it. What kind of love is it, if you have to share it?"

"Don't pine before it's time," said Supardi."But it's true, polygamy makes a person into livestock. We nationalists must not trivialize it. For us ourselves, I mean. Other people consider it carefully. There's no danger if we don't oppose it. But whoever calls himself a revolutionary will not be able to stay quiet when a woman is seen as lower than him."

Sulastri, sharp and ironic, her face filled with lines and her lips pursed, said with a sidelong glance at her husband, "Theoretically, all men are considered equal. In practice, you make a slave of a woman."

"Well, well, am I such a fierce bulldog? But it's totally fitting that you're always whining and complaining...." Sudarmo then choked back several sarcastic sentences that he'd thought of tossing out and went on in the usual way about everyday events, school, friends and the party.

After their guests left, the couple had a conversation. They discussed how, if Supardi were forced to go so far away, his wife would accompany him. Certainly, someone like him could never bear to break up his marriage for something like that. Then Sudarmo had an idea: "Let's us take their child. It would lighten their hardship."

"What kind of an idea is that! As though a mother could be separated from her child so easily! A man can't begin to imagine the love of a mother for her own child. Do you really think that rational thinking could influence it? I'm sure you'd say that on the contrary it couldn't be out of love that a mother would let her child be stricken with malaria and live in danger of demoralizing influences. But in this case, a mother feels better being stupid than smart. Oh, I also know how I myself would act in such a difficult situation."

"If I were facing such a future, I really should leave you and our child," Sudarmo admitted. "But you don't know how you'd act in that kind of situation. Perhaps I would be the first to regret it if you stayed here. Supardi and Juhariah realize what they are going to do, so no problems will suddenly arise for them. I respect Supardi for how he achieved such a high position with just an average education. But it's not that. Education is meaningless in this matter. It's character that counts. He's poured out his heart, with the warmth of his humility. And he feels at one with the soul of the people. He feels their hardships. If he weeps at seeing scrawny little children holding out their hand to beg for something to eat, it's genuine. I can't be like him. I'll tell you frankly, there's a wall between me and the common people, maybe because of traditional attitudes and practices or, more likely, because of my intellectualism. I really do have honest intentions, but the people are afraid of me. And if I try to get close to them, they are suspicious. If I'm friendly, they get confused; they forget their manners and don't want to listen to what I am saying."

Sulastri said, "You really are arrogant. You look down on uneducated people. You feel other people are different and there's no connection between you and them. People say we're condescending because you and I can't get to the depths of their hearts. Our colleagues don't open up to us, when in fact we are truly concerned with their interests."

"I'm irritated that these colleagues of ours have no interest in modern education, that they're only like machines, so stuck to old-fashioned methods. They have no strength because they're crippled by their everyday difficulties. I give them books to read, but this tribe of 'illiterates' doesn't read them, they just daydream on them. How can we progress with people who aren't alive? And nationalist education has to be served with blazing ideals.

"Yes, they're loyal, very loyal, when you recall that Harjono has worked here for five years and has never had any pleasure besides his gramophone. Sometimes I see them as really believing in this, but then why do they have such a dreary attitude toward new issues? They've studied the Croes method at school, so they hold on to that method. This is just one example; there are other problems. Really, Tri, we've become stones here. How can you make progress if you have to work alone? It's not that they treat us badly, but the 'yes, yes' attitude, just like ducks, and the lack of performance of the regulations that have been agreed to.

"Prawira still comes late. Miss Jukro teaches the children to read with a tedious chanting tone. And Jamil, he teaches using difficult lessons from those heavy books. The children can't understand what he's teaching when he sounds like some old grandpa. Waluyo sabotages, that's clear, but no one will be sorry if he goes. In the end, an administration employee is a luxury for us, to say nothing of someone who's always showing up late. And it's not true that he works for the party. That's nonsense. I've asked for him and people say that he can't be found anywhere. Jamil's begun to imitate him. He doesn't come in to teach, just goes for a walk. He's not sick when he doesn't show up for teaching, because people see him out strolling around. And these are even my friends and fellow-party members. If I acted fairly, I should be reprimanding them as I do with the others. People are slandering us for all sorts of things."

Such were Sudarmo's grumblings, and Sulastri yielded to him. Even if he was ruthless when it came to the regulations, and thus inevitably made enemies, he was honest and tireless in his work. When the school let out for the day, he stayed in the classroom to straighten out the chairs and benches. He even helped carry benches when the school relocated. He helped the coolies when they lifted heavy furniture and fittings, and that night he complained of chest pains and lay down exhausted on the divan. His physique wasn't strong and several hours later he spat out a little blood. Sulastri went pale with fear when she saw the blood on his handkerchief and heard his hoarse, labored coughing. She hugged him and for a moment placed her head on his chest, which heaved with his coughing.

Sulastri still remembered all so clearly how, before they married in Batavia, he would walk with his sunken chest, and cough medicine in his pocket. He was so skinny then, you could have broken him into two. He was afraid he had tuberculosis because several family members had died from it, and so he frequently went to a doctor who was well-versed in this disease. When he had asked whether he had TB, the doctor snapped at him and said things he shouldn't have said, so he recovered out of fear. Nonetheless, when he was younger, he had been strong, an excellent athlete, and quick to anger and happy to scrap, until one day he fell and badly injured his spine. From that moment on, he began to be sickly. He couldn't sit without a piercing pain. From a fit and lively boy, he became a cynical and irascible youth who frequently lost his temper, was easily offended and always felt let down. And so Sulastri got a shock because of the blood and she was afraid his heart had stopped beating. Sulastri forced him to go to bed and she massaged him solicitously and intimately until he closed his eyes to hold back the tears. At that time, Sulastri wanted to bear the hardships together with her husband, if by doing so, this could lighten the pain in his body.

It was two months since that happened. Now he was refreshed and the sensation of illness had gone.

But Sudarmo felt very disappointed that none of his colleagues truly cared about the fate of the school. He was sure that the moment they got home, they forgot all about the place. Maybe they didn't know that Sudarmo couldn't sleep nights because he was searching for a solution to the school's revenue, which kept dropping because of the departure of children from the school. The Nationalist Party had initiated a large-scale competition for building a school, one with very low tuition, so that children of the members of that party could go to the school themselves.

This development had a big impact on Sudarmo's school, because the students were the children of party members, whether of the Nationalist Party or the Marhaen Party. They were all genuine children of the common people. There were also some children of customshouse officials and senior clerks, but they were either "slow learners" or had been dismissed from the government primary schools. Sudarmo often expressed his regret that his school could almost be said to be a school for "slow learners," because the Marhaen children were truly backward in their thoughts if compared to children of the same age from fairly prosperous families. They had to be given basic lessons in sanitation. Even speaking was often difficult for them. And while teaching them, one got the impression of speaking to the benches, even when the subject matter was trivial. During this time, the school seemed to be lacking in every way. The teaching aids were inadequate; there wasn't even money to buy ordinary maps. If it weren't for the devotion and sacrifice of the teachers who didn't place their own interests first, this school might have had to close long before.

It was understandable that Sudarmo's thoughts were flooded with the school's problems and ignored unrelated issues. He isolated himself from his colleagues and they complained that he very seldom attended ononparty meetings and rallies. Over time, they came to see him as someone who could no longer be used for party work, even though they knew that in spirit he would never leave the party. In any case, intellectuals were said to be useless, so for that reason, Sudarmo stopped giving political courses to the inner party members.

Waluyo incited his colleagues using the clichéd word "dictator" about Sudarmo. These colleagues, who didn't really understand the situation, followed along with Waluyo in opposing Sudarmo. People from the Nationalist Party wanted someone from their own membership, a young poet and a former teacher from a private teacher's school, to become head of this nationalist education school. They took devious routes and betrayed Sudarmo, who at first didn't know about this and still visited Sukarno, until he clearly saw their insidious guiles. And at that same time, he also realized that Sukarno had shifted from his friendly attitude to one of hostility. Sudarmo felt that he was surrounded by enemies and gradually lost the foundation he stood on.

On Idul Fitri, Jamil received an unwelcome gift, the government's prohibition from teaching. Waluyo was dismissed because the teachers felt they couldn't afford to provide food to such a lazy administrator. Because he often repeated his old errors, Waluyo had been given a warning: come on time or don't come back at all. He chose to go. As a result, Sudarmo was all alone and faced enemies on three fronts. They opposed him secretly or openly. His hands were tied as he tried endlessly to find a solution to his difficulties. Then he got the idea of opposing them using their own weapons.

He needed someone who could continually visit the parents of the students to influence them. Such a person would have to be able to face slander from left and right, so he must be someone who understood the ways of politicians. Therefore, Sudarmo invited a friend of his brother-in-law to come to Bandung from Central Java. He would have to confront crafty people from the Nationalist Party. Gularso, the name of his in-law's friend, had been exiled because he had been a fiery propagandist for the communist party, the PKI. His influence was so great, people said, that all of Bandung had obeyed his commands. However, his time in exile had broken his image as a tough guy. He corrected his behavior so he could be called civilized, and after five years the government pardoned him and allowed him to return to his hometown. In the meantime, his reputation as a bold and trustworthy person lived on. On his return from exile, he brought with him only a broken heart and a certain apathy. Rabowo, Sudarmo's brother-in law, was unaware of this when he wrote that Sudarmo ought to take on his former schoolmate and close friend. And so, one rainy day, Gularso arrived at the side veranda carrying his suitcase. Sudarmo and Sulastri had in mind the different, earlier Gularso—passionate, with a sturdy body and a brave countenance.

This person dripping water, though, was scrawny and sunken-eyed, one who impressed you with his sloppiness and lackluster expression. He wore a sarong and sandals, and his clothes were so shabby that for a few amazed moments Sudarmo didn't say a single word. Then they quickly greeted him in a friendly manner and invited him to sit and to change his clothing. After some coffee, the fatigued expression became somewhat refreshed. Sudarmo described the situation at the school and went on to say, "Mas Gularso, you will have a room at the schoolhouse. You will eat with us and will be as if in your own home. You must help me, because we need your help. You will soon see for yourself what's going on. All right then, let's eat."

Sulastri made their guest comfortable. But Gularso didn't need much looking after. He already felt at home. He laughed and chatted about Digul and influential people and ate without paying great attention to what the food was. Then they sat about on the side veranda and listened to the heavy rainfall. When Gularso went to his room, he seemed calm. Sudarmo yawned and remarked to Sulastri, who was still tidying things up, "I'd like to know if my idea is going to work. I suppose he can be trusted. He's so simple in every way."

Sulastri stopped what she was doing for a moment and tried to bring Gularso's face to mind.

"Yes," he said. "He can be trusted. He'll be our friend, and so we won't be so lonely anymore."

"A comrade-in-arms," she thought. "A friend in the struggle. A comrade." And her thoughts revolved around those words, words that had deep meaning for her. As she fell asleep that night, her way of breathing seemed to show the hope that had arisen with Gularso's arrival.

8

A month passed. Gularso had become perfectly familiar with his work. He not only taught but also handled administration. His face was now more agreeable. Where it had once been thin, it now had become more filled out and youthful. His hair, formerly unkept and dirty, was now wavy and clean. His eyes, once sunken and listless, were now bright black, and could now blaze and sparkle. He seemed to be a different person, with his neat clothing and growing plumpness. His comradeship with Sudarmo was clear and without artifice. The three of them often took walks together and at night would sit together. Gularso talked about the stupidity of the rich.

"If they come across a snake," he said in a pleasant tone of voice, "they'll light a fire as long as the snake itself and not cut it into pieces. They'll enjoy eating it for several days until their bellies stick out and they can hardly walk!"

Sulastri and Sudarmo had him tell stories, both funny and sad things that had happened while he was in exile. Once, when they were discussing how lazy Waluyo was, he told them, "I was in the first consignment. One day after we arrived at Digul, I was handed an ax and told to build a barracks. For that we had to cut down trees in the jungle with clouds of malarial mosquitoes all around us. If you didn't obey, they'd stick a bayonet in your chest. Could we refuse? We used every bit of our strength working and if we rested, here came the bayonets; we were cursed endlessly and beaten like animals. We had to pound the unhusked rice ourselves. My wife pounded it furiously and at night, when we were supposed to be asleep on our mats in the barracks, she'd have me rub her back. We went to sleep on command and we worked under the bayonets. That's the way to make Waluyo work. He has to go through something like that. Fever, fighting, beatings... it was like we had plunged into hell. Who could last long in conditions like that? I got wounded by a saber, here on my shoulder."

Gularso held one of his shoulders and tilted his body at them as they listened with rapt attention.

"My friends considered me a traitor, because I worked hard in the administration section of the hospital. A squabble broke out, it became a fistfight, and I landed on the floor, covered in blood. My wife almost fainted, she was so scared, until I opened my eyes in the hospital. I figured there was no use in sabotaging and thought it'd be better for me to use my brain than to get thrown in the camp of the irreconcilables. Later, we weren't so poor anymore, and I got a little money from selling pineapples my wife grew in the garden. When we returned from exile, we had about *f* 600 saved under our pillow. We bought a complete set of jazz band records as well as good clothes. But even though we had a little income at Digul, I was overjoyed to see my village again."

He stopped and, scratching his leg, chased off some bothersome mosquitoes.

Sudarmo smiled and said, "But a lot of people live in abject poverty there. You see all that from your own point of view. If it were me, I'd suffocate because of my need to be in a human environment. But if that had to be bought with promises, then no, Mas, it would be better for me to go to the camp for the irreconcilable prisoners."

He broke off there suddenly, pursing his lips and scoffing. Sulastri said soothingly, "That's all right, it's not possible to do political propaganda among the rich. I don't know what would be better."

They stayed silent for a while until they heard someone's footsteps on the gravel. A Javanese man appeared out of the darkness and stood under the lamplight. There was an interesting and titillating feeling among them as they wondered who it was. The man broke out into friendly laughter, almost neighing like a horse. His rotund shape, short neck, and a nose that was quite big over his full and well-formed lips, gave the impression that he was both a person of means and possessed of a friendly disposition. His well-cut jacket indicated fashion-consciousness and that he considered this clothing symbolic of the culture of the gentlemanly class. Whatever the case, he looked like such a dandy that Sulastri thought she smelled the fragrance of perfume. Because of that, she observed him playfully. Sudarmo stood up and bowed in the manner of the Javanese receiving a visit by one's elders. Indeed, it was his uncle.

"Oh, just stay nicely seated as you were," the guest said smoothly, with the accent of Central Java. "How would it be if I joined you in sitting here, assuming it wouldn't be inconvenient? Oh, don't get up, Mas, I am just an ordinary visitor. And, little sister, are you well?" He bowed to Sulastri and sat down. He then took out his handkerchief from his jacket pocket and mopped his perspiration, of which in fact there wasn't any. This fellow Pak Joyokuno usually felt hot, even when the breeze was chilly enough to make you shiver.

"Ah, it's so hot," he sighed. Sudarmo offered him a cigarette which he firmly declined.

"No, no, they're too strong. I prefer the lighter ones."

He took a little box from his pocket and offered them expensive cigarettes, took one for himself and smoked it with evident pleasure. The three of them waited for what he would say and followed the movement of his big fleshy hands.

"In another month, I must take an examination. I study very hard, but can a thirty-year-old person study three foreign languages at the same time? My Dutch, well, it annoys me, though only the spoken part. For written Dutch, I feel at ease, oh, yes, a composition about a servant who's run off and is given delicious spices, that's not so difficult, you know. But they ask for more than that. God only knows how hard I've tried to get rid of the b's and d's from my pronunciation. You've got to use a mirror for that. If I speak normally, you don't hear it much. But if I get excited when I'm talking, well, that's when it happens...." He laughed so amusingly that they all burst out laughing. Joyokuno was the typical product of the Higher Training College for Native Teachers who had diligently applied himself to studying modern streams in education from the headmaster's certificate textbooks. "Pedagogic teacher" was the most important thing for him, and he studied very hard with a charming sense of responsibility. Thus, his books were filled with blue and red underlining, because he considered just about every sentence as important.

"I can imagine it, Pak. Do you know the device I use to eliminate it?"

"What? I want to pass this headmaster's certificate exam. It'd be just too embarrassing to have four children and not pass the exam, you know." He pursed his lips, sucked on his cigarette and then stubbed it out. Sudarmo didn't reply right away, creating a leisurely mood. He knew that his uncle spoke Dutch according to certain rules of his teachers, who were typical of headmaster training schools, always changing the subject from something important to something trivial.

"Pronouncing the words is the most important," said Joyokuno and gestured with his hand, earnestly and impressively. He pulled the hem of his jacket forward, spread his knees with his hands resting on them, and appeared short of breath. Sudarmo gave an amused smile and said earnestly, "It's true, people say that it's easier to become a professor in Dutch than to take the headmaster exam with good grades in that language. A Dutch farmer or a soldier will always be better at pronouncing that language than us. It shows what the examiners are made of. Let's just say, Indonesians aren't allowed to take the headmaster exam with good grades for Dutch."

Joyokuno nodded and then asked, "What device do you say should be used?"

"Burn incense the night before every Jumat Kliwon, then scrape your tongue with a gold ring like they do with parrots and you are sure to get a voice deeper than a drunken Dutchman."

They laughed, Sudarmo the most of all.

All this while, Sulastri had been watching her husband with a look that said, "Be careful," for she saw Uncle Joyokuno laughing a little sourly. But Sudarmo, happy as a fish returning to its own pool, criticized the people in education, to say nothing of their arrogance in thinking they could explain away all problems. He related an example of one such conceited inspector.

"One day a school inspector came here accompanied by a supervisor of native schools. I wasn't married at the time. The inspector entered the schoolyard like some sort of peacock, chest all pumped up, while I was playing chess with a boy. I was in national attire, a sarong and peci cap. The inspector signaled one of the children and asked to speak with the principal. The pupil told me about this and, before I could go and meet him, he was standing right there next to me. He asked me, a bit shocked and with eyebrows raised, "Sir, are you the principal?" I answered politely and escorted him here and there. But, when he walked around like a turkey, criticizing this and criticizing that, I just let him be. Jamil came in with his bear-fur peci, looking like he was going to pull out a dagger and stab him. The Tuan Inspector was silent for a moment. When he came to the pavilion, he saw all my books.

And, whether he intended it or not, sharp words came out of his mouth, 'Did you really read these books, sir?' and I replied, 'Yes, and others as well.'

"He looked at me mockingly. He seemed on the verge of saying something else, but then held his tongue. You could see on his face that he was going to ask if I understood what I actually hadn't read. Then I told him that I wasn't taught to be a teacher. Yes, Dutch people have to be dealt with differently. If someone behaves simply, they will see him as stupid and scared."

Joyokuno agreed with him, but weakened it by saying, "Right, right. But if it weren't for your teachers, you wouldn't be so clever."

"No, rather they wrecked me. I'm actually like a monkey, because I want to talk like them, and I'm also a fool. Why do I feel hurt by their criticisms about my Dutch? They've ruined my life with their language rules and all their insulting talk. 'Better to be a peasant and wield a hoe than to go to a MULO school.' Oh, those Dutch! They've got to be smacked to shut their mouths. So I've opposed your method of parroting and following their lead in everything. The time we waste learning Dutch would be best used on other things."

Joyokuno could offer no answer to that. He laughed rather stiffly and spoke about other things. Gularso and Sulastri only listened. Sudarmo would occasionally reply with scattered thoughts. The moment came for Joyokuno to go home. He invited Sulastri to visit him at home, said a genial goodbye, went into the darkness and out of sight.

Gularso was still sitting with them and said casually, "Be careful not to get into trouble with that newspaper. They can confiscate it and then all the work we put into it would be wasted." Sudarmo shrugged, but after Gularso left, he felt an inner tension which he tried to dispel with logical thoughts. It's too bad, he said to himself, because the cost of printing can be covered by the revenue of each run. The children are energetic in selling it. And one confiscation would automatically stop its publication, because the initial capital would be gone with it.

Gularso's fears weren't without cause. In the morning, when the newspapers arrived from the printers and were to be distributed, a young man came to the school. Sudarmo believed he knew him as a pupil at AMS the year before, when the youth had made an impassioned speech on national problems at the Young Indonesia rally. But Sudarmo was a bit dubious and then asked bluntly, "Are you Idih from Batavia, comrade? I think I've seen you." The visitor confirmed this, but in a voice that was a bit shy and hesitant. Then he introduced himself as a civil service candidate who was detailed to the PID. He had been given the assignment of confiscating newspapers because of some offending words. He showed Sudarmo one of the papers. The offensive words had been underlined in red. Out of curiosity, Sudarmo read the underscored lines. Idih apologized by saying, "I'm very sorry, but it's my job and I've got to carry out my superiors' orders. Please forgive me, comrade."

He said this in a sympathetic tone and his youthful expression matched his words. Without thinking, Sudarmo replied affably, "Of course, that's your job. I won't be angry at you in the slightest. I only feel disappointed that this has happened."

Sudarmo stood up and invited Idih into the classrooms, where each teacher was facing a pile of newspapers. Idih took these, and in this way, he arrived at Sulastri's classroom with a large bundle of newspapers. She nodded her head rather tensely and told him that she had already distributed the papers. The youth was embarrassed and said, stuttering and stammering, that he had to take all of them. Sulastri asked the children to give the papers back, but they didn't understand and placed them on their desks with amazed expressions.

"Get them yourself," she said bitterly. She gave him a disgusted look and stood right in the doorway. Her visitor stooped deferentially as he passed her, apologized, and passed Sulastri on his way out. Then Idih approached Sudarmo who drew out his last card.

"In your view, isn't it too much to say that my newspaper is inciting the children? The little ones can't read all that well, while the older children just scatter copies of it around. And anyway, there's no incitement in these newspapers. Wouldn't it be reasonable if I compare a government school with a nationalist education school, and if the government doesn't also deserve to be criticized in its management of education? One hundred and eighty HIS institutions for sixty million people. Tell me frankly, is that not saddening? Ki Hadjar Dewantoro has in ten years established the same number of schools and without any capital other than his enthusiasm and fervent desire to raise the position of the people. And according to what the corn-haired, cat-eyed people say, you, comrade, as an Indonesian, cannot say I'm lying. I say things as I see them. Look for yourself at your boss's hair and eyes, too. His hair's just like corn silk, and his eyes are like cat eyes. Why are the police offended and why do they order these newspapers seized?"

Idih didn't reply. He again apologized and proceeded with some difficulty to carry his pile of newspapers to the *dokar* that had been waiting there. Yet again, Sudarmo was reminded of the tragedy of colonial society, where brown-skinned people are sent to harass other brown-skinned people to perpetuate the rule of the whites. Now Idih was still apologizing for performing his job as an employee. But, in a year, maybe five more years, if the civil service had become his flesh and blood and if he carried out his work in the manner of an employee of the civil service, then he would consider those who struggled for independence as his enemies, as villains who deserved to be insulted and humiliated. If a raid had been launched on them, he would see it just as the opportunity to be promoted and an honor for himself if he could arrest one of the troublemakers and trample what they did into the mud.

The confiscation of this newspaper signaled to Sudarmo that there was something going on.

That afternoon after school was dismissed, he rummaged around in his clothes closet and took out several small boxes. "Tri, get together all our letters and private correspondence," he curtly ordered his wife. "Put them in this basket." And when Sulastri looked at him questioningly, he said, "We'll burn them. Just go through and select them."

Sulastri examined the pile of letters, setting aside the unimportant ones and putting others into the basket. Sudarmo checked his bookcase and removed several brochures. "Into the bonfire," he said, laughing. Sulastri reread the love letters from before they had been married and she recalled how it all had been in those days. But Sudarmo's voice roughly put an end to her nostalgia. "Don't be so sentimental, just get on with it. Imagine if our love letters were put on display at the police station!"

He foraged through the boxes, throwing piles of letters into the basket. Then he brought the basket outside. Under the berry tree they lit a fire. Sulastri, a sad look on her face, tossed the old letters one by one into the fire. The fire blazed up, time and again as it was fed new food.

"That is our love," she whispered, "Memories of you in my poems."

She gazed into the flames which greedily devoured the paper. Sudarmo placed his hand on his wife's shoulder and comforted her.

"If we think back, we sacrificed a few stamps and time on those letters. And you, your attention and dreams to become a writer.... It's sad, yes, but this has to be done."

He threw brochures into the fire, stirred them around with a pole so that the flames rose higher. He brooded, and tears covered all this from view. Sulastri's eyes were also rimmed with tears as she stood silently in front of the bonfire. When the fire had died down and only black ashes were left, she kicked it about, and, unheard by Sudarmo, murmured sadly, "You've all gone, your memories from the moments I awaited and hoped for. I've consigned you to the fire. But, no matter, you are clean and pure and the best in my heart that I've committed to Sudarmo."

"What're you saying? Tri?"

"Oh, nothing... that we're afraid of letters that can slander us."

"That's not true. It would be so stupid if private letters between you and me were given to the police archives. How'd it be if they read them?" Sulastri nodded in assent, treading on the ashes and feeling fatigued and lightheaded. She went in and lay down on the bed and tried to hold back sickening feelings.

For the following days, they were in an atmosphere of extraordinary tension. The sense that a disaster was impending stayed with them and then was proven by a rough surprise: Sukarno was taken into custody. Sudarmo read it in the newspaper.

"Well, there it is," he sighed. He felt a certain relief and could breathe easier. He thought, this is the end of the demands of the Nationalist Party members, demands on the schools and on the Marhaen Party; but he heard the depth of his heart speaking and he was ashamed of his pettiness.

"Something happened?" Sulastri asked.

"No, no." Then he corrected himself. "Read this news. Now it'll be the turn of the Marhaen Party. They're going to have to be very careful."

Sulastri paled as she ran her eyes over the news and noticed Sudarmo's closed expression. Sudarmo was sunk in thought, his fingertips touching. He looked broodingly at the street. There was only someone passing by quickly. Sometimes the street emptied of pedestrians. The garden seemed to be filled with dancing shadows in this daylight, calm and clear. The bougainvillea and grass gave a dark and harmonious cover to the bright lawn, over which the shadows of flying birds threw down moving, dark-colored clots. It all seemed so calm that they felt they were alone in their gloomy thoughts.

9

The school revenue kept shrinking. If action weren't taken quickly, things would get even worse. Sudarmo was well aware of this, so he recommended that the school be located in just one building and the teachers live elsewhere.

"What about the classrooms then?" protested one teacher. "Wouldn't this building be too small for so many classes?"

Sudarmo shook his hand as if to show they needn't worry and spoke firmly and concisely. "I will try to make everything all right."

Because he had promised he would fix things, for the next few days and nights he kept looking for a way to solve all this, until suddenly he had an idea.

"A tent," he thought. "Not just one, but two. So I won't have to ask permission from the city, as if I were making a shed." This thought stayed with him and he went over it again and again with Gularso, describing his plan, measuring the area of the lawn and making a sketch of where a tent would be raised with a flag on top, and how this would provide a solution to the predicament. He immediately bought bamboo and calico cloth. Sewing the cloth was Sulastri's part and she looked with distaste at the piles of calico. But he didn't wait any longer. The next day, people saw a bamboo frame under the cempaka tree. A school employee, Sabirin, bound strips of bamboo as tightly as he could with thick cord. In doing so, he attracted the attention of the pupils, who were always commenting on this and that.

Urip had been let go after Waluyo left. He had opposed Sudarmo and asked for a decision at a meeting of the teachers, but Sudarmo, who had previously been happy with him, now felt he had been burdened enough by such a lazy fellow. Besides that, Urip had become a scout of the National Guides. He went around in the uniform of a scout and felt too elevated to hold a broom, even though the schoolyard was covered with dead leaves. The teachers were pleased to see Urip's tough luck. After he stopped being the favorite, they paid no further attention to him; then they took revenge on him because of his rude attitude in earlier days. Sabirin in contrast was obedient, diligent, kept his mouth mostly shut—an ideal servant who knew his job.

The teachers laughed at the tent plan, but during the day Sudarmo joined in to work tirelessly, as did Sulastri, who appeared to be putting on weight. The calico cloth was sewn by a female servant, someone nimble and clever. Sulastri taught her to sew in half an hour. Two days later, the calico cloth was unfurled across the bamboo structure. The tent held thirty school benches. The red and white nationalist flag fluttered from a pole at the very top. People laughed at such a strange classroom and likened it to a circus. No one had any desire to teach there: they didn't want to be conspicuous.

Sulastri was annoyed at the complaints and grumbling of the teachers. Thus, over the next days, she taught Dutch in the tent to grades one and seven. Now no one was laughing at her. But it rather bothered her that the children were watching the trees in front of them or the small birds bobbing about on the gravel. Once in a while, a chicken came to class and that interruption made for boisterous laughter.

The white cambric of the tent would surely have to be painted to make it rain resistant. So Sudarmo bought white paint powder and mixed it with a waterproofing base. He began painting the same day, standing on a ladder and assisted by the school staff. As he squatted mixing the paint, Ibu Sarjan approached him. This woman, together with her female friends, took French lessons from Harjono in order to understand the contents of films. She was very modern indeed, from her rouged face to the nail polish on her fingers and toes. She moved in a free and quite thrilling way, much like a film actress, and astonished people at how her eyes played with married men or bachelors, flirting and caressing them in front of everyone. Sudarmo couldn't stand her. If this woman had been younger, Sudarmo might have paid attention to her. Now, though, he didn't look up from his work.

"What are you doing?" Ibu Sarjan asked coyly and threw him a flirtatious look as he mixed the paint. "Can't you see for yourself?" he snapped. "I'm painting." And he kept on working. The woman stood beside him, then started walking slowly around the tent, her hand securing her chignon, but in the end, she left feeling hurt by Sudarmo's coldness. He pretended indifference and went back into the classroom. Sulastri watched this scene from a distance and smiled with amusement at Sudarmo's display of hostility, but she was actually pleased. So, she helped him with the painting from time to time. After about two days, Sudarmo had finished painting the tent. One more classroom was added to the "circus" class, and these spaces became the coolest and nicest of the classrooms, even with the many disturbances from the various worms and caterpillars during that season.

One day a child got a caterpillar on his neck. He scratched his neck and then his face until the itching became so bad it made him cry. Sulastri rubbed the red spots with coconut oil until the liquid glistened on his nose and cheeks. The other children made fun of him, running behind him and shouting "Dayak!"

Because the annex of the school had been moved to the big building, the teachers who had recently lived there were now forced to move into a tenement not far from the school. This again created a disgruntled atmosphere. The teachers saw more clearly the difference between the pavilion occupied by Sudarmo and their small rooms with woven bamboo walls and clay tiles. These cubicles comprised a kind of housing barracks. Their rooms were constructed around an open yard and housed up to fifty people. A washroom was built in the yard, open and shaded by a large cape tree. The Europeans who lived there were unemployed. They received unemployment funds, more money for hanging around, drinking beer, and getting into fights than Prawira earned with his hard work for his wife and children. These people even got allocations of milk and soup, and sometimes cakes. It was very painful for the teachers to have these dismissed employees as neighbors who lived better than they themselves did. In the eyes of his colleagues, Sudarmo was too bourgeois, because they were envious of his calm pavilion. Those hidden feelings of envy seeped into the teachers.

Gularso had sent for his wife Mientje, a Eurasian. He lived in a little house not far from the school. At first, Mientje was friendly and nice to Sulastri and frequently came with Gularso to call on her and Sudarmo. But one day she came alone. Sulastri received her in the sitting room and offered her cakes. Mientje, a bland smile on her wrinkled face with its clear European features, declined them. With her greenish eyes, Mientje often resembled a magician. All this time she looked over the furniture and red curtains with side glances and sighed, "It's so nice and peaceful here. Where we live, we're always being bothered by the neighing of the horses in their stalls."

Mientje's sharp eyes saw the shining wood of the chair embroidered with plush fabric. She rubbed its arm rest with the sleeve of her kebaya. "You're good at taking care of the furniture, Zus."

Sulastri didn't reply and bent over to pick up a page of the newspaper that had fallen. When she lifted her head again, she noticed a coldness in Mientje's eyes.

"Oh," Sulastri said indifferently, "This is furniture from when I was a girl." She raised her cup, stirred the sugar, and went on about the school as she sipped her tea. It appeared that Mientje's mind was elsewhere and she was not listening to her very closely. Then Sulastri went silent and waited for whatever her guest would say. She didn't understand the odd tension emanating from Mientje and how she seemed so distracted, but she didn't place much importance on it. When the time came for parting, Sulastri saw Mientje off a rather long way and watched her walk away, a woman quickly aging, with a large waist, and tall of stature but stooped and stumbling as if her legs were unable to bear such a girth. Her facial features were disheartening, what with her rather disheveled white hair. Perhaps in the past her hair was curly and of a fine brown shade. Sulastri didn't mention this visit to her husband. Gularso's visits also became gradually rarer, and that was why Sudarmo himself visited him one day.

Usually, Gularso received Sudarmo the way someone welcomes a dear friend. Today he apologized for not being able to provide a good place to sit and couldn't serve nice tea. And Mientje added, "This tea tastes flat. If one visits a poor person, there's usually nothing good. Everything's a mess here."

She made an irritating show of tidying up the exercise books. "Our home is so cramped," she complained. "It's too stuffy for you, Mas Darmo, yes?" She laughed rather mockingly and, wiping her hands on her waist, she went off, making noise with the plates in the kitchen in the back. Sudarmo got the impression that the very walls were watching him with scorn. Gularso spoke listlessly, as if he didn't feel like talking, and with his head bowed low. When he got home, Sudarmo related this visit to Sulastri. She thought about it and concluded that something was going on with their two friends. Sudarmo shrugged.

"It's not possible. Last week I just said to him to come on time and not to leave before time. Gularso's actually lazy, just like Waluyo, but can't a friend speak to him like that?"

Whatever the case, Gularso avoided Sudarmo and Mientje didn't visit anymore. Gularso's attitude of having been admonished rekindled feelings of resentment by the teachers against Sudarmo which had never subsided. Gularso himself was unaware of why he disliked everything about Sudarmo, and he watched him intensely to confirm his feelings. Mientje was always complaining about money, and she fell sick. But, even though Sudarmo and Sulastri expressed their sympathetic concern and helped them goodheartedly, none of that ended Mientje's efforts at slandering them out of her uncontrollable envy.

The teachers' hostile attitude to Sudarmo grew all the greater out of envy. You could see it by the way Gularso kept away from the pavilion and in his stiff manner when he greeted them, and also in his insinuating remarks that carried a hidden enmity. Even in Gularso's written administrative work there was much scratching out and evidence of his extreme dislike. Sudarmo never saw what was going on and only recognized it if matters became irreparable. Still unwilling to admit his friend's treachery, Sudarmo gave advice to Gularso and didn't see that his friend was barely listening to him. Gularso even told his workmates that Sudarmo's words, which in fact were good, were the trickery and policies of a "dictator." Sulastri, who was normally guided by her intuition, remonstrated with Sudarmo for his boundless trust. She pointed out things that had a certain meaning.

"If Gularso's got to go through the pavilion, he'll take the long way around. He doesn't have time now if I have to tell him something. There's something not right, Dar."

Her husband made a big mistake when in all candor he said to Gularso, "It seems that you have become someone else, Mas Gularso. You never come to chat with us anymore."

Gularso answered diplomatically, "I have a lot of work at home now." And when he perceived the sharp and sarcastic look on Sudarmo's face, he said, "An acquaintance from 1925, just before the big PKI uprisings, now often visits. And now I'm doing my job correctly and carefully. May I go? I still have a lot to do in the office."

He left nervously, as if there were someone following him, and stumbled down the stairs. This gave Sudarmo something to think about, but he refused to entertain the idea of betrayal.

He often visited Supardi. Juhariah, who felt that danger lurked in waiting for her husband any day now, readied herself to confront the arrival of the worst kind of fate for him. Her expression revealed calm in the face of misfortune, like someone who sees with a tranquil and pure heart the angel of death. While she could give birth to her child at any time, she didn't complain about exhaustion or oppressive difficulties. She always looked cheerful, going about doing all the tasks that occupy a housewife.

One day when Sulastri and Sudarmo came to visit, they saw Supardi on the front veranda enclosed by a rather high wall. He was deep in thought, his chin in his hands, and was looking into the distance. From the way he sat, it was clear that he was agitated and fearful, and more than once he looked like he would suddenly leap up. When Sulastri climbed the steep stairway of that tilting stilt house, she greeted him in her usual warm and friendly way. Even so, she noticed a flash in his eyes and something in his manner that was different.

Sulastri wanted to just go inside and had taken hold of the door handle. Supardi held her back, "My wife... she's feeling it."

And at that moment he grew very pale, and his guest understood. "Ah," said Sulastri, and she opened the door slowly and then entered the room. There she saw Juhariah on the mat on the floor, coiled up in excruciating pain. Her eyes began to brighten, she smiled, and signaled with her hand, but stayed silent.

"Ju." Sulastri knelt, feeling pity for such a big body, writhing from the sharp, recurring pain. "Ju," was all she could say and she sat down. An old woman, someone Sulastri only now saw, was sitting beside her. The *dukun* approached respectfully and whispered in her ear. "It'll still be a long way off. Just go outside for a while."

Sulastri shook her head and took hold of Juhariah's hand, but was shocked when she saw the whites of her friend's eyes under her eyelids, which taken on a purplish cast. Juhariah let out a groan as Sulastri placed a hand on her stomach and fell back on the pillow, resigned and weak. Her breath came in short spurts and her forehead shone with tiny beads of sweat. Her dampened hair stuck to her neck and shoulders in sodden strands. Sulastri groped for a handkerchief and wet it with eau de cologne and wiped the pale forehead. She saw bottles of medicine on the bed and the sagging low rack about to collapse. The air in the cramped room was very hot. Everyone was quiet, and only these two were alive: the pain and the baby wanting to free itself.

Again, contractions convulsed her body, and again, her limbs stiffened in pain. Again, she was daubed with the eau de cologne, and a meaningful look went between Sulastri and Mak Dukun. Sulastri felt a strange constriction in her chest. She heaved a sigh and at that nearly inaudible puff of air, Juhariah opened her eyes, smiled and said, "A unique spectacle, isn't it. Still have a while to go, Tri. It won't come out, I guess."

She tried to cheer up, but her lips curled bloodlessly, although there were red marks on them from having been bitten.

"Hmm, the eau de cologne is so nice, Tri. Now the pain's gone for a moment."

"Don't talk," Sulastri whispered. Juhariah tried to smile, but her effort failed because her white, bitten lips looked too sad.

"Supardi has come a few times to look in just now," she whispered. "I chased him away and told him: you're not the one giving birth. All you're doing is just making everyone nervous."

"Shh," said Sulastri, "don't talk."

Mak Dukun held Juhariah's stomach, nodded and said, "It's sure to come out later in the day." She inserted a quid of betelnut and sirih leaves into the corner of her mouth so that her lower lip stuck out. Sulastri looked at her with disgust and shivered a bit as she thought, "Why would Ju place herself in the hands of a such a filthy woman?"

Mak Dukun talked with a trembling voice about all the times she helped deliver babies. "It all went well," she said with pride and, with her red, tearful eyes resembled a cockatoo drowsing on its perch. The dukun sat with her legs folded back and began to make a new sirih quid, carefully smearing lime paste on the leaf and biting a little pinang nut, as she glanced at Sulastri at her side. Sulastri was spreading out a handkerchief on her lap, rolling it up, and spreading it out again, as if she was unconsciously beating back her fear and inner turmoil. Juhariah had fallen asleep and was breathing calmly, so Sulastri went outside, taking her leave of Mak Dukun with a gentle smile.

Out on the front veranda she saw Supardi and Sudarmo sitting across from each other, Sudarmo reading but Supardi staring straight ahead with a wretched expression on his face, looking like a cat dunked in water. This man who could laugh at any time, now seemed confused, unstuck with distress at seeing suffering in the one he loved, and helpless to do anything about it. He looked at Sulastri, devastated. "Ah, everything will be all right, Mas," she comforted him. "Yes, we'll leave now and come again later."

Sudarmo and Sulastri slowly walked down the steps.

They didn't say anything to each other along the way. They barely heard the little *dokar* carts or the people in the crowded streets. And it seemed as if the sun had grown pale and trembled sympathetically out of fear for Juhariah's big body. Sulastri was barely aware that they had arrived home. Without feeling anything, she changed her clothes and still saw the fear in Juhariah's discolored eyes. That was something she was going to go through, and she was going suffer just like that. She shivered without knowing it and stroked her waist where she had felt a quiver. Then she had to laugh at her childishness and picked up a stack of exercise books for correction outside in the tent classroom.

Ibu Prawira passed by on the street, a parasol shading her head. From a distance, she bowed to Sulastri, who signaled her to stop for a moment. Sulastri quickly drew near her and saw that this woman was also expecting a baby. Her face was like a flower in blossom, and her condition gave her a freshness that made her attractive and gracious. Even her hair was now curly around her temples and her skin looked firm, though her steps were a bit difficult. Sulastri invited her into the house. Ibu Prawira shook her head and apologized that she had much to do, but promised, "Some other time. I would like to visit Zus's home. But how could I do that with such a big family as I have?"

She dabbed her lips with her handkerchief, where the red of the sirih juice gave a fresh color which was appealing and not beyond the bounds of decency. Sulastri was pleased with this woman. She was always dutiful, a mother and a gentle wife for Prawira, who was often domineering and spoke harshly to her. She was always full of love and acceded to the will of others. Her worst quality was her untidiness, which was understandable in someone who had as many children as she did. Also, her uncle was senile, and this added to her difficulties.

"Oh," Sulastri urged her, "Just for a moment." The other woman declined politely and salaamed, and so Sulastri went back to work. This didn't go very smoothly, because her thoughts were flying to all sorts of problems and the people around her. Then she brought the pile of exercise books into the house and sat down next to Sudarmo, who suddenly exclaimed, "Tri, Uncle's had his exam. Let's go to his place this afternoon to see him." But the moment he said this, Joyokuno himself came in wearing his sarong and head cloth. He began speaking even as he collapsed into a chair. "I'm ashamed to say it, but I didn't pass. I failed my Dutch test."

He said this very sadly, his breath choked and his voice very low. Then he related that he had forgotten the pronunciation of the word "*literatuur*" and had applied stress on the final part of the word. His teacher had said words borrowed from French were emphasized on their final part, "And that is why I had mispronounced it." Then he giggled, "I pronounced it, "literatoor..."

Sulastri felt rather sorry for him, and Sudarmo asked him if he would be able to retake the test in the following year and still be able to get the study subsidy?

"Oh, it's all right. I'll go home now," he said, declining Sulastri's invitation for him to dine together with them. The real reason he declined was because he always ate well at home. His table was always covered with delicious things cooked by his wife herself. This goodhearted fellow who loved to eat only got angry if the food wasn't to his taste. Everything else was of minor concern. Even his failure to pass the exam didn't particularly bother him. He never stinted when it came to eating but was extremely tightfisted with everything else. He'd prefer to return home in the rain rather than buy a more expensive ticket if the lower class tickets were sold out. He scrutinized all his outlays, and his underlying principle was "spend money in line with income." Sudarmo, whom he had known as the primary "Dutch-language expert" in the small city of his birth, laughed when he heard the way his uncle tried to pronounce Dutch precisely and according to the rules. Besides, Joyokuno liked to use foreign words, because it made him look like an intellectual among ordinary folk.

After Joyokuno left, the atmosphere got rather heavy. Sudarmo was bored that there was nothing to do. He climbed the *sawo* tree and tossed some unripe brown fruit into the upright hands of their servant Sari. This Sari was good at catching sawo, and Sulastri brought a basket into which Sari put the fruit. Sudarmo loved climbing trees, and he'd tread even small branches like a monkey. He'd wave broken branches or leap about to show that such and such a branch was strong enough to step on. Sulastri considered climbing trees inappropriate for adults. So they often argued, but how was she to oppose someone as stubborn as Sudarmo? People shouldn't see him moving about the tree like an ape, waving his handkerchief, while he forbade the schoolboys to act like that.

That afternoon, the news came that Juhariah had given birth to a boy. Supardi couldn't say anything when Sulastri and Sudarmo returned. He only said in a surprised tone of voice, "His name is Jemena."

"You're so pale, Mas," Sudarmo joked, "It's like you're the one who gave birth."

Sulastri signaled her husband, but Supardi joined in the laughter and ran his fingers through his wavy hair. Then Sulastri suddenly realized that he possessed an interesting passion in his slightly startled eyes. Juhariah was lying on the bed and next to her was a little human being who would add to her work but would also be the source of happiness and love in a mother.

"How are you, Ju? Does it still hurt?"

She shook her head. Sulastri sat on the edge of the bed and noted her friend's face which was calm again now. Then she noticed the narrow window, through which you could see the wall and some of the roof of the house next door. There was no yard at the side of the house, nor at the front; only in back was there a place to dry the laundry. This little leaning house seemed squeezed between other nondescript buildings that looked close to collapse themselves. The floor was made of bamboo strips, but so flimsy and brittle that you had to walk like a cat, soundlessly, gently and barefooted, because with each step, everything wobbled, including the table. The bedroom had a door which couldn't be locked, because the key was rusty and made a snapping sound whenever turned. The little lamp cast the room in a dim yellow light which caressed every object and gave each a different, brooding quality. But there was something in that house that couldn't be seen: a calm atmosphere, where Juhariah's love, warm and refreshing, did away with the ugliness of the dilapidated walls. It was here that Supardi felt peace of mind after completing his party work, and dispersed his thoughts about the strife and discord which of course did go on. On that shaky table, he had written his mesmerizing articles and in the washroom with its slick tiles he had sung of his happiness over his work, which was growing by the day. You don't feel poverty when you are loved by someone courageous, who threw out all of your complaints like ephemeral things, and when there was a pair of eyes that shone with serenity. Sulastri envied Juhariah her grit and fortitude.

She observed Juhariah's serene expression again and felt frustrated that she herself was unable to provide anything other than her attention. Feeling very moved, she asked, "Is Mak Dukun still here? Who helps you bathe and so forth?"

Sulastri noticed the dark rings around Juhariah's eyes. "Goodness, do I need to be helped? I've just bathed in the washroom to clean off all the polluting mess. You know there's always a lot of blood after giving birth, right? I did it myself."

"Ju, oh Allah!" Sulastri spoke, startled. "Oh, Allah! Isn't it dangerous? Your auntie isn't here? You should be staying in bed. Oh Allah! Why are you like this...?"

Sulastri stopped short and called Sudarmo and told him about Juhariah's condition. Sudarmo had come in with Supardi and shook his head. "That's really dangerous, Zus," he advised. "Just sleep now. Oh, you don't know why? Our ancestors could do that. They were different from us."

Juhariah laughed and put her hand on her head.

"Who can help me? I don't like to inconvenience people. And anyway, it's nothing. Really, it's nothing. If I don't do this, I'll be ashamed my whole life. I'm healthy! Imagine if I just lazed about and other people served me."

She laughed again, also because she saw how miserable Supardi looked. Supardi apologized. "I've told her. She's so stubborn, let her feel it herself."

"But Mas," said Sudarmo, getting a bit angry now. "It's not being lazy. It's a necessity. A woman who's just given birth, oh, why didn't you tell me? We can help Zus."

Juhariah didn't reply. She was proud of not inconveniencing anyone. Mak Dukun came in, and moving on her knees, she tidied up here and there. Sulastri noticed her long black fingernails. After a lengthy conversation with Juhariah, Sulastri and Sudarmo went home with the vision of how poverty made a mockery of health. One year, two years from now, Juhariah would be so thin from all the difficulties and hardships of home life. Sulastri thought: the same sort of suffering is pending over me—but Sudarmo isn't embarrassed to light up another nice cigarette. The sharp contradiction between those two very different things should put a person to shame, if there was nothing beyond the right to go on living and to sustain yourself. In this way, all deeds would be lost, but where would the justice be in all of this? Sulastri felt very gloomy and sad. She shivered and wrapped her shawl about her shoulders. The wind howled through the houses, mixing the street smells with the aroma of pretty flowers and took this across the roof tiles and the garden into the unseen distance.

10

There was loud knocking on the door, like that of some angry and impatient person. Sulastri, awakened from deep sleep, whispered to Sudarmo, "What's that?"

Sudarmo tried to shake off his sleep, but began to drift off again, and the pounding on the door became even louder. He got up and went barefoot to the front door. Peering through the gap in the curtains, he saw something very white in the darkness. He was going to open the door right away, then thought better of it and put on his pajamas. A presentiment made him whisper to Sulastri, "It may be the police. Get dressed."

She understood and nodded, her heart pounding. Sudarmo opened the door, and before it was fully opened a very tall Dutchman pushed his way in and sneeringly introduced himself. "Good morning, my arrival is disturbing, no? I'm from Political Intelligence and I've got to search this house."

His tone of voice sounded more arrogant because he was looking down from his height at Sudarmo, who answered shortly, "Please come in. You're very early."

Sudarmo stepped back. Three men came in, one of them without removing his hat and looking red-faced with anger, and another a bit more polite in his demeanor, short and broad, like a good-natured Dutch farmer. The third was a young "native" police official. He wore a lornette on his nose and with his head tilted upwards, he had an air about him of someone very important and displayed a functionary's sense of responsibility.

Sudarmo went over next to Sulastri and said very softly, "Police." Then he stood with his hands in his pockets next to the bookcase, watching rough hands opening his books as if to say, "Well now, isn't this nice? I've got you now."

It was almost daylight outside, cool from the morning dew, and the lights had been extinguished. All of a sudden, Sudarmo sensed the irony of this incident. Those three were sniffing around like animals, while he himself had been ordered to the side, to watch helplessly as his books were being thrown down until they piled high on the floor.

Sulastri, having dressed and combed her hair, now looked on quietly, filled with hatred at the hands searching everywhere, hands that certainly had never caressed a book. The young detective showed some lines in one of the books. The sentences had been underlined in red. A sense of justice or something similar seemed to arise; nonetheless the Dutchman with the hat studied it for a while, hesitated, and then gave a definite signal to throw the book onto the pile. Then the native official picked up a collection of poetry and took it with him. Sudarmo couldn't resist saying caustically, "Beautiful poems."

This got an angry look from the fellow and a warning glance from Sulastri. Sudarmo crossed his arms as if wanting to say, "I'm not standing here for my own fun."

This fool of a native policeman appeared to be more energetic than the two Dutchmen, who frequently whispered to each other. Lofty nodded and Shorty tossed the book he was holding onto the pile, which now numbered at least fifty books, among which were the children's stories *Book of Heroes*. So thorough was this detective that the name of the book seemed to be dangerous, regardless of the contents. It was the word "Heroes" that was threatening. The police station would examine this for possible evidence. Here they didn't need to weigh what was right and what wasn't. Sudarmo said, even though the atmosphere didn't permit it, "That book you're holding should be put back. It's one hundred percent reactionary."

Lofty looked at Sudarmo for a moment, shrugged and replied, "I know what my job is."

Shorty, looking on a bit suspiciously, caught Sulastri's glance and whispered to Lofty, who had just said, "You'd best not make those comments. Otherwise, we know what we've got to do."

This threatening attitude vanished when they saw the mocking look on the faces of those being threatened. Sulastri opened the window and saw the morning clouds like a grey film over the grass. She shivered a little in her flannel kebaya and went outside. But there she saw a plainclothesman standing under the *kedongdong* tree and perhaps someone else near the fence. She was pleased with this surveillance and called Sari to make coffee. The girl was a long time in the kitchen but didn't display any sign of surprise at so many visitors, and did all she had to do, just as she would have on ordinary days. Sulastri went to her bed and folded up the blankets, shook out the pillows so that they billowed out again, and spread out the bedcover.

Then she abruptly felt her blood rise to her cheeks when she remembered their calculating looks as they were searching under the mattress, trying to determine where she and Sudarmo had been lying. She put the key in the clothes chest, and quietly watched what was going on. She went back to Sudarmo, who was standing by the window with his head lifted high. Lofty with the hat said, "Finished. Let's look here."

He opened the desk drawers, saw letters and gave them to Shorty, smiling that he had finished, as he thought. They were letters from parents of the students. The student essay books also landed on the heap. And Sulastri saw her comments and lecture notes thrown there too. She whispered to Sudarmo, "Lofty may have a boil on his head. He never takes off his hat."

"I think so too," replied Sudarmo. "Maybe he's the tribal chief, because even at the police station he doesn't take off his hat to the police commissioner."

Imagining that there was a boil under that genial hat brought glee to Sulastri's heart. Just then, they pulled out a cash book. Lofty demanded it be examined. Shorty did so slowly and then came to a halt on seeing a receipt.

"Ah," he sighed with happiness. "What's this? Tell me what this receipt's for."

"Which one?" Sudarmo coldly observed the smiling face, read the receipt, and then said officiously, "After Waluyo left here, he received from the school a pension of *f* 10 for his three months here. It was his right."

"Indeed, indeed." Lofty nodded his head, as if wanting to say, *You're finally caught. You lost and that's that.* "Well, officer, throw this on the pile too."

He gave his orders like a general. The functionary came quickly and took the cashbook with satisfaction as he smirked at Sudarmo. Sulastri went back to the bedroom. Lofty gave a coded signal and the official went out to tell the plainclothesmen to stand in front of the room.

"Those fools," thought Sulastri, "What if I give them a cup of coffee?"

"So, let's look here now." Lofty pulled the curtain aside and entered the bedroom. He opened the clothes chest and rifled under the clothes. He opened Sulastri's diary in which she had written a number of comments. Shorty looked over the hat tree, under the mattress, shook the pillows, foraged under the bed, even on top of the mosquito tent in case anything was there. The functionary rummaged in the kitchen drawers and came back saying, "Everything's been checked, sir," and went to stand next to the two others. In the sitting room, the five of them looked at each other without saying another word. Lofty, mockery and disdain in his eyes; the Indonesian, standing at attention, his feet tightly set together. Making a show of investigating, Lofty ran his eyes over Sulastri's body, and she had the feeling that his eyes were stripping her as she stood there, a woman with a body the same as any other woman's body.

"Can Nyonya give me your assurance that you are not concealing anything under your clothing?"

"No, you can believe me, sir," Sulastri replied coldly.

As Sudarmo stood there staring into space, that strange investigating look and the mocking smile on Lofty's face returned, and he said, "Keep on with the search, Detective. The man is coming with me."

"Fine," said Sudarmo. "May I get dressed first? Wait for me on the front terrace."

The others hurried out bumping into each other, so that in any case, they still could be said to have been polite. Lofty remained, scanning the surroundings, as though afraid of missing something that still needed raiding. He stood next to the door, examining a print on the wall. Then he took it down and looked closely at the frame. Then he put it back. It feels strange if you can't interfere with people who enter your home without permission. Because of this painful, nauseating feeling of helplessness, Sulastri lay down weakly on the bed. Sudarmo dressed calmly, fixed his tie, and smiled in the mirror at Sulastri.

"Oh, it won't be that much trouble," he said. "Have her bring me some coffee. I'll be back very soon, dearest." The extraordinarily soft tone of his voice was as if he was still thinking about sweet things between them before they married. He drew near his wife, stroked her hair, and took her hand and helped her sit up.

"I don't think you have anything to worry about," he said and went out.

She smiled weakly and then stood up with some difficulty near the door and called Sari, who quickly appeared with the coffee. Sulastri took the tray and brought it to the terrace, where Sudarmo was sitting nonchalantly with his legs crossed.

By now the policemen had gone into the school building and were carrying out their search. No drawer was overlooked, no paper went unread. They performed their job like police dogs and, for the two Dutchmen, perhaps their loyalty to their mother country could be understood. But when it came to the Indonesian police, why were they so full of hatred for the nationalists? Were they afraid that if the nationalists won, they themselves wouldn't be given any chance for livelihoods?

"It's strange," Sulastri whispered to Sudarmo, "I now understand the Dutch even better."

Sudarmo slowly finished his coffee, lit up a cigarette, and waited for Lofty to tell him to come along. Behind him was a plainclothes detective standing next to the books. Perhaps if this were a normal situation, such a person would be goodhearted and understand other people's feelings; but now he was arrogant and had assumed an odiously suspicious attitude. Finally, the three returned from searching the classrooms. The last one was the Indonesian policeman. He was weighed down by a pile of books and exercise books. So heavy was this weight that he had a hard time walking upright. He handed the pile over to one of the plainclothesmen. Now they were walking out of the yard, Sudarmo between two Dutchmen, looking so small and skinny that it was almost funny. The plainclothes cops followed close behind without saying a word.

Standing on the terrace, Sulastri watched Sudarmo get into a *dokar*, followed by the two Dutchmen. He sat so squeezed between the two sturdy men that he seemed to be hiding in their midst. And so they went, in two little carts, with the books—as if they were weapons seized after taking some stronghold.

The streets were unusually quiet, and to Sulastri it seemed as if the very leaves were holding their breath from all this tension. She calmed her panic and went about her work with some composure. All along she had the feeling that there was an emptiness about her, like the high heavens, and everything had become vast, far too vast, and she was too small and helpless. The raids were not aimed only at them; she knew that. At this time, throughout Java, there were surely people, mouths shut tight, just like Sudarmo, astonished they had become criminals, but who nonetheless had faith that there was a justice different from what the police had just carried out.

Sudarmo was back before eleven o'clock that same morning. There was sweat on his face and a certain restrained anger in his eyes.

"And so?" asked Sulastri. He had thrown himself onto a chair and was wiping the sweat from his forehead, a distant look on his face. Then he said hoarsely, "I was allowed to go home because I'm not a member of the Marhaen Party leadership, and also because I haven't taught courses for a quite a while. But the others—Waluyo, Supardi, Pramono—all of them were taken by car straight to jail. When we met, we were surprised. Hey, we said, you're here too? And you too? The police commissioner rubbed his hands for joy, I suspect, all the more because Waluyo was picked up too. Waluyo, who could usually answer him correctly and still mock him. Never mind, they didn't ask me much. We're just waiting for what more will happen." He stopped speaking and looked tired out from all his tension.

"And Lukmono?" asked Sulastri. "Was he there too?"

"Yes, white as chalk, shivering and unable to take the stress. He's a goodhearted person. He couldn't kill a fly. The police arrested him for being on the board. All that time, he never did anything dangerous. They got the wrong person in arresting him."

"As I recall, that time he was here," said Sulastri, "and called us part of the bourgeoisie, all that time he was saving money to buy a house."

"Oh, don't talk about that again. Let's go to Juhariah. Her fate is certain. Tri, their child! Ah, all right, we spoke about this before."

They moved quickly on the street, where people were going to their daily work. They didn't realize that the good friend they worried about would soon would be going far away from them.

There was no one on the front veranda, so Sulastri just went inside, where she found Juhariah and the baby in the bedroom. They understood each other. They didn't need to utter a word about the arrest. Juhariah only said, "I'm going to my mother in Ciputat. She'll be happy to see me come back."

They talked about meaningless things, never daring to touch on the important ones, and Juhariah felt it better that way. Sudarmo only briefly talked about running into his friends at the police station and then said no more. A heavy atmosphere hung over them, one that oppressed, one that saddened, a tension which showed in their nervous hand movements, in the melancholy gaze through the window and in their leaden and monotone voices. Then Sudarmo and Sulastri said their good-byes with glances full of pity and sympathy. And for the first time, they realized how heavy the burden of isolation was on that slender woman. When they turned from the steps, they sensed Juhariah's sad look after their departing figures, so they looked back and waved.

Then Juhariah was there by herself, with the baby and his "auntie." For Juhariah, the full heat of the sunny morning was coldness itself. Life's hustle and bustle was mute here. Suddenly she noticed her hands, pale and delicate, in supplication to hear the laughter again that would never return, the unruly hair that she'd never stroke again. Tears welled up in her sunken eyes, red from her suffering. Then, for a moment she wept, sobbing. But the baby began to cry and she took him up to her with a graceful sweep of the hands, as if she wanted to declare all her love and hopes in that movement.

That night, "The Great White Press" rejoiced in the success of the ever-vigilant police. You could read in large letters:

BIG RAID
SEVERAL HUTS FILLED WITH
INCRIMINATING EVIDENCE.
NO WEAPONS, TOP INSTIGATORS ARRESTED!

11

Time moved on. The leaves turned and everywhere you felt the blossoming of new life on the branches when the first rains fell. The grass was fresh, soft in its delicacy and coated in a grayish color when the sun baked the earth. Here its light cut across the tips of the grass, rooted in the damp soil, where new life raised new sprouts from the center of the earth, which contained the seeds of growth of every sort that lived.

The general mood was tense from the arrests and raids that had been raging throughout the archipelago and then eased into listless discussions about what would happen next. There was the daily work, which demanded full attention. Only during idle moments did pain revive from memories of the spirit of struggle that was crushed with unusual violence, and of those friends who saw their future days in jail as the sign of a long journey.

In the vacated rooms of the party buildings, voices whispered their sorrows and curses against the persecution by those in power, but no one dared to raise their voice. Desolation was everywhere, and those who were afraid returned to their peaceful lives in the offices. Previously, people who stayed working in the government would be criticized as cold and calculating; now there were sounds of regret, and envy of those who hadn't been willing to sacrifice anything. And so the days went by, filled with feelings of desolation and emptiness, a sense of living adrift in a very strange atmosphere.

For days now, Sulastri's baby had been announcing its arrival. Its fluttering movements became fiercer and fiercer and on one day she couldn't teach. She lay on the bed awaiting the midwife who was coming to examine her. The result of her examination was that the baby would come in three weeks' time. Sulastri, who had full faith in this woman, didn't trouble herself over the medicines and other preparations, and reminded herself that these distresses would be soon over and gone. It was at night that the pain was worst. Sudarmo, reading a book next to her in bed, joked about it, but was alarmed at the twisted expression on his wife's face. At first, he was afraid that she had been poisoned when Sulastri threw up a lot and supposed that she was never going to give birth. He made her drink two tins of evaporated milk out of certainty that would get rid of the poison. Later, he called a doctor. She had faith in the midwife.

While Sulastri was suffering in this way, she had to laugh at Sudarmo, who was too nervous to stay calm in the room, until she ordered him to fetch the midwife. Once again, Sulastri felt the irony of that situation when she saw the servant sobbing under the table, while Sulastri herself was the one suffering and actually happy that she could soothe and steady the girl. The pain came and went. She felt the urge to roll about on the floor and lose herself in unconsciousness, where she wouldn't suffer. She rubbed her hands together, clenched her teeth, took a deep breath and realized that this was harder than outright dying. Deep breathing, in and out, painful shrieks as if sharp daggers were in her body. She was weak and fearful and tired—so tired. All of a sudden, she saw her mother when she had suffered this pain. So quiet, like a stone, that small woman. Not a complaint came out of her mouth, as she rubbed her body and inhaled with lips shut tight.

"Mother," thought Sulastri. Her memory was hazy about her movements, so patient and yielding, nonetheless still friendly. Now she was suffering like her, just like her mother had suffered with Sulastri, without crying and sobbing, but with an extraordinary joy.

"Hang on, Lastri, hang on," she told herself and she revived the conceit of not uttering complaints. When she was still little, she had managed to stand fast when her father cuffed her. As a girl she had tense quarrels with Marti, her older sister, and disregarded her pinches and slaps. She'd just endure the pain rather than scream, and this pride made Marti even fiercer. She struck Sulastri with her angry fists, which Sulastri didn't want to feel, until her body was full of blue marks. She just stayed cold, quite happy to see the anger of grown-ups.

"Little Satan," is what her large family jeeringly called her. And for Marti, she was always that little devil. All of this, Sulastri recalled in her loneliness, with the servant crying her heart out under the table, and she no longer felt how wet her eyes had become. Back again came the driving pain, worse than before and now almost unbearable, with Sulastri angrily fighting to keep the pain at bay. Then the midwife came quickly back into the room. She threw her bag onto the floor, held Sulastri's hand tightly and told her, "Breathe slowly with your mouth wide open."

Sulastri did as she was told without realizing it, and so a mystifying event took place.... She felt her body come light, so free, until she could breathe in with pleasure and happiness, because she heard the first crying that escaped from the baby.

"A girl, ma'am. And she looks just like her father." Then the midwife asked where her clothes were.

"Baby clothes! I haven't made them yet. You said I would give birth in three more weeks."

"Yes, yes, it came too quickly. Give me a piece of old cloth."

Sulastri gave the midwife a piece of cloth. A bucket of warm water was brought in, and the baby was bathed. Then the midwife tore the cloth into several pieces and wrapped the baby in them and then in a blanket. From her bed, Sulastri observed all this unusual midnight industry and thought, "Is this me lying here or someone else?"

Sudarmo came in hesitantly. All this time he had been outside endlessly smoking and feeling, he said, frightened. Sulastri pointed to the baby. He looked with amazement and muttered embarrassedly, “She looks like me? I’m not so ugly, am I?”

Sulastri answered teasingly, “Her face has the same oval shape as yours.” He looked closely at the facial features of the sleeping baby and turned to his wife, and it was as if he were seeing her differently than before, so pale and small, that he all at once gave himself over to his feelings, and tightly grasped his wife’s hand. Sulastri smiled joyously, wordlessly, and looked at the ceiling, as though she saw there a shadowy image of their days ahead.

“Now you’re a father. How clever you are,” she said sentimentally. Sudarmo looked again at his baby so cautiously, that the midwife, perhaps thinking this funny, winked at Sulastri. No one slept that night. Sudarmo spent the night on the divan, and frequently came in to see how things were. He couldn’t wait for morning to come to proudly show off his first child. When the first light of dawn streamed into the room, Sudarmo was no longer at home, but had gone to Joyokuno’s to borrow some baby clothes. He came back with Joyokuno and holding some flowers. Joyokuno’s wife also came along and showed her interest by saying. “Well, that baby came right on time. So much hair!”

But the midwife bathing the baby stuck to her view that the baby had arrived early. Which of the two were correct, Sulastri didn’t know, only that she supposed that the midwife felt guilty because her eyes twitched. They telegraphed Marti the news of the baby’s birth and asked if she could send someone to take care of Sulastri.

That evening, Sulastri’s mother came. She was a small and rather chubby woman, and her face gave the impression of simplicity and an amiable childlike quality. She came in shyly in that same girlish way, so that Sulastri gazed at her, captivated. Her mother took the baby up from the bed and observed her with gentleness and deep affection.

"Who does she look like, hmm? Not you," her mother laughed. Sudarmo moved next to the older woman and said, "She looks like me, isn't that right, Ibu?"

Visitors see it as an obligation to compare the baby with its father or its mother, and to praise its robustness and large size. Sulastri had to smile at the humor of it all if a guest said the baby looked like its mother. With the arrival of Sulastri's mother, the clash now began between tradition and modernity. The mother wanted to cover the baby's navel with a *jarak* leaf.

"Because," said the mother, "jarak leaves will deflate the baby's stomach, which is most important for a girl child." Sudarmo grumbled. He couldn't stand to watch the old-fashioned ways with leaves, herbs and spices, and jasmine. Sulastri's mother felt she had done something wrong and looked ashamed, but she kept at it and took care of the baby in her own way. If the baby cried, Sulastri's mother carried and rocked her, and held her close.

Sulastri felt hurt when her husband consistently saw their various customs as stupidity, such as when the placenta is buried in the traditional way. When Ibu asked if they would be holding a *selamatan* after the umbilical cord had dried, Sudarmo firmly rejected this, saying, "The baby won't become healthy because of a selamatan. In my view, it's useless."

Sulastri's mother gave in, complaining that she worried about the attitude of non-belief among the young. To Sulastri she said, "You've become so clever because on Selasa Kliwon, the day of your birth, I always fasted. It's a sin against Allah if you ignore rituals and do not heed our customs passed down to us by our ancestors. These have become our traditional practices and attitudes and if you disregard all of that, you will surely be courting disaster."

Sulastri began to doubt herself and to fear Allah's punishment. Deep within her, she was still rooted in the old ways, even if intellectually she these found these ineffectual and her Westernized education made her see those thoughts and practices in their true perspective. Sulastri was hesitant, but it was Sudarmo who decided in this matter that there'd be no selamatan. Financial difficulties also played a part in this decision. Ibu secretly burned incense, and she and Sari made simple yellow rice with chicken.

Work colleagues showed interest in the baby in customary visits to the baby's mother. Prawira appeared amazed at the baby's looks. He stroked his face with his right hand, a personal habit, and said in a pleasing tone of voice, "Look how big and bright she is. Of course, she should resemble her father and mother, who are both clever." He clicked his tongue and, gently taking hold of the baby's hand, he nodded his head as sign of praise. The baby stared at him wide-eyed and meaninglessly, then suddenly began to cry, so that the embarrassed Prawira had to speak some sweet words to calm her.

Only Harjono didn't visit. Perhaps he didn't feel safe in the room of a mother and her still red and mewling newborn. The schoolchildren lowered their voices when they passed through the room. Sometimes they'd pace back and forth in front of the door and when Sulastri called them to come in, they were very pleased and proud to see the baby.

Sudarmo was radiant. He went back and forth, busy as could be, giving instructions, looking at the clock for the baby's feeding time. Over these days, he seemed to be overflowing with joy, and behaved like someone of importance when he told Sulastri that the ordered life was crucial for a baby. All this bustle revolved around the baby, now named Rustini, who placidly sucked her hands and paid no attention to the adults, who acted so comically because of her.

Marti sent Sulastri a draft of *f* 10 and Rustini's first set of baby clothes, which weren't being used anymore. Marti had the habit, upon a new birth, of using the previously born child's clothing, and didn't buy anything new unless it was needed.

She wrote to Sulastri that she had needed to spend a lot of money over the past months, so she wasn't able to send more than she did now. With this money, Sulastri ordered baby clothes made, and she herself worked with needle and thread while in bed, and in this way the baby clothes increased to an adequate amount.

Sulastri's father came on the tenth day from Garut. Ibu was then in the room carrying the baby in a sling against her hip and talking to her. Standing behind her, Bapak said to his wife, "Have you been here long, Bu?"

This was a surprise to her and an unusual and quavering smile crossed her face as she put the baby on the bed. Then, shyly as any girl, she asked him, "Where are you coming from, Bapak? I didn't know you would come."

He didn't reply but put his walking stick in the corner and looked around the entire room. Sulastri, entering, approached him and kissed his hand, as was the custom in their family. She wondered at his clothing, so neat and youthful-looking. Bapak took the baby's hand, asked her name, then said, in a by-the-way manner, "Bu, I've gotten married to Ratna in Garut." It was as if what he said meant nothing at all.

"What? Did I hear right?" Ibu's cheeks and lips turned pale. Sulastri felt nailed to the floor.

"Yes, married to Ratna." He took the baby's hand again. His wife slowly turned away and Sulastri was afraid of seeing her mother like this. There was a long silence.

Then, "Why didn't you pick someone else?" Ibu asked dispiritedly.

With a conscious and upright attitude, he replied curtly, "I don't care what other people think, I really have married Ratna, not for me alone but for our daughter Marti, to shelter her from a wretched fate."

Ibu's expression was a question mark and with it, an appeal for pity. She murmured as if struck by a blow. "For our daughter? Why? Why not someone else?"

This last sentence evaporated at the end of her other words. She stood there, at once pitiful and brave, the sweet Ibu holding back her anger. All her life she had been calm in every stressful situation. She always placed herself in the background, so that you almost never saw her and sometimes would be surprised that she, too, could become angry or happy. She usually accepted everything her husband did, so that one need not have considered what she wanted, or even have noticed her flowing tears. Ibu was Ibu, a soft woman, who only wished for peace in the family. After a long silence, Bapak invited her to go with him.

"Listen, I'll explain, Bu," he said. "No, Sulastri also has to know. Marti's husband wants to have a love affair with Ratna. That would be the end of Marti's trust and happiness. So I married Ratna, for your child. Do you understand this? How would Marti react if she heard what her husband wanted to do? Our daughter's happiness is in your hands, Bu."

This man who usually spoke engagingly, who managed so many words so glibly, now spoke clumsily. "Is this person my father?" thought Sulastri, "the father whom I so respect?" She noticed those familiar facial features now looking so different, as if lit with erotic love and hidden intimacies, and beneath, feelings of shame and the realization that with just one blow, a child's love and reverence had changed into hatred. This event, filled with unspoken feelings, would determine Sulastri's outlook all her life. Her mother was helpless in the face of her husband's calm demeanor.

"And how does Ipah take this?" Ibu protested softly. Her forced smile appeared to say more than her words did. Ipah was her mother's cousin whom Bapak had married as well as Ibu, with the excuse that he had to cure Ipah of her frequent nervous tension.

After her grandparents, that is, her mother's parents, died, Ipah lived by herself in her own parents' house, with its surrounding broad and spacious yard, and even more broad and quiet than her yard was the village around it. Ever since she was young, Ipah had weak nerves and now they disturbed her more. She cried and shouted angrily at people incessantly. In short, she disturbed the public peace.

Sulastri's father, who had to keep a watchful eye on her, had felt compelled to marry her. In this way, he was chivalrous, a warrior of sagacity and prudence. What the real issue had been, Sulastri didn't dare wonder, and she never discussed this with Sudarmo, who himself had a very low and barely concealed opinion of his father-in-law. In any case, though, Sulastri's love of her father was stronger than her sudden realization about his egotism. She tried to see him as unblemished, as she did when she was a child. That didn't work now, and she felt she had become a beggar, like someone who denied her sufferings and lied to herself that she was a princess.

What name could she use to voice this sense of shame, combined with her self-contempt, since she was a part of that person, of his own blood, begotten of his desires. A chasm yawned between her and her father. She felt as if she were clearly bonded to the vicious circles of that reality. Previously she had seen the frame of this portrait only vaguely but as very beautiful, varnished with her feelings of reverence toward her father. Ratna had lived with Sulastri's parents since the age of sixteen. Ratna of the storm-tossed nature, who had married an old haji and was divorced after seven months; Ratna, the lazy young woman who annoyed Sulastri's mother, was now Sulastri's father's wife number three. The reality of this truly hurt. How could she conceal this shameful matter from Sudarmo, from Prawira, who himself came from Garut? It was as if all her feelings had gone mute, as if she had been beaten unconscious, so empty she felt in her head, in her heart.

Bapak went on in his usual voice, "We'll talk about this later, Bu. You're the wisest of us all and will make your choice. Tri, your baby has a wonderful name. Better than that of Marti's first child. This name was chosen with true discernment and subtlety. Bu, let's you and I talk in the guest bedroom."

Bapak's glasses flashed. Behind them you could see such gentle brown eyes, which could flash with a fine light, so you'd have to forgive his many faults. His face was round, an earthy *sawo*-brown and fresh, with rough features that now aroused repulsion in Sulastri, for deep inside, she saw hiding behind that face the male egotistical spirit. The driving force of all male behavior was the desire to copulate, which it conceals with polite excuses. Sulastri had to admit that he was intelligent and had character. Even lying to her mother, he was uniquely different. And did Ibu dare complain? No, that was her destiny; to rebel against that fate would bring a curse upon herself and her children. And Ibu didn't want to be called a "wicked" mother.

Sulastri's parents went out together. She noticed that her father's back was broad and suggested a stubborn character. There was something in his rolling gait that aroused her disgust. And as she sat there and wondered how her mother would face all this to come, Sudarmo came with a smile that was both jesting and intimate.

"What's with you, Tri? So lazy, sitting there with your hands in your lap..."

She turned toward her husband and replied in a toneless, rather absentminded way, "Oh, nothing at all. Just daydreaming. Bapak's here, Dar."

"I don't see him. Where's he now?"

"With Ibu in the back room."

The secret was on her lips and wanted to be spoken, but Sulastri restrained herself just in time. She swallowed and then talked about their baby as Sudarmo proudly looked at the little pink foot sticking out from beneath the blanket. Sudarmo hugged his wife's shoulders and they gazed at their baby, the embodiment of their love.

That night, Bapak and Ibu sat on the side verandah and praised Sulastri's haughtily upright sunflowers. Under the light of the lamp, the flowers looked unusually big. Dark shadows were hidden between the murmuring leaves. Slim stems glided down to the earth in the caressing dark. The flowers appeared to be alive with their odd and witty faces. Sulastri and Sudarmo were in the room when they heard a rather long and drawn-out voice, as if the speaker was weary and indifferent. Sulastri heard, "I'm glad our daughter has a home as good as this, isn't that right, Bu?"

"Yes, with its big yard. Early in the mornings, I shiver from the chill." Ibu paused and then with a quite different tone went on, "I'm going to say to you that Ipah will have another breakdown. I myself don't care. Don't I already have a lot of children?"

Bapak was hurt and reacted angrily, "I just told you now why I did it. If you don't care about the happiness of our daughter.... Don't be so narrow-minded like other women. Ipah has to accept all this. In the end, people's good intentions are more important than their deeds. It's better for me to be mocked than for Marti to suffer."

He expressed this convincingly, firmly, and abruptly in a trembling voice.

Their conversation could no longer be heard, so Sudarmo pricked up his ears. Sulastri tried to turn his attention to other things by joking, but she noticed her husband listening tensely. They didn't talk again. Perhaps both were sunk into their own thoughts, perhaps also they were noticing the beauty of the visions that came and went among the sunflowers.

Then Ibu's voice was heard in reproach.

"You only think of your own pleasures, Pak. What will our children think? They will be ashamed. You've got grandchildren and you behave like a bachelor who still wants to have fun in life." Then she teased him, "An old man who acts like a teenager. Aren't you ashamed of this?"

Then they heard Bapak refute Ibu's derision in a calm, emotionless voice. "Allah's rewards for a good person are great. Aren't you more pleased to obtain happiness in the hereafter? If so, you have to forego happiness in this world. Really, Bu, you've got to accept all these things. What's more, my love for you is different—it's spiritual, not of this world of illusions."

Then the two voices stopped, perhaps, because they were outside, they were again looking at the sunflowers, which couldn't speak, only display grandeur on their golden faces.

"What is it, Tri?" asked Sudarmo, concerned.

His wife shrugged and answered indifferently, "Oh, family stuff, nothing important to us."

Sudarmo wasn't satisfied with this answer and looked at his wife suspiciously, but Sulastri, her face turned away, started laughing and jokingly invited him to go out.

Sulastri's mother stayed with her daughter for another month, her father having gone back some time before. During that time, Sulastri tried to get her mother to ask for a divorce. Again and again, she said, "Yes, yes, of course it's not right that he didn't ask my permission first. When I go home, I'll definitely ask him to divorce me."

Sulastri knew on the contrary that her mother would not ask her husband for a divorce, even if the whole family prodded her to do so. Ibu's love for Bapak was a devotion that forgave everything he did, a love that asked for nothing, and even derived happiness in being good to him. All her life she had sacrificed, from the first child she carried on her hip to her youngest one. She always had to sew and mend their clothes and those of her nephews and nieces. Her hands, so diligent and nimble, would be busy far into the night, and on the next day she'd endlessly look for work to do in the house. Ibu found it boring to rest and laze about. She had to always be busy, for in being occupied she wouldn't feel her hardships. And so her sadness because of Bapak would abate and then she would feel bound tightly to her children. She never dared give advice to them; she was too humble. Without her realizing it, her children grew to be more mature than Ibu herself, and she felt surrounded by wise and sensible faces who advised her, so that her motherly voice became requests or one or two mild words of regret. But actually no one wanted to make her sad, and her children clung very closely to her. Even her nephews and nieces felt as if they had emerged from her womb. She *was* Ibu and would always be so. Because of her, the relationship between Sulastri and her cousins still stayed close.

Ibu spoiled her daughters. Sulastri remembered when she despairingly tried to sew a kebaya with her clumsy hands, because previously Ibu had always been ready to do it. When Sulastri was somewhere else, far from her family, she felt the love from her mother's attention and she regretted having often snapped at her impatiently for some silly little thing.

"Ibu is so stupid." She often justified herself like that, but it wasn't true. Ibu felt frustration in the face of her children's foreign skills. They spoke in foreign languages around her and sometimes didn't bother answering her questions and concerns, which she had raised very hesitantly and doubtfully.

A month passed. After her mother had returned to Garut, Sulastri realized for the first time that her departure had left an emptiness everywhere, even though when she had been there, they hardly noticed her presence.

Schoolwork recommenced for Sulastri. And sometimes, standing half-heartedly and without energy in front of the class, she felt she would faint. Nonetheless, she held up and gradually she became the Lastri of old, who would walk about tirelessly in the schoolyard. The rather strange feeling of lightness in her now slender frame had gone away and she felt weight returning to her body, becoming curvaceous and filled out like before. Her pallor was replaced by warm blood quickly flowing and bringing color to her cheeks.

Sudarmo noticed this change and felt disappointed that his wife was filling out again. He was happier with her interesting paleness. Human esthetic sentiments ask for something different than daily routine.

Relations between Sudarmo and his colleagues went back to being difficult, as they eventually saw the baby as nothing unusual. Once again, their conversations became forced, now that they no longer needed to talk about the baby, and the wall of hostility grew ever higher until some split between them would push two people to a future neither of them recognized.

12

Sudarmo was now officially banned from teaching. This was a blow against their lives and became a weapon in the hands of the teachers who opposed him. And they began to move intensely. Several months beforehand, Sudarmo had a presentiment of this. He discussed it with Sulastri, but once the ban was issued, there was no longer any use in talking about it. Gularso openly opposed Sudarmo and the situation could no longer be maintained, especially after Sudarmo could no longer teach.

Sulastri began to count the furniture, and made a list of everything to be sold to anyone who wanted it. They packed their books in boxes and waited for the time when they had to leave. And that is how several weeks passed, during which they organized the lessons for their replacements, so that the schoolchildren wouldn't suffer from this development. Sulastri, in her heart, had already bid farewell to those unforgettable students. All this while the baby was growing and could now lie on her side and move about. In the afternoons, when they sat with her on the mat, they would listen to the spotted doves in the *kedongdong* tree. The tremulous voices of these birds were filled with enchanting rhythms, and the leaves seemed to capture the sounds and launch them to very tips of the trees.

"Listen to such beautiful sounds, Tri. They mean we'll be moving away."

"Umm," she replied almost without hearing, for a gloomy feeling came to her from deep within. To leave all this... the earthen-colored *sawo* fruit also wanted to know and peered from behind all the greenery and spoke to her, and everything around her seemed to be bidding her farewell forever.

"I have detached myself from all of this," she thought and regretted that their work, as planned by Sudarmo, had been nowhere near finished. In that plan, they would have achieved a financial improvement in the first year, cultivated relationships with the outside world in year two, and in the third year, they would have achieved a real modernization of education. Now they had almost reached the third year. The work, begun with such great enthusiasm, would be halted, all because of a petty incident, Sudarmo's receipt of that treacherous letter from the provincial governor. Sulastri immediately realized that they would have to lead a new life and abandon forever all that had gone on before. Everything around them was in bud and must grow into trees, but even the buds would desiccate before blossoming.

"*Kur, tikukur, kuk,*" the enchanted crystalline sounds quavered in the throats of these birds and resounded deep within the melancholy hearts of the listeners.

"*Tikukur, kuk, tikukur, kuk.*" Baby Rustini, laying on her stomach, wriggled herself closer to one such yellow bird in the grass and grasped at it, squealing with laughter. Sulastri and Sudarmo watched their child and listened to the charmed songs in the tree.

"*Tikukur, kuk, tikukur, kuk.*" Birds were bringers of happiness and also of woe. The premonitions and presentiments supposed to be buried in their hearts, resurfaced and affected them both.

"*Tikukur, kuk, tikukur, kuk.*" The small bird spread its wings and was gone. Its voice, though, still echoed amidst the trees and floated on the gentle breeze moving through the cempaka blossoms.

The next day, a few pieces of furniture were sold.

"Here's the money." Mientje carefully placed seven rupiah in Sulastri's hand. Sulastri felt like hurling the money away, but what good would that do? Seven rupiah had their own worth, especially for empty wallets.

Mientje, her hand on the sofa, examined and then took hold of a lampshade and the door curtain. Then her gaze crossed the hat rack. All of these belonged to her now, and for all those things she had grandly counted out those seven gleaming rupiah coins.

For Sulastri, this was Mientje's real character: a childishness in the hauteur of a woman who was clever for her husband, a woman brave enough to reach out her hand to work, but at the same time, petty-minded from envy and very affected by her ageing face.

"Poor old Mien," Sulastri thought without feeling any animosity toward her, but rather pity. Sulastri almost believed that a person could become like that by a deep craving to own something. Mientje's rupiah felt as if they were burning Sulastri's hand, because Mientje had the right to express her criticism of this and that item. But Sulastri reminded herself of her journey, remembered that she perhaps would stay with Lurni, her sister-in-law, for several months and thought of the days after that, which took on a frightening shape in their drifting lives.

After pieces of furniture were taken one by one and their trunks were packed, there was still a lot Sulastri had to do: taking leave of her colleagues and the students' parents. Among the teachers were those who suddenly felt what it meant to see the pavilion which would soon be empty, even though they had actually wished for this all along. They could look on Sulastri as a friend again, now that they no longer had to be concerned about their own interests. They unhesitatingly declared their regret that Sulastri would be leaving in a few days. In their hearts, they were good people, rather stupid, but in truth quick to forgive the faults of others.

But why, in all the preceding months, were they so nasty, at least as Sulastri had seen it? She couldn't find the answer. Given the current situation, they made peace and all parted as friends.

Sulastri would go first with the baby. Sudarmo would follow, as there were still many matters to be settled first. Several days later, Sudarmo escorted his wife and child to the station. They were going to Yogyakarta.

On the train, alone with her baby, Sulastri sensed that she wasn't leaving just Bandung, but other things as well, to which she felt tightly bound: her ideals and her mental strength. She felt shattered to the core, and old, as if she had lost a bet with stakes that had been too high and was now impoverished, her spiritual resources a wasteland. She looked out the window. The far-off mountains were hazy and then with a turn in the tracks vanished entirely. She turned her head back and found herself looking right into the eyes of a young soldier who had been observing her all along. He gave a quick smile and asked where she was going, perhaps not supposing in the least that the woman in front of him was an intellectual. Nevertheless, he spoke in a voice that was half ironic and half cordial, until Sulastri reminded herself that she was a woman. She thus turned away, barely replying, even though she could not have reproached his behavior. In fact, it was rather surprising to have as a travel mate a woman journeying alone with her baby. Sulastri could guess what was on the soldier's mind; still, she saw the soldier as good-hearted when he took the baby onto his lap and let her play with his buttons when he couldn't bear to hear her crying.

"Well, look at that. She thinks I'm her father," he said sheepishly and on his face was a smile so friendly that in spite of herself, Sulastri felt a certain tenderness toward him. However, she understood that were she let that show, the atmosphere would become complicated, and so she was afraid of the soldier, a fear that may have been passed down from parent to child, because the soldier was a symbol of repression, authority, and the violation of women. This fear could not be dispelled and it throbbed in her breast, oppressing her, and so she tried to calm herself by reading a book.

She took out a book about Caesar and, though she hardly saw the letters of the words, the book created a chasm between her and the soldier. The soldier himself eventually stood up and went over to his friends. It had just so happened that the train was filled with privates, corporals, and sergeants who perhaps were on leave. Near the window across the way was a soldier's wife wearing a sarong with blueish-white flowers, white kebaya, and a length of cloth covering her head. She was rubbing one of her legs and had both legs placed on the bench in front of her. She kept complaining to her husband about feeling dizzy. He was a sergeant from Manado who couldn't be bothered with answering her and grumbled—*hem, hem*—about everything. His wife then angrily set to rubbing her leg again. Sulastri felt like she herself was sitting on thorns and being scrutinized by eyes that dirtied her by their measuring the shape of her body, up and down.

"Sudarmo has put me in this maddening situation," she thought. "Why doesn't he know what it means for a woman to travel alone!" But then she promptly felt extremely stupid for being afraid without any reason at all. She put the baby to sleep on the pillow, stroking her gently, and then went back to reading. All the while she kept having the feeling that she had experienced something extraordinary in her life. She had never understood that the soldier was a human being just like her. She normally viewed soldiers as "animals" and she was hit by the thought that a soldier could also love a child, just as a civilian did.

When the soldier returned, she was no longer afraid of him. He played with the baby when she cried again, and Sulastri felt grateful to him because during the journey she didn't have to take care of her by herself. The soldier closed the window and took care lest wind get in through an open door. In short, perhaps he had not been as friendly as he was now. In the meantime, he noticed Sulastri's calm and studying look. It was a look that diminished his inappropriate behavior, transforming it into the gestures of a teenage boy and his attitude, so cocky before, into a show of awkwardness.

Yogya was near. Sulastri felt she could breathe comfortably, for it was very hot in the train carriage. She opened the window, but remembered with alarm that she had to manage her baggage. So she counted her bags, combed her hair, and waited tensely for the train to enter the station. Yogya for her meant being forced to stay with her sister-in-law, even though she didn't yet know her very well. In any case, she would stay with her for the shortest possible time and look for a house. She would get *f* 15 a month for three months because Marti didn't want to take back Sulastri's wristwatch just like that. That watch was the only luxury item that could produce a little money. It was a gift from Marti, but what was its use, if a person so greatly needed money and in fact had gone bankrupt from working hard for two years in a nationalist education school? And taking care of a baby was a heavy chore now that Sulastri was no longer producing milk and had to feed the baby from a bottle. It wasn't surprising that Sulastri was looking more and more sad, and her gloomy appearance would increase as the years passed. And yet at this time she was still young, a little over twenty years old, although young didn't mean the same for everyone.

She had a sense that she had already become an old woman who had to see little pleasures in her life, which seemed empty and disappointing. Now her baby gave her consolation and that was very good. "Sudarmo only thinks of himself," she thought, "Fate has given me the same thing as other women in my situation: hardship and the deprivation of everything that gives pleasure. I feel old now and so very tired. Will I ever be able to be happy again?"

The sun's glare made her shut her eyes, then she looked out the window again. "Yogya, Central Java, and here they speak a language that I don't know." She brooded again and always saw her own face: Sulastri who was exhausted, who no longer had high hopes and whose nerves were on edge.

When the train stopped at the Yogyakarta station, her eyes scanned the people on the platform, and she spotted her sister-in-law Lurni and Ribowo. She waved at them and moments later she was being hugged by two affectionate arms. Lurni carefully carried the baby, and in this way, they walked down the platform, not saying much but stepping fast.

"This is Yogya," thought Sulastri, "I wonder if I can live here. It could be my spirit will be crushed in this environment, but never mind, only one person will be lost."

She didn't see the shops they passed very clearly. She realized that all of this was foreign to her and that those mountains that had gone out of sight earlier had to be wiped from her memory if she wanted to live in peace and happiness. Sulastri loved the Priangan highlands, the region where she had been born and where, as she felt, she had left her soul, because Sulastri in Yogya was a different Sulastri, someone unaware of herself. Sulastri, the dimly perceived and of an unclear form. Only a shadow, like a leather puppet against the screen and her voice an echo. Her mind was thus elsewhere and she gave only vague replies to Lurni's questions. And so she didn't notice her sister-in-law looking at her curiously.

Lurni set the baby in her lap and was surprised at the faces of both Sulastri and the baby. The baby stayed silent, strangely enough, and Lurni was unsettled by her listless expression. She just kept sucking her fist. Lurni didn't understand why Sulastri would want to live so simply to obey Sudarmo's preferences, and she looked destitute in those clothes. Lurni was embarrassed by Sulastri's excessive simplicity. Lurni herself was dressed in the latest fashion: a gracefully worn sarong wrapped in a way that showed off her slenderness, and a flowery kebaya with a simple brooch, while her large chignon was ornamented by a beautiful hair pin.

Her oval face and slanting eyes made her look lovely. She resembled Sudarmo, though in a somewhat different way, for Lurni could be said to be pretty, while Sudarmo, with his sharp features, would not be called handsome.

Ribowo sat next to the coachman. Sulastri observed his bent back and his white jacket tightly hugging his corpulent body. That back was a sign of Ribowo's character: affable, goodhearted, of normal intelligence, extremely stubborn and childish in some matters, generally speaking; someone trustworthy, but without much initiative. In other words, a man with a firm character, who could work diligently .

Lurni, on the other hand, would frequently get angry over small things. Because she was sturdily built, she even dared to get rough with others if she felt she was being treated unfairly. It was hard for her to forgive an insult, but she never took revenge. She was sensitive only to people's attitudes toward her, good or bad. In fact, Ribowo wasn't a suitable match for Lurni, and in this regard she always felt, though without reason, disdained by people. That sensitivity and her mistaken notions cast a shade over Lurni's honest and courageous character and made her melancholic. In her outings and in her work for the women's movement, she looked for ways to rid herself of such anxieties. Actually, Lurni should have married someone of good rank, because she couldn't let go of her habit of wearing jewelry and fine clothes, so that her marriage brought misfortune to her, while otherwise she might have been a sweet and cheerful woman.

Sulastri's sympathy toward Lurni was based on her respect for her activities, but for sympathy to become love, more was needed than just that. Mutual respect, mutual acknowledgment of accomplishments, and a similarity of character. But at that present time, there was no warm mutual appreciation; their ties were not strong because they weren't soulmates. There was always something unclear in their relationship, and Sudarmo would then be between them and never understand why he saw the caustic aspects in Lurni and Sulastri, though there was no explicit hostility there and it was hard for him to determine his attitude between the two of them.

When their *andong* drew up in front of Lurni's home, the first thing that appeared to Sulastri was a garden filled with pebbles. A small, cemented path led from the gate to the house. Right in front of the house, the path became brick. The front verandah was dark and cool. Potted palms and maidenhair ferns in the front and at the side had a cooling effect on the heat of the sunlight and made for an impressive old-fashioned atmosphere. A circle, planted with flowers was enclosed by a low cement wall, so that this circle appeared raised above the gravel and planted with vinca flowers which grew in a disorderly huddle. There were roses, dahlias, and tiny lilies. Around this were more pots with rose bushes not yet in blossom. Their long branches crept over the pebbles and crossed the low wall of the circle of flowers. A shady *jambu* tree ornamented the garden with the last of its red fruit. This tree threw its shade over a wall bench, where one could sit and relax. Then there was a mango tree and a coconut tree in the front yard, something that was familiar for Sulastri, for in her region fruit trees were always in the back of the house. These trees created a captivating atmosphere for they provided coolness.

"Welcome to our home," said Lurni, turning to Sulastri, who followed her slowly. Ribowo drew a breath, for he felt the heat, and called the servants, who fetched the bags. Then Sulastri entered Lurni's room, where the baby was lying on her stomach on the bed.

"Oh my! So sweet!", Lurni exclaimed and, bending over a little, looked at Rustini. "The very image of her father! Mas Dar exactly!" and when she saw a skeptical look on Sulastri's face, she added, "When he was little, not now. Now he's ugly."

Sulastri laughed. Lurni joined in and patted her sister-in-law on her shoulder. Sulastri wiped the dust from her face with a handkerchief and replied languidly, "She looks just like Mas Dar, it's true. I hope she'll be different in other ways."

Lurni looked at her in surprise, but that's all that was said and she asked Sulastri about a number of other things. Sulastri, feeling fatigued, replied lackadaisically, but was sarcastic about school matters, something that Lurni had no interest in. And while Sulastri was talking on the bed, in came a woman of about thirty years of age, Sudarmo's and Lurni's surviving aunt. The other members of this family, including their mother, had died several years earlier. This aunt, Mintarsih, was two years older than Sudarmo. She was slender, quite lovely, and with her ivory skin and narrow eyes looked more Chinese than Javanese. Her wavy hair was combed smoothly with coconut oil and her large chignon was neatly tied at the back of her neck. She spoke in a hesitant and shy way and she had a placid look about her, like someone of social stature, but also like a girl, for in her expression was the impression that she was seeking sympathy. Sulastri took both her hands and they exchanged greetings. Then she waited for what this *bibi* of hers, Mintarsih, would say next.

"You've come by yourself, child? And when will your husband come? And is this Rustini? She's so big. There now, she's laughing. Oh, how sweet!"

Mintarsih picked up the baby and praised her clear skin and long eyebrows. This really was a pretty baby. Sulastri was surprised to have such a pretty child, but Sudarmo saw this as it should be, because for him, the father was the most important for the physical form of a child. This was certainly Sudarmo's personal theory of biology.

"Now," said Lurni, "take a rest first, or would you like a cup of tea? Let's just sit in the inner veranda."

Sulastri sat on the sofa next to Lurni and looked outside, where a gardener was watering the plants from a sprinkling can. The flowers, the gardener, the sprinkling can all aroused memories of the days of her past life. She gave a start, when suddenly Lurni asked, "And what are Mas Dar's plans for work here?"

Sulastri shrugged and sampled the tasty crisps, then turned to see a fourteen-month-old girl being carried in a shoulder sling by her nanny.

"Your second child, right? What's her name?"

"Teja, but her official name is something else," Lurni laughed. Indeed, it would be a bit strange to call a baby by three names, all long and each having its own meaning.

Sulastri took the baby from the nanny, but she resisted and started screaming. Lurni soothed the child on her lap. Now she was still whimpering a little and looked sideways at Sulastri, who was feeling awkward and tried to get on the child's good side by giving her some cake. Ribowo clapped his hands to get his child's attention. He loved Teja in his own way, but was unable to speak endearments to her and usually said the same thing every time, which he voiced every day with a pleasant laugh. If the child cried, he would calm her down shyly: "So, who's that crying there? Not Teja, right? No, no! Teja's quiet. What animal is that? A gecko? Oh, a gecko!"

For Sulastri, Ribowo was comical with the short gestures of his round hands. He was plump, so that he resembled a woman, especially when he was wearing a sarong. His wife was irritated to watch his behavior and unfashionable clothes. Ribowo was the type of man who indulged in his eating. But the food he most liked was of the simplest kind. He had the talent of being silent and keeping his mouth shut whenever he giggled, which made others start laughing as well. Moreover, he appeared to live quietly and to be full of love for his wife. Lurni said a bit mockingly to their child,

"Don't look at your father! He's so tiresome." And then to Sulastri, "All men are tiresome. I'm always asking myself why I ever wanted to marry."

"You were the one who asked me to marry you!" Ribowo joked and winked at Sulastri, who smiled for a moment. Lurni suddenly got angry, as though jabbed with something sharp. "Oh, yes? Who wrote the letters from prison, those letters that begged and pleaded? Tri, I felt sorry for him and that's why I'm saying it. Yes, even though I—" She stopped, surprised at her sudden anger and, with a smile, apologized to Ribowo. He looked at her tensely, but then calmed the unpleasant atmosphere by saying, "Ah, I don't think you're being serious. Those aren't words from your heart."

Her eyebrows were still raised, but a subtle look full of pity spread across her face and gleamed in her dark eyes. Ribowo teased Lurni, but she replied apathetically. She appeared to see, clearly and with melancholy, many incidents in her past, and to see as deeply as possible into her own heart. Sulastri, because of that, stayed silent and did not feel involved. Ribowo stood up finally and hummed a tune, pacing up and down, cakes in his hands. Teja went under the table and pulled at the tassels of the table cloth.

The inner veranda, where they now were, was large and divided by a wooden screen. The furniture was very simple. The room seemed bare, because the walls were devoid of paintings, but at the same time grand: there was a glass cabinet filled with crystal and chinaware, all arranged neatly and in good order. Through the window could be seen the neighbor's front veranda, which stood on high pilings. The key lime tree was full of yellow fruit and its branches were higher than the wall that separated the yards of the two houses. The custard-apple tree was bearing its green fruit for the first time.

"Mas Dar is alone in the pavilion now," mused Sulastri. "Is he thinking of us?"

Lurni saw her sister-in-law so silent and distracted, so she roused herself to gladden her guest. She told Sulastri about the work at school and about her friends, but Sulastri was paying only faint attention to her stories and had to force herself to listen closely. An uproar of unruly voices—laughing, singing, and shouting—came to them from the back rooms.

"Still so many children here, Lurni. How many of them?

"Thirteen. Some from the MULO school, several from the teacher's school. It's always this raucous. We can't converse calmly. When we have to discuss something, we just go out for a walk. The house is never peaceful."

Lurni had a dormitory, and this helped pay for the electricity and rent. There weren't any other benefits, but she was able to rent a bigger place in a good neighborhood; otherwise, she might be forced to rent a small house from their salary at the nationalist education school, which according one joker, was too much to starve to death on and too little to breathe easy. Lurni and Ribowo were the oldest teachers at the school, which had only one branch at that time. Nonetheless, the school principal was not very happy with Ribowo, because he was a member of the Marhaen Party leadership and had a bit of influence on the parents of the students. For his part, Ribowo was unaware of the hidden worries of the principal and dedicated himself and all his energy to the school. He had only two character flaws. He wasn't obsequious, and he dared to say what he thought was right. The principal, though, in spite of his many good qualities, liked to be surrounded by sycophants who saw him as the foremost defender of Javanese culture. Ribowo was prosaic. He didn't know Javanese literature and would nod off if he saw a *serimpi* court dance. On the other hand, he was the center of all sorts of work, while the radical youngsters, because Ribowo was a member of the executive board of the Nationalist Education Schools, gave their energies to the school out of sympathy for him.

Without Ribowo, many small branches would separate from the core school. The principal knew this and suspected that Ribowo worked against him. In fact, Ribowo didn't in the least think of making things difficult for the principal. Under these circumstances, Lurni and Ribowo gave lessons, and they still remained teaching only because they were honest and loyal. In the end, they weren't working for the principal but precisely for the nationalist interests. Like Sudarmo, they had to experience unpleasant treatment from their colleagues. They allayed these worries with their naive belief that good people would be rewarded for their goodness.

Then Sulastri asked, "And what's the attitude of the principal towards you two?"

"Oh, nothing special, indifferent, but we don't care. It doesn't matter that we receive less than what we contribute. In this regard, we thought all of that over thoroughly at the outset. But, you, Lastri, what are you going to do here?"

"I don't know. I want to rest a while, if I may, I mean, if..."

"Yes, I understand. You all can stay here with us for a while. If there's food for twenty people, there'd certainly be enough for twenty-seven. Really, you're no inconvenience for us. Actually, we're happy. It's so much work taking care of a baby."

What the two relatives discussed, and it wasn't much, didn't offer a solution; but Sulastri now knew she wouldn't be by herself if Sudarmo at some point was awarded work as a civil servant. Sulastri couldn't bear the life of suffering as she had done recently, because the desire to live had been melting away little by little and she was slowly being dragged back to the precipice of devastation. You begin work with tremendous enthusiasm and in the end you're exhausted. But still, there's something else that you have and that is the shame of losing your convictions. From that moment on, Sulastri wasn't going to take other people for granted. She would pay extra attention to people's character or the look in their eyes and feel humiliated over silly little things. She would often ask herself, "And why do they act like that to me?" To find the complete answer to that question would require her whole lifetime. It would be a good thing, too, for Sulastri to go through a crisis and rediscover herself as some insignificant person, no more valuable than the next one.

One evening, Sulastri visited Windarti, one of her childhood friends from when she lived for several years in East Java. Windarti was different. From a girl who liked to joke and paid no attention to her conduct as prescribed by custom, she had become a real housewife who often quarreled with her servants and studiously poured over cookbooks for new recipes. Parsono, her goodhearted husband, was a fat man with a handsome face, much like an Arab, with a plump double chin, which because of its weight stuck to his broad chest. He had the respectable air of a *bupati*, something rather odd in a person as young as he. When Windarti was still a girl and, along with Sulastri, visiting Marti for several months on end, the two friends enjoyed the happiest period of their lives, bathing together, squabbling, and gadding about, and this way were never separated until Windarti was summoned home by telegram and fell into the trap set for her. She was to marry Parsono, who had long and faithfully loved her. This had worried Sulastri, for she didn't see Parsono as a proper match for Windarti, who had the possibility of developing her mind, while Parsono was nothing more than a good-natured obscurity. Windarti had grown precisely in the direction Sulastri had feared, and she was sad to hear Windarti going on and on about the things they needed in their daily lives like some old woman, while there were other matters where her attention could have been directed in this time of nationalist development.

It was such a loss of the growth of her intellectual gifts and a downward pressure for her as a person. But Windarti was satisfied, even excessively satisfied, and she seemed not to feel the loss of anything other than her freedom. Parsono was the principal of the nationalist commercial school. Why this school would have been called a nationalist commercial school was a mystery. Perhaps because at the time the word "nationalist" was very much the mode and had to cover all sorts of cargo in the boat. Parsono stayed in the pavilion giving lessons in the evenings in bookkeeping and filling his free time by making lecture notes. He didn't bring any extraordinary character to his school. He travelled along the road that he had long been used to travelling, and people praised him only for his great diligence and persistence.

When Sulastri entered the nationalist commercial school yard, she had the feeling that she was entering a different milieu. While she was on the road, she had the sense of being in a new world, so calm and tranquil it was. The homes, the people, the streets, even the soil, was different from her own region. The atmosphere had the quiet calm of a village, its rhythm evident in the indigo color of people's jackets, life that was painted by the *andong* carts that moved slowly, and all within dust-filled air and sunlight. That's how Sulastri saw Yogya, a city anchored in tradition and ceremony, culture and aristocracy. The houses were cool because of the *sawo* trees in the front yards, dark because of their shadows, and secretive by being unrecognizable, but, nonetheless disappointing, because they looked dirty and hid themselves out of sight, as if there were things within that could not be shown without damaging something sacred or simply couldn't be revealed to the common folk. In fact, Sulastri considered this environment with antipathy. She, with her fresh disposition and style, rebelled against the overly refined culture here and felt frustrated by the languid movements of the people and the shadows in the dark shade of the trees. She was aware that these moody feelings came from the differences between Java and her native Sunda, based on the ancient hostilities of the ancestors.

She felt herself a foreigner who stood out clearly in a setting consisting of thousands of people who were all the same. On the streets she felt as if she were floating in the air, pulled outside from all of this. In her thoughts she recalled something distant, left behind, and as if she no longer had any senses; dead, and insensitive to everything, as if she had lost herself, who could give color and life to all people.

Without realizing it, she had entered the yard of Parsono's home and smiled at Windarti who joyfully jumped up from the steps and with outstretched hands greeted her and embraced her as if they were still girls. Windarti swung Sulastri's hands from side to side.

"Lastri! My God, why do you look like that? My dear, I'm so happy..."

Windarti let go of Sulastri's hands, then grabbed them again nervously, laughing loudly, delighted to take her friend by the hand up the steep steps and into the pavilion. The front veranda was empty. Two flowerpots with dry, straggling growths tried to ornament the wall with its worn-away paint. The cement tiles were cracked and split here and there. The faded deep-red doors all spoke of poverty. Windarti opened the front door and the inner veranda was unimaginably messy, like items of furniture at an auction piled up any old way. The guest chairs were brown, the bookcase old-fashioned, the desk was black, and the divan was upholstered with green cloth that revealed dusty circles here and there. There were some photos on the wall, arranged with no particular style or taste, as in the atelier of a professional photographer. Windarti moved a chair over to Sulastri and quickly went inside, calling her husband and telling the servants to make tea. She took over her child from its nurse, and complained about that she couldn't make the housework run smoothly.

"This is the way it is, if you're the mistress of the house. Do you remember back when we were still girls? What time it was when we usually got up?"

"Yes, you had to be shaken awake. We usually stayed up until late at night playing Patience on the bed. Do you recall how annoyed you'd get because you couldn't get a match?" Sulastri laughed.

"And early in the morning, you'd always say, 'Huh, this water's wet' and you'd shriek when you'd spray me. And remember how we could finish off hundreds of *duku*? And the so delicious durians from you? Oh, Tri!" Windarti joined her hands and went on happily, "They weren't very nice, what I'm going to remind you of. When we'd had our fill of the durians and had to go the meetings, we'd use a lot of *odeurs* to get rid of the durian smell, but in fact the smell of them was too strong. Even if we used perfume, people would smell it with disgusted looks and we'd giggle away. No one would suspect that such elegantly turned-out girls were the source of the smell. I couldn't breathe from laughing and several times you said that the smell of durians is more piercing than *quelques fleurs*, so tell me, in your opinion, what's the strongest smell in the world?"

"Okay, enough, Windarti, I'm ashamed to remember that. Now we're so polite, no one would suppose we used to be real rascals."

"Do you remember that Batavia fruit peddler who said to us, 'Don't buy too much, I'd take a loss,' because he thought that he sold his things too cheap? And do you remember when Marti wanted to get us to do something and we stayed quiet as mice in our room? And that fortune teller, do you remember him?"

Windarti suddenly burst into uproarious laughter.

"He predicted that I would marry someone with a little mustache. And that's right, isn't it?"

Sulastri shook her right hand and they laughed again out of sheer delight. Windarti's child looked at them with wonder, and Parsono, just now entering with heavy footsteps, joined in laughing, too, while greeting Sulastri with a friendly salaam. Then he started teasing her, "You look so beautiful, Tri, because you're quite slender."

"Don't flatter me, my dear Parsono! I know, you've become a distinguished person. A real bourgeois."

"Distinguished, Lastri! My goodhearted husband here is a model of happiness and prosperity."

Parsono was rather angry. He wasn't happy when he was teased like that, because his fatness was a subject never to be touched on, even if he didn't much care how his face looked. It pleased him the most to be called "hardworking and diligent." Could someone who was hardworking and diligent be so fat? He sat down on the divan and, bent over like that, he resembled some giant. But Sulastri saw his wavy hair and the sweetness in his eyes. She observed him somewhat challengingly, glancing briefly at Windarti and said scornfully, "So, you think the Sulastri of now is prettier and nicer than the Sulastri of before. You're wrong. Guess why you're wrong."

He didn't understand what Sulastri was saying. He took a cake and, frowning, asked, "What do you mean?" as he looked quizzically at Windarti. Windarti shrugged and began to busily talk with Sulastri about her relatives. Parsono looked at Sulastri with new eyes. "Strange," he thought. "Our Lastri was a good kid. If she had been more gentle and amenable, I would have definitely asked for her hand." He appeared sunken in reveries and memories, not speaking and eating cake after cake, all the while looking at Sulastri and then back to Windarti.

Windarti's listless and gloomy eyes shone and her entire lethargic face was like a flower's return to bloom, her pale lips came to life with the flow of blood, and her slender, elegant hands moved quickly and spiritedly or were clenched like a young girl's. Sulastri and Windarti had become oblivious to everything around them and often laughed, while Parsono echoed their happy laughter. Then Windarti said, "I hate men like him. They ask for everything from you. They're all egotists, from their feet to the hair on their head."

"Yes, Windarti, a person who's gotten married has no freedom, but to tell you the truth, I'm happy that I have Sudarmo. At least I have someone who's there to help if I'm in trouble."

"But to have to live with that person for years on end, with someone who doesn't know how to talk, who approves of everything that you do.... Oh God, I can't breathe from boredom."

Parsono interrupted her. "Who's bored, you or me? Marriage is indeed most irritating! It should be abolished." He spoke sharply as if he had something else to talk about. Sulastri spoke as if she didn't care, "Oh, I'm quite happy. But... oh, I don't know. I don't know. At this point in time, Sudarmo's the only one for me."

They chatted on about marriage and discovered that difficulties in marriage weren't easy to resolve. The only result from this conversation was that Parsono and Windarti faced each other glumly. Luckily at that moment, Ribowo and Lurni came to fetch Sulastri, so that those dark looks turned suddenly into warm laughter, and Sulastri watched the two couples with amusement. Lurni picked up Windarti's child, now seven months old, and put it on her lap. It wasn't able to do anything yet, only looking around and calling out fretfully. It looked a little odd.

"It looks like a tadpole with its big head and its body so tiny. Will it become a normal child?"

The other two people comforted Windarti, saying that she was only seeing an image that wasn't real. Actually, the child was rather strange-looking and this made her sad. She held the view that when she was pregnant, she had once suffered a terrible shock. Lurni and Windarti were not particularly fond of each other, but didn't want to be open about it.

"Give a course to the members of our association, Win. You don't have work at home, do you?" Lurni said.

"Don't have work?" Windarti restrained herself, for she was getting angry. "Yes, and what about my baby? What I think is, it has to be cared for first and only after that are there any other things. No, no, if anything happens to my child, I'd never forgive myself for as long as I lived. And what courses would I have to give? Zus is the smart one. Let Lastri be the one to give them."

Sulastri protested. "Not me. I panic seeing so many people. I'm really not at ease doing things just by the book, if that's the way it has to be done."

"And your big sister, Marti, she's so active." Lurni said sharply.

"But Lurni, do you want to make your women's association a family business? It's best if you are in it. In Bogor, my adopted big sister and brother-in-law both are members of the board. Soon we can, you know, become an oligarchy." Sulastri scoffed, Windarti laughed and Lurni became angry. Then the men came up to them, so that their squabbling was gone with the wind, and they parted in a friendly manner.

On the following days, Sulastri adjusted herself fully to Lurni's life. With so many schoolchildren boarding there, it meant, first of all, the food was unappetizing and tasted as if it was from a soup kitchen. Second, there were ears listening everywhere. Third, it was a noisy bedlam from morning to night. Then, the washroom was always in use, making people wait at the door for their turn. And finally, in every issue you had to be accommodating and forego your own wishes. Sulastri was amazed at how Lurni could be calm in this life, with hardly a moment's quiet. But Lurni actually felt lonely on holidays without all that uproar. There was no way that Sulastri could live like that.

Only when sitting on the stone bench under the *jambu* tree could you feel at peace, because from there the entire yard was clearly in view.

If Lurni and her husband wanted to dine well, they usually went out to a restaurant. They were of the view that everyone in the house had to eat the same food. Because people's stomachs sometimes deviated from that view, they had come upon the excellent solution just mentioned.

Two weeks later, Sudarmo arrived with the remaining baggage. He was thinner, talked nonsense, and for Sulastri, he was like some foreigner. He was happy to see her and, taking Rustini upon his lap, said that he had looked for work in Batavia.

"But, oh, there's nothing for us there. I think it would be better for Sulastri to look for work here. I intend to issue a journal here. I have the money for the first issue from our furniture. After that, we'll see what happens."

He was certain that he would succeed. Because Sulastri wasn't happy about living at Lurni's house, she told Sudarmo she wanted to live in their own home. They looked for one, and Sudarmo found a small, nice pavilion. The rent was four rupiah and so they moved there on a nice day. This pavilion would be their home for the time being.

Sulastri did not get work and her time was spent taking care of the baby. Lurni would send food to them daily so they didn't have to start feeling panicky. The pavilion had only one room and was made of bamboo slats. They put Sudarmo's books on a rack he made himself from old kerosene cans piled up in the form of a pyramid. In front of the dwelling was an unusually large papaya tree now in fruit, and two rose bushes.

The owner lived in the big house, a post office clerk, who was startled to see someone with so many books living in a rather impoverished neighborhood, and he didn't want to know why an intellectual wasn't rich or didn't have a car. For him, cleverness was tied to rank and a good situation in society, and he often gazed at Sudarmo with disbelieving eyes. He also wondered why Sulastri seemed not to differ greatly from his own wife. Not only this clerk but everyone around wondered about this couple and speculated about this and that; they actually appreciated them for having briefly stirred up and surprised such a drab and boring neighborhood.

Rustini could stand up by herself and was put in a box of spotted bamboo where she pulled at the roses and laughed happily. And so, three months of their idealistic life went by and the cuckoo dove of their neighbor left a poetic imprint on it, a life which actually had to be filled with someone's grumbling and complaining.

13

How would you react if someone invited you to eat noodles together at night under a banyan tree? You'd wince because of being invited to dine "inappropriately" and being compelled to agree to it lest you hurt the feelings of the one who invited you. Apart from that, it would tickle you because this invitation was extraordinary, and you, the invitee, would go along, always feeling inside that you were being watched.

Under the great banyan tree, Sudarmo, Sulastri, Lurni dan Ribowo sat on low bamboo benches, closely watching every movement of the noodle seller, who was expertly sautéing red onions in a black iron pan. They saw the seller and his assistant moving about in complete mystery under the yellow light of their kerosene lamp. Other people were sitting in the dimness, and over their heads were the deep-dark leaves of the banyan treen like a great umbrella, a frightening and gloomy atmosphere, like a haunt of demons and vampire-ghosts. Sulastri looked upward and felt the saw-edged shadows showed a person's face in the starry light-blue heavens. They almost couldn't see the other people's faces, but heard their voices, full and loud, and all the more clearly for being invisible in the darkness.

"It's nice here, all right, but my thigh itches," whispered Lurni as she stood up and searched on the mat covering the bench, then sat down again. Then she whispered again, "Insects, Lastri. Don't you feel anything?"

This surprised Sulastri, for all this time she had been silently watching the noodle vendor, who tasted his work and, with a nod of his head, apportioned the noodles into each bowl. Two plates were on the tray and the thickly steaming noodles made everyone's mouths water. The vendor's assistant brought the food over.

"For us?" asked Sudarmo and he put down his cigarette to take over the bowls. But the assistant was gone. Ribowo laughed, and Sulastri felt that Sudarmo must have gone red right to both his ears, for those noodles had been for someone else. You breathed in the aroma, you watched as the assistant passed back and forth several times with plates brimming with food and you felt irked at having to wait so long, while others had started eating. Sudarmo went up to the vendor and said rather peevishly, "Sir, could you make it quick in helping us, and with *uritan*?"

The noodle cook nodded and, taking a handful of yellow noodles from the load on his shoulder pole, stirred them into the broth, and then moved them into the bowls. He had sat there for hours, mincing spring onions, stir-frying shallots, and hour after hour serving the hawker who was under him. He appeared to be nailed to his low footstool and unable to do anything other than silently nodding his head, cooking, and giving change. But the customer who valued him as the best noodle cook didn't in the slightest regret having to wait half an hour or even longer. You went there to eat noodles, period. And for half an hour you dove into your own thoughts or reflected on other things.

Finally, the assistant placed the plates before Sudarmo and Ribowo and handed them spoons.

"Give us chillies and pickles," said Sudarmo, as he dipped his spoon into the hot noodles. It was as if he were seriously explaining some very important issue.

"That way, bacilli germs drop dead." He moved his spoon about, collected a few noodles and put them into his mouth, but all of a sudden, he made a slurping sound. This may have been because his tongue got scalded, because he said in a strange voice, as if his tongue were folded, "Really delicious!"

Sulastri and Lurni laughed, first because they were happy to see Sudarmo punished for his greediness. Ribowo moved his bowl over to Lurni and he went off for a moment. Lurni passed the bowl on to Sulastri, and she herself waited for the assistant to come back. Sulastri ate with the sense that there was something else mixed into the noodles, for she had noticed the rag that was being used to wipe the dishes. The rag looked awful, nor was there any color to it, making Sulastri suspect that it had been used for several days without being cleaned. Nonetheless, this event was a sensory delight, and Lurni, now beginning to eat, added, "He truly ought to be treasured. He's renowned."

"Who?" asked dimwitted Sulastri.

"The noodle man, of course. Did you think I meant Ki Hadjar? Oh, this fellow is more renowned than him! And he's even more popular among young people," Sudarmo scoffed. Lurni retorted sharply, "Don't talk like that, a noodle man and Ki Hadjar.... That's a sin and you'll be punished for it." Then she turned to her husband, "And you? Aren't you eating this?"

"I don't like noodles," Ribowo said.

Sulastri burst out laughing. So it wasn't out of respect for his wife that he told his wife to eat before him.

"He doesn't like eating food that's delicious. One time we visited my cousin, who had prepared beefsteak, a specialty of his, but my husband wouldn't even look at it. After eating, I asked him why he left the food untouched, he was surprised and apologized, saying that he didn't like eating raw meat."

Ribowo was sitting bent over next to Sudarmo and he stretched out when someone brought a plate to him.

"What's that, hey?" Sudarmo looked at it and chuckled.

"My God, bean curd, when the noodles here are so famous for their taste," he said, a bit taken aback.

Lurni felt a little hurt, but Ribowo calmly and quietly ate the bean curd, as if this was normal for him and then said, "I don't know, but I am not keen about these foods. I like *tempe* fried in beef fat, saté also, but noodles, no, to say nothing about it's being Chinese food."

Here he stopped, because Ribowo was educated in Islamic school and furthermore the son of a *naib*, an important mosque official, so from when he was little, he had already tasted something of Arab culture in the form of goat meat, beef fat, and all sorts of other Arab food. During his youth, he faithfully prayed daily, fasted, and now, in an age that ignores religion, he fasted every Ramadan in accordance with the obligations of a Muslim, even if he no longer cited the Quran when he spoke.

Sudarmo asked for another portion and greedily finished the fatty broth, while Lurni and Sulastri wondered who that bunch of other people were who only made themselves visible by the movements of their cigarettes. Sudarmo praised the noodles again and again, and after they finished eating, they went home. It was in an air of happiness they walked through, the streets only dimly lit. One or two other people passed by. The dark calm of the entire city seemed strange. Everything was so quiet in the streets that their own voices sounded loud, so they spoke in low voices, almost whispering, so as not to disturb the silence everywhere around them. They soon reached home and blinked at the bright lights; and because they were used to these lights, they felt they had come back to their very own world.

They stayed chatting and listening to the neighbors on both sides talking also. And when Lurni and Ribowo left, Sulastri and Sudarmo sat outside to watch the stars gleaming through the leaves of the papaya tree. Now there was silence everywhere, occasionally broken by the bamboo *tik-tak-tik-toc* of the noddle peddlers or the shouts of the cake sellers, because the distinctiveness of the Yogya streets wasn't the multitudes of people passing back and forth but the tireless vendors peddling their wares right until morning.

It was something new for Sulastri to still be able to buy food at two o'clock in the morning. In her own region, food vendors were fast asleep at twelve midnight. There, at night, the streets were not alive as here. These were the invigorating forms of life in Yogya and easily expressed poetically, but Sulastri still also wanted a fresh atmosphere from the friends around her. Yogya was too narrow-minded to give those who were not civil servants a cozy, home-like feeling. Speech always revolved around "That wife, you know, she has to ask for a divorce" or "He can't make friends with anyone at all, not even with his own children. A strange person."

Or people went on about some fashionable woman's party: "The governor was there too, and the floral wreaths were made from real flowers. And the orchids had been ordered specially from a Dutchman's garden." The speaker would lift up her hands and look upward. "Oh, just wonderful, they had to have spent hundreds of rupiah just for the decorations alone."

The men even paid attention and calmed the quarrels that sometimes broke out between the two women. At such times, Lurni felt like a fish in a pond, even though she gave courses to Marhaen women and taught them that upper-class women were parasites.

The tidings about unpleasant issues in the city came to Windarti from someone's lips and via someone else to Lurni, so that all the events that roiled the skies were sure to be known to everyone. In such a small city, people who spoke Dutch all knew each other, and, just for something to say casually, people could precisely report the color of the kebaya some lady wore on this day and on the next. More and more, Sulastri stayed quiet and kept to herself when there was a gathering. They whispered about her, "She yearns to write poetry, so she floats in the clouds. I don't understand such minds, but according to what her sister Marti says, she often writes poems. And we believe Marti. She's able to judge her, isn't she?"

But Lurni shrugged with the certainty that it was all just pretense and took her revenge again and again by answering vaguely whenever Sulastri asked her something, because certainly, you could be very distracted over the problems of the women's movement. And Conscious Women, Lurni's own association, had many difficulties indeed. This association had only a handful of members, about twenty. Sometimes the course leader overslept and arrived when everyone was at the point of going home. Sulastri watched Lurni go stalwartly to her association building and later come back, books in hand, erect in posture, to Sulastri and Sudarmo's home, chat for a moment or two, check the flowerpot filled with ferns, which Sulastri had borrowed from her, and ensure their roots had been watered.

"Not too much water or they'll die." She was disappointed that Sulastri wasn't all that attentive to her plants. One day, Lurni asked for a pair of scissors. She cut them down and left black twigs in the pot and, after one week, green whorls and curls came out of the soil, promising the beauty of new fronds.

Sudarmo loved his younger sister, who was exactly like her mother. From when they were little, they were taught together by their uncle, because their father had another wife and their mother of course had to go back to her older brother. So the bond between older brother and younger sister became all the more abiding over the years that followed. With her social activism, Lurni increased her brother's pride as a family member, and his greatest delight was when people showered Lurni with praise and respect. Sudarmo wished that Sulastri was more like Lurni, but Sulastri seemed to be increasingly secluding herself and retreating from what Sudarmo wanted, so as to find her own path in life out of the sight of people.

Sudarmo's journal *The People's Livelihood* came out with a cover of light green and contents consisting of his own writings, though people thought him unable to wield a pen.

"People said that I could barely fill one page. I've proven to them that I can fill twenty full columns." He spoke with sardonic resolution on his lips.

And now this journal existed, for which Sudarmo had labored fiercely for several days. Sulastri proudly read his articles, stroked the cover, and observed her husband with total attention. He was passionately reading out a part to her in which he attacked the movement of *serimpi* dancers and the singing as reactionary. Then he noted the cover with satisfaction where his name as chief editor—*hopredaktur*— was grandly displayed. He winked at her to gauge its effect and sighed with pleasure.

Suddenly, slapping the table, he patted Sulastri on the shoulder and giggled like a teenager. Sulastri thought he was just being silly, but joined in the laughter, infected by his overflowing happiness. She helped him until late into the night by writing addresses and sticking on the ribbons. Everything hung on that journal. If a lot of subscriptions came in, they would be helped. They drew up a list of their friends and acquaintances as well as other prominent people. A week later, Sudarmo carried a bundle of his journals to the post office while Sulastri carefully put the remaining copies on a rack at their home. Now came the days of waiting patiently for money orders to arrive. Their hopes and expectations made them forget reality and they saw themselves as owners of a big printing house. Waiting for the postman was more suspense-filled than when they were still engaged, and it was Sulastri's duty to check the mailbox. On the wall next to the front door all this while was hung a large board on which was written in dark red artistic letters:

The People's Livelihood—Editing and Administration

The base of the nameboard was silver, and Sudarmo could fittingly stand in front of it for a few minutes with praise in his heart. Then he'd walk up and down the street, while glimpsing through the rose bushes to get a sense of how someone passing by would see the beauty of the board. Then he got Sulastri to join in the act, which made her rather doubtful, but her husband made an angry face so she hurried out to the street.

When the money orders first arrived, they made plans to enlarge the operation. It could even grow into a daily newspaper. As luck would have it, only friends signed up for subscriptions of *The People's Livelihood,* and the money that came in amounted to only seventeen rupiah and fifty cents. The result was that, despite their wishes, issue number two couldn't come out, even though the copy was ready for the printers.

At this time, Marti wrote a letter to Sulastri saying that there was a place for a volunteer at her husband's office and would Sudarmo want it? She could go to Batavia to take a look first, and then they could see if there was any work for Sulastri herself. For the time being, Sulastri could stay with Marti. In short, Marti still thought of her sister as in the old days and she would try to give her the courage to lead a new life. Marti had heard from someone that Sulastri had lately been isolating herself. So, because of that, and because of Sulastri's letters so filled with complaints and laments, Marti felt obliged to pay attention to Sulastri's fortunes.

Office work wasn't to Sudarmo's liking. At first, he refused it and scolded Sulastri, saying it was too late for him to become a government employee. It wasn't appropriate for someone thirty years old to begin by becoming a clerk and suffering the jibes of his friends. Sulastri stayed quiet and turned away, but in this short interlude in their daily conversations, she made Sudarmo realize that he could not keep on living this way. In the end, Sudarmo went because he felt a responsibility for his wife, who had surrendered her whole existence to him. Lurni gave him travel money, and Sulastri's gaze followed him until he was gone from view at the street corner.

The first letter expressed his unease at working in an office; and in the second, he said that he was going to come back very soon. But before a third letter—or he himself—arrived, Sulastri had stopped paying rent on the house and ordered the furniture be moved to Lurni's place. She wrote that she was coming to Batavia on the following day and that he should accept this job, even if only temporarily.

When Sudarmo received this letter, he was on the verge of returning to Yogya. At a time when final decisions needed to be made, Sulastri showed that she had become someone different from whom she had been. She was released from her death-like feelings and she now saw clearly the faces she knew, the land where she was born and voices that spoke a language she understood. If she had just waited two days, or if she hadn't abruptly become self-aware, their lives might have gone in another direction.

Now Sulastri went with Rustini to Batavia and Sudarmo would meet them, infuriated perhaps, and perhaps also deep inside happy to see them again. But she didn't bother her head about this. She only thought of what was pleasing and promised herself to be smarter and enter the future with a grip on her intuition. She observed Rustini, sitting quietly on her lap, then looked out at the brown land and the green stands of trees rushing into view, until she saw nothing beyond the green hillocks and brown lines and she took a breath and felt very light inside.

A policeman helped her along the way, exactly like that soldier before, and she had to smile at the irony of the coincidence, that a person who was tasked with maintaining power helped her with such minutiae.

A woman, still young but faded, sat opposite her. She wore a head covering and sat hunched over and fearful, all of which signaled that she was a village woman in an environment that was foreign to her. She observed Rustini with a gentle but timid smile. When Sulastri asked where she was going, she answered hesitantly, not wanting to be straightforward: "To South Sumatra, Lampung," and then was silent, possibly afraid of a slip of the tongue. Sulastri glanced at her several times and, putting Rustini in her lap, they chatted off and on, until the woman had to change trains. She nodded shyly, fixed her head covering, and went off, her body hunched over.

"She is like me, still young. I really have to be grateful I don't suffer as she does." And with a sudden rush of joy, she kissed Rustini so hard that the child was surprised and was about to cry. But Sulastri calmed her by giving her a cake. When the train arrived at Batavia's Gambir Station, Sudarmo was already there with trembling knees, in shock and with lips tightly pressed together in anger.

When Sulastri saw him, she greatly regretted having acted so quickly and assertively in following her husband, and when she stood in front of him, she said softly, "I've come. That's my luggage."

Sudarmo's face was pale and cruel. He frowned when a policeman politely saluted them and he said curtly, 'I don't know what I'm going to do with you, but you disgust me. You're not honest."

Then he walked on ahead without a look at his wife and child. Little Rustini appeared happy to see her father again. She was like a little imp with her dress and cap of wool, very cute, but her father only indifferently touched her cheek with his fingers. They didn't speak in the taxi, and they turned away from each other. Only the little girl laughed squeakily and clapped her hands from happiness. The taxi stopped in front of Marti's house, a building with a loft and a pavilion next to it, on a good street where there were similar two-story houses.

Marti, now grown plumper, was very talkative and welcoming. She ran to greet them and laughingly took the child from Sulastri. "Oh my, so sweet! Like a dove with such big eyes!" and then looking at Rustini more closely, said amiably as she held the child away from herself, "She doesn't resemble you. She's really and truly beautiful."

Marti's two children drew near them, and the older one, Kemal, greeted his aunt rather shyly. Then he said to his mother as he looked at Rustini for some time, "Her eyes are dancing about, Ibu."

This boy was smart and his face showed it, with his short round nose and his big handsome eyes. The second one, a girl with a *sawo*-brown complexion, was potbellied and resembled her father, though not exactly. Marti held the child by her shoulders and said to her sister, "Yes, very much like Bibi Sulastri, right? Just as stubborn."

Sulastri laughed at the odd tone of voice used by Marti and she caressed the girl, who at first didn't want that, but then abruptly snuggled up tightly to her aunt.

"It's hard for me to believe you've had a child. Yes, yes," said her sizable brother-in-law Kartonegoro, who came languidly out of his study. Eyes big and round, a round face, a round body and a round head as well, with short curls; moreover, the demeanor of a respected and rather self-controlled person, one not quick to make friends, languid and yet always alert: this was how Sulastri saw her twenty-nine-year-old brother-in-law. His sharp intelligence always raised a wall between him and his friends. He affably nodded at Sulastri and asked, "And... how are things with you?" He sat down and obliquely observed Sudarmo, who had quietly taken a chair and was sitting down on it.

Kartonegoro lit a cigarette in his characteristically languorous manner, shook the burning match stick and placed it carefully in an ashtray. Taking a spot of tobacco from his lip and puffing smoke with a feigned nonchalance, he smiled at his wife's sister, who said nothing more or less than, "Oh, as you can see, quite well."

"And your husband is beginning to feel at home. Well, it will be nicer for you to be here too."

Sulastri shrugged and helped Marti who was just then busy with the tea and cups. Then they talked about whatever was most important to them at that time, about working in offices, about what Sulastri had done in Yogya, and about families. But that was where the conversation stopped. The men moved to the study, while Marti tried hard to calm Sulastri and always tried to treat her like her little sister of earlier times. Influenced by past memories, Marti supposed after their conversation that Sulastri still saw her as her older sister. Marti had no idea that after Sulastri's own life had been burdened by her sense of responsibility, she no longer considered older people smarter than her.

At night, when Rustini had gone to sleep and the Kartonegoro family had locked the main door, a little light brightened the pavilion. The plant-filled front veranda was dark. There Sudarmo and Sulastri sat, silent and miserable. In their room Sudarmo barely glanced at his wife. Now in the darkness it was still the same, as if they sat together as strangers, each hating the other's bodies. For Sudarmo, a heart oppressed by worry. For Sulastri, melancholy and an impulse to rid herself of that feeling by breaking out sobbing. The street was pitch black, deserted in the drizzling rain which added to the sadness. The windows of this big house did not impart a friendly impression, nor did the mute allamandas, looking sullen but barely visible on their soaked and drooping stems. Only the little cananagas with their dark colors spread their astringent fragrance, deepening the mournful atmosphere. Sulastri was the first to end their silence.

"And you weren't happy to see us return, after that long week?" There was a trace of intimacy in her voice. Sudarmo said nothing.

Then, responding to a sudden desire, Sulastri moved over to him, slipped between his arms and rested her head against his chest. The arms that resisted her, she wrapped around her body. But her husband seemed to have gone cold, so stiff and tense was he. Sulastri put all the blame on him, charged him with a hurtful and uncaring attitude, and finally she released her deep resentment in tears and weeping.

"Oh God!" Sudarmo exclaimed, "Still so emotional after all your foolishness caused this situation. You wanted this clerk's life so much! Well, you've got it now. Be happy that everything has gone your way."

He shoved his wife away from him, stood up and then lay down on the bed, listening apathetically to the slow fall of the raindrops. Sulastri went in, stood there, hesitant in the doorway. Then she closed the door and gently approached her husband. She took his face in both hands and begged with a look that sought pity to regain his love, which had frozen in his heart.

At first, he had no desire to respond, then warming, he pulled her to his body, so that he felt the fear-filled throbbing of her heart beating against his own and he put all regrets out of his mind, and remembered that she was here, the only person who had lightened the burdens of his life. Outside, the rain still fell softly on the roof tiles and onto the plants and sang a kind of hissing song, but in the room there was the heat of a hot night in Batavia.

"Dar, the light is disturbing."

"Oh," he replied, "all the doors are shut tight."

14

Sulastri told Marti that she wanted a home of her own.

"No," Marti said, "You don't have enough money live in a separate house. Don't misunderstand our good intentions."

"But I'm not happy like this. You know we're used to living independently."

"We're doing all we can to keep you from difficulties. But you don't have any sense of gratitude if you don't want to stay with us. What kind of a house would you rent with such a small salary as your husband has? On the other hand, if we move out to another place, you'll get the pavilion for yourselves."

Sulastri said nothing. She knew that Marti would still act as her protector. That would be good for the time being, but the feeling of pressure, that she always had to be helped, wouldn't go away. This was eating a beggar's meal, and the situation would undeniably give rise to a feeling of great indebtedness. Before they moved to a bigger place, even living by the side of the road would be preferable. Marti was annoyed at Sulastri and called her an ingrate because of Sulastri's having said it wasn't always suitable to live together. With the color drained from her face, Sulastri listened to that criticism and didn't say a word in reply, but went to her room in the pavilion and locked herself in there to calm down her sudden anger.

Marti had been on edge of late. She felt sick to her stomach, a condition often arising in women having a nervous breakdown, for Kartonegoro was paying attention to a young member of Conscious Women. If there was a meeting, this particular member would usually come first. Kartonegoro would arrive and sit with her, speaking with great energy and feeling. He would joke and direct his gaze at her lovely face and shapely neck which ended in a pretty and softly-formed chest.

"Just hit those bourgeois women hard, with hot and sharp words, Zus!" Kartonegoro would say with a laugh and then winking, whisper, "I'll be listening upstairs."

The young woman answered flirtatiously, well-aware of her obvious beauty. When Marti came in, her husband would hurry upstairs, a stack of papers in hand, and would not appear again. Sulastri brought him croquettes and salad upstairs, Marti's repast for the attendees, because her view was that with a selamatan and tasty food, she could attract new members, even though she said that those selamatans were merely casual affairs. "Lectures are the most important things," she explained. But more time was used in preparing the selamatans and no new members registered themselves.

After these meetings, a squabble would break out over trifling matters, and usually the issues involved the purchase of this or that item that Marti considered unnecessary, or something about one of their children, or the lack of money at month's end, or other things. But their voices sounded filled with anger and you could hear Kartonegoro say, "And why can't I send money to my mother, which is what I want to do?"

Marti, shrill and angry, would retort, "Of course you can, but she doesn't need it as much as others do!"

"Quiet, you, or I'll hit you. The neighbors hear us, you know!"

Then Marti would say, even more sharply, "Who cares about the neighbors! You just need me to be your slave. Go ahead and hit me if you dare!"

A momentary silence would ensue, and then the sound of things knocking together, sobbing and weeping by Marti, and finally Kartonegoro's soothing voice and then calm. Occasionally Marti would be heard again, now with a I'm-going-back-home-to-my-family tone. After quarreling like that, Marti would go about with reddened eyes, but smiling again, as if nothing had happened. Sometimes girls would visit and Marti would be hospitable and Kartonegoro would be in a happy mood, but once the visitors had gone, angry voices again sounded from the study. Sulastri thought her sister foolish for having given away the secrets of their marriage with all the shouting. Of course, you feel insecurity, but it was frustrating when the servants tip-toed in and out of the rooms, because of the angry voices.

Marti's uncontrollable nerves and Kartonegoro's silent treatment as a way of hurting her frequently raised little quarrels to great heights, so that for people who observed them, it seemed that they were in a living hell. Marti's feminine instincts were finely honed and read extreme meaning into insignificant incidents, such as her husband's being late coming home or when he returned at night from working overtime at the office.

Sudarmo and Sulastri felt squeezed in a difficult situation and they often looked at each other with shocked expressions, but they had become used to pretending not to hear the bickering.

After they moved in, the pavilion became a place of refuge for Kartonegoro on dispute-filled days. There he chatted and smoked or expressed his complaints to his childhood friend Sudarmo. And Sudarmo could only undermine Marti's position and of course justify that of Kartonegoro.

Strife in the home grew worse, for Marti's youngest sibling came to live with her as well. This boy, born nine years after the youngest daughter, had been indulged in by all members of the family, partly because he appeared to be somewhat backward. Undeniably, Kartonegoro was worried about the boy's stupidity and foolishness. Kartonegoro often said, "It looks like his parents had run out of steam when this child grew inside his mother's womb. I don't understand why he has never been promoted in school, even though we've tried our best to have a teacher give him extra lessons."

Didi called his brother-in-law "Father," because he had been taken in as their child, but being addressed like that made Kartonegoro vaguely uneasy, which later became clear when he said sharply, "Make him learn how to speak good Dutch, otherwise our own son Kemal won't be able to get into a good school."

This really hurt Marti. She said something in reply and a clash flared up again. Not only this, if one of Marti's family members came to see her, she gave a little travel money and apologized, "This month I have to spend a lot of money on Mas Kartonegoro's motorcycle and also subsidize my woman's association because its cash is almost gone."

And when their relative had left, Marti would say to Sulastri, "I feel sorry for her. She went to so much trouble to bring us a gift, but I really have no more money," and once again began to apologize.

Marti's and Sulastri's older brother, who from time to time came in the morning, told Sulastri, "Actually, I'm not all that happy coming here, because I suspect Marti's husband isn't pleased with our visits."

The feeling of difference in circumstances unintentionally insinuated itself, but Kartonegoro felt he was able to connect with others affably enough, to say nothing of his being a member of the Marhaen Party. When Marti's father came, Kartonegoro greeted him brusquely.

"Oh, Bapak," he said and then, smiling ambiguously, went into his study and didn't come out again. But the older man wasn't hurt by this and was very proud of his son-in-law, who was descended from the high aristocracy and known for the brilliance of his mind. Marti respected her father who ascribed to Kartonegoro extraordinary inner strength, but Kartonegoro just shrugged because he didn't believe it.

Not long after they married, Kartonegoro bought a male pigeon, which in fact turned out to be female. This pet bird laid eggs and Marti's father said, "This is a miraculous bird. Eat its eggs and you will gain extreme good fortune!"

Marti ate the eggs, one by one, nine in all, from the sweetheart bird. But Kartonegoro who came to know of this afterwards, got angry and shouted, "That bird isn't some chicken raised for its eggs. Stop doing this, or else...." At this point, his voice failed him and he grew pale from his anger, and Marti burst into tears. But at the time, they were newlyweds, so this squabble soon ended. Marti even asked for advice from her father when they were moving house and later whether there were ghosts in the new house. And her father drove away those spirits with incense or he had a tree planted or buried a charm as a protective antidote. In short, Marti held to the old ways and this ignited Kartonegoro's anger. It was all the more so when her mother-in-law influenced her as well, because she, too, believed Marti's father was very intelligent, and this complicated problem increased the tension between husband and wife.

Marti told her sister, "I think Mas Karto doesn't want to see Bapak under the current circumstances. But, Bapak says, the time will come when he treats him differently. Once he turns thirty, he will know that there is a supernatural power that he can't understand now with his brain. Mas Dar will also see things differently and not ignore Bapak." Sulastri stiffened. She didn't like people criticizing Sudarmo.

"I think your husband is rude," Marti went on, "when he doesn't want to come out of his room, because he doesn't want to see Bapak together with Mother and Auntie Ipah. Bapak won't forgive him."

Sulastri bit her tongue and said nothing. Marti, who felt she was actually being encouraged, said scornfully: "If Bapak were the *wedana*, certainly...!"

"For sure there'd be no Sulastri and I wouldn't have married Sudarmo," her younger sister interrupted her hotly. "Mas Dar is respectful enough. He has apologized to Bapak, but that's not enough for Bapak. What's more, after Bapak married Ratna, he lost the respect of his son-in-law. And you yourself, where are you now, really, with your principles on monogamy?"

Marti got angry, and grew pale, her lips crinkled. "You bitch, you! You dare to speak like that about Bapak? His *kualat* will fall upon you and you'll regret it!"

Her legs trembled and she held on to the edge of the table with all her strength. But Sulastri just said calmly, "Let the kualat fall on me."

"What?" Marti stepped forward, here hands clenched in fists and her eyes bulging. "I have a lot more to be upset about from you. You're ungrateful and disgusting!" Marti had become incoherent.

Sulastri didn't care and spoke clearly and slowly, as if none of this mattered, "I don't want to be intimidated by oaths and stories about kualat. My fate is in my own hands and I don't give a damn about other things."

"You dare to... be so...? You dare? You dare?" Marti screamed but Sulastri had left her and locked herself in. Her older sister followed after her, still shouting, and rattled the doorknob and pounded on the door, but Sulastri covered her ears and felt ashamed. Why did she continue this quarrel so violently? On the other side of the door, the angry voice was implacable, booming on in her ears. Her sister's angry words stayed with her. They pierced her heart and insulted her.

On top of that, Sudarmo often complained about the pain in his back from all the sitting in the office chair, and he blamed her for having put her husband in an intolerable situation as a clerk. Feeling guilty, Sulastri massaged her husband's aching body and tried hard to relieve his pain, but Sudarmo kept brooding over little things. Contentions piled up inside Sulastri until in despair she tried to empty her mind by reading a novel or by recording whatever restraints she was feeling at the time.

Marti entered the room and asked to see the book. "Always novels," she said sarcastically. "Read better things, something useful for our women's movement. Or write an article for our journal." And when she noticed the notebook on the dresser, she headed over to it, but Sulastri was quicker and grabbed it first and put it away jokingly. So then Marti felt insulted and said dejectedly, "Listen, I can appreciate your poems too. Let me take a look." Then, afraid of Marti making fun of her literary aspirations, Sulastri went quiet.

"So sentimental," Marti said caustically. "Noting down personal problems. As if that were useful for the outside world. It's not useful to anyone at all."

"It's useful to me," Sulastri retorted. "Why does everybody have to be like you? Are you happy if there's a Marti the Second by your side? Or do you only want me to be your soldier, only enough to fill the ranks for you?"

Marti was fuming, but although she felt stabbed to the heart, this time she said nothing. She became friendly, and in the end talked about everyday things and invited Sulastri to go to the auction on the following day. While she was still a girl, Marti could spend money like nothing else mattered. Now she was proud of herself for buying things more cheaply than other people and in this way, she was competing with Sudarmo, who was animated by the same compulsion. Sulastri laughed at Marti's gestures, which made her feel smarter and more competent, and this helped her to ingeniously listen in calm to Marti's jibes. And this made Marti furious.

Preparations for the Indonesian Women's Congress were underway. Marti was busy, running here and there, reviewing the short notes made by Kartonegoro, skimming through books, writing on several sheets of paper, then tearing them up, and being unable to finish her lecture. To work calmly she brought a pile of books to the village where her father lived, but after two days she came home again because she couldn't stand living there. Kartonegoro examined the sheets of paper she had written and said, "Get rid of the analogy of bourgeois women with tapeworms, otherwise we'll have trouble getting together with our friends. And that will create difficulties for us, too, now, as we still need them."

In the meantime, people were meeting at Marti's home. That night, after it was over, she proudly said, "They elected me chairman. They're all on my side and they accepted all my motions. What's more, the representative from the Priangan Women is my cousin and another one is my friend—"

"Wow, you're in luck," Kartonegoro cut in, "That way it will become a family get-together." Everyone laughed.

"I drove that pro-polygamy Saridah crazy. She said again and again, 'How does that verse go? I memorized it before, but I've forgotten it now.' I replied, 'Things as good as that are never forgotten, comrade'."

"Well, you've hit them all good, so, thumbs up to you," Kartonegoro joked, and he did just that. Marti blushed for joy.

But the congress became chaotic. Marti tangled with Saridah and because of that, according to Marti, the general meeting made fun of the Conscious Women group. When Marti went home after the meeting was over, she ardently related all that had happened, and when they asked what Saridah had actually said, she replied, "She said, 'Narrow, petty-minded people who cannot appreciate good things and try to create divisions.' Well, when she said that, it was of course Conscious Women whom she meant."

Kartonegoro didn't believe it. "Was it really you all who were accused?"

Marti held to her account, but Kartonegoro knew his wife and didn't want to pursue the issue.

The Women's Congress meeting concluded safely, but there was a split between the Conscious Women and other women's associations. The Conscious Women left the Indonesian Women's Congress and thereby lost influence.

Two, three months passed and Sudarmo now could be said to know his job, but he kept grumbling and going on about starting another school.

"Let me look for work here," said Sulastri. "So our lives can become more stable."

She looked for work, but found all doors tightly shut. During that period, Sutrisno often visited them. He was a student at the Law Faculty. He was depressed at being expelled from the student's association.

"How could I stay dishonestly silent?" he said to Sudarmo. "The police pressured me, appealing to my moral feelings, and I told them who the author of that article was."

"But why were you so foolish as to tell them that? There's such a thing as solidarity." Sudarmo looked hard at his friend. Sutrisno, with his constant shifting about and restless hands, now sat tense and upright. "That was the reason," he replied. "They had appointed me to be editor, on paper only, not to work. I'm not someone who can lie or go to the police either. I feel like I'm falling to pieces. Now you know it as well, Mas Dar. Sometimes I want to end this all by killing myself."

His voice was hoarse and his eyes were wet because he felt deeply moved. And he went on in the same tone of voice that showed his ardor. He said he couldn't sleep that night and was still awake at three o'clock. He felt disgust toward everyone.

Sulastri saw the thin face of the youth, where his lively eyes sometimes blazed, then softened again and weakened into a dim, dreamy look. She thought, "How overflowing his feelings are, and his nerves are so very taut. But he's a good young man, friendly, simple and refined."

She was pleased with Sutrisno, this young man of twenty-five, and offered her feelings of honest sympathy to him, who probably would likely drown in his psychological contradictions. His wife, Herwati, nine years older than he, loved him from the depth of her heart and behaved as a mother toward him, but would sometimes annoy him, because she wasn't clever and paid no attention to things beyond the environment of the home. Sutrisno would sometimes observe Sulastri as she filled his and Sudarmo's cups and inconspicuously sat down with them. Sutrisno was impressed at how Sulastri was different from other women of her age, different also from Marti, calm, simple, but with a self-awareness which rejected all inappropriate cordiality. Sutrisno thanked her with a smile for the tea she poured, and Sulastri reciprocated because she was grateful for the attention of a young man. When they were still girls, it was Marti who'd catch the eyes of everyone, and only occasionally did people notice Sulastri. Sulastri's only role was to be Marti's little sister; everybody was attracted to Marti's intelligence and liveliness and ability to give the right answers to whatever others were saying. But now Marti had grown plump and just wore comfortable clothes, not caring for the cut of her kebaya. She no longer looked the vivacious girl of before. And Sulastri herself—

A question from Sutrisno brought an end to her ruminations.

"And, what book interests Zus the most?"

Sulastri thought for a moment, "All books. Just give me any one of yours, but not those by Jo van Ammers Küller or of Querido. Those are Marti's favorites."

"Have you read Nico van Suchtelen? His *Demonen* is really excellent. A clear analysis of a human being's soul. Shall I bring it sometime?"

Sulastri nodded to please Sutrisno, but said, "Actually, I am bored with Dutch literature. I mean, it's not something I need now. There's not a lot that impresses me from that country. Everything's slow and heavy and massive and tiresome. It's different with Multatuli, of course. He has ideals he has to express."

"And *Camera Obscura*?" Sutrisno turned away. Sulastri noticed his messy and overly long hair and then saw Sudarmo, a momentary strange light in his face and who was smiling, as if his wife were still a child.

"No, even though in that book, he describes with clarity the true characteristics of a Dutchman. No, now I prefer not to read Dutch literature. I really am happier reading international literary works." She said that with a frown, as if issuing a challenge.

Sudarmo diverted that conversation by touching on Sutrisno's despondency, "I prefer to read Freud over van Suchtelen's *Demonen*. If you want to perfectly know the devil in someone's soul, read as well Marx and Fritz Künkel. It's not lust that tempts and seduces one's heart, but also the stomach that starves and thirsts for praise. This is to say nothing of the desire to dominate others, often concealed behind grandiose ideals and elaborate words. If Mas Tris, for example, had read Künkel's essay "Character formation through self-education," you would obtain a clear vision of what drives people's actions. By this we arrive at self-criticism. This has helped me, because without it, I might not be able to shoulder the hardships in this life of mine. I'm not living here. It's like I'm dead. Only my wife knows joy."

Sudarmo's voice was sour and shriveled, while he stared in front of him as though lifeless. Sutrisno began to console him, and Sulastri thought that if she had the opportunity to correct her faults, he wouldn't treat her as he did.

And the opportunity came. Sudarmo devised a plan to move to Bogor to establish a school for her. One afternoon, he went there and on the next day looked for a house and a carpenter to make simple school benches; he made a budget for the costs to be incurred. Marti immediately went into a rage again, and every day was filled with saddening hidden conflicts because she ridiculed their plans and thought it foolish if people wanted to take on the uncertainties of the future.

"Right, right!" said Marti, who really did mean well, but in the wrong way, in wanting to hold her younger sister in her power. "Sudarmo hasn't the talent to lead people. My prediction is that the school is going to hit the rocks."

And Sulastri's father said, "People look everywhere for the food to fill their bellies, while you're so foolish as to only look for dreams while your belly is rumbling? Don't follow your husband, he's too spoiled."

But with all that talk, she actually succeeded in obtaining the opposite of what she intended. Sudarmo had found a house in Bogor that was both big and cheap, and was preparing for their move. At this time, he noticed a plainclothesman always shadowing him, from the office to home and from home to the office. He spoke about this to Kartonegoro and, to make sure, one night they went out by motorcycle and some man tailed them in his car. When they returned, another man was waiting unobtrusively next to the streetlight in front of their house. Kartonegoro became flustered and thought that those people were tailing him because he had been an important figure in the Marhaen Party, and it was easy to understand his tense attitude. And Kartonegoro often worried about being let go, when in fact he previously had intended to leave government service and open a law firm in Kalimantan. At the time, he often went about unkempt in his sarong and peci, buying peanuts at the roadside and gesturing in imitation of "Marhaen" people. It was a new day now and because of that he was frightened. The conclusion of such secret movements came when Sudarmo was called to the police station and received the proof that his ban on teaching had been withdrawn.

Now the road ahead appeared to be quite smooth and Sulastri joyfully made a list of the things she would need for the household. One day, after shopping in the market and returning home with pots and pans and other such articles, Marti watched her apathetically, but didn't say much. Sudarmo began a month of going back and forth between Bogor and Batavia because he desperately needed his salary. Then, as soon as there were sufficient students enrolled, he was going to resign as a civil servant and get back to teaching, children early in the morning and adults at night. Their calculations were intense. They hadn't the slightest idea that an event would send all of that scattering to the four winds. At the time they weren't afraid of anything, and when a taxi brought Sulastri, Sudarmo and their child to Bogor from Batavia, they thought they were facing a glorious tomorrow.

The Bogor house was situated on a hillside and was spacious; moreover, in the back, a kitchen and outbuildings had been built in a circle around an inner yard. The front veranda was supported by stone pillars and its floor was made of stone tiles. The high staircase went from a dirty yard to the veranda. The house belonged to an Arab, and the stone walls prevented anyone outside from looking in. From the front to the back, the land slowly slanted downward, so that man-sized pillars were needed to prop up the back of the building, and someone on the back veranda would have to descend an extremely steep staircase to reach the back yard.

The floor inside was made from bamboo slats. Furthermore, the secretive ambience was felt everywhere, because the back was dark, the well next to the stairs was also dark, and the back yard with its *jambu* trees and its walls weren't very friendly either. In short, people sensed that this house was haunted. But Sulastri was satisfied with it and she stretched out a thick blanket on the floor for when they went to sleep at night. Only Rustini would be sleeping as usual in her bed. Because they only had diminutive chairs for the future students, they sat on a mat. Only on the front veranda were there old rattan chairs borrowed from Sutrisno.

Sutrisno and his wife came one night, together with young Yusuf and his wife and Sutrisno's friend Muhammad, bringing with them fried bananas and peanuts. They snacked and joked, and Sudarmo and Sutrisno talked on and on. After they guests had left, Sudarmo said, "Now I'm breathing fresh air. Now we're going to have good times. Also, Sutrisno has the same ideals and dreams as we do. We'll build a library, come out with a newspaper—oh, Tri, there's so much work for us in the days to come."

They talked for a long time. Outside the cold wind whistled through the houses. Sometimes you could hear prayers being recited. And then it was silent, so dead quiet you could hear your heart beating inside you. Sudarmo hugged his wife and sighed in happiness, as though on that night he had found hope again. But there was something that bothered them again. When Sudarmo was in the office the next day, Marti came to Sulastri's house quite agitated and told her, "A secretary from the personnel department telephoned to tell Mas Karto that the PID had asked his boss about who had recommended Sudarmo to be accepted as a civil servant. Mas Karto has been thrown into a state of confusion. It means that he could be fired from his job. You know, don't you, Tri..."

And as Marti wept, it just so happened that Sudarmo came home then as well and related the same story.

"I don't know what to do," Marti said as Sulastri comforted and calmed her. Sudarmo just stayed quiet. Marti began again, "Mas Karto can't sleep. He doesn't want to eat, and just walks sadly back and forth in the house and won't go to the office tomorrow, he's so upset and confused. He's in a very bad way, because really this means getting the sack. Mas Dar had been stamped red and Mas Karto asked his superiors to find a place for him. And... and...." Marti burst into tears again, her body swaying and her handkerchief pressed against her eyes.

Then Sudarmo asked, "What is it you actually want, Marti?"

She didn't answer at first and then said firmly, "Ask that you be laid off, and right away. That's the only solution. I went to him just now and that was what he advised. What do you both think?" She daubed the tears in her eyes and stared at them, one by one.

"We don't have a single cent," Sudarmo replied. "You've made all this into a big mess. How are we going to eat?"

Marti was overjoyed that she now had an argument. "Naturally, we will help you during the first months. That's what we'll discuss further. Come to the house tomorrow and we'll take care of everything."

A feeling of love suddenly arose in him toward Marti, and Sudarmo agreed with her. When Marti had left, he said, "We owe a lot to them. I had to agree."

The next day, Sudarmo came back from Batavia with a long face. "We spoke together about it with Uncle Rachim. He said, 'You'll lose five hundred rupiah if your husband is let go, Marti, and Sudarmo only fifty. If you subsidize him with thirty, you'll still make out all right. Sudarmo has no money, he doesn't work, and so it's very fair, if you, Marti, send him and his wife at least thirty rupiah a month until their school begins to make money.' And Marti agreed to do this. Well, now I am dismissed. And now, my dear Lastri, steel yourself, for we are facing a very shabby future."

As it turned out, those words were truly spoken, because when Sulastri asked for money from Marti for household needs, her sister sent her five rupiah by letter in which she abused and vituperated Sulastri with very ugly words.

Two days after they moved, while Sudarmo was visiting Sutrisno, Sulastri's father came. He examined the building everywhere, all the rooms and the well. Then he told her, "Stay calm, I have driven the bogeys aways. The fate you must bear, Lastri, is your own. It'll be better for you to live impoverished now and live well later, rather than the other way around." With that, he sat down on the mat, but five minutes later he excused himself. "I can't sit on the floor because I'm sore all over. I'll just go now." Sulastri accompanied him for a little while to her cousin's home, and there her father said proudly, "My other son-in-law now has a very high position. He's a Bachelor-of-Law."

"And this one?" the cousin asked without meaning anything in particular.

"Oh, this one," her father said indifferently and with a slight shrug. "She's just a teacher." His attitude was humiliating, and Sulastri returned home feeling sad, as if someone had hit her. Up to now she had always felt a sense of respect toward her father. Now, she knew, everything was shattered, and she bit her lips in vexation.

She told Sudarmo about her visit, and he said, "That was a lie about his leg being sore. He was ashamed to see your poverty."

Actually, a week before this event, Sulastri had planned with Sudarmo to visit her father, but how could they, if all they had was two cents and there the only food in the house was a bit of uncooked rice and a sticky rice snack. Now that very hurtful letter came from Marti. This is how it read:

> *Sulastri,*
> *You both have always been a bother to us. Your husband is a wild man, ill-bred, someone who doesn't know how to show respect. Why hasn't he met Bapak? Bapak couldn't stay long in your house because of his rheumatism, and also because he couldn't bear seeing that you had no furniture there. It made him cry, he told me. He said that you said*

> *bad things about him and therefore you will not be happy in life. People like you, self-centered people, are real egotists and cannot respect a father. This is the last time I will be helping you. From now on, I won't be able to send you anything more. Money can't grow on my back. We have so many bills to pay.*

The rest of the letter was filled with insults. One would really have had to laugh. This was Marti with her dreams of justice. Sulastri tore up the letter and gave the paper money to Sudarmo. Then, driven by a need for solidarity, she showed him the torn fragments of the letter which he put together again. After he read it, his face got red. Sulastri felt overcome by misfortune, by an urge to tear up the money and spit on it, and she would have taken it all from Sudarmo's hand, but he forbade her to.

"People without money will always have to go through things like this," he said sadly. "We're never right and will always be blamed for everything. But no matter what, I don't want to be treated that way. Betrayed like that, even though I was better and nicer toward your father than Kartonegoro was. But it's appropriate, because in this matter your father has usually been indulged in and he wants me to crawl to him. I don't want to and would rather be destroyed by kualat than to lower myself like that. I've never done anything to him. If he only knew what Kartonegoro says about him. But even if he knew, he'd just smile and see it as a joke from his highborn son-in-law."

"I'm going to send the money back," said Sulastri, her lips quivering.

"No, we need it too much. No, Tri, we actually have a right to that money."

Sulastri looked at her husband, then burst out weeping, feeling pain gouge at her heart.

"Don't cry, Tri," said Sudarmo, trying to calm her. "I'm right beside you. Whatever sorrows will come, Tri dearest, you have to be able to shoulder them with fortitude."

He held her tightly in his arms and she leaned into him. Rustini came up to them with tiny steps, looked her bapak and ibu in wonderment and giggled with delight.

15

Sulastri did their laundry under the tap in the back yard. She crouched as she scrubbed the clothes on a washboard. To make her work easier, she folded her sarong higher and tied the ends of her kebaya. The sunlight beat down and made dark circles on the ground where mounds of white jambu flowers were scattered about. Rustini gathered these up and went up and down the steps, as Sudarmo leaned against the railing of the back veranda and kept an eye on them both under the *jambu* tree. When Sulastri stood up several times to hang the clothes on a line, her dripping sarong clung to her legs. She felt tired from the work and sat on the lowest step and stroked her child. Sudarmo sat down too. A breadfruit tree spread its broad leaves over the high wall. Its fruit looked like little round green hedgehogs, amusing and familiar. The wind blew dry leaves from their branches and rustled Sulastri's hair into little locks on her forehead. It was a place of solitude. Occasionally they heard a peddler calling out his trade.

Sulastri looked at the back of her hands which were turning red and starting to swell. "The work's hard. I feel like I've just been in a fight," she said with a smile at her husband, who had glanced at her naked arm.

"Rub it with Purol ointment. That'll make it better. Working with the hands makes you strong." He patted her on the shoulder.

She didn't answer and leaned against the veranda wall.

"Oh," she said, "how long will I last like this? But luckily, I fall asleep the moment I touch the pillow."

Sudarmo didn't reply. He turned the subject to Sutrisno, who came by almost every day.

"He'll be here again soon," Sudarmo said, "I feel sorry for him. It's not so good to be married to a woman who's nine years older than him. In this, he may have unconsciously copied Karno, because before he married, he had admired the man."

"His complaints about himself are much too exaggerated," Sulastri criticized. She sensed that Herwati was unhappy, because everything she did irritated her husband. "Herwati's a good soul and she loves her husband with a love I can't give to you, Dar. Truly, Sutrisno asks too much from her."

"Yes, I agree, but that's the way he is going to fall into a pit. It's too bad, because he's an innocent young man. Truly, Tri, there's only one person who can appreciate me at this time, and that's him. He still has ideals."

Someone was knocking at the back door. Sudarmo got up, expecting something, and quickly opened the door. This door opened to the garden, and there stood Sutrisno and his little daughter, Juniati, who closely resembled her father, with impressive brown eyes and a little soft mouth.

"Hello, Mas!" Sutrisno waved his right hand warmly upon seeing Sulastri on the steps and he laughed with an odd giggling sound. Behind him, broad and plain, stood Muhammad, with his robust head, strong mouth, and Arabic-looking black eyes and eyebrows. Near him, Sulastri felt tense and rather shaken inside. She glanced at him, but quickly lowered her eyes. Then she pulled her sleeves down to her wrists. Sutrisno and Sudarmo, together with the child, entered the house and went into the front veranda. The other two stayed for a moment on top of the stairs, then also went in. But Sulastri felt a heaviness in her heart and that something had begun to change. She combed her hair in her room and applied a little powder to her cheeks, changed her clothes, and then went and sat down shyly with the others. All this while, she tried to become of aware of something but wasn't successful. Muhammad didn't speak, and she listened to Sutrisno explaining and driving home his argument with both hands; she felt bothered by Sudarmo who repeatedly interrupted him.

"Mas Darmo says that the village can become a strength for us. But how could we ever turn those buffalos into real people and make them into a fortress that could resist any authority at all?"

Sudarmo replied slowly, as though he was trying to concentrate his thinking. "The struggle for independence is always close to my heart. Anyone who has sworn to devote themselves to that purpose, will never find peace of mind with this life. I see the village as a means. It's independence that is the final goal that we must achieve. I've read Boeke's *Restoration of the Village* and Kraemer's article in the journal *De Stuw* and those writings have convinced me that we can develop an extraordinary energy in the village."

They spoke most nimbly and briskly. Muhammed gave Sulastri a sidelong look. He spoke hesitantly as he held Rustini's hand. "She's very pretty, isn't she?" Then, with an inquisitive look, he said, "It doesn't feel lonely, so far from town?" Sulastri nodded and stroked her child's hair. All this time, Juniati had pressed close to her father, who was energetically carrying on his debate with Sudarmo. Muhammad shifted his chair a little back.

"Come, Rustini," he said, "You'd like to sit with Uncle?" The little child looked at him in wonderment and then at Sulastri, who wanted to give her to Muhammad. As she passed her over, their hands touched for a moment. Sulastri felt as if her heart had stopped, but she turned away and said in a normal voice, "She has gotten heavy."

Muhammad kept looking at her and Sulastri was in ecstasy, piercing and bitter, though she hoped this feeling would stay. And so, she said, "The silence is nice here. I like to have silence around me. But I only feel nervous at five o'clock in the morning when I listen to the muezzin."

Muhammad looked outside, where the sky had become a hazy light blue and the birds, which were now quiet, revealed themselves as black dots on the roof tiles.

"But why is Mas Darmo building a school in the town?" Sutrisno, his voice insistent, wanted to know. Sudarmo looked at Sulastri for a moment, as if she had known all along what was in his heart, and replied, "I want to reach the villages from the town. In town I feel at home, and so I think the best thing is to have a psychic connection to the villages. Here in town are the consumer cooperative and a distribution office. There in the villages the cooperatives are for crops. Let me put it honestly: I haven't known the villages for a long time. And I don't dare oppose the influences of the civil servants and the religious elite there. When I feel I would be strong enough to put up with living in the loneliness of a village and can confront its influences calmly and steadfastly, that's when I will dare to prefer the village as my permanent home."

"Yes, yes, I agree with all that," stated Sutrisno. "I also feel out of place in the villages. Villagers look at me with suspicion. I seem to have been equated with contract coolie recruiters and the like, but there's no interaction between the villagers and us, and even if I lived there my whole life, relations are hampered by our intellectualism."

"That's right," Muhammad put in here. "Intellectuals don't pray and so are considered disbelievers. So if you—"

Here Sudarmo interrupted in a manner clearly intended to take over the discussion.

"If we want to win their hearts and gain their trust, then we have to defeat the religious leaders with their own weapons. Mas Muhammad is right. We have to pray and fast and learn their traditional customs and outlook."

Sulastri gave her view. "The narrowness of those villagers is actually a shield to parry with smiles the blows in their lives."

Absorbed in their discussions, Sulastri's feelings had vanished, but she regretted it, because she could now, without hidden thoughts, look at Mohammad openly in his face.

"Zus Sulastri is correct," Sutrisno said, nodding, as though expressing his gratitude for what she said. "We don't know the conditions of their lives. That they're so ignorant and too submissive, that's proof they can't find a way out of their many hardships. And we have to admit our own mistakes, that we're not all that concerned about the sufferings of these people. Yes, of course everyone feels moved by their suffering, but no one does so to the point of feeling afflicted by it themselves. I sometimes hate myself because I know all this, but lack courage because of my fear."

"We know—no, we believe—that we can do something good there, but hesitate to act. In people's hearts there's more cowardice than we suspect, even in the hearts of some who from the beginning were blessed with extreme courage. I think that the basic instinct of fear of the angel of death is what often makes us have that disappointing attitude," Sudarmo said.

"That's correct, what you say," Sulastri laughed dryly. "At three o'clock this morning, when you had to go outside with such uncontrollable urgency, you told me to stand night watch under the *jambu* tree."

They all laughed at this. Sulastri was pleased at having poked fun at Sudarmo, because he was dumbfounded.

"This house is haunted," Sudarmo weakly excused himself. "Really! If you look into the dark rooms from the back, for sure you're—"

"*Aduh*!" Sutrisno laughed. "And Mas Dar says he doesn't believe in ghosts. People say that ghosts are afraid of lamplight."

"There are many, many bats in the back," said Sulastri. "That's why it seems that someone threw something at you. A falling *jambu*, for sure!"

They laughed again and Sulastri mockingly observed her husband. Well, now his discourse that had been so important had been shattered and his efforts to return to discussing serious issues in the middle of this hot day didn't succeed, because all of a sudden Juniati scratched Rustini's eyelid, causing shrieking and crying as the child sought refuge with her father.

"Don't, Ati," admonished Sutrisno in a gentle and soothing voice, as he usually used with this child. "Rustini's still little, dear." He held Juniati's face. The child gazed at her father with a blank look, but nonetheless in an ashamed way with her head tilted to the side. Meanwhile Sudarmo was holding Rustini, soothing her, and, without realizing it, glaring at Juniati. He said frowning, "Don't scratch, Ati, you both have to play nicely."

Whatever the case, after this tiny incident, the atmosphere became uneasy. The mood of intimacy had been lost and the sense of inhibiting isolation would have been much worse had not Muhammad tried to fill this void. This goodhearted fellow didn't understand why the atmosphere became so cold so suddenly. It had felt so hot on the road and likewise in the house. The sun was not visible but was felt blazing behind a screen of terrific heat. Sutrisno stood up in surprise.

"Oh!" he said, rubbing his jacket pocket as he looked for his missing pocket watch. "The morning's getting on and Ati's mother may be home now. I'll just say goodbye."

"Just a moment," Sudarmo held him back, himself full of regret. "Wait a little longer. The day's still early. Really!"

The mosque drum sounded, and the guests who didn't feel like going but actually had to, were still in the front yard, occupied with conversing again with Sudarmo, while Muhammad stood near Sulastri, silent, with a sympathetic and calming expression on his face. Finally, they left. Muhammad looked for a moment at Sulastri and nodded at Sudarmo.

In the cool house, Sudarmo began. “I’m not happy at that Ati. Look at Rustini! Her eyelid’s bleeding. Such a sweet child.” Gently, he drew his child close to him. Sutrisno and he were equally pleased with their children who perhaps also resembled their fathers in disposition. Sulastri tidied up the front veranda. In the inner part, where there was only a white mat on the floor and on the wall a board with bottles, she prepared a simple midday meal: rice, salted fish and some vegetables, the leftovers from yesterday’s meal. Even if they were poor, the plates were set neatly on a tablecloth. The high windows, from which you could look down on the tiled roofs of the other houses, were strengthened with grilles. The floor was covered with shining palm fronds, which looked cool and clean. The walls in the lower parts were also covered with these fronds, light brown, fresh and in no need of any adornments at all.

“Come over here,” Sulastri invited her husband. “Just sit down, we’ll eat a king’s feast.” She gave him a plate of rice and passed over a plate of the salted fish, then began to eat with zeal. From time to time, she gave rice with vegetables to Rustini.

“We are now living pleasantly. There’s no work, each day is a day off, and we have rice to cook,” said Sudarmo with a slight laugh. “But now it’s beginning to get truly difficult,” he went on. “If no more than the five students whom we have registered come, we’ll be bankrupt. And Lastri, what will we do then?”

Sulastri shrugged. Hardships were normal, so that if there were more, she wouldn’t care. It was Sudarmo who encouraged her several times. He hoped there would be more students. Whatever the case, it wasn’t yet the time to despair, and looking for a job as a government employee was humiliating. Yes, it would destroy any sense he had of self-respect. Only if later, there were no alternative, then such things could be considered. But crying before the struggle would only make the journey more difficult and heartbreaking.

Because of all that, he frequently got angry with Sulastri, and also because sometimes people could see that Sulastri couldn't keep on living like this. This fact really hurt him, but occasionally when he was lying down quietly before falling asleep, he would feel sorry for her, remembering that she was only twenty-three years old. But then, he would argue, wasn't she free to leave this suffering if she no longer wanted to live with her husband? His wife was still young. Why did people let themselves be tied down by trifles?

And Sulastri thought that she had made every effort she could to be cheerful and if she couldn't do that, she wasn't to be blamed. Sudarmo often criticized her, "You don't dare to live. You want to treat me again like you did in Batavia? That time you got your full punishment because you felt humiliated too, that you only were able to make me a clerk. We live in poverty now, but free, and no one dictates over us, other than our stomachs and these are satisfied with very little. Just so long as our hearts can live and we're not just eating and sleeping."

Sulastri bowed her head at her husband's harsh words to her, but the chasm between them reappeared as if they were living in two separate worlds. However, the chasm wasn't all that troubling for her, when she again saw in her mind the sight of Muhammad's dark eyes.

Sutrisno came back in the afternoon, this time alone. Right away he began by saying, "My God, that woman is so stupid and narrow-minded! Oh, Mas Dar, sometimes I feel smashed to bits because of my love of Herwati. I can't stand being at home. I feel like I'm locked in a cave and always witnessing the same things around me, that love that terrifies me!"

He heaved a sigh. "Mas Dar at least can talk with Zus Sulastri," he went on. "My wife, the moment she comes home, she goes right to sleep. She only has time for her child. Sometimes I find that kindness and consideration of hers so tiresome."

"That's right!" he began again, this time at Sulastri. "She loves me totally, she never asks for anything, but I can't live in a coop, always around her." His ears were red, his eyes were almost popping out of their lids, and those gesticulating hands of his, slender as a girl's, looked cold and full of tension. Sulastri and Sudarmo just kept quiet. They knew that Sutrisno saw his depression about everything as being caused by his wife, so that Herwati would gradually feel at fault, but not know why. Herwati then became a figure who drew compassion and for whom no one felt any dislike. Herwati couldn't be blamed if she didn't appear moved by the most beautiful poems, read by her husband in a resounding voice and in rhythm with quivering of his heart. Nor could she be blamed if she replied to the lyrical missives sent by her—then fiancé—husband, with only short notes which expressed something of her job and daily experiences. In this town, where she had lived since she was little, Herwati was like a little gray mouse in her lane who wanted to spring into the wide world but was afraid to do so.

She felt as home here in Bogor as vegetation would in sunlight, and she couldn't understand why her husband longed to leave such a peaceful town for unknown experiences. Apart from that, Herwati only rarely had brilliant thoughts. She was just an ordinary and average person, and if you didn't love her for her good-heartedness, you would say she was by nature extremely tedious. But Sutrisno adorned Herwati with characteristics she didn't possess, and so he was greatly surprised that his wife was as ordinary as his neighbors and friends—delighted with nice clothes, proud of her child, and most importantly, the special demeanor of a mother. Sulastri knew Sutrisno's faults and calmed him down.

"In marriage, everything depends on the husband. If you're looking for happiness for yourself and your wife, you are the one who has to find it. The man can make anything at all of his wife."

Sutrisno turned his head away and looked up at the ceiling, where the lamp made circles of light. "No," he shook his head. "That's the way people are. Mas Dar, I envy you. Sometimes I want to kill myself. Oh God, if I think about that... but I'm a coward, too afraid to carry it out, I suppose."

He stopped there, perhaps driving away an awful image from himself, because his lips puckered and he shook his head. Sulastri and Sudarmo looked at him quite bemused. Rustini came in her short steps and continued her games on the floor.

"Don't give up, Mas. In the end we need more courage to make this happiness better," Sudarmo said in a voice that was unusually gentle. Sutrisno said nothing and folded his hands on his knees. Then, as they were concentrating their thoughts on this very same matter, and just as Sutrisno rather regretted having made that abrupt utterance, four people came out of the darkness of the front veranda and into the lamplight: Herwati, a true mother, calm and friendly, and wearing a shawl over her shoulders; Jusuf, tall and good-looking, with a face as refined and soft as a cat's; Farida, his wife, arousing and lively in a nervous way: and behind them, Muhammad, smiling broadly.

Their hosts stood up. Sulastri went up to Herwati while Sudarmo, tidying up the newspapers and books on the table, greeted them with a laugh and a friendly "Come in!" There then began bursts of laughter and chuckling, the sound of chairs scraping on the floor, and in the room appeared a friendly light that shone on the wall and passed across the delight-filled faces. Sutrisno, quiet at first, soon came back to life, chatting about this and that, as he suddenly rediscovered himself. Joke after joke went flying back and forth, occasionally interspersed with serious discussion.

"If we are depressed," Sudarmo began seriously, "Künkel can become our road sign. He teaches us to smile, even if we are overwhelmed by humiliation."

Jusuf nodded non-stop, as if he was in complete agreement with Sudarmo, and then said in a drawn-out of sort of way, "I guess it would be useful if we studied Künkel together at night like we're doing now? When you say that, many difficulties will disappear by doing that—"

"Say, that's a good idea!" Sutrisno cut in. "Why hadn't I thought of that? We could learn to see some aspects of our lives from another perspective."

Muhammad nodded silently, but there was in his eyes an enthusiastic light that he rarely displayed. Sulastri opened her mouth to say something and intentionally turned toward Farida, who wanted to speak with her, but Sudarmo anticipated her and said delightedly, "What a terrific idea! Let's start next week. One of us will open the conversation and we'll discuss the issues all together."

"Let's just have Mas Dar start," said Jusuf quickly, but Sulastri glanced at Sutrisno, who looked happy because his mood had lightened, and said, "No. Mas Sutrisno should be the one. Mas Dar talks too much." This sarcastic jab made Farida laugh uncontrollably until tears rolled from her eyes. She was not all that pleased with Sudarmo because he was too self-concerned and forgot to pay attention to a woman's beauty, even if only out of politeness. Because what was more important was that he didn't want to endanger this new and tender friendship and perhaps make Sulastri jealous. And Farida knew that she was exciting, and connected to that was her unconscious dislike of Sutrisno, because he would rather talk with Sulastri than to her. Now all eyes had turned toward her laughter. "Be careful, otherwise you'll choke," Herwati said. Sulastri touched Farida and she started laughing again until everyone else joined in as well, even though Sutrisno laughed like someone with a toothache.

It would appear that this was a happy night, for time passed by without anyone noticing. It was past ten o'clock when the guests sped down the hill to town in an *oplet*. After they had gone, Sudarmo sang in a low voice and Sulastri was surprised to see him so youthful again, after being her husband for so long. Then he began to bother his wife again and she saw this as childishness but pleasing, nonetheless. And when the wind whistled around the house, rattling the windows and bringing down many *jambu* from their branches, there was a feeling of warmth and intimacy, and the lamps seemed to wink in a special way, like old and dear friends, as if knowing about many things hidden in the hearts of husband and wife.

A week after this gathering, "Künkel Night" was held in Sutrisno's home. He read from the book he held in his hands. The others listened around him, Herwati next to her husband, so glad to see her man the center of their collective attention. Jusuf nodded his head at the parts that impressed him and had the most significance. Muhammad, who had not felt overly impressed, but had not dared to show it, finally slipped his hands between his knees to cover his stiffness, and looked down at the floor so that his thick eyebrows were more visible. Sudarmo's face glowed from pleasure, and Sulastri, who felt stiffness in her back, didn't dare shift her position but imperceptibly stretched her back, because Sutrisno's look was now directed at her and Sudarmo; then he looked into the book again with full attention.

"And so...," he started, placing his hand on the page, "About a person's role as the subject and at the same time as the object, I am able to better clarify one example with an image." He paused for a moment, and then in a serious voice went on. "If a person eats too much sugar, he will get sick to his stomach...." He observed the people listening attentively, when all of a sudden, Herwati's sweetly caressing voice was heard: "People get toothaches from candy, not stomach aches, right, Tris?"

With an angry glare from her husband, his wife realized her mistake and made a kind of snorting sound. Sudarmo frowned as he repressed his desire to laugh. Sulastri's lips quivered and Farida nervously moved her slippers about. Jusuf lightly coughed while Muhammed maintained his stiff demeanor. Sutrisno shook his head until his hair hung disheveled and, with eyes blazing, he angrily said, "You're always spoiling the mood. I'm serious, Herwati. If you're not interested in my lecture, there no need for you to please me by sitting there."

Herwati looked so small and shriveled that no one dared to glance at her and instead looked tensely downward. Finally, Sudarmo's voice broke this tension. "Zus Herwati's right, Mas, people do get toothaches from eating sweets. The main point is, all examples must be evaluated with the physical consequences of actions by people as subjects. The moment someone suffers a toothache as an object, all that is appropriate."

Everyone sighed with relief and laughed, but Herwati slipped out like a mouse, went into her room, and didn't come out again. Sutrisno read again, they exchanged views in a debate in which Sudarmo and Sutrisno became the main debaters, while the others were the audience and with their attention, they made the wrangling even more exciting and fun. It was almost eleven o'clock when they parted, and on the way back, Farida spoke again with pleasure about that event just now.

"That Mas Trisno," she giggled. "Oh my goodness! The way he glared, and Herwati, oh, so pitiful."

Sulastri laughed, but brought the levity down, "Oh, Mas Trisno takes everything so seriously. It's not right for him to treat his wife like that. Such a nice person, am I right?"

Behind Sulastri, Jusuf and Sudarmo walked along, absorbed in conversation. Jusuf with his affable "Yes, yes," and Sudarmo, pleased at having a listener who agreed with him.

The following days were filled with friendship, earnest conversations full of revived enthusiasm. Sutrisno would visit

Sudarmo's house every day and talk about his problems. He'd be there in the morning and stay until midday. Herwati was grateful that her husband seemed to have come alive again and rarely talked about his intention to commit suicide. For that, she was pleased with Sudarmo and considered him a friend who could be totally trusted.

But when the school was opened, the number of registrations turned out not to have increased and stayed at only five; and these five had been enrolled by the Criminal Investigation Department. Therefore, no one else showed up and Sudarmo seemed to be struck in a daze watching the morning turn into midday. Sulastri, who dressed neatly to teach, changed into everyday attire and she cooked in the back yard.

When Sudarmo silently came up to her, Sulastri didn't look at him. They both knew what the other was thinking.

"So, Tri," he began, "we have to leave. Where to, we'll discuss later."

Sulastri didn't answer. She suddenly felt so thickwitted that all thoughts left her. In her heart she felt the steady knock that said, "We have to go, enter a new life, leave this, to where, I don't care." She felt drained, as she saw clearly what it meant, going here and there to an unknown destination.

Later in the day, Sutrisno came to ask questions with his usual attentiveness and what Sudarmo said right off was, "Mas, we're thinking of going to Semarang. When we had just arrived in Batavia, Hapsoro had deliberately gone to Yogya to ask my wife and me to work in his school. We couldn't at the time, because I had just started working in Kartonegoro's office. Now, I'm going to remind Hapsoro about that request. Perhaps he still needs me."

Sutrisno was shocked and asked, "Is Mas thinking of staying a long time in Semarang? In the end, there's no need to go so far simply to work to keep a stomach filled. You can do that here too," and, in an urgent voice. "Just stay here and together we can work for one goal."

In his heart, Sudarmo had to laugh at Sutrisno, who had no clue of what it meant to have to live off the wind. Sutrisno had never known the lack of money. The only person who could fully understand these hardships was Muhammad, who had come almost penniless to Batavia to be a student. Now Muhammad was living at Sutrisno's home, contributing a little money for food, and in this way, he felt so deeply indebted to Sutrisno that he often discussed his benefactor's mental suffering and asked advice as to how he could help him. If Sudarmo left, this meant that Sutrisno would relapse into his psychological difficulties. Sutrisno had begun to feel these and grasped at all the possibilities of keeping Sudarmo close by him. Now Sutrisno asked if Sudarmo could stay here with him, continue on with this school and establish a model school where they could work toward a relationship between rural and urban. Sudarmo didn't agree with him, because he had nothing except his books. But Sutrisno didn't want to let go of his dreams and held tight to the possibility that he could realize them. He was like a man who was almost drowning and begged his friend not to go away.

He was filled with anxiety. "Surely we don't have to be intimidated now by a lack of funds when we are on the threshold of new possibilities! I'll take care of the money. Mas will just teach. My wife is of the same mind as me, to contribute *f*50 monthly for the school. She's paying attention to this and would be very pleased if you both would stay here."

Once again, Sudarmo voiced his reservations and didn't come to any decision. That night Sulastri, who had no idea of this, innocently went along with her husband on a visit to Sutrisno's home. The men chatted on the front veranda while the women talked at the dining table. Sulastri was taken aback when Herwati suddenly said to Farida, "All right then, we agree, helping other people with Sutrisno's remaining money. That's more useful than buying a plot of land like you talked about earlier."

Farida nodded and looked at Sulastri, who had now gone pale. Who had to be helped? Her? Why would she have to be helped, when she could work equally well somewhere else, even at a very low salary. She always felt humiliated, always had to be helped, while she was smart enough to overcome poverty as far as she could. But Sudarmo would perhaps see it differently. And Sulastri was beginning to give in, because she knew she couldn't prevail over Sudarmo's obstinacy. It would be better to wait with a light heart for all that was ahead of them, to happily join in taking a role in this, because she felt oppressed in again confronting the squabbling and depression in the future. Sulastri was sunk too deeply in her thoughts to hear Farida's question, and when she looked at Herwati and Farida, they burst out laughing.

"Mas Dar has decided to set up a school with Mas Sutrisno," said Herwati. "The school building and all the other things will be for us to take care of. I'm so very pleased that Trisno now has something that will make his life happy."

Sulastri stood up and went over to Sudarmo and asked him hurriedly, "Is it true? I'm only now hearing what the both of you are planning?" She stared at Sudarmo, tense and with a strange light in her eyes, as though now waiting for him to say something.

"Yes," Sudarmo said, "we will now be working to realize one goal, which I have always dreamed of. Now we're discussing several issues we have in common. Just sit down here, so Zus Farida and Zus Herwati can hear too." Then in a soft tone, because Sulastri would not accept it immediately and wholeheartedly, he said, "You remember what you promised me?"

Sulastri stared at them one by one and Sutrisno explained. "I begged Mas Dar to stay here. Zus will agree, right?"

There was a hope in his eyes, and Herwati whispered to Sulastri, "We've urged Mas Dar. You know that Tris feels lonely here and Mas Darmo is the only person at this time that can distract him from other things."

Sulastri just kept quiet. Once again, she sensed the hollowness in her heart, as if she had to part with something that she desired above all else, the feeling that she was not tied down by anyone. She heard them saying something in a muffled way and it was like she had no interest at all. And she let it all pass over her.

"But," she debated with herself, "Trisno appreciates me and he expects even more from me, from his own wife. If they knew that I'm as insignificant as Herwati and am not brave enough to live like this with its consequences, that is, being misunderstood by others, being betrayed, and sacrificing everything..."

There was still something that disturbed her but she tried to push it away. She heard Sudarmo speaking. "There's one condition, and that is, Mas Trisno has to take my books in payment of the base capital. If not, I will not be able to rid myself of various kinds of obligations."

Sutrisno at first refused this offer, but Sudarmo pressed him and he then presented this idea. "We will gather my books together with Mas Dar's for a complete library that we can make available to the community. In addition, there's also a job for Mas Jusuf, something just right for a librarian!"

Such a solution produced a lighter feeling in her, but Sulastri was still gloomy, though she tried to think her feelings away. After these discussions came days of busy work which Sutrisno threw himself into with gusto. He forgot his inner pain and Herwati saw the joy on her husband's face. Even Farida, who until now lived like a butterfly, fluttering from here to there, joined in too, and sometimes overdid the praise. But her enthusiasm was welcome when she diligently listed Sudarmo's books, which had arrived at the same time as those of Sutrisno and Jusuf. You would often see Jusuf half-dressed typing long lists on the typewriter at Sutrisno's home. Farida would be sitting beside him, dictating book titles, and playing with Rustini, whom they treated like a cute doll. Sutrisno and Sudarmo tirelessly searched for an appropriate building for a school. It had to be cheap, large, habitable for living, and located on a good street in town. As they walked around the town, they would debate energetically, and on such days, Sutrisno's eyes would light up with happiness, while Sudarmo spoke warmly to his wife. The result was that Sulastri emerged from her tense indifference, and she searched for books for her lectures on the day the school opened.

Also, during that month, they found a house, behind the station along the main street. It was big and strongly built, but had to be repaired first because it was in a distressingly filthy condition. Sutrisno requested the help of an *opséter,* who oversaw this work free of charge. The old building was painted, cleaned, given new floor boards, and just when it truly began to look good, documentary announcements about the construction of new schools were circulated. Seventeen students had been enrolled, a respectable number, because the school only opened in October. This was the result of a stratagem by which prominent people in the town had been asked to sit on a supervisory commission, so that the school's continuation for the outside community was at least assured. They had simple benches, chairs, and desks made, and a sign was artistically painted with the Sanskritic name of the school, "Loka Siswa," which meant "Student Heaven."

For the building repairs and other items, Sutrisno spent about *f*200. Herwati was a bit startled at such a large outlay, but she remembered Sutrisno's new courage for living, and so did not consider that he paid too much for these things. Now there were new discussions, and Sutrisno decided that he would temporarily pay the building rent and the electricity and water, while Sudarmo would provide the food and pocket money of *f* 10 per month to be paid to him and Sulastri. Sutrisno would collect the school tuition and hold the position of administrator.

Soon the school building was complete, and Prayitno, Sulastri's older brother who owned an electrical installation agency, was connecting the power lines at a quite low cost. September was almost gone when Sudarmo and Sulastri left their home, spent a few nights with Sutrisno and Herwati, and then moved into the school building, where they were to have two back rooms, a bed, closets, and a desk and chair. All of these belonged to Sutrisno; only their clothes and Rustini's bed and a few other things were their own. This made Sulastri joke with Herwati, "We're just like nomads, owning nothing but what's in our bags," which made her friend laugh.

They moved in during the late afternoon, and the three of them ate dinner under the smokey light of kerosene lanterns, because the electricity had not yet been connected. They sat on the large back veranda, with its big doors on the right and the left. In front was a dark lane, and one in back, so that they had the sense of being submerged in darkness. The wicks in their lanterns flickered and their light passed across Sudarmo's face, casting circles of brightness on the walls and the bamboo racks. The food tasted good, even if there was a strange ambience about everything around them. They groped for their bed in the darkness but didn't sleep calmly, supposing they heard strange sounds everywhere. It was with a light heart that Sulastri opened the strong windows as dawn broke on the next day.

16

The following days were spent cleaning the school building and arranging the school furniture. The front and back yards were swept and after a few days, the refurbished building gained a pleasing appearance. You could sit nicely on the front veranda and see the broad, quiet street, or, if sitting and chatting there, you had the impression you were at your own home. Rustini walked here and there, carrying pebbles from the yard to the low house. In the front yard were several straight-standing clove and nutmeg trees, while below there was a little garden, both narrow and unsightly. After that, a low wall that separated the yard from the street. Along that street to their right and left were shady trees that gave the impression of a leafy tunnel. If you looked out from the veranda onto the street, you would see broad and peaceful fields with lines streaked with sunlight or circles of sparkling brightness, giving you the impression of morning passing into midday. Across the street were sheds, stands, and the warehouses of the station. Trains passed by, their whistle sometimes reminding Sulastri of when she was young. After that, the morning was usually calm and tranquil, just as it was in the villages, and not in the middle of a town.

On both sides of the veranda, which resembled an open-air pavilion in Central Java, there were two front rooms with doors leading into the school area. In these front rooms were the library and common reading rooms, with book cases standing against the walls. Here Jusuf worked, and the tick-tack of his typewriter sounded all day long. Here also Sudarmo and his friends discussed their efforts at raising the level of autonomous activity of the people so they could grow into a principled people's movement.

In these front rooms, ideas were conceived and those who thought them felt so bound together, so passionate, as though the days were coming when the world would be at their feet. And the books in their fresh covers behind the glass doors witnessed their earnest debates, which always ended in laughter and friendly goodbyes until the next day.

From the front veranda was a narrow lane that went to the back veranda, where, to the right and left were the rather small bedrooms for Sudarmo and Sulastri. Then, down a high set of steps from this veranda, you would come to the back yard which was next to a ravine. This ravine was densely overgrown with bamboo trees and descended to a river. In later days, the dark brown water of this river would often make Sulastri remember its gentle sound.

The environment they inhabited in the ordinary school building raised the suspicion among many people that the lessons being given there weren't as good as those in ordinary schools with their unfriendly classrooms and benches. And because of that, there were only seventeen students, even though the school fee was only one rupiah. People took a wait-and-see stance on how things would turn out. Sudarmo and Sutrisno looked after the bookkeeping. Several days later the accounts were presented. Sutrisno expounded on his plans and the listeners noisily voiced their approval. Then Sulastri gave a speech and read it out in a normal voice, although everyone understood its intention. She was pleased at the words of congratulations and various comments she heard right after the speech. Sutrisno's face lit up with happiness, and after everyone else had left, they had a final conversation that grew quite fiery, in which Sutrisno expostulated, "Truly, Mas Dar, we will make this dead town come alive again. I've seen with my own eyes, buses full of farm crops coming in from the villages and giving it to our distribution offices."

Sudarmo carried on with this thought. "I've seen this school become a model primary school together with teachers' training and farmers' schools."

And Jusuf laughed heartily and shook his head. But Muhammad wasn't present because his betrothed had invited him to go out for a walk. On the back veranda, Sulastri and Farida seemed to be busily discussing the events of a few minutes earlier. In fact, Sulastri was listening to Farida's chatter half-heartedly.

"And, Zus, Muhammad's fiancée," said Farida with amusement in her eyes, "she's like a zebra in that kebaya with all the stripes." Farida related this and recounted that, but she didn't reach her listener's heart, because Sulastri was listening to her as she would a small child.

On several occasions, Sudarmo's laughter sounded louder than anyone else's and Farida giggled and said, "They're so happy. I'm really and truly pleased, everything's turned out wonderfully." When Farida and Sulastri went over to the men on the front veranda, the conversations continued. Sutrisno kept smoothing his hair back; Jusuf's refined fair face was full of amiability, and Sudarmo sat at the reading table, swinging his legs.

"And after this," Sudarmo gave emphasis to his words, "our journal. We will write articles for it, so that all of Bogor will wake in amazement. Mas Trisno, you say will be able to raise the initial capital. If so, tomorrow we will look for a printer—uh, no, I can't, because I have to teach. No, Mas, just find a printing company that's cheap."

Sutrisno nodded in compliance and Jusuf stopped thinking about printing and the journal when he said, "I've got several members for the library and have divided up some tasks. And almost all the books have been listed, but I don't know where to put them."

Jusuf stood up and went to the bookcase and took out a new book. The others looked at him and finally decided under what rubric it would be listed. In this way, the day was advanced when they departed. But that night, Künkel evening was to be continued at Sutrisno's home. This time everything went smoothly, other than Farida laughing too much and Sulastri's brooding, while Herwati just thought of patterns of sleepwear for children. However, the men didn't notice this and once again they parted in good fellowship. And every day there was some new event. Once, a new member of the library came. Another time, a question arose about education, to the point where the men were so intent on their discussion that they didn't pay the slightest attention to what was slowly going on in the background. On one occasion, Sutrisno complained, quite angrily, to Sudarmo. "Zus Farida has taken her typewriter away and now I can't type a thing!"

"What?" said Sudarmo, surprised, "Is she as bitchy as all that?"

"There always something going on with that woman! What do I have to do with a sewing machine?" Sutrisno replied, his anger getting the better of him.

"A sewing machine? How so?" asked Sudarmo.

"What I mean is, a few days back, Farida borrowed Herwati's sewing machine and yesterday when Herwati had me bring it back, because she herself had sewing to do, Farida came and without a single word took the typewriter right from under my nose and went home with it."

"Oh God!" said Sudarmo laughing. "And then what happened?"

"As Mas can see, now I am the victim." Sutrisno was sitting with a long face, but when he saw Sudarmo's expression, he laughed too, and griped, "Those women! Those women!"

But Sudarmo had an idea. He borrowed the typewriter from Farida, and Sutrisno borrowed it in turn from him, so that the moment came when Farida was amazed to see the typewriter back on Sutrisno's desk. Nor did she dare say anything, especially when she saw a sardonic look on Sutrisno's face; but she then took it out on Herwati, saying Herwati was the most tedious of people. Luckily, Farida, as usual, forgot about her revenge and came back again a few days later and made it all up to Herwati, laughing and giggling.

Meanwhile, a printer for the journal had been found. To hold down the printing costs, the chief printer was made a member of the editorial staff, so he felt flattered and wrote a spirited article in Sundanese. There was money for the first printing, so they diligently started to write the first essays which would introduce *The People's Economic Education* to the public.

Sutrisno went from store to store to find advertisements. Often, his face beaming with happiness and even covered with sweat, he said that he had succeeded in persuading a number of shop owners to post ads. After some debate about the cover of the journal, the first edition of *The People's Economic Education* came out early Saturday morning. The journal was to appear regularly once a week. Its cover was light green, not all that attractive and more like a movie theater program than a journal. However, Sudarmo and Sutrisno regarded it with affection, stroked its pages and gazed at its cover with great satisfaction, happily appreciating the artistry of the cover.

The names of Sutrisno and the head of printing as editor were printed on the cover. Farida, in her girl scout's uniform, distributed the journal from house to house and collected subscription funds. Jusuf, Muhammad, and Sudarmo competed at landing subscriptions so that on the next day, they had satisfactorily obtained quite a lot of money. All of that meant that publication of a second edition was assured. And Sutrisno was tireless, as was Sudarmo, and even Herwati joined in with handling the administration of the journal.

But with issue number two there began to be problems at the printers with the typesetters and other workers. They had to work hard for very little pay, so that sometimes only a few of them showed up. Thus, the publication of *The People's Economic Education* was late in coming out. This in turn worried the subscribers. So Sutrisno would help with the printing until late at night. The printing was old-fashioned, by hand, and he worked under a kerosene lamp. Then Jusuf, Herwati, and Farida came by to look in on him and stayed chatting away so that it was almost midnight when they returned home. Herwati sometimes brought fried bananas for the printers, and she was so happy when Sutrisno and she walked together along the deserted streets and spoke enchantedly of all their feelings and experiences. Sudarmo and Sulastri sometimes also stopped by, if only briefly, because on the following days they were obliged to arrange for the folding of the journals and divide them up among the older children for distribution in town.

When Saturdays were over, they took a breath, but Mondays forced Sudarmo to write fast for the next issue, and when Fridays were coming up, Sutrisno ran panic-stricken from here to there from fear that the journal would come out late. Then he worked hard until the break of dawn. His servant Sanip helped him diligently and finally, after the weeklong tensions, came relief on Saturday and the satisfaction that work had been completed as best they could. Sutrisno couldn't write anything more because of his work in the print shop, and it was Sudarmo's responsibility to fill the pages with content. This was not easy for him to do; but Sulastri and his friends helped, and he was somehow able to find the way to complete the empty columns. Often, he was up all night long, typing the articles on his bed, while Sulastri, worn out from her daily routine, slept peacefully. Sudarmo placed his typewriter on his pillow between his stretched-out legs. After typing a few sentences, he would throw himself onto the pillow to straighten out his sore back and give some logical thought to the next sentences. Sometimes on Friday night there'd be a message from the print shop that two columns were still empty, and then he would panic and hurriedly compose something and bring it himself at midnight. There, Sutrisno would be sitting on a kind of high footstool, wearing a western-style shirt and scrutinizing the printing. But often, after Sudarmo had tensely tried for three hours, he was unable to achieve material for more than one column. They then would find the solution by the technique of interlacing.

Muhammad, who at first loyally translated Sutrisno's articles into Indonesian, thought it would be better if he wrote his own articles and that's how he began his own several short articles in that language. These writings were smooth and pleasant to read, about legal problems that occurred almost every day, and were informative for readers. And the success of these issues of the journal was so great that all of Bogor was wide-eyed with amazement and kept wondering if this wasn't just something being done for fun by some young intellectuals. People spoke about it and praised Sutrisno's extraordinary energy in searching for advertisers and subscribers. On the other hand, Sudarmo's pen was full of a certain scorn, but clearly illuminated other aspects of the cultural movement that was being trumpeted with new energy. For the comrades, there was no more time to talk about mundane and quotidian matters.

And it was especially so when Sutrisno considered it so very bourgeois if Farida sometimes ridiculed her friends' attire. Herwati simply kept her thoughts to herself when they gathered, as did Sulastri, but after the men left, the women would talk about things other than what was allowed in the conversations with men.

During that time, Sulastri was even more aloof than usual. She had noticed how Sudarmo liked to joke around with the young women who occasionally came to take books. One of them, who could joke back, was quite flirtatious, quite cute, and at the least a girl who could steal a man's heart away. When she came for a book, Sudarmo showed her newly arrived items and stayed for rather a long time in the library, throwing glances her way. On the next night, he got angry with his wife over nothing at all. Sulastri didn't say anything, but felt all the more hurt. In the evenings, if Muhammad had to supervise the library, she would be sure to talk with him—in a calm way, even if people could see that this meant something quite different for Sulastri than just friendship. They would sit together on the bench near the fence of the front veranda and look out onto the street. On one such occasion, Muhammad's fiancée with two other people passed by in a *dokar*. Plump beyond her years, she was an example of a "society" girl, who only wished to shine at parties and to shrewdly choose her future husband. Did Muhammad know this?

Sulastri felt frustrated for Muhammad and she very much wanted to lighten his life. His fiancée waived at them, and Sulastri, with a sidelong glance, saw Muhammad give a calm greeting without demonstrating the slightest feelings or giving any other indication that he was pleased with her. When the *dokar* was out of sight, Muhammad said blandly, "They're going to their friend's."

Sulastri said nothing. Then they chatted about the school routine and finally they came to the tenderness of love in marriage. Muhammad said, "Oh, for me, if there's no more love between a husband and a wife, they should just separate. Marriage is a gamble and there's nothing wrong with trying." He said that, because the people around him all advised him not to marry this girl because she was shallow and had the character of a slanderer. And why she had such a character was because of the influence of her mother, who was a wildly ambitious social climber and who was seen at every function that provided the opportunity to be noticed. Muhammad didn't think of his future, and as far as he was concerned, everything would go just fine.

Sulastri disputed this wearily. "Of course it's a gamble, but shouldn't the very best possibility of winning be considered? But, oh—" she stopped, shrugged, and then looked at him in a certain way and said simply, "The thing is, we really hope for the very best for Mas and because of that...," she hesitated for a moment, and then forged ahead, "We actually advise Mas not to marry her."

Muhammad looked her squarely and quizzically, and Sulastri held his glance. Then he said gently, "Those who don't dare gamble, won't ever win. I want to bet on it. Of course, I think Partinah will change in marriage. We've actually seen that girls whose hearts are cold, become caring wives." Silence enveloped them. Sulastri looked long at the street and felt inescapably wistful. "Why didn't I meet you earlier in my life?" she thought, "Now it's far too late." Unconsciously, she heaved a sigh and intertwined her fingers. She sensed Muhammad's sidelong glance at her, but she realized that in a person's life there were other things than the love of someone else. Could such a feeling be called love, the feeling of wanting to run and meet that other person and look into his eyes so very deeply as he looked into yours? Was this just wanting to have a close friend or was it searching for romance in the tedium of everyday work?

And Sudarmo? She saw her husband in her mind's eye with his melancholy and sarcastic mouth that could say so many biting words, his desire to dominate, and the pettiness of Sulastri herself, because she always gave in, so that she was left by herself with stinging feelings, left feeling she had become only a useful object, someone against whom Sudarmo could hurl his apprehensions and worries. But what about her husband's trust? Muhammad was his comrade. Did Muhammad love her? Sulastri kept her rigid bearing, so that Muhammad also sank into that atmosphere and saw her as the real Sulastri, a young woman who still loved to laugh, but couldn't because of the seriousness of her life and work that demanded her entire attention.

And so there grew a subtle relationship between the two of them, which could grow stronger if it weren't for something else, and that was the moral awareness, the sense of something not permissible. Muhammad waited. But Sulastri hesitated. She didn't dare betray Sudarmo by doing such a thing. But no one, let alone Sudarmo, would ever have seen that inner game; and if he did find out about it, he'd just have smiled, because he was so self-aware. That Sulastri would choose Muhammad over him was for Sudarmo was just not possible. Certainly, a brief love affair was possible, but more than that? No. Sudarmo also knew that Sulastri was too intelligent to dare throw herself away in a passing love. Moreover, Muhammad wasn't an aggressive person, and Sulastri was too fearful by nature.

There was no time to deepen those unconscious feelings into love, and traditional attitudes and behavior constrained them from drawing any closer to each other than just carrying on a hesitant conversation, so that Sulastri, gradually aware of the chasm yawning ever wider between her and Muhammad, sunk back into her own solitude. One night, when Sudarmo was teaching several people, Muhammad came and sat down next to the dining table where Sulastri then was, and he spoke with an unusual brightness in his eyes. "Come, let's go out and buy *duku* together. I just saw a huge amount."

Sulastri looked up. She wanted to quickly accept that offer with pleasure, but she thought of something and lowered her head in embarrassment. She sensed that now was the time that determined something in her life. Muhammad watched her tensely. And there was a challenge in his look. Sulastri had never seen him like this.

"Yes, let's go." she replied.

She stood up, looked all around her and then at Muhammad, who assumed a waiting stance and then saw Rustini next to her. She scooped up the child and looked at her bright eyes, and then sat with her in her lap and stroked her hair back from her forehead.

"Let's go," Muhammad urged. Sulastri shook her head and said in a tired voice, "Ah, no. Some other time. Mas Dar won't know where I went."

And abruptly she realized that she was still happy with Sudarmo, and she would be pained if he was saddened, if he felt bad. She bit her lips. Muhammad's look was so insistent and had such an odd brightness that she didn't dare look back at him, afraid of blushing. Then she began to speak about just ordinary things with her face averted, all the while caressing Rustini.

Sudarmo arrived back and, speaking passionately about this and that, invited his friend to the library. Sulastri stayed back by herself.

"It's too late now," she thought. "But it's just as well this way. I'm too good for just a quick affair, and would Muhammad love me like Sudarmo does?" She stayed like this for quite a while, never moving, and when she heard Sudarmo's voice, she felt the deepest of pleasures. And when Muhammad came up to her, that temptation was lost and she laughed at him with a soaring gaiety and a challenging brightness in her eyes.

There was hidden discord among the women. Now it was between Herwati and Sulastri. Sulastri felt that she was living parasitically on Herwati's salary, because Herwati often complained that she couldn't buy this or that, so that Sulastri felt at fault since Herwati had to economize on her expenditures. Herwati's home was rather smaller now and she had to buy furniture for the house that was somewhat simpler. Previously, her home had been big and built with stone, while now the bamboo floor shook under their quick steps. Before Sulastri arrived, Herwati and Sutrisno had lived comfortably from their salaries that were more than sufficient. Now they had to spend money for the schoolhouse rent and food and pocket money, so that Herwati's moodiness could be understood and forgiven. And increasingly Sulastri felt that she herself was at fault. That is why she said to her husband, "If it really needs to be, Dar, I'd be happier eating from the school income, so Mas Trisno would pay only for the lighting and building rent. I feel so impoverished, almost like a beggar who lives on alms."

Sudarmo got angry at her and explained, "We're not eating off anyone. We work hard for what we are trying to do. We teach class from seven-thirty in the morning to one in the afternoon. And from five to nine o'clock at night we teach again. At least three times a week I don't sleep at night because of our journal. And we aren't asking for much for this work, just a bedroom in the school building, a plate of rice with leafy vegetables and salted fish, and ten rupiah for pocket money. I don't feel like a parasite, because we're bringing every bit of our energy to bear. Whatever the case, no one will be able to say we're lazy, and we certainly aren't rich. If you want to devote yourself to the national movement, you've got to put bourgeois morality aside. And don't even be afraid if someone needs to be killed. Just remember the main role of Gladkov's Dasya."

"No, we're not lazy, but it's extremely hard for me because the one who pays for it isn't Trisno, but Herwati. She gripes that she's always short of money every month, and can we accept all this from her without feeling anything? I feel I'm shouldering a really heavy load, Dar. I have a sense that everyone's criticizing me. Oh, let me try to live carefully with what we have, no matter how little, no matter if we only have to eat rice and salt fish. Right! It would taste better to me!"

Sulastri looked at her husband. Hearing the sadness in her voice, he felt stung and so he tried to calm her. "All right, I will make peace with Trisno. And he will just give us income from the school and there'll be no need to send us food or pocket money. Just remember, Tri, it's not a lot, just twenty rupiah."

She nodded happily and quickly said, "I don't care. Anyhow, all this will be different for me, even if—" Here she stopped and talked about other things. Sutrisno agreed with him, but spoke sharply to his wife, because women can be petty-minded. The work required their full attention. Such concerns had been forgotten and as usual Sulastri was busy working everywhere, while she sometimes thought for several days of writing an essay. Then she composed something on a single sheet of paper, tore it up again and again, but eventually the piece did get completed and she received a nod of approval from her husband. He had again shown his love for her with his teasing, or strolling together, or patting her on the shoulder as though she were a teenager. Farida came more frequently than usual, bringing a rather nervous excitement, and her giggling resounded happily in the library. And at night Jusuf would stay to chat with them, as did Sutrisno. But one day there was a change in that intimate comradeship.

Sudarmo's avid desire to feel in command showed itself in little things. When composing headlines on the cover of *The People's Economic Education*, he was determined to win in every debate. Sutrisno made Sudarmo uneasy, because he no longer wanted to write articles and often, he found excuses for releasing himself from his obligations as editor, administrator, or for finding advertisers. Whatever the case, Sudarmo faced a great amount of editorial work and he had the feeling that his friends had intentionally left him in this job. During this period, Sutrisno often spoke of living in a village to research life there. He said that there was one unforgiveable sin, and that was if an intellectual forgot himself by not working and only argued.

"Work," he said, "we have to work, for what's the use of just theorizing if there's no attempt to put it into practice? I want to try to form my ideas in the village." He spotted the gleam of mockery in Sudarmo's eyes and he flared up again, "We, the intellectuals, always just want to pick the fruit, but we're loathe to roll up our shirtsleeves. In the village I will try to buy the crops and sell them here in town. I've never lived in a village and would like to see the people in their happiness and suffering, Mas..."

Sudarmo just kept silent and Sutrisno grew anxious at his friend's coldness. Sutrisno now insisted, "Herwati will join me.

Truly, I cannot waiver in my idea. I want to roll up my shirtsleeves. I want to live a real life and I want to experience all that as a lesson."

Sudarmo had long known about Sutrisno's plans but never dared suppose that he would really go through with it. Besides, Sutrisno wasn't a person to bring something to fruition in a practical way. So Sudarmo said, "You've considered everything? Sometimes in the village there's a silence that suffocates. And you've got to be able to pray, because if not, you won't be able to enter village society or penetrate into the innermost hearts of the villagers who are fenced in by their silence and their aloofness. Mas Trisno, think a bit more before going. Here you have the journal, which at this time, demands all our attention."

"Journal... oh, we have Mas, don't we? Just let Mas replace me as editor, and in the end, it'll still go on."

Then Sutrisno began again in an even more passionate tone of voice about the unknown fervor of the village, but Sudarmo suspected that this was a place to run away to from the position of editor. And even if Sutrisno proved with his arguments that he needed to go there, Sudarmo couldn't dismiss his suspicion that Sutrisno had betrayed their endeavor.

"You're running off," Sudarmo finally said in his normally harsh and honest personal style. "You want to leave this, though the work is beginning to grow under our hands. Do you realize what you're doing?"

Sutrisno got angry and his eyes lit up with his fury now boiling over. But, restraining himself, he said, "You suppose I have thoughts that I don't feel or I don't want. We still work together, each in our own field. Isn't the final goal the development of the rural areas? You work from the city, I from the villages, and in this way, we will meet at a point that we have agreed upon and has always been the idea we've held in common." He shook his hair back and ran his hand across his rather prominent mouth with his fine, tightly shut lips.

After this exchange, Sutrisno visited his friend less and less, so that neither knew what the other was doing. They lived as strangers and each reverted to managing his own daily routine.

Herwati in fact complained to Sudarmo: "Trisno now has yet another new thing he wants, a village. Soon he'll forget about it again, and we'll have to come back, and naturally that will involve a lot of expenses. Can you speak with him to drop this plan? You've always had a lot of influence on him."

Sudarmo promised Herwati that he would try to get Sutrisno to change his mind. Sutrisno would soon cancel his plans, once he experienced what it meant to live in a village. But Sutrisno wouldn't listen to him and saw Herwati's concerns as bourgeois petty-mindedness, narrow and cowardly. This even provided an extra stubborn impulse to prepare his move to the village. Herwati gave in. What could she do, if Sutrisno remained glum for several days and barely ever talked to her? Her friends pitied her and tried to find a middle way for Sutrisno. One night they gathered at Sudarmo's home. The atmosphere was fatigued and full of worry, consisting of the contempt of one and the veiled opposition to the other. Muhammad and Jusuf behaved as usual. The women sat on the back veranda and Herwati complained, "Trisno's annoyed at me, but if I don't give in, I'd never forgive myself for as long as I live. I go wherever he goes. He's so puny and sickly. Who'd take care of him in the village?"

Farida kept the pot stirred. "In fact, don't go with him. It's too exhausting for you, right? If you refuse firmly, Mas Tris would cancel his plans, you know."

"Yes," replied Herwati tonelessly and then she stood up and went over to his friends and began telling of her concerns about going to the village.

"What do you think about Trisno's plans?"

Sudarmo replied, “It would be better if Mas Trisno saw for himself what it’s like in the village. At the very least, he has to find a place to stay and so forth. It couldn’t be justified if Mas Tris lets his children face dangers that might arise on the road when they move.”

Back and forth they went, and at last it was decided that Sutrisno go by himself first. After that, Herwati and the children would follow. This satisfied her, but Sutrisno made a sour face and tried to get rid of his gloom by intense debates with his friends. A good mood, though, didn’t materialize, and their shouts were only tired and sharp-sounding. They broke up late that night, and this time Sudarmo’s greetings were perfunctory, even though Sutrisno seemed to want words of warmth and friendliness. In their bedroom, Sudarmo said to his wife, “So, now he’s going to the village, he’ll be back in town on the day after, and like that, this big boy will always bounce back and forth, never making a final decision and never releasing himself from Herwati’s love. Kartonegoro was right when he said that Sutrisno is a leaf on a tree, changing colors and unable to stay firm. And always abandoning his responsibility. This is what cowards do.”

Sulastri didn’t say anything and Sudarmo sat for a long time in reflection, as if he realized what it meant to feel alone.

“He’s broken off with me,” he thought bitterly. “Was it my need for control that made him run from me? Am I so bad that all my friends desert me? Sutrisno has kept himself away for a long time. It was actually he who always listened to me. He was so stubborn just now. As if he were smarter than anybody else. And I meant well by him. He might be the only person I truly love.”

17

Sutrisno went to the village and lodged with an old haji, intending to stay there for a month. After three days, however, he was back, and he stopped by Sudarmo's home before returning to his own.

When he entered the front veranda, Sudarmo was standing in the doorway and greeted his friend with, "Hey! You're back?"

Sutrisno laughed, rather awkwardly but gloomily. "Yes, but I'll soon be going back again," he replied. He saw the surprised look in Sudarmo's eyes pass over his clothes, and explained. "Yes, I wear a pajama top and sarong, because I don't want to stand out in the bus and I don't draw attention when I go about like some villager."

Sudarmo laughed and needled him, "But the way you move your hands and how you speak is too intellectual for a villager."

Sulastri, who recognized Sutrisno's voice, came out and greeted him. "Is this really Mas Tris? Am I dreaming? Dressed like that, Mas really looks like a schoolchild."

Sutrisno felt exposed under Sulastri's scrutiny which was full of teasing and curiosity. This made him angry but he tried to hide his embarrassment by retorting, "Why must we be so bourgeois and reject these clothes? This is really what villagers wear."

"Uh, no," Sulastri said soothingly, "I don't want to humiliate you, but it's so clear that Mas Tris is still our very own Mas Tris, in spite of going about in such clothes."

Sulastri laughed and gazed at him playfully, and Sutrisno laughed as well, although it was a bit forced and sour. Then he said, "We know about such prejudices, but of course those people are very narrow-minded and they regard little issues through a microscope."

"Little issues? It seems to me that's the important point, if Mas wants to totally adjust himself to village ways," Sudarmo said in all earnestness. Then he went on, "In fact, don't brush your teeth anymore and don't use soap."

"Yes," Sulastri added, "most importantly don't brush your teeth because all the toothbrushes are made with pig bristles. To be consistent, you should brush your teeth only with pumice. And your towel must be kept in your luggage."

Sutrisno looked at Sudarmo and Sulastri in turn and was worried about this, but he noticed Sudarmo looked directly ahead as if nothing was the matter and saw a crease in Sulastri's forehead, and suddenly he began to laugh and they laughed too. He said he felt caught out. "There's some truth to that, but to act that way...." He shrugged, looked away a moment, then lit up: "The silence at night sometimes sets the nerves on edge, and then there's the voices of the people reciting the Quran all around me."

"But one can capture the poetry of all that there, right, Mas? And isn't Mas Tris charmed by the clumps of the rustling bamboo?" said Sudarmo and he winked at his wife.

"And in the morning," said Sulastri in a high voice, "the fresh breeze and dew that vanishes slowly and mysteriously and captivates our desire to get to know that closed remoteness. Oh, there I will feel happy and always feel enchanted when I see the rustling stalks of golden yellow rice."

"It depends on the person, from what angle he sees those conditions and situations," Sutrisno said despondently. "I don't look for poetry in the villages. I'm too empty to search out only things that are pleasing to the eye." And in quite a different tone, he said to Sudarmo, "Come with me to the village, Mas. You will get other impressions."

At first Sudarmo was unwilling, but in the end, he agreed, and they took a bus to the village. That night when they returned, Sudarmo began a lively account to Sulastri and Jusuf. "Pak Haji's house is on a little street, and I entered it filled with expectations, since Trisno had told me about it, and also this haji was religious and a clever speaker. We came to a little raised house next to a prayer house. Next to the prayer house was a small pond with brown water, where you have to wash your hands and feet as *wudu* before praying. Trisno explained to me that he had to wash his mouth out as well with that water and that he hasn't been able to bring himself to do that. I had to laugh seeing the catastrophic look on his face, but dodged the thought by asking about the old haji's family, as though I had some great interest in them. As Trisno told it, he had three girls who were always giggling in the room next to mine. They disturbed me with their laughing, but I pretended not to hear anything.

"When I teased Trisno, saying 'Be careful, Mas Tris! Zus Herwati can't know about this. That haji wants you to be his son-in-law!' he got angry. 'I'm already married.' Then I teased him more, 'That's no obstacle for a haji'. Well, I then got to meet that Pak Haji."

"So, what was he like?" asked Sulastri, curious.

"I had supposed he'd look like one of those religious scholars, white goatee and all, but actually, he was a fierce-looking guy, a real businessman, with a dirty *peci* and green teeth. There wasn't the least indication of him of being a religious master, only his fatherly attitude toward Trisno. Then we debated a bit about verses in the Quran, and Trisno sat with us like some little kid. And those three young girls, all were equally ugly and stupid."

Jusuf took hold of his chin with his right hand, nodded and said, "Oh, that Mas Trisno, he brings trouble on himself."

Then he laughed, and Farida, who had just come to fetch her husband, joined in laughing, even though she didn't know what it was all about and asked, "Why are you all laughing?" This tickled Sulastri all the more, and she shook her head as she laughed. Sudarmo explained it all to Farida and then continued, "When the bus left, he looked at me so sadly, like he was going to ask me to just stay there. I turned my head, but truly I had to laugh, it was so funny. I waved at him and saw him go into that little muddy street with his head bowed."

They laughed again and Farida's laugh was the loudest of all. As she explained it, "I'm sure he'll come back fast," and everyone present agreed with her. A week after Sudarmo's visit to the village, Sutrisno came again, his left arm bandaged up. His left hand was bound against his chest and there was a look of pain on his face. He looked very ill. He kept touching his left arm with his right hand, and screwed up his mouth and face. This irritated Sudarmo who asked harshly, "What's the matter, Mas?"

"I sprained my arm. *Aduh!*," Sutrisno replied and he stroked the cloth that bound his left arm. "My arm's swollen and now I have to see a doctor about it."

"Does it really hurt a lot?" asked Sudarmo sympathetically and with an ironic glint in his eyes. Trisno moaned "*Aduh*" again and grimaced with curled lips. "Really, I couldn't sleep at all last night. I have to stay here a week at the very least for the doctor's treatment."

Thus, Sutrisno stayed at home for a week as his arm healed, even though he often said that improvement was slow and that he should be getting back quickly to the village. Herwati took care of him, and she was so gentle and sweet that people were amazed to see how busy she was around Sutrisno, who let himself be spoiled and looked recovered, even if he didn't really want to admit it. Friends came by to look in on him and came back on memorable nights, even with Sutrisno's demeanor of seeming to ask for pity, because Herwati solicitously created a welcoming atmosphere.

At home, Sudarmo told Sulastri, "Mas Trisno is faking. Why

doesn't he just say that he wants to come home and be with his wife and kids?"

Sudarmo discussed Sutrisno's situation with Jusuf and Muhammad, and Jusuf said, "Mas Trisno can't live without Zus Herwati. He's going to ask her to go to the village to keep him company in his isolation there, for sure."

The others nodded in agreement and Sudarmo said, "Yes, let's just let it be.... He's definitely got some scheme or other for asking his wife."

And that suspicion was totally correct, because when his arm had healed and another week had gone by, Sutrisno came to Sudarmo and said in bubbling high spirits, "Isolation in the village inhibits me and, what's more, every night I hear people reciting and praying everywhere. Those voices in the silence are just so annoying and they're still in my ears right up to now. On the train I hear it sliding along with the sound *la ilaha illallah, la ilaha illallah*. I feel my nerves getting all tense. Those voices seem to be following me even to this place. No, I am going to go crazy if I stay there by myself any longer."

Sutrisno went silent and looked at Sudarmo somewhat oddly. Sudarmo, choosing his words, said, "Come back home, Mas. You're just staying temporarily at Pak Haji's, right?"

"No," Sutrisno shook his head tenaciously, "I won't abruptly let go of all that, if you can imagine, simply because I can't stand hearing that buzzing sound in the silence. No, I'd be ashamed of myself, if I abandoned my plans just like that. I asked Herwati to come as quickly as possible to the village."

"It hasn't occurred to you, Mas Tris, what kind of situation it would be for Zus Herwati, if at the crack of dawn, she had to come here and only return home? And this goes on every day? Are you aware of what it means to draw yourself totally into the village? You don't intend to become a hermit, do you?"

"At this time, I need a different environment around me. This isn't escaping, but rather one step in convincing myself. From there I can see objectively a lot of things in their individual colors. Here I feel submerged and like I'm sinking myself into trivial things."

"But it's precisely here that we need you," Sudarmo argued. "Especially seeing that everything is growing, why must we pick on each other and sometimes not understand each other? I think you aren't contributing your energy to our endeavor, if you're looking for your own happiness in that village."

This made Sutrisno angry and sharp words were ready on his lips, but he just stroked his face. Once again, Sudarmo's sarcasm came out. "It's not for introspection that you stay there. Besides, I know a lot of people who examine their souls their whole lives and up to now still haven't reached any realization of themselves."

Sutrisno replied indifferently, as if he didn't care what his friend thought. "People can think what they want. I'm not going to go through life quacking like a duck. I want to be free," he said with a shrug.

"It's not a quacking duck that we want from you, Mas. It's courage to carry through a job until it's completed. Besides, Mas must remember Zus Herwati. Aren't you aware how tough village life would be for her?"

"If I didn't dare to sacrifice my life for an ideal, I'd have no right to keep on living. And if Herwati doesn't wish to be with me in this, let her find out for herself!"

"Hold on, Mas. It's clear you want to go to the village and you want Zus Herwati and the children to go there too. There's no use in us talking like we're in a stage play. In the end, this doesn't just affect Mas only! I see this as a waste of energy in trying to do all those things. I mean, for a temporary notion, you're risking the love of your wife. And because of that, it'd be better to continue on for another month of living there by yourself. Moving to the village with your family will cost a lot, as well as being troublesome, and... for Zus Herwati, it will be exhausting to move there now and then return later to town."

This struck home and Sutrisno didn't want to say anything more. He paid his respects and went home.

That night, he came back with Herwati, and immediately she started in. "We'll be going to the village next week. I feel it's my obligation to be by Trisno's side in everything."

Sudarmo and Sulastri said nothing and looked with extreme concern at Herwati, who seemed suddenly very contented. It was as if she felt Sutrisno's love was in her hands and there was no need to share that love with anyone else. Then she went on, "I'll be very happy in the village. Will you both come to visit? Tris has gotten a house with a broad field in the back and to the side and by the village office. I will be going and coming by *oplet* and it will be fun to live in a different environment."

Then Sutrisno added, "I'll raise chickens and sell the eggs. Besides that, I'll encourage the villagers to pound the rice themselves and not take it to the mill. And I'll recommend that they make coconut oil. If you all in town want to propagandize hand-pounded rice and medicinal oils, then we will have moved a few steps ahead toward cooperation between village and town."

"Yes, yes, and we'll be giving work to the farmers because they're forced to be unemployed for six months; but it's also quite hard being a *kulak* and at the same time a propagandist for the *kolkhoz*," joked Sudarmo, and the warm atmosphere returned. They all took turns teasing each other until late into the night. Sudarmo and Sulastri accompanied their guests when they left, but they were all talking so much that they went farther than intended and found themselves in front of Sutrisno's house and only there did they part, promising to visit Herwati in the village.

The day of Herwati's move arrived. Before that, her friends and acquaintances were all aflutter about Sutrisno's plans and their pity for Herwati, because of her whimsical husband who was always busy devising new experiments. Herwati responded by saying it was only temporary, and that if Sutrisno knew what Herwati said, he wouldn't forgive her.

But people *did* consider Sutrisno eccentric, someone who wanted to bang his head with all his strength because he intended to experience his fate to the fullest. Sudarmo said with a smile to Jusuf, "Mas Tris will come back for sure. In the end he has to find out about the bitter side of life. And each defeat will either raise his prestige or bring it down. It's my guess he'll be experiencing some new crisis."

The Sutrisno family moved to the village, and that was the last people heard of them. Once in a while, Sutrisno would come to town, and one day he came offering hand-pounded rice to several prominent people, who ordered a little, but afterwards said that it was inedible and even their servants didn't like it. And Sutrisno grumbled that he couldn't reduce the price because the wages paid to pound the rice was too high. And so he lost a bit of money and then tried with cassava.

Although Sutrisno was no longer seen in the circle of his colleagues, their work went on. The journal came out in an orderly manner, and Sudarmo's articles were the talk of everyone. The library got new members as time went on, and the colleagues still visited each other as before to enjoy conversation. They often discussed Sutrisno. Farida came almost daily to chat, and she saw this and that in the Sudarmo family. One day she came with cream-colored sandals with high heels. She approached Sulastri and thrust them into her hands, saying, "Put them right on, they're still brand new!"

And because Sulastri said nothing, she added, "Come on, they're of no use to me." At that, Sulastri regarded Farida, deeply moved, and then joyfully gazed at the sandals. She walked back and forth and asked for praise from Sudarmo, while Farida stood there with her own overflowing happiness. Sulastri's old slippers were worn no more and now she wore those sexy sandals, with the click-clack of the heels sounding happily on the wooden floor.

On another occasion, when Sulastri visited her family, her mother gave her a piece of cloth for a kebaya, saying as usual, "For you. You don't deserve to wear a kebaya so worn out as that one." And her daughter, who at first was going to refuse it, accepted it, and even felt moved by the pity that she had unintentionally aroused. Because she didn't wish to speak about the situation at home, she pretended that they didn't need to feel any pity. In her family everyone knew what the situation was like and Sulastri, who sometimes liked to daydream, aroused their sympathy and they blamed Sudarmo for such an impoverished existence. For this reason, Sulastri kept away from her family.

One day at the end of the month, Marti dropped by to look in on them and upon parting stuck a half-rupiah in her apathetic sister's hand as she said, "I haven't had any money until very recently. If I have any, I'll give you more." It was true what Marti said, because she was usually short of funds, and sometimes had only a few cents at month's end.

"Oh, no," Sulastri refused, "Don't. I already have all kinds of things at home." But because Marti pressed her, she said wearily, "Thanks, this is fortunate."

When Marti left, Sulastri got a scolding from her husband, but she let those sharp words pass and with the money bought a tin of sardines and, for the overjoyed Rustini, a piece of chocolate. After Farida, Jusuf came and rather stiffly gave a shirt to Sudarmo, who thanked him warmly. He clasped the fine cloth and his face showed the brightness of his pleasure. After Jusuf left, he said to Sulastri, "I didn't have it in me to refuse that shirt. It pleased him to give me even some little joy."

They felt they were even closer in friendship during this period. Muhammad, who now lived at his fiancée's home, came as usual, loyally not saying much when he had to take over the library. He even began to be more voluble, and one day he told Sudarmo about this and that aspect of his life and also about his fiancée. After he spoke so freely, Sulastri considered him even more sympathetic, even though she felt odd at now being able to converse with him without the slightest bit of tension. Sulastri even began to tease him about his betrothed, and it seemed that he enjoyed the teasing because he repeatedly spoke about her. People were surprised that he was so delighted with that girl, while Sulastri without realizing it deprecated that delight. And gradually Sulastri saw him as a man who in time would submit to his wife.

"What does he see in her?" Sulastri asked Sudarmo. "But, all right, that's his own affair. Still, I feel sorry for his lot in life."

"He has little awareness of his own worth," Sudarmo replied. "With his title of bachelor of law, he could get dozens of girls like that later on, because everyone looks up to someone with a university degree like that, even people I'd never expect."

Sulastri looked out the window and the sky seemed to shimmer from the sun's heat. She wiped her brow and burst out laughing, as she quickly stood up and went to sit on the steps next to the kitchen. Sudarmo sat next to her at first and then invited her to the edge of the stream. The brown water below them roared, at first contracting before running straight again. The water looked so fresh in the heated air. A little path carved into the riverbank led down to the water. Sudarmo bent under the barbed wire and he followed the steps down, signaling Sulastri to copy him. But his wife stayed standing as she watched him slowly make his way down. Jusuf stood behind suddenly and without her knowing it. He giggled when he saw that Sudarmo was below them.

"What's he down there for?" he asked.

"Oh, he wants to see if he can make a little pond there, and if so, we will raise big carp in it."

"A very good idea." Jusuf nodded his head in appreciation, and he bent low under the wire and went down to the side of the stream. When the two friends came back up, they cheerfully planned on directing the water into the pond in such a way that there'd always be water there. But all discussion came to an abrupt halt, for the young journal administrator, who had been appointed with a 5 guilder allowance, food and free lodgings at Sudarmo's home, came with the news that the head of the printery was sick and thus they were still short one article.

What should they do? It was already Friday. Sudarmo had done two articles. Advertisements for the library had been printed bigger and wider, and newly arrived books had been publicized. Thus, they decided to reproduce a part of *Jean-Christophe* and the most apropos part would be about women. And so they took the section about Amelie, and Sulastri had to translate it into Sundanese, rather difficult for her as she didn't have a Sundanese dictionary. When the translation was completed, Sulastri wasn't satisfied with it, for she considered the sentence sequences were more like Dutch. Writing in her own language was very difficult, when people always treated people who taught it with scorn. She remembered a teacher of Sundanese in primary school who always awarded a grade of 4 to her compositions, because she was too fanciful. That was his view and Sulastri didn't like him. And so she worked for a Dutch teacher, and she now very much regretted that she hadn't been so smart back then. Now she had to write articles in Sundanese, because Sudarmo was buried with work.

There was a lot to do at home, too, and strolling about in the evenings was out of the question, as was going out and having fun on Sundays. To take a break from daily work, Sudarmo made a model of a small kitchen cabinet. He carefully sawed board sections according to measure, and he was so meticulous that he was at it for two days before he could nail the top and sides. He nailed a piece of green wire mesh on one side, and when he finished, he proudly displayed the result of his work. Now all that was left was to catch and caulk a few cracks between the boards. As he was painting it, Sutrisno unexpectedly showed up and was interested in what his friend was doing.

"A great cabinet!" he gushed.

"Yes," his friend said, calmly painting with long swipes.

"Sulastri needs a cabinet, so I made her this, so that food can be stored properly. This still needs red borders and after that I'm done." Sudarmo stood up and put away his can of paint, and unconsciously rubbed his hands. Then he sighed, "I went through a lot of trouble to make this, but now I dare to make a rack."

"Goodness," Sulastri said ironically. "If a carpenter needed as much time as you..."

Sutrisno laughed, but now Sudarmo heard his friend's amusement as mocking when Sutrisno said to himself, "It's so annoying to always be tinkering and fiddling. It'd be better to use the time for some other job."

Sudarmo retorted, "Oh, yes, if you measure everything with the results... but the pleasure is in doing something, that's the thing."

Sutrisno's expression was strained. He took this as innuendo.

Jusuf was sitting in the reading room, but when Sutrisno joined him, conversation didn't go smoothly and Sutrisno quickly bid goodbye. Sudarmo gave him several sheets of their journal which shook him inside, though he didn't show it, and then he invited his friends to the village.

On the following Sunday, Sulastri, Sudarmo and Rustini went there. Muhammad came along as well, but Jusuf and his wife would only come later, as they still had work to do at home. Muhammad bought an orange at the train station and when they arrived at the little stop, they got off and went by *sado*. They passed though winding streets, cassava trees on both sides. They went over a bridge crossing a rock-filled stream with almost no water. They ascended and descended slopes. Finally, they saw Sutrisno's home. In front of the house, a little to the side, was a leafless tree, almost reduced to its trunk from being struck by lightning. It stood there, frightening, black and melancholy. Sudarmo pointed to it, "The guardian spirit of the village," he said and when the other two exclaimed in surprise, he laughed and whispered mysteriously, "Sutrisno knows how to talk about it. Ask him a little later."

Herwati was sewing in a little garden in front of the house. She didn't jump up when she saw her friends, but knotted her thread first. This attitude wasn't her usual one, and her visitors looked at each other briefly. Sutrisno descended a little set of wooden steps and he expressed his joy a bit overflowingly.

"Hello, friends, I'm happy you've come." He told his servant to bring chairs to the little garden and the visitors had an opportunity to look around them.

Sulastri, who had imagined an idealized view, was disappointed when she saw the only garden covered in dense grass, but in every respect no different from their garden in town. A jackfruit tree with its fruit in cracked husks provided a bit of shade. Then a green fence and several flowers were visible here and there, as if shy to be seen; but the dusty road and the houses across the street were low and faded in color. Next to the garden was a plot of land, broad and unplanted, that stretched to the rear of the house and descended gently to the river, and after that became a hillside, which in the distance looked green and fresh in the sunshine. On the piece of land in front of the kitchen were several long bean plants propped up with bamboo, and a smattering of green vegetables. Under the jackfruit tree along the fence, some of the earth had been dug up and a few stunted banana trees rose from a deep excavation; they looked like they had just been planted. Sutrisno followed the close interest of his friends who noticed all that, and he explained, "The owner of the house, Pak Lurah, says I can cultivate all the land on the side and around the house."

"Excellent!", Sudarmo said approvingly. "Will you be using artificial fertilizer? But you would have to stay here a long time. It would be terribly frustrating if you were to work so hard for someone else."

Sutrisno did not take that bait, but gave a little laugh and invited them to look around some more. The raised house was quite neat and tidy. Only the white bed was not in harmony with the unpainted windows, and the place for washing one's face was a little strange-looking and the glass cabinet too modern. In this house, so simple and no eyesore, it felt painfully conspicuous because there was no room for a buffet, so that the buffet was in a place where it shouldn't have been, thus giving the impression of the little house being cramped for space. The dining room was an annex and had a brown dirt floor. In the kitchen there was an open stove, and here the servant was cooking the cassava and sweet potato that was to be served to the guests. In the rear of the house, a part of the yard was fenced off by little bamboo stakes.

"For the chickens," explained Sutrisno.

"Oh, a chicken yard," said Sudarmo. Muhammad suspected that civets could come and get in there.

"Yes," said Sulastri, "It's got to be tightly guarded, Mas Tris. In my village we were always troubled by civets. Do the chickens here have to nest in this modern coop?"

"No, I am ready with one sketch. This is the coop for walking around. The coop for sleeping had to be built first and I have researched a number of things about chicken husbandry."

They went almost to edge of the drop off and looked out into the distance, where the blue of the sky began to pale and several white spots evoked memories in Sulastri of the time she was a little girl hunting egrets. She stood there in silence and immersed herself in the passion of the silent view that spoke so much to her.

A fresh breeze swept the heat from her cheeks and brought a wistfulness to the village of her childhood. She thinks she hears the dim sounds of mortar on pestle, the clean bright sound of a loom, the cheerful voices of people joking or whispering mysteries, and the noise of *sado* wheels rolling on gravelly streets. She remembers a lumpy durian tree. Under it, she had sought its yellow-brown fruit, fine as velvet. She made dolls from the big fruit, whose names she is unable to say.

This was only because of the wind and the distance so pale, but the images of bygone times reappear intensely within her. Marti with her bangs, fierce eyes, and sturdy legs. And she herself with a palm frond rib smeared with jackfruit sap catching dragonflies in the hot sunlight. She would sing high notes offkey that usually brought laughter. Then she sees Marti again, eager to sell rambutans from their garden. She's tied them up with several bindings and angrily throws the coins back into the face of the buyer, considering the two little coins too cheap for that heap of sweet, fresh fruit. Marti is only five years old then and Mother tells how the buyer grabbed hold of Marti, but Marti scratched and bit him and went after him until he gave back the rambutans. Then there is that scary night when two leopards tore their dog to pieces. Her uncle goes with a rifle to look for the leopards and she and Marti stay by themselves in the house, glued to each other and imagining they hear the scratching and the roaring of the two leopards. And Mother is away and Bapak at that time is always gone, so they hug each other ever more tightly. In that wide night, they can feel and hear their hearts beating.

"Oh, the Marti of those days," thought Sulastri and her eyes filled with tears. Why should something totally insignificant, like that mischievous wind, be able to call up different events that she supposed were buried very deep, dead and forgotten. She turned and noticed she was by herself. She turned around again to the view in front of her, but it was no longer as captivating as before and she had to give a silent laugh. It was all just a dream, she thought, and she slowly walked behind her other friends.

Herwati was standing by the kitchen feeding her second child, a one-year-old boy whose face brought to mind Herwati's father. That's why Sutrisno's love for this child was not as spontaneous, and often his love got mixed up with something he wasn't aware of. Sulastri stood there briefly chatting, and again Herwati spoke of the hardships in her home, how the servant had to wash the clothes under a tap down below at the side of the stream, how she bathed there, too, how there was nothing to be bought here, and how she herself always bathed early in the morning behind the kitchen with water stored in a barrel, because it was too dark and too dangerous to go to the stream. Sulastri nodded in understanding, but she wondered why they didn't come back to town.

An autobus sounded a long blast from its horn. People descended from it, and when Sulastri looked that way, Farida and Jusuf were among them and waving. Farida came over and entered the yard, lively and kittenish in her long Minangkabau kebaya with its purple flowers, worn over a sarong of Javanese batik. She loosely held a bag and a folded shawl.

"Hello, Zus Herwati, Zus Tri," she said, greeting them with a smile. Farida held Herwati by the arm and, looking at her face, she suddenly exclaimed, "You're really dark. It's really the healthy skin color of the village."

Herwati laughed, but there was an embarrassed quality in her expression that rejected these words. Then, scrutinizing Farida from her head to her toes, "You're dressed so prettily, but I guess you could be more frugal about it too," she said.

"Yes, you could cut off several meters and maybe there'd be enough for another kebaya," mocked Sulastri.

Just then the men came up and Sudarmo joked, "Your chitchatting is correct, but it's more decent like this, although—"

He stopped and Sulastri picked up the thread, "Yes, Zus, this blouse, light and cool, right?"

Farida reddened under their calculating gaze, and wanted to say something but held herself back, and looked back at them, one by one, until Sudarmo gave the signal to laugh all together. Jusuf even had tears in his eyes. Farida herself joined in but concealed her embarrassment by going up to the long bean tree, picking one and biting it slowly. Just then, she noticed the ground that had been hoed and, fully interested, asked who had done that. Sutrisno indifferently admitted that he'd worked at it for two days but quit when his hands got blisters.

"Hah!" exclaimed Jusuf, amazed. "*Aduh*, ibu! Mas Tris," and he broke out in giggles so noteworthy that everyone laughed too. Then Farida asked derisively, "So, how many months would be needed to hoe ground as wide as this?" Then, Sulastri sarcastically calculated, maybe a year.

Sutrisno was embarrassed, but Farida kept poking, "A few more months and we'll be seeing cabbage, beans, fruit trees, flowers… oh for sure, it'll have become a *park*."

"We'll go and have picnics there and try not to step all over the plants," added Sulastri.

"Such a fantasy," said Sutrisno. "Never mind, Mas Dar, let's go sit there under the tree."

The men went ahead, with the women walking behind, and now they started their own conversations, with Farida's and Herwati's voices prominent, and those of Jusuf or Muhammad occasionally heard. The rest were silent, immersed in that strange atmosphere. Numerous buses passed by, raising great clouds of dust.

"It's noisier here than in town, in front of the school," Farida commented. Jusuf nodded and said, "A good village, and I wouldn't feel I was in one if this house had a bathroom."

Sudarmo once again pointed to the blackened tree and whispered, "What did you say just now? This is a village, because in town there's no way we'd have a tree like that. There's a story linked with that tree, isn't there, Mas Tris?"

Sutrisno's face reddened, which piqued Farida's curiosity. Herwati looked at her husband, who began in an unremarkable tone of voice. "Oh, that's where the village guardian lives. As new residents, we had to hold a selamatan and on that occasion, we smoked opium, because that spirit had that habit of old or maybe still does. At first, I didn't want to, but Pak Haji urged me on something fierce, and we did it, even if I didn't believe the story." He shrugged, and Farida shouted, "Oh God, Mas and that narcotic drug?" They all burst out laughing and Sudarmo thought that this would bring on inner tranquility, precisely because it was strange that sometimes you do something according to ancient custom, even though you know it's not really right, and he gave this as an example.

Then Herwati told a ghost story, and in this way without noticing it they were prattling away, until Herwati remembered with a shock that the visitors had to eat.

In the dining room with its tiny windows where there was only space for chairs, they ate heartily of red rice, fish and other side dishes. Seeing the greens, Sulastri said, "Red rice, salted fish, spicy relish, all eaten in a little hut amid the rice fields, the sunshine about you—so delightful! I should be jealous of the peasants!"

"Yes," said Muhammad, "I remember when I was still small, I loved to eat like that. But I'd be happier sitting on a dike in the rice fields, my feet in the water, and not in a hut."

And so, they went on and on about the poetry of life in the village and how Sutrisno seemed to have been refreshed. He expanded happily on his plans and the others stopped chatting because they wanted to just listen respectfully while Sutrisno spoke on and on and only stopped at the sudden arrival of the servant bringing peeled citrus fruit and roasted yams. This gave the group of friends a reason to open their mouths in praise of the yams. Farida began to rattle away again. She couldn't sit still and from time to time took hold of Sulastri's arm.

After the men had eaten, they again sat down under the jackfruit tree, but the women went to take a look at the village office next to the house and picked the deep-red soldier-button flowers from the garden being tended there, while Rustini and Juniati played with stones in the road, under the watchful eyes of a twelve-year-old. This village office was spacious and furnished with benches and didn't look any different from other ones. It was cool in there and they sat down. Farida just went on joking and Herwati and Sulastri only laughed. However, the shadows in the roads and streets and the yards were gradually lengthening, leading Sulastri to consider it was time for them to return home. They approached the men who were still absorbed in their discussions.

"Those robbers have threatened to come here," related Sutrisno. "In the end, Pak Lurah ordered this house guarded, and they robbed elsewhere, but to feel calm, I've borrowed a rifle from my brother-in-law."

"Mas Tak knows how to use a rifle, is that right? Aren't you afraid of shooting by mistake?" Farida interrupted.

"Not for shooting robbers, but for shooting your own shoulder," said Jusuf artlessly. "And that rifle can fall on the floor, but Zus Herwati would most likely be next to you to pick it up."

Sutrisno laughed accommodatingly and replied, "Feeling that there's a gun in the house gives you an inner strength over those robbers, even if you don't know how to shoot. But I admit that I'm still rather scared."

Sudarmo winked at his friends. “It really is frightening. Let’s go back quickly to town, even though you could say this village is right at the edge of town or the gates of the town.”

“Mas mocks everything, but he’s not necessarily right,” Sutrisno answered hotly.

Here was a reason for debate, but it wasn’t taken up, for the servant brought in three baskets of yams, souvenirs for the guests. Sudarmo got one basket, as did Jusuf. Muhammad got one for his betrothed and got teased once again by everyone.

They had to wait patiently for the final bus to come.

18

A year had slipped past their notice and many difficulties and hardships loomed again for the days to come.

On the first days of the new school year, only five children were enrolled, much less than they had hoped for, and Sudarmo was in despair. Jusuf and Sutrisno were with him, the former looking sadly ahead, but Sutrisno spoke matter-of-factly, "Herwati actually encouraged the messengers and other office workers to enroll their kids here."

"Oh," said Sudarmo and he shrugged to cover his dejection. "Surely more than that will come, maybe this week. They're trying to find a place in a government school or a subsidized one first. Then they'll come here."

Jusuf nodded and spoke sympathetic words about how in the morning he had been feeling sad and moody. Sutrisno in fact had a lot to say, but his words came across as devoid of meaning and it seemed that he said them merely because he had to speak. Sudarmo just stayed silent, sometimes glancing at the street. Occasionally he tried to joke, but he sounded flat and lethargic, and anyone could see the real situation.

After Jusuf and Sutrisno left, Sudarmo and Sulastri sat facing each other at the dining table. Suddenly Sudarmo sprang up angrily and said, "This is what's come of Sutrisno's fooling around! Besides, your father, who knows a lot of people in this town, isn't pleased with us. He may also have had a bit to do with tripping us up and that can be understood. Don't believe in kualat, when Marti attacks and hits you with such words."

He stopped for a moment and looked outside, where the clove tree showed its dark, mossy branches. Sulastri followed his gaze and she abruptly realized that those familiar green branches might soon live only in her memory because they might have to leave them again. She felt so depressed and weak that she had to force herself upright to see normally. Several days before, they had discussed this possibility and were full of doubt as to what was the best course of action, to just stay or to leave again. Now, after Sutrisno had displayed his strangely calm attitude that very morning, almost indifferent, Sudarmo's hesitation was gone and he said bitterly, "There's no use in staying here."

Sulastri replied soothingly, "You don't have to be so sad. This is the result of your comical criticisms. The result of having a principled attitude. If you want to compromise... but in this way, we stand more purely with the national struggle and for me that's a good feeling. That we don't lower ourselves to get this and that!"

She looked at her husband and some gleam in her eyes made Sudarmo heave a sigh of relief and form new plans.

"I'll write to Hapsoro and see if he'd help us. Before, he had asked you to work for him and for a while you would get *f*25. What's more, he would issue the journal with me and I'd be paid for it. He also wants to hold night classes."

"Good," said Sulastri. "And Herwati promised that she would provide a subsidy for one year and now that year has passed..."

Sudarmo wrote a letter to Hapsoro and a week later a telegram came in response: "Come right now." And so, their hesitation ended, and they got ready to move. Sudarmo wrote Sutrisno to come and discuss school matters, and when Sutrisno came, with his couldn't-care-less, calm, and even remote attitude, his friend showed him the telegram and simply said, "We're going to Semarang at the end of the month."

Sutrisno didn't any show any emotion and he seemed to feel it his obligation to ask, "You can't wait three months more? Herwati wants to extend her subsidy by three more months."

"No," said Sudarmo firmly, "If we haven't succeeded in one year, there's no use in extending any more. Let's settle all of this and see how best we'll do it."

Sutrisno tried to argue him out of it, but because their friendship no longer felt so deep, his counter-arguments sounded almost disappointing. Three days after this conversation, the friends all gathered in the reading room. Now there was someone else, Buntaran, who had just entered this circle of comrades. Broad-shouldered and with an open face that clearly showed his sincerity, he soon won everyone over. When Sulastri asked Sudarmo about Buntaran, he replied with certainty, "Honest and brave." But Farida said, "Strong inside and outgoing," which gave Sulastri the impression of something hidden about him. And possibly so, because Buntaran liked to visit Jusuf, even if he didn't speak much with Farida.

Sudarmo opened his speech by presenting his plans. After a momentary silence, they came to the discussions. It was decided that the students would be transferred to a nationalist education school in that town, that Buntaran would continue the journal, while Jusuf would head the library. Furthermore, Sutrisno would replace Sudarmo as the leader among the circle of comrades, but for that he would have to move back to town and stay in the school building. It was almost ten o'clock before Sutrisno bid them good night, and when Sudarmo asked him in surprise why he didn't just stay with them, he answered vaguely that he really did have to go home, that he would wait in front of the market for a truck to take him to the village.

"Just wear my jacket. It's good for keeping out the cold," Sudarmo said. At first Sutrisno refused, then he took it, moved by Sudarmo's offer which had come spontaneously from his heart, and went into the cold night. A wind had come up so strong that the nuts from the branches of the *kenari* tree fell with a sharp "tok" to the ground. Their other friends were still standing by the wall of the front veranda and shivering. The wind was blowing so hard into the house through the veranda that the lamps swayed and the palms waved elegantly. That evening Jusuf had kept quiet and now spoke to Sudarmo in doubt, "But really couldn't Mas stay here?"

"No," replied Sudarmo, shaking his head. "Mas himself knows our situation here." He stopped and regarded his friends, who were all looking down, filled with their own thoughts. Jusuf said again, "No matter what, maybe we could try to—"

Unexpectedly, Buntaran interrupted with a regret that couldn't be hidden. "Now, after I have met you, Mas, and joined in helping you, you are actually leaving us. You may not know that I have suffered much and will soon be recovered, but now...." Running his hand across his forehead, he went on, "It's my lot, of course, to have bad luck in everything." He smiled, but his smile pierced the hearts of everyone, and Sudarmo said quickly, "People can meet again in our lives, but do the journal well and that work will give you the courage to live."

Buntaran nodded and spoke about his plans. The atmosphere remained tense and when they left, there was note of frustration in Jusuf's voice, while, for the first time, Muhammad looked quite moved. Finally, they were lost in the darkness beyond the light of the streetlamps. A cold breeze blew through the streets, raising leaves that had fallen there, in spiral movements. The nutmeg trees with their dark tops and leaves briefly gleaming in the light, stood indomitable and bewitching. Light from the reading room fell on the steps and passed over the gravel and spread from trunk to tip while rough circles of light formed on the ground beneath the trees.

Sudarmo slowly climbed the steps and went onto the front veranda and listlessly shut the windows and the doors to the reading room. On the back veranda, Sulastri was reading. When Sudarmo came up to her, he said straightforwardly, "In a few more days, we're going to be again leaving everything that I know here." They both knew that they would be experiencing strange days but that during those same days, they would learn to appreciate many things with care.

After they took the decision and everything was in order, including transferring the students to the nationalist education school, all that remained now was to bid farewell to their acquaintances. Sudarmo went to Batavia to say goodbye to the Kartonegoro family, though Sulastri stayed at home to pack. When Sudarmo returned, she asked him about this and that, and Sudarmo said, "Marti asked that you stay over at her place."

"Oh God." Sulastri frowned, caught by surprise, making Sudarmo laugh. "When I was there just recently, I had to run to my room to avoid their flareups."

Sulastri's laugh was full of derision, but she continued by forgiving him. "He wants to convert people too much and doesn't understand that people laugh at him. At the end of the day, I really feel sorry for Marti."

He shrugged and they didn't speak any more about Sulastri's older sister.

They had farewell visits, as dictated by custom, alone or together, and knew nothing more than that their departure was near. For the past few days, their comradeship felt ever closer. It seemed that Sudarmo and Sulastri saw their friends one by one and got from each the qualities that were so pleasing: Farida, with her laugh like a turtledove, Jusuf with his gentle face, Muhammad with his loyalty and silent character, and Sutrisno... but here their thoughts halted, because Sutrisno was still behaving indifferently.

Herwati only came briefly after Sudarmo and family had said goodbye to her in the village, and she was perfunctory, which was not in character with her, and they sensed in her a hidden hostility.

The final day arrived and Sutrisno seem to suddenly realize just what these two people meant to him. He had lost about six hundred rupiah, hadn't followed his law classes for about a year and now had only a modicum of self-confidence.

He spent that night with them. The next day the Sudarmo family would leave by the first train for Central Java and with that they would be ending a collaboration between friends who no longer remembered those everyday trivial issues. They gathered together until late that night. Sulastri's mother and her relatives also came. Her mother only looked at her child and said nothing. The atmosphere was cordial and courteous on the front veranda, where the men sat, and on the rear veranda where the women were helping pack things. Sulastri joked and laughed. She said over and over that she would return. Gradually that happiness switched to quickly saying something, then something else, because in a while there would be no more time to say anything; but they were all too moved, and so stayed silent so as not to touch the feelings stored in their hearts. In the front room as well, they were silent. The guests departed one by one. Only Sutrisno still stayed behind, chatting a little, but the night was far gone when they went to sleep.

Sulastri was up at 4:00 am. She made coffee and dressed Rustini warmly. Then she herself was ready to go. A little later Jusuf, Muhammad, and Buntaran arrived and they went wordlessly to the station through dark streets. Rustini thought the streetlamps were funny, and Jusuf, who liked her very much, was moved and took hold of her hand. "Oh, Rustini, when will Uncle see you again?"

There were only a few people on the platform, so that as a group they stood out. Occasionally, someone would talk, though with no real appetite to do so, as if everything appeared empty to them at that time. They looked for seats in the coach and after that they bid their final farewells, nodded, waved, and the train entered the cold of the morning. Everything that they had experienced was behind them and the days ahead were in the distance, and they would have to be experienced again with all their consequences. The wheels rolled and the houses flew past.

"Sutrisno stood there as if he wanted to say something else," thought Sudarmo and he looked out and everywhere the grass was covered with dew.

"Ibu was so quiet last night, and Farida was gushing with happiness," thought Sulastri. She remembered it all and it was painful for her to watch the surroundings seeming to run backwards. Depok, Manggarai, Gambir, then Marti with her children were standing there together with Sulastri's younger sister with her husband. Marti looked quite flustered in excusing her husband—"His foot hurts."—and she pressed five one-rupiah bills into her hand and gave her a basket full of food. Marti glanced over at her little sister and there was emotion in it. Sudarmo was now down from the train and Kemal had climbed on his back.

"It's going to be really hot later on," said Sulastri. "Your citrons will be refreshing." She smiled at Marti and had a feeling she couldn't hold back, to break out weeping.

The train started off again, its wheels turning forward. There were tears in Marti's eyes just then, but that didn't mean much, because she always blew hot and cold, and that pretty much summed up Marti. On the train they didn't much speak, Sulastri sitting in the corner and trying to read, while Sudarmo yawned and then held Rustini on his lap again.

It was getting hotter and hotter. The sun shone down on the unremarkable fields. Mountainous West Java was now behind them and now the train went along the coast of the Java Sea.

"Look," said Sudarmo. "There's the sea, in between the gaps in the rubber trees." Brown waves came rolling in with their white crests, and behind them, a dim blueness where the sky touched the earth. Sulastri looked at the sea with intense concentration, but it was too hot in the coach to immerse herself in the poetic atmosphere, so she returned to her book.

Finally, Semarang. The baking air brought beads of sweat to Rustini's forehead and Sulastri felt the perspiration slowly trickle down her back. Sitting back against the seat made her uncomfortable because she felt dirty from being covered with dust.

"Soon you'll get to know my cousin," Sudarmo said as he wiped the sweat from his brow, "a hardworking guy and trustworthy, even if he likes to visit his women friends, but that's another story. His wife is goodhearted and fat. You'll still make friends with the two of them, even though they have a quality that's not so good. I mean, they are extremely frugal."

He talked about what they were like, and Sulastri had the impression that they were courteous but very attentive to etiquette. That actually pleased rather than unnerved her.

The taxi came to a stop in front of a brick house, rather low, in a residential area owned by the municipality. A plump and broadly smiling woman with thick eyebrows and a skin tone like the *langsat* plum, came forward. She took Sulastri's hand and shook it like a long-time friend. She invited her guest to sit, took Rustini in her lap, and apologized for how hot the air was here. It was truly hot and even iced syrup was unable to refresh their parched throats. Outside the sun baked everything mercilessly and dust got into the clothes. Everything seemed to be covered in dust.

This woman, Sumiati, bustled about as if it was hard for her to reassure her guests. Then her husband Mas Hambali came in, a tall man, quite dark of skin, and from first glance, someone to be trusted, if rather gloomy-looking. But he appeared honest and respectable, with his erect poise and incipient belly bulge. He smiled at Sulastri and asked her trivial questions. Sumiati was meanwhile preparing food on the narrow back veranda, with space enough only for some chairs, a sideboard, and a rattan sofa. On a rack next to a window hung a beautifully painted birdcage. In it were turtledoves, bringers of good fortune, as Mas Hambali said with a little laugh. There were too many kinds of food to mention, and the servant standing quietly in the doorway looking down, silently refilled the plates. A cuckoo dove began to call out and the sound was strange in a house in this city. This small, narrow house felt suffocating, and Sulastri felt that she, too, was in a birdcage. Sumiati constantly encouraged her guests to take this or that side dish. And as she chattered on amiably, they finally reached the "mouth cleanser," that is, dessert, which consisted of the tiniest of bananas, all quite amazing to Sulastri.

After eating, the guests were allowed to rest in the bedroom. Sulastri wasn't able to rest, though, from feeling so sweaty and asphyxiated that she thought she was losing her mind, so she went out and sat in the inner veranda. There Sumiati was sitting with her handiwork. The furniture was sturdy and the chairs belonged to the set on the front veranda. Sumiati explained that the chairs were there when Sudarmo was still attending the MULO school and they still seemed still seemed fine. Buying cheap becomes expensive was her motto. So, she bought strong and expensive things and even Mas Hambali's pajamas lasted years. Mas Hambali had a good salary as a supervisor in the municipality office and a nice red car. He went to work in the car, but chose to live in this little house, which had been built by the city under his own supervision. He had personally financed its improvements, so it would be a waste if they moved away. So here they had lived for almost twenty years and didn't mind if they lived there forever.

"Goodness, what a long time you've lived here," Sulastri began. "We fly here and there and every time we meet with something new."

"Mas Hambali hates moving around," his wife said, stopping her lacework. Sulastri said she well understood that, but wasn't Sumiati bored, always doing the same things? The older woman looked at Sulastri in surprise and shook her head. She explained in a rather flat voice that she couldn't adjust to life anywhere but there. It was true that they had gone on holiday somewhere, but that was only for a few days.

"No," she said firmly. "We're happy here, though I would like to change this heat with the coolness in the mountains. But how could I ever leave all my friends here?" Sulastri laughed at Sumiati's worries, and it now became Sumiati's turn to ask if it was nice living in such an unsettled way.

"Oh, we're like a kind of bird that goes to the hot lands in the winter and back to the cold country in the summer. Back and forth."

"We'll try living here for a while, and if things don't work out, we'll go somewhere else. The world is wide," Sudarmo said.

Now Mas Hambali joined them sitting there. Tea was poured, sugar cubes added, and cheese pastries were served. Sudarmo winked at Sulastri as a hint that Sumiati didn't serve cheese pastries to just anyone at all. Sulastri felt very much at home here and saw them as outgoing and hospitable.

That evening Sulastri and Sudarmo visited Hapsoro, who lived in a large house on a broad street. There was a shade tree in the front yard, then a high veranda and the usual fence wall, marble tiles, albeit broken and discolored here and there, several sets of chairs (which didn't fill up this space) and screen doors in back. Hapsoro greeted his guests warmly. Tall and not in the least handsome, with a kind of dent right between his eyebrows, and wearing a sarong and a headscarf, Hapsoro looked old-fashioned and modern at the same time when with *politesse* he invited Sulastri to take a seat.

A moment later, his wife arrived. She was a pretty woman of a little over thirty, with a full body, white teeth and a dark brown complexion that was usually downcast but now smiling.

"We telegrammed you," Hapsoro said, "because there is teacher who has married and will be leaving us the day after tomorrow. Could Zus teach in front of a class full of hooligans?"

"Of course," said Sulastri, rather stung. "I could hold my ground against that possibility."

There was sarcasm in her voice and Hapsoro replied soothingly, "So then, it's taken care of. Let us be reconciled now. For the time being, Zus will receive *f*25 and then I will see whether there's a place for Mas Darmo as well. And furthermore, these are night courses." He scratched the back of his ear and quickly added. "Oh, that will be taken care of, too."

Hapsoro's wife had come in briefly and a servant brought glasses of a syrup drink. Karlinah placed the glasses on the table and apologized by saying, "This sour syrup I made myself, so perhaps it's not so tasty, but it's good for people who are thirsty."

"Oh no, of course it's tasty," said Sulastri politely and she began to taste it. It was too sour, but she nodded and gave a sign of praising it.

"Don't we have any other syrup in the house?" broke in Hapsoro.

"No," answered his wife, rather ashamed, and Sulastri wondered why she should be as ashamed as that.

Sudarmo had called Hapsoro a passive poet and Sulastri had tried to imagine Hapsoro as a poet, but just couldn't, because his face was too real and his belly bulged. It was true that his eyes were intelligent, and he looked like a person with curiosity behind his glasses. However, his tendency to small talk disappointed Sulastri. Was he speaking that way out of courtesy in front of an ordinary woman? He didn't need to take such an attitude with her, as Sulastri was used to conversing with men, without taking account of gender.

"Just the usual, very disappointing, not impressive," thought Sulastri and recalled with pain when she had sent her poetic drama to him for critique, "but was Sudarmo wrong-sighted?" She followed the course of her own thoughts, which was not being polite, because you normally expected from your guest an amusing comment. Sulastri knew that this was disappointing about her because she often repelled people with her silence, even though she didn't mean anything bad by it. Sudarmo took over the responsibility for conversing out of courtesy by chatting. Sulastri felt tired and they said goodbye and returned by *dokar* to Mas Hambali's home, where the family was awaiting them for dinner. Mas Hambali was precise in everything and Sudarmo apologized for his negligence in arriving late because of being detained by Hapsoro. Mas Hambali laughed, and a happy atmosphere returned to the dining table.

All through their conversation, Sudarmo annoyed Mas Hambali about his bird. Mas Hambali answered appropriately. "The turtledove is more modest than the radio and... it brings to us the atmosphere we need."

Sudarmo couldn't find a reply, and that was disagreeable to him. Sulastri laughed because of the look on his face which showed he'd been bested.

After the meal, they kept talking and Sulastri conceived the notion that these two cousins were like people from different eras, even if they had been born in the same century and notwithstanding their modern clothes and home. When it came time to retire, Sulastri slowly changed her clothes, thinking "This is Semarang. Perhaps I'll find my happiness here, perhaps not, but it looks as if life will be more pleasant here than before."

She was totally mistaken, but she didn't know that yet and she asked Sudarmo what his impressions were of this day. His face showed how tired he was, but also happiness, as well.

"Hurrah!" he exclaimed, sticking his head out of the mosquito net. "'Don't despair', say the Dutch, who praise their hero Coen. We're called the intellectual proletariat, Tri. Doesn't that make us happy? We are truly the intellectual proletariat, even if we sometimes obtain a place of refuge in the homes of the bourgeois."

"You're praising me," said Sulastri, "I don't deserve that."

19

Sulastri was astonished at the tears that had welled up in her eyes. Why so terribly sentimental? She who wanted to be an Indonesian woman, able to struggle, and who actually was this? Why couldn't she see her memories calmly and with fortitude, write it properly on paper and in that way defeats them forever? She thrust her shoulders back, peered from beneath her hands that she had reflexively placed over her eyes to see if Sudarmo was paying any attention to her. No, he was totally absorbed in reading a propaganda brochure and was full of criticism of it. In any case, he was frowning and reading with all his attention, not noticing his wife. Sulastri wrote further. How had it been then at Mas Hambali's home? These recollections were closer to the time it happened than those other ones, but Sulastri didn't dare confront them forthrightly. She was afraid of experiencing that over again. Why was her life always distressing then, why did hardships always return, as if predestined, unavoidable? Was that in fact the answer, that she didn't have to explain the law, the reasons why someone like Sudarmo and her, intellectual people, who lived like free people, outside the ranks of the civil service, had to experience the things they had?

And would she have the grit, if she knew for sure that, if she held fast to her principles, she would suffer right into old age? She wrote again, "It can't be denied that Mas Hambali loved his wife. But in his own way." Sudarmo had explained it, and when Sulastri looked at him in surprise, he added, Mas and she had married according the old customs and traditions, and thus their parents played the important role in that marriage. But that didn't mean that Mas hadn't been smitten by her. In the beginning he sent her a photo of himself on a horse in a horseman's attire. She thought him handsome, and so the marriage went forward. At the time Sumiati was fifteen years old and Mas was almost twenty-five. She came here, and in this house, learned from her husband to manage a household, and in this way her love, solicitous and respectful, was quite adequately illuminated. By contrast, Mas Hambali was extremely patriarchal, something that in fact Sumiati liked.

Sulastri had actually seen this in them. When Mas Hambali arrived home from the office, Sumiati quickly went to meet him and take his briefcase into the house, for that was a statement of her respect for him. She served him at the dining table, and she spoke of trivial matters most sweetly. Never did she look at him in anger, even though Mas himself sometimes displayed his own. And that was because human beings usually from time to time want something else, and so Mas sometimes came home late at night, but Sumiati quietly accepted her fate, somehow concealing her inner life behind a patient smile.

"Does she have a soul?" wondered Sulastri.

Sumiati often slept in the inner veranda, on a carpet, because it was too hot in the room, she said, but the truth of this Sulastri saw in her hostess's reddened eyes. Sumiati was childless, nor did she have any hope to give birth. This made her often more withdrawn than her usual way, but luckily, she had her cats. With soft shiny fur and bright eyes, two cats padded soundlessly about the house and she took care of them more attentively than she did her niece. This niece had become their adopted child at the age of fifteen and had just recently failed the final exams at the Fröbel Teachers School. She was the child of Mas Hambali's younger sibling and seemed to have become frozen, according to him, in all things, serene and polite, as if she were twenty-five years old rather than eighteen. This child with the earthy brown complexion smiled and rarely spoke, and when she did, usually joked as if afraid of causing a scene.

It was very clear how she and her adopted mother avoided any squabbling with each other and only spoke together of trivial matters. This wasn't a sort of family life in which a wife would explode in anger and quarrel with her husband or where children created an uproar. For Sulastri, this marriage was like a fairy tale, like a marriage in the previous century. So, she herself became attracted to this ambience and became softer than previously to her husband, and precisely because of this, Mas Hambali respected her. He rarely acted that way with his own wife.

"There are two kinds of women," said Mas Hambali in a deeply reflective manner, so deeply that you had to listen to him. "A wife and a coquettish, seductive woman. And there are only three women from this generation whom I respect: my wife, Zus Lurni and Zus Sulastri."

Seeing the way Mas Hambali behaved with his wife, Sulastri preferred to be one of the enchanting and seductive women, whose lives were not so boring and didn't need to be silenced with moral principles. What's more, the enchanting ones were quite pleased with their independence and no one bothered them except when making them bear the consequences of their deeds.

That night, while enjoying a cup of tea after dinner, they had an example of the atmosphere of the city.

"The youth of Semarang have become irresponsible," Mas Hambali said contemptuously and his intention was to criticize his nieces. One them was beautiful, flirtatious, lively and used makeup, and Sudarmo's sidelong glances followed her stealthily, because he didn't want to hurt his wife's feelings.

"Is that so?" asked Sudarmo in surprise.

"Indeed, it is, but what annoys me even more, is their attention to automobiles, clothing and silly things, which we don't want to bring into our conversation. Truly, I feel as if I am in a village. Only Hapsoro is still refreshing."

Hapsoro.... Sulastri's pen couldn't move forward because of her anger. It was to work with Hapsoro that they had come to Semarang, and it was because of his attitude toward them that they had left it. He had turned out to be uninterested in people and had become harsh, like a businessman looking for workers to carry out his orders. All that was not so troubling at the time. What really disgusted her was knowing that Sudarmo had been such a fool in his estimation of Hapsoro that he even urged Sulastri to give Hapsoro her poetry to ask his advice.

The difficulties that arose with Sudarmo after their life in Semarang may have been rooted in feelings of disillusionment and disappointment, because her husband simply did not understand people. And Sulastri had been the one to suffer for it. It was true that Hapsoro didn't express his decision in so many words, but had let Sulastri ask to be let go because he didn't want to provide a paid leave of several weeks after she gave birth. And Hapsoro well knew, as did Sulastri herself, that she even had to borrow money for the requirements of her delivery.

One word was enough for Sudarmo once he clearly saw Hapsoro's soul. And in that way they left Semarang, right on time, and they stayed for a while with Lurni in Yogya. Even though they had only been a few months in Semarang, it felt like years of spiritual desiccation.

And also, afterwards, Sulastri remembered well, there was only one event—clear and still stored rather dramatically in her memory—and that was her quarrel with Sudarmo that caused them to return to Bandung. It seemed her life in Central Java had not become completely real to her, even though during that time she had a second daughter, and at that time, too, they had stayed for several days with Lurni, who was suffering financially, so that she didn't receive them as royally as before. Did she need a return to the atmosphere of the Priangan highlands for self-awareness? Perhaps too, her physical weakness was due to the heat of Semarang, her working too hard and giving birth.

Several hours after arriving in Yogya, she was lying in a maternity clinic with a new baby beside her, which forced her to stay with life, although that night she had been certain that things would have worked out better if she died.

And for the next week, she sat around, not working and in solitude, far from the busyness of her sister-in-law, and without Sudarmo, who was then staying with his uncle in Surabaya while he looked for work. Sometimes she shut her eyes and she saw in revolving circles the mocking face of Marti and that of her father with his face of the religious scholar of high attainment, the sharp features of Sudarmo's face, and Rustini's funny eyes.

Marti had written in a letter that Sulastri had to see her tribulations as a punishment, a kualat from her father, and that perhaps all that would make Sulastri gentler and more humane toward others. Sulastri couldn't understand why Marti, herself precisely a nationalist, would consider life off the main track, safe and protected by the government, so bad and why she should be rejected by her.... Must all the struggles of nationalists, who grope along their way, often times tripping on stones, be called the acts of mad people, she wondered, and would all firmly resolute nationalists truly fall like that because of kualat? Then, cooping up her thoughts, she began to write a novel in Sundanese in Lurni's garden, under the *jambu* tree, with butterflies fluttering about her. She tried to put aside her sadness, but she succeeded in dispelling only some of it.

But that was the beginning, as Sulastri thought about it now, of what she was doing at this time: recording her memories so as to deliver herself from them. But before that, at Lurni's home, surely the weakest moment in her life, she hadn't seen herself so very clearly. She had thought that she could release herself from that decision of hers without seriously delving down to the bottom of her experiences. That the Sundanese novel would not be realized was in fact just one step toward what she was so industriously doing now. But before arriving there, she had to rediscover Sudarmo, and Bandung and daily life with all its cruel side. It was this, the latter, that she wanted to record.

When Sudarmo was back from Surabaya after a month, for the first time in her life, Sulastri was not happy with her husband's return. He seemed odd, exhausted, but cheerful too, and he enthusiastically attempted to relate his experiences. His tone was almost hysterical, his hands gesticulating rapidly, and the words seemed to almost slide from his mouth without giving the listener time to catch them.

"Before I didn't believe in Pak Mulyodiharjo's skill in massage, but now, after seeing with my own eyes, I'd say it's very strange. He takes hold of the patient and then there's a kind of electrical current that enters the body and he automatically moves the body. The body is needed to loosen up the taut nerves. In that way he cured a crippled person, people who suffered from nervous disorders, and even tuberculosis patients. The way he cures them doesn't disturb anything, but his results are astonishing. He said that he could release the secrets of his curing to me in six months and that I could receive that mystical power from him. How would it be if you were the wife of a *dukun*, Tri?"

She laughed nervously and her eyes rolled under her eyelids. Sulastri pursed her lips with contempt and said firmly, "Let me just ask for a divorce." Lurni laughed in a whistling way and Ribowo was silent, feeling struck in the unpleasant atmosphere.

"You don't want to be the wife of a dukun? But nowadays dukuns bring a lot more income than people with law degrees."

Sulastri paid no attention to his chatter, stood up and went into the bedroom. It pained her badly to see Sudarmo like that, and she had a feeling of complete contempt and hatred for him.

"Have I tied my life to a man who is so irresponsible?" she thought to herself. "Lastri, you are now cured of your great love for him." She took a breath, thought of Muhammad, then took up the baby and gave it her breast. Rustini didn't immediately recognize her father on his return, but a few moments later called out "Bapak!" after which her father lifted her up and kissed her. After nursing the baby, Sulastri sat with the others on the inner veranda and asked impatiently, "You talked about this and that, but what about a job there?"

Sudarmo again related all about Pak Mulyodiharjo, and also that he was honest and well-wishing.

"But now there's another thing," Sulastri began. "How are you going to live in Bandung?"

He shook his head and said there was no certainty that he knew of, but certainly there had to be a school and a journal. There wasn't much else that could be discussed and he departed again two days later. Sulastri's brief comment was, "I only pray I will be following you sometime soon."

Sulastri received a few short letters from Bandung. Sudarmo hadn't been in the least successful in finding work for himself or for Sulastri. After waiting for a month, Sulastri didn't wish to stay on any longer with Lurni; besides, there was a change in Rustini from a brave and independent-minded little girl to one who was spoiled and seemed unable to be taught well. This was because Lurni let her child be minded by a servant.

Sulastri then made up her mind and wrote to Sudarmo that she wanted to go to Bandung now and Sudarmo must find a house. How he should get the money was up to him. Whatever the case, Sulastri was certain she should leave Lurni, and if Sudarmo couldn't finalize things for her, then there was always divorce. Sudarmo, for the first time in his life, saw his wife's boiling anger and acted firmly, backed down and borrowed money from a friend of his.

"The house is ready," he wrote back, "It doesn't come with furniture; only one bed, a set of chairs and a chest of drawers. You should know yourself how to overcome difficulties here." Sulastri's novel was given to a specialist in Sundanese literature, who considered the writing style to be vivid and honest, but the syntax Dutch and its form rather modern, not the usual.

Gularso, Sudarmo continued, would meet her, because he had to be in Solo for a few days. Gularso did come, and he spoke of a number of things, interspersed with short words to say he was sorry to have caused so much suffering to Sulastri; then he was so friendly that she felt moved. A few days later, Sulastri left. On the train, Sulastri placed the baby in a rattan basket beside her. Gularso sat across and kept an eye on Rustini. Sulastri had to change the baby's diapers and Gularso was always ready to help.

The countryside passed by her eyes and finally she recognized the fresh green valleys of the Priangan. She started to sing almost soundlessly with Rustini on her lap, looking out the window with tears in her eyes and thought of herself as being sentimental again. It was strange to feel tied to one region, while the land of her birth was said to be this vast country.

Bandung—and there was Sudarmo standing with Mientje on the platform, the former thin, pale and dirty, and the latter, sturdy and, after her own fashion, affable; over these three years she had become even older.

Bandung—and the *dokar* stopped in front of a house. It looked quite alright, with windows whose glass was trimmed with tin. Sudarmo opened the door and invited her in with a sweeping gesture. "Our home! Six empty rooms..."

Sulastri laughed and went inside with curiosity. The house was better that she had expected, but it was cold everywhere and the many high windows made it so chilly that she shivered for a moment. Next to the third room was a terrace, over which hung young green mangoes, which promised a wonderful harvest. From the terrace could be seen the high wall of the house next door. There was almost no yard, a handicap because this made the rooms rather dark.

"I'm going to have a hard time losing my fear of these empty rooms, even in the daytime," said Sulastri, and Sudarmo told how he had slept here lately, night after night.

"I sleep with all the lights on," he said, "and I always have the sense of being watched by invisible eyes, Tri, and the result has been, I have never slept so badly before."

Sulastri laughed, but was unable to shake off the same feeling.

In the days that followed, she didn't have a chance to speak at length, because she had to do the laundry, cook, and do everything that a household required, so that she was exhausted by nighttime. The next morning, she quickly started the work all over again. Sudarmo helped her and was always nearby. Sulastri of course noticed that all along he looked different. There wasn't the slightest sign of his childish mercuriality of before. This man was phlegmatic and cynical.

"Everything has changed, Tri," he said sadly. "People who didn't count before can now voice their opinions. And no one thinks of refuting their assumptions, or even doubting them. I feel like someone speaking about ideals and dreams in an empty room. These are now said to be the thoughts of a crazy person because they don't produce immediate results. And the strangest of all is that I feel I myself am out of luck."

Sulastri said nothing, knowing that Sudarmo was right, and over the following days, she too felt she was in an oppressive atmosphere. During that time, they started having some real quarrels for the first time in their life together. And how could it be avoided when both of them were quick-tempered, tense, and only saw difficulties in the days ahead? Disappointment and frustration every day, the poverty that only with great effort was concealed behind their smiles; worries, and angry arguments. It would be too sad if Sulastri were to portray such a time of suffering. And not only suffering, but also the boring rhythm of this period. There were days when all they had was rice and coffee without sugar.

"Turkish coffee," Sudarmo called it with a laugh and he drank it cheerfully, while Sulastri actually felt happy enough to joke with him.

Five months passed and in that short time, they experienced the most destitute of proletarian lives, frequently borrowing money from friends to pay for water and electricity, practicing forbearance towards Marti's poisonous letters, because, during this time of difficulty, Marti had sent *f*7.50 each month, even if she always complained that sooner or later the time would come for Sulastri to stop bothering people. Psychologically feeble, physically frail, after five months, Sulastri saw herself having become years older. And she had the sense that she would never be able to laugh again. But this period just dragged on. Then one day...

Sulastri was tidying up her exercise books which contained her essays. She seemed to have been saving her memories in those books for perpetuity.

"My magic books," she said with a smile to Sudarmo, who looked quizzically at her. She recalled her father's hidden power and shook her head when she remembered Marti's fear of retribution.

"I don't know what to write anymore," she said in reply to Sudarmo's look. "We've gone through a time filled with suffering and is our luck any better now? Our situation is no different from our nature. Maybe our situation won't change, but... but one morning I noticed that we never were as close before as we are now. I really just realized it this morning, Dar. If our lives were different then, maybe our lives now would also be different."

This is what happened one morning. Rustini was quite sick and Sulastri herself got up late, being worn out after caring for the child all night long. Sudarmo had gone out. The sunlight shimmered on the tiles. She could see the tiles from the windows of her room and from that open window she admired the dark yellow flowers that were hanging nearby. It felt like she was seven or eight years old in her father's house, before there was any danger of cosmic retribution. She felt still tied to Marti, whom she perhaps never truly did cut loose in her heart. But what had separated their lives? And how different were the lives they had chosen! Sulastri had felt fainthearted toward what could grow from the "bourgeois" seed within her, but she was surprised, for suddenly she heard familiar steps outside. And she realized that was a good thing. Sudarmo and she lived together and what had made her smile just now was just like in the past, that crazy retribution, kualat. She quickly went to welcome her husband.

"Rustini's begun to recover, Dar," she said. "Sit next to me for a moment. We're both damned, so we both go in the same class."

The sunlight shone in Sulastri's eyes when she said that, and that sunlight was also in the way she looked, she felt, when she looked at Sudarmo. Her hand moved the exercise books slightly away. Was she writing this for Indonesia? Of what use were her memories for other people, even if everything really did happen and held lessons in them? She taught at an unauthorized school, a "wild" school. Sudarmo taught at another one. Nothing terrific or heroic, and yet...

"You're elated," said Sudarmo," Yes, stop writing if you're feeling exuberant."

"Then, hey, what should I do if I'm elated, Dar? Cakes for Rustini? Would the PID and the women's movement allow it, if I make cakes for Rustini?"

"Don't always be joking," said her husband. "One day they'll come to chop you to pieces, and then what?"

Glossary

AMS	Abbreviation of "Algemene Middelbare School," the pre-WWII senior high school in the Netherlands East Indies.
andong	The four-wheeled horse-drawn taxi once ubiquitous in Yogyakarta and Surakarta (Solo).
Balai Pustaka	The "Bureau of Literature," was established in 1908 by the Netherlands East Indies government as *Volkslectuur* ("People's Reading") to promote, control and shape local literary activity. It may be rightly credited for publishing many of the great classics of early modern Indonesian literature. It exists to this day.
Bezoldigingsregeling der Burgerlijke Landsdienaren 1938	The then-prevailing pay scale for civil servants in the Netherlands East Indies.
Boven Digul	Located in today's Papua province, a notorious malaria-ridden dumping ground of exile for Indonesian independence activists during the late Dutch period.
Bung	A many-nuanced term, ranging from "bud, buddy, bro" to "elder brother," and in this sense was used in affectionately addressing and referring to important public figures, especially of the Revolutionary Era, such as Sukarno, Hatta and Tomo.
bupati	The title of a high-ranking official in provincial-level civil administration, usually translated as "regent."
danyang	A guardian spirit of a tree, house, a village, etc.
Dayak	A large and differentiated indigenous ethnicity of Indonesian Borneo and East Malaysia, who traditionally dwelled in longhouses close to rivers. Here meaning "savage, uncultured."

Dispereert Niet	"Do Not Despair," the motto of the much besieged, indomitable and brutal Jan Pieterszoon Coen (1587–1629), first governor-general of the Dutch East Indies (1619–1623 and 1627–1629).
dokar	A diminutive two-wheeled horse-drawn carriage.
duku	The sour plum-like lanson fruit.
dukun	A traditional healer, herbalist. *Dukun* also refers to someone, usually male, who is adept in the white and black magic.
Garut	A town in West Java to the southeast of Bandung.
Gladkov, Fyodor	One of the earliest Soviet social-realist novelists (1883–1958)
HIS	Abbreviation of "Hollandsch-Inlandsche School." During the colonial period, these schools were open to a limited extent to the native elite and geared to preparing a higher level of native bureaucrats.
Indonesia Raya	"Great Indonesia"—Indonesia's national anthem introduced by its composer, Wage Rudolf Supratman, on October 28, 1928 at the Second Indonesian Youth Congress in Batavia (today's Jakarta).
Inggit Garnasih	Sukarno's second wife (1888–1984) whom he divorced around 1943.
Juma'at Kliwon	"Kliwon Friday"—a day in the Javanese calendar system with mystical implications, such as being a favorable or likely time to come into contact with supernatural beings.
kebaya	A woman's long-sleeved blouse worn over a sarong, or skirt-wrapping.
Ki Hadjar Dewantoro	(1889–1959) A famous advocate for universal education and Indonesian national consciousness from the early 20th century and founder of the *Taman Siswa* school system to this end in 1922 in Yogyakarta.
kualat	The term for a kind of cosmic retribution for violating crucial traditional norms and attitudes, such as familial relationships.
Künkel, Fritz	(1889–1956) German psychiatrist and later an American educator.

la ilaha illallah, la ilaha illallah	(Arabic) "There is no god but God. There is no god but God."
Lampung	The region, later a province, in the southernmost part of Sumatra
lurah	The formal title of the head of a village in Java and elsewhere in Indonesia.
Marhaen Party	"The Proletarian [or "Plebian"] Party," founded by Sukarno in Bandung in 1927 and so named to evoke the poor indigenous masses of the Indonesian archipelago.
Mas	A polite form of address in Javanese for males of social status and age equivalent to the speaker and frequent substitute for the status-laden second person singular pronoun
MULO	Short for "Meer Uitgebreid Lager Onderwijs," the junior high school for Dutch and native pupils.
Multatuli	The Latin-derived pen name ("I have suffered") of Eduard Dowes Dekker (1820–1887), a prominent Dutch writer, most famous for his novel *Max Havelaar; or the Coffee Auctions of the Dutch Trading Company*, a sensational, satirical exposé of the injustices of the plantation system (*Cultuurstelsel*) in the 19th century the Netherlands East Indies.
Nyonya	A somewhat dated formal title and form of address for a married woman.
opium	Opium smoking was a widespread practice in Java during colonial times. James Rush's study *Opium to Java: Revenue Farming and Chinese Enterprise* gives an excellent and highly readable account of this during the final century of Dutch rule.
oplet	An informal urban passenger transport vehicle
opséter	A supervisor, overseer
Pak	The affectionate and familiar abbreviation of the formal *Bapak* ("mister, sir, father") and is the equivalent of "Dad, Pop, etc." The female equivalent of *Pak* is *Bu* or more formally, *Ibu*.
peci	The dark velvet, shorter version of the fez, popularized by Sukarno and the early Indonesian nationalists.

PID	(*Politieke Inlichtingendienst*) the Political Intelligence Service.
pikul	Equivalent to $133^{1/3}$ lbs. in most places in Asia where this unit of weight has been traditionally used in wholesale and retail markets.
rambutan	A tropical fruit with a sweet lychee-like fruit over a pith and enclosed in a "hairy' reddish-yellow rubbery skin.
rujak	An Indonesian and Malaysian sweet, sour and spicy-tasting unripe fruit salad
sado	A two-wheeled horse-drawn passenger transport, roughly like a *dokar*.
selamatan	The ancient commensal blessing and security-invoking ceremony involving varying numbers of a community, depending on the purpose of the invocation.
Selasa Kliwon	"Kliwon Thursday," another "spiritually charged" day of the Javanese calendar system, believed to be good time to be in contact with God through prayer.
serimpi	One of the ritualized court dances of the Central Javanese sultanate/kasunanan of Yogyakarta and Surakarta (Solo).
Srikandi	Also "Dewi Srikandi." One of the two archetypical heroines in the Indonesian version of the *Mahabharata*. The other being Sumbadra. A wife of Arjuna, Srikandi symbolized the indomitable woman-warrior.
Sumbradra	Also "Dewi Sumbadra." One of the two archetypical heroines in the Indonesian version of the *Mahabharata*. The other being Srikandi. A wife of Arjuna, Sumbadra, symbolized the gentle, graceful, and refined—the idealized traditional—female/wife.
tumbal	Often something living that is sacrificed to sanctify an undertaking or (as here) dedicated as a charm simply to placate the spirits of a place.
uritan	Premature, i.e., shell-less, eggs which seem to be a street-food specialty of Yogyakarta.
warung	A roadside food booth, usually with seating provided

wedana	Title of assistant provincial regent in the traditional Javanese civil administration and mainly preserved under Dutch rule.
zakat fitrah	The mandatory charitable donation incumbent of all Muslims at the end of the Ramadan fasting month. This requirement is one of the Five Pillars of Islam.
Zus	From the Dutch, meaning "sis," and a friendly and polite way of addressing a female about the same age as the speaker.

Afterword

A Life Free from Trammels

Suwarsih Djojopuspito's novel, translated here as *Against the Grain*, was originally written and published in Dutch under the title *Buiten het gareel* (Out of Harness) in 1940 but then, several decades later, rewritten by the author in Indonesian and published with the title *Manusia Bebas* (Free People) in 1975. The novel contains the strongly autobiographical record of the experiences of a young married couple working at nationalist schools in several towns in Java.[1] In Sulastri, the character through whose eyes we witness the events narrated, we recognize Suwarsih herself; in Sudarmo she depicts a portrait of her husband Sugondo Djojopuspito. Both Suwarsih and Sugondo belonged to the group of Western-educated young Indonesians who preferred working for the education and improvement of their own people to a reasonably well-paid job in a government school. This choice meant an uncertain existence, which led to many disappointments and

[1] Earlier I wrote on this subject in "'Suwarsih Djojopuspito', a so-called 'Levensbericht,'" in *Jaarboek van de Maatschappij der Nederlandse letterkunde te Leiden* (1978-1979), p.39-48. A list of Suwarsih Djojopuspito's main writings was added to this article. In *Indische Letteren*, vol.1, no.4 (December, 1986) one can find three contributions dealing with Suwarsih Djojopuspito and her work: Robert-Henk Zuidinga, "Suwarsih Djojopuspito, E.du Perron en de roman *Buiten het gareel*," A. Teeuw, "Een buitenbeentje in de literatuurgeschiedenis," and Gerard Termorshuizen, "Een leven in isolement."

often made them doubt whether the ideals they cherished could be realized. Living in bitter poverty most of the time, this group formed an intellectual proletariat in whose lives the nationalist movement had occupied a major place even while they were still students.

It becomes clear from the unpublished reminiscences of her youth how much this applied to Suwarsih Djojopuspito.[2] In her memoirs she looks back to the first eighteen years of her life and describes the difficulties which a simple *desa* girl had to face, before she could work for her people.

Suwarsih (her family and friends called her Tjitjih) was born in 1912 in the *desa* Cibatok, some twenty kilometers southwest of Buitenzorg (the present-day Bogor), on the main road to Bantam. She was the third of six children of a mixed marriage between Raden Bagus Nursaid Djojosaputro, a descendant from the Cirebon dynasty, and Siti Hatidjah (1892–1958) whose family were rich Chinese who had converted to Islam. Thanks to their wealthy Chinese grandparents, Suwarsih and her brothers and sisters had a carefree childhood. The mother was a gentle, somewhat shy woman who remained in the shadow of her much older husband, a man who liked to play the grand seigneur, but at the same time proved to be a bad administrator of the business capital entrusted to him by his father-in-law. He occupied a leading position in the *desa* community on account of his abilities and education. Adventurous by nature, he had seen much more of Java than the small Cibatok, where he settled later. He was a gripping storyteller and a talented *dalang* who used to give performances with his own puppets. Coming from a family that attached great importance

[2] In 2021 I put the memoirs and other documents in relation to Suwarsih Djojopuspito (among which personal correspondence) at the disposal of the Literatuurmuseum in The Hague.

to education and learning, he used the prestige of his aristocratic background to gain places for his children at schools in Buitenzorg, where Western education was provided. The fact that in doing so he treated his sons and daughters equally—"progress lies in the hands of woman," he declared in his *desa*—was characteristic of his advanced outlook.

The so-called "ethical movement" at the beginning of the century had given state education for Indonesian children a considerable stimulus. But opportunities for girls were still very limited. It was therefore very important that Kartini schools, Dutch schools for girls from the indigenous aristocracy, were founded from 1913 onwards. This happened on the initiative of Conrad Theodor van Deventer (1857–1915) and his wife Elisabeth van Deventer-Maas (1857–1942). The Kartini school in Buitenzorg was opened in 1914 and Suwarsih entered it in 1918, two years after her elder sister Suwarni (1910–1967). Their schooling was paid for by their grandparents for whom this became an increasing burden in the course of the ensuing years. At first the sisters lived in the boarding house of the school, but when later this became too costly, they stayed at home with their parents.

In her memoirs Suwarsih speaks with gratitude of the Dutch lady whose task it was "to teach us to speak proper Dutch, to acquire Dutch table manners and to give up the habit of sleeping at irregular hours; she also watched over our moral development." Both sisters were gifted pupils and also attended the advanced elementary school known as *Meer Uitgebreid Lager Onderwijs* (MULO) in Buitenzorg. Some figures will explain what this meant for an indigenous girl in those days. In 1918 Suwarsih was one of about fifty girls who were admitted to the first form of the Kartini school. Thirteen of them completed all seven forms, but only four were allowed to attend advanced education. Thus Suwarsih and her sister were in an exceptional position. They themselves became sharply aware of this, when for the first time they came in contact with European and Eurasian fellow students. The experience of being considered "inferior" by their classmates and the impossibility of breaking through the dividing lines between themselves and the others, strengthened their feeling of being "different." Of that period Suwarsih was to write: "Although we were still very young at that time, we realized that life would not be easy for us and that intelligence and learning would be the only weapons with which we could overcome the numerous difficulties."

In their uncertain search for their own identity, the girls' nationalist feelings were playing an increasingly important role. Both of them joined "Jong Java" (Young Java), a nationalist youth movement. Even at the age of sixteen, Suwarni—rather Nining, as she was always called—was one of the prominent figures in this movement. She was, for instance, the moving spirit behind providing education for illiterate women from the kampongs. Even as a child she was always the center of attention. She found it easy to get along with people, was quick-witted in discussion, and full of ideas which she was able to communicate persuasively. She was a born leader. Mainly from 1930 onwards, when she had become Ibu Pringgodigdo, she played a very important role in the feminist movement in Indonesia.

It was inevitable that the more introvert Suwarsih, who as a younger sister was always taken under Nining's wing, should for a long time remain in the shadow of her admired sister. The feelings of uncertainty with which Suwarsih struggled not only in her youth but also later, may be partly explained through this relationship with her older sister, which was also the reason why developing her strong personality was such a difficult process. In the mid-1930s it became clear how unyielding Suwarsih could be even towards her sister, when she opposed Nining's constant suggestions and advice and, together with her husband, continued along the difficult path which she had chosen much earlier.

After MULO, Suwarsih attended the European teacher training college in Surabaya from 1928 to 1931. She received free education, and her room and board were paid for by the Kartini fund. She was one of only two Indonesians selected for a class of thirty students. In her memoirs she talks about it: "At the beginning my Dutch classmates were slightly contemptuous of the two little Javanese who had been chosen to study with them. Their attitude was understandable and I could forgive them, because in their eyes at that time Indonesians were considered inferior. Keeping a school 'white' gave style and standing to such a school. Because of our presence its status had been seriously damaged." However, she also writes that they gained the respect of their fellow students on account of their excellent records. Her Dutch teacher gave her high marks for her essays: "This was a token of great courage, given the situation in those days; if he had given lower marks, nobody would have protested, because the difference between the Dutch and Indonesians was so great and seemed so unbridgeable."

The same teacher told his students about Multatuli (pen name of E Douwes Dekker, 1820–1887) and read from his works. The great importance of Multatuli's influence on young Indonesians showed itself also in Suwarsih's case: "When my teacher had read something from his novel *Max Havelaar* (1860), I no longer felt lonely at home. My life had become meaningful again, and I realized which direction I had to give to my future. I heard the girls next door laughing and enjoying themselves. And I said to myself: 'My life differs from theirs. One can say that we have no 'youth,' but 'youth' is not granted to us, young Indonesians. For, as soon as we have left school, a difficult task lies ahead of us: to be leaders of our people. It seemed arrogant to put it this way, but in later years it appeared that my generation had to contribute a lot to the nationalist movement, albeit only as small contributors, not as the leading figures we had earlier imagined.'"

It was in those Surabaya years that Suwarsih came in contact with nationalist education. It happened in Bandung where she often stayed with her sister Nining during school holidays. Together with some of her friends, Nining had opened a small school, a so-called "wild" school—not subsidized by the government—where Indonesian children were brought up in a nationalist spirit. These nationalist schools had existed from the beginning of the twenties, but since then their number had considerably increased. The development of this unofficial education had been reinforced by the fact that the government had failed to meet the rapidly growing demand for Western schooling among the Indonesian people. This schooling gave access to the European labor market in the Indies. Dutch primary schools for native children, linked with secondary education, were far too few; from 1932 onwards, mainly because of far-reaching cutbacks, no more new schools were founded. In these circumstances the Indonesian nationalist leaders decided to deal themselves with the enormous problem of illiteracy among their people—about 95% in the 1930s—by founding their own schools.

As the native teachers in these schools had themselves received a Dutch education, it was a matter of course that the materials and methods they used were Western orientated. Moreover, the nationalists understood very well that the schooling they gave had to meet the requirements of modern society and that such a Western direction was in the interest also of their own future state. At the same time, however, they had to think about the way in which the Indonesian identity could be retained in their schools and the nationalist consciousness could be developed. In this regard, the founding in 1922 of the Taman Siswa movement by the Javanese aristocrat Ki Hadjar Dewantara (1889–1959) was an important event. This organization, as soon became apparent, was a great success; in 1940 there were about 250 Taman Siswa schools. They were based on a program which emphasized national cultural values, but at the same time remained open to enriching elements from other, especially Western, cultures. In order not to alienate the children from their own environment and way of life and also to keep the costs as low as possible, Taman Siswa schools used simple classrooms and materials. Ki Hadjar Dewantara's ideas determined not only the character of his own movement, but also exercised considerable influence on the "wild" schools in general.

As we have seen, Suwarsih had become acquainted with the nationalist education while she was a student. She had experienced how poor but idealistic teachers, together with the equally poor parents of their pupils, tried to organize ways of raising the money needed for classrooms and teaching materials. Now, she herself was taking an active part in the feminist movement, giving instruction in childcare and other practical subjects to women in Surabaya. In her memoirs she writes about the fate of women: "Married at fifteen, three or more children, hard work, drudgery in fact; not yet thirty when the first bloom is over, repudiated by their husbands, without money to take care of the children. Such was the fate of these ordinary Indonesian women." The education of children and the feminist movement occupied a significant place in Indonesian nationalism during the 1920s and '30s. Gradually the conviction developed that women could also make an important contribution in the struggle for independence. But in a society in which women traditionally had an inferior position and polygamy was widespread, Suwarsih saw herself confronted with the tremendous task of making men recognize her as an equal. One of her aims in life was to become the equal partner in the struggle for a shared ideal.

After finishing her studies at the teacher training college—she was one of the very first Indonesian teachers with a European certificate—Suwarsih taught at a nationalist school in Batavia (now Jakarta). Soon afterwards she married Sugondo Djojopuspito, who was working at the same "wild" school. It was an "open" marriage, in other words a marriage held together by the partners' free choice, which until recently had been absolutely impossible in Javanese society.

Sugondo Djojopuspito was born in Tuban, East Java, in 1905. He first went to Hollandsch-Inlandsche School (HIS), the Dutch-language primary school for indigenous children in Tuban, and then to MULO in Surabaya. Subsequently he attended Algemene Middelbare School (AMS), the Dutch secondary school, in Yogyakarta. From 1925 he was a student at the School of Law in Batavia and got his first degree in 1928. Then he broke off his studies in order to work for the nationalist cause. In 1927 he was appointed chairman of the Perhimpunan Pelajar-Pelajar Indonesia (Federation of Indonesian Students) and one year later he chaired the second Indonesian Youth Congress which became famous in Indonesian history for its Sumpah Pemuda or "Youth Oath," in which the unity of Indonesia was stated for the first time. Thus, like Suwarsih, Sugondo was a nationalist from the very beginning and, like his young wife, considered the provision of schooling for the children of the common people his main task.

When Suwarsih started her work in the service of the nationalist movement in 1931, times had become more difficult. From the end of the twenties—after the Communist rebellion of 1926 in Bantam and the founding of the "Vaderlandsche Club," an association of colonial diehards as a reaction to this—the differences of opinion between the Dutch government and Indonesian nationalists were considerably sharpened. Increasing police action led to the arrest of the main political leaders and their deportation to the notorious Boven-Digul and other camps. Of course, in this atmosphere the pressure on nationalist education also increased considerably. Dutch control of nationalist teachers had existed for years, on the basis of the Wilde Scholen Ordonantie (Wild School Ordinance) of 1923, but now repression was increasingly felt. The fear of arrest or at least of a teaching ban, the daily improvisations in order not to succumb economically or psychologically, and the tensions in their own circle taxed the idealism and endurance of these people. It often meant a constant struggle, and for Suwarsih and Sugondo it also led to a nomadic existence in Java.

The period in Suwarsih's and Sugondo's life which was described first in *Buiten het gareel* and now here, in *Against the Grain*, covers about four years, from 1933 to 1937. The year before, as the novel tells us, Suwarsih, who had gone from Batavia to a teaching post in Purwakarta, West Java, had again joined her husband, who had just become headmaster of the Taman Siswa school in Bandung. In 1937 she was again in Bandung, but now unemployed, after disappointing experiences at a nationalist school in Semarang—in the novel this is Hapsoro's school—and a stay with her family in Yogyakarta. With the information we have about Suwarsih's life, it is not difficult to show how much the author used her own experiences, usually preserving their chronological order, as the starting point for her book. This affects not only episodes and events, but also certain individuals. One could even call this novel a roman à clef. Sulastri and Sudarmo stand for Suwarsih and Sugondo, and Marti and Kartonegoro are modeled on Suwarsih's sister Nining and her husband Abdul Karim Pringgodigdo (1906–1961). In Sutrisno, who with Sudarmo opens a little school in Buitenzorg, we recognize Sujitno Mangunkusumo (1909–1947), a brother of the prominent nationalist Cipto Mangunkusumo (1884–1942). Also Gularso, an ex-prisoner in Boven-Digul and a colleague of Sulastri and Sudarmo, must be drawn from real life. Suwarsih's parents are also present in the book. One character even figures under his own name, though only vaguely depicted. It is the nationalist leader and future president, Sukarno (1901–1970).

Suwarsih Djojopuspito wrote her book in Dutch. This is remarkable in itself and had to do with earlier events which, in part, are described in the novel. After her disappointment in Semarang, Suwarsih had found shelter with her family in Yogyakarta. Sugondo was somewhere else looking for work and their marriage went through a crisis. To take her mind off things and considering that she could perhaps be useful in some other way, she wrote a short novel in her native Sundanese about the problem of the relationship between man and woman in marriage. The novel describes the unhappy married life of a young woman whose husband is unfaithful to her. She sent the manuscript to the state-owned publishing house Balai Pustaka. However, it was refused because, according to Balai Pustaka, it was not didactic and its style was too complicated. In short, the novel was not traditional enough and therefore not suitable for the reading public. Many years later, in 1959, the novel was published under the title *Marjanah* by the same publisher.

The refusal of her manuscript deeply disappointed Suwarsih. Sometime later, in 1938, she and her husband, who had found employment again in Bandung, met Edgar du Perron (1899–1940) who had recently come back to his country of origin. This contact had come about through *Kritiek en Opbouw* (Criticism and Construction), a progressive, anti-colonial magazine which had been founded in Bandung by the social-democrat DMG Koch (1881–1960) in 1938. In the course of that year du Perron had joined the editorial board, on which Indonesian nationalists were also represented. This was unique, given the colonial situation of those days. Suwarsih, who had contributed some articles to the magazine, and her husband were in touch with this group.

The short period during which Suwarsih and Sugondo were in contact with du Perron, who returned to the Netherlands in 1939, was a high point in their lives and turned out to be of great importance for their future. With his sharp insight into human relationships, du Perron immediately noticed their social and especially their mental isolation. In an atmosphere of mutual respect and trust and through completely frank discussions of their problems, they regained their self-esteem.

Du Perron heard of the rejection of Suwarsih's manuscript and persuaded her to take up writing again and to describe her own experiences during the last few years. He suggested she should write in Dutch, the language she could handle better than her native Sundanese. And thus she began writing *Buiten het gareel.* Du Perron coached her and gave her his essay *Uren met Dirk Coster* (Hours with Dirk Coster) as an example of a plain, honest and personal style. As he himself had just finished his *Het land van herkomst,* (Country of Origin) he could talk to her about the problems of the autobiographer. We find this concern for "writing" in Suwarsih's book; it even decided the final form of the novel. I am referring here to the first chapter and part of the last one in which, as it were, the real story is embedded and where Sulastri does not figure as the main character, but as the woman who is confronted with the complications and the possibilities of being a writer. It is very likely that du Perron exerted a decisive influence on this structure, which was something new in modern Indonesian literary prose.

Du Perron took the manuscript with him to the Netherlands, looked for a publisher and wrote an introduction. In 1940 it was published by De Haan in Utrecht, but on account of the war it did not reach the Indonesian reading public. During the turbulent time following the declaration of the Republic of Indonesia in 1945, the reprint of 1946 fared no better.[3]

---

[3] After 1946 the novel was reprinted twice: in 1947 the third printing came out, and in 1986 the fourth appeared (published by Nijgh & Van Ditmar, Amsterdam). For the last reprint I wrote an afterword.

The importance of du Perron's influence on *Buiten het gareel* becomes clear if we look at the novel against the background of pre-war Indonesian literature. In addition to its innovative form, compared to the Indonesian literary norms of the time, there are also new elements in its content. Overwritten descriptions and moralizing passages were significant ingredients in Indonesian literature during the thirties. Suwarsih's novel, however, is not "overwritten," and the book offers no didactic message. It is modern also in the way Suwarsih depicts her alter ego Sulastri and analyses her feelings with self-critical irony, especially when "sentimentality," which is always in the background, threatens to carry her away. Her honesty at these moments is one of the most striking characteristics of the book.

As we read the novel, we can hear Suwarsih's voice and detect her compelling need to put order into that jumble of experiences and emotions of the last years, to clear her mind in order to prepare for the future. She knew that the future, too, would be difficult. Du Perron's words of farewell, "life has nothing to do with career; self-esteem is most valuable," were to serve Suwarsih as guide and comfort in the future life.

Against the Grain is a nationalist novel. The main characters are nationalists who try to realize their ideals in the classroom. In the book, attention is concentrated on the characters themselves, on their tensions and conflicts. The struggle of Indonesian women for emancipation is also emphasized: the fight of women who want to have the same rights and responsibilities as men. It was the fight of Suwarsih Djojopuspito herself and we meet her in Sulastri, to whom it is of great importance to be the equal of her husband Sudarmo in marriage and in her career.

Suwarsih and Sugondo were working in Batavia when the Netherlands was occupied by Germany in 1940. As intellectuals who believed in democracy, they were aware that cooperation with the Dutch was necessary if there was to be a chance to stop authoritarian imperialism from Japan. In a startling article in *Kritiek en Opbouw* of August 1941, Suwarsih made an urgent appeal to the government to release the imprisoned nationalist leaders and to wage a joint fight against "the menacing fascist power" for the sake of "the democratic principle." Her plea proved to be in vain. Even earlier her wish for cooperation with the Dutch had led her to take another, no less remarkable step: she had accepted a job at a government school in Batavia, a decision which stemmed from her profound democratic convictions.

With the Japanese invasion in March 1942, Dutch colonial rule came to an end. It was under the new masters that Indonesia prepared for its future existence in freedom. In 1942 Suwarsih and her husband moved to Yogyakarta where they remained for the rest of their lives. Between 1945 and 1950 they were members of a national council which advised the Indonesian government. For a short time Sugondo was also a minister in the government. In 1951 they retired from public life. As democratic socialists—they belonged to Sutan Sjahrir's (1909–1966) circle—they felt increasingly alienated from the political and social-economic policy which Indonesia pursued. In a letter of 1973, Suwarsih, writing on poverty and social injustice, noticed: "We have paid and are still paying a high price for our freedom." They were condemned to a new isolation, "thrown away like a rag" as Suwarsih used to say bitterly. And continually she had to worry about the money they and their three children needed to live and, later, about insulin for her diabetes. Now and then she became seriously ill. Moreover, she suffered from feelings of uncertainty and doubt about the usefulness of her struggles and her life afterwards. She yearned for some recognition and appreciation, which she did not receive even as a writer of Indonesian short stories. When, at the beginning of

1976, she received a literary award, she wrote with some pride in a letter: "at least some appreciation and some money." She found relaxation in handicrafts; she made woolen toy animals for her grandchildren and little table mats and beautiful crochet stoles. She enjoyed doing this and, moreover, it provided some extra income: "I do not want to burden anybody, certainly not my children who have their own difficulties. Then I can die with the feeling that I bothered no one, and that I did my best during my whole life and that I always remained good-humored, however difficult things were," she wrote in a letter. In this she did succeed, cheerfully and with courage. She could tell gripping stories and sometimes speak sharply about the many disappointments in her life, but all the time with humor and irony, for she could laugh at herself.

It was not surprising that Suwarsih—spontaneous as she was and open and direct in the way she approached people—had trouble settling in Yogyakarta. The Javanese atmosphere oppressed her, as it oppressed Sulastri in *Against the Grain*. Moreover, Suwarsih found Central Java gloomy. She constantly felt homesick for the bright skies, the fresh green and the mountains of the Preanger, her native soil, and for the people there with whom she felt at home. Only rarely could she go there. What she especially remembered of her visit to Holland in 1953 at the invitation of Sticusa, a Dutch cultural organization, were the fresh greenery, the smell and the colors of spring which reminded her of the early mornings in Cibatok.

In June 1970 I met Suwarsih for the first time. On that evening and on the following evenings we talked about her novel and its background. She felt glad that there were still young people who read her book, that she had not been entirely forgotten. Some years later, when she read the passages which Rob Nieuwenhuys (1908–1999) had written about her work in his *Oost-Indische*

Spiegel (East Indies Mirror)[4] and received the anthology *Het laat je niet los* (It Won't Let You Go) in which a fragment from *Buiten het gareel* had been included,[5] she wrote in April 1974: "I did not know that what I wrote at that time would remain valuable and would attract attention today." A few months later Andries Teeuw (1921–2012), professor of Malay and Indonesian language and literature in Leiden, and I made a proposal to translate her novel into Indonesian with financial help from the Dutch government. Suwarsih translated the book herself and it was published in 1975, thirty-five years after the first printing. She felt, as she wrote in a letter, "the happiness of an old woman who sees herself again as a young woman of forty years ago, and now feels that she has not lived in vain.... I consider my book as a kind of last will and testament for our young people, a simple thing which I can offer them. Life without ideals is barren and dry."

With the money she got for her translation, she had her house redecorated and painted in bright colors: "It is more cheerful this way than the dark green which depresses and reminds me of the grave [...]. Now I am not thinking of illness or other unpleasant things. I feel something like a new life, a kind of early spring, which will enable me to write something new."

Suwarsih translated her book under the title *Manusia Bebas* (Free People).[6] This "means a human being," she writes, "free from

---

[4] Rob Nieuwenhuys, *Oost-Indische Spiegel; Wat Nederlandse schrijvers en dichters over Indonesië hebben geschreven, vanaf de eerste jaren der Compagnie tot op heden* (Amsterdam, 1978). Published in English under the title *Mirror of the Indies: A History of Dutch Colonial Literature* (Amherst: University of Massachusetts Press, 1982).

[5] *Het laat je niet los; Een keuze uit de Indisch-Nederlandse letterkunde van 1935 tot heden*, (It Won't Let You Go; Dutch Literature on Indonesia from 1935 to the Present) edited and introduced by Rob Nieuwenhuys, p. 138-142.

[6] Suwarsih Djojopuspito, *Manusia Bebas* (Jakarta: Djambatan, 1975).

prejudice, free from fear, from conventions and traditions. In my efforts to be mentally free, I often experienced failures and met hostility among my own people. I am aware that a human being must first be liberated before thinking of building a better future for the nation."

During the first months of 1977, my wife and I often visited Suwarsih and her husband. Her unfailingly bright and dynamic mind made one forget her physical decline. She was eagerly looking forward to a stay in her native region, but this plan came to nothing: the doctor diagnosed lung cancer in her husband and she had to take care of him. A few months later, on August 24, 1977, she suddenly died of cerebral hemorrhage. Sugondo followed her eight months later, on April 23, 1978.

Gerard Termorshuizen

Biographical Information

SUWARSIH DJOJOPUSPITO was born on April 30, 1912, in Buitenzorg (then known as Bogor), West Java, to a well-to-do middle-class family with progressive ideas on female education and equality. She commenced her education at a Kartini School and went on in the Dutch-medium MULO and Europese Kweekschool, a training college. After this, in the second half of the 1930s, she undertook a series of teaching assignments and, now married, was actively writing and editing material for various Dutch-language journals and publications in the Netherlands. Locally, her first attempt in 1937 at achieving publication of her first novel *Marjanah* was frustrated by official restrictions on nationalist thematic expression.

Several years later, encouraged by the Dutch literary critic Eddie du Perron to write a novel in Dutch, she wrote *Buiten het gareel* ("Out of the Harness"). This strongly autobiographical work realistically incorporated her experiences of economic hardship and social isolation while teaching in the so-called wild schools (proudly nationalistic institutions that refused government funding), association with the young Soekarno and members of his political group and representatives of the world of the Netherlands East Indies society of the 1930s. It also highlighted many of the issues she campaigned against in her writings, such as polygamy and the abandonment of women by male-oriented divorce practices, to say nothing of political repression under the colonial regime.

Suwarsih's literary output of both novels and short stories was impressive in the years following Independence. *Buiten het gareel,* was at long last translated by her into Indonesian as *Manusia Bebas* (Free People) and published in 1975. She died two years later and is buried in Yogyakarta.

George A Fowler began studying Malay and Chinese in Singapore at Nanyang University ("Nantah") in 1970. He moved to Indonesia in 1971 to research and co-author *Pertamina: Indonesian National Oil.* Subsequently, from 1973 to 1975, in between semesters at the University of Toronto, he returned to Indonesia to do field research for *Java: A Garden Continuum*, essays on Java's culture and history, another co-authorship in book form. From 1976 and for the next 24 years, he worked as a commercial banker throughout the Asia-Pacific region, including in both China and Indonesia. In 2002, with an MA in China Studies at the Jackson School of International Studies at the University of Washington, he began a second career as a freelance translator of commercial Indonesian, Chinese, Malay and Tagalog and subsequently as an Indonesian-English interpreter.

George began literary translation of Indonesian and Chinese in 2009 with the publication in 2011 of *Sitti Nurbaya* and *Old Town*. He has translated 15 other works of fiction, non-fiction and poetry from these two languages, including *Islam Dalam Bingkai Keindonesiaan dan Kemanusiaan-Sebuah Refleksi Sejarah* (as *Islam, Humanity and the Indonesian Identity: Reflections on History)*, by Indonesia's prominent public intellectual, the late Ahmad Syafii Maarif. He and Scholastica live in Woodinville, Washington, USA.

Gerard Termorshuizen (Rotterdam, 1935) studied History and Dutch language and literature at the University of Amsterdam. Between 1970 and 1975 he worked in the Dutch Department of the University of Indonesia in Jakarta, and afterwards as a research fellow at the Royal Institute of Linguistics and Anthropology in Leiden. In 1988 he obtained his PhD degree with a thesis on the East Indies journalist and novelist, PA Daum (1850–1898). Since 1969 he has published a significant number of books and articles on the subjects of East Indies colonial literature and journalism, among them a two-volume handbook on the Dutch-language press of the Dutch East Indies and several biographies of well-known Indies personalities. He lives in Sassenheim, a village near Leiden.

Translator's Acknowledgments

My primary acknowledgement is of course to John H McGlynn, Lontar's co-founder and director of publications, for introducing and giving me the opportunity to translate Suwarsih Djojopuspito's extraordinary novel, one of the earliest examples of modern feminist writing in Indonesia. Although on the whole written straightforwardly, it is not without a certain stylistic opacity in some parts which offer challenges to the translator. I attribute this to the filter of linguistic influences on the author's own translation (published in 1975) into Indonesian from her original Dutch novel (published in 1940) and which latter in fact had its own literary antecedent written by her in Sundanese (Suwarsih's first language) possibly in the early 1930s. In this project I have been relieved at certain puzzling junctures by the timely assistance of Roggie Cale, Dwi Elyono, Meyta Korompis, and Alan Stevens.

Finally, yet another translation of mine has now been made readable by my excellent editor, a partner in many literary endeavors, Diana Darling.

www.ingramcontent.com/pod-product-compliance
Lightning Source LLC
Chambersburg PA
CBHW031321230926
51848CB00001B/36